HER

TORTURED

BEASTS

A Note on the Content

I care about the mental health of my readers.
This book contains some themes you might want to know about
before you read.
They are listed at www.ektaabali.com/themes

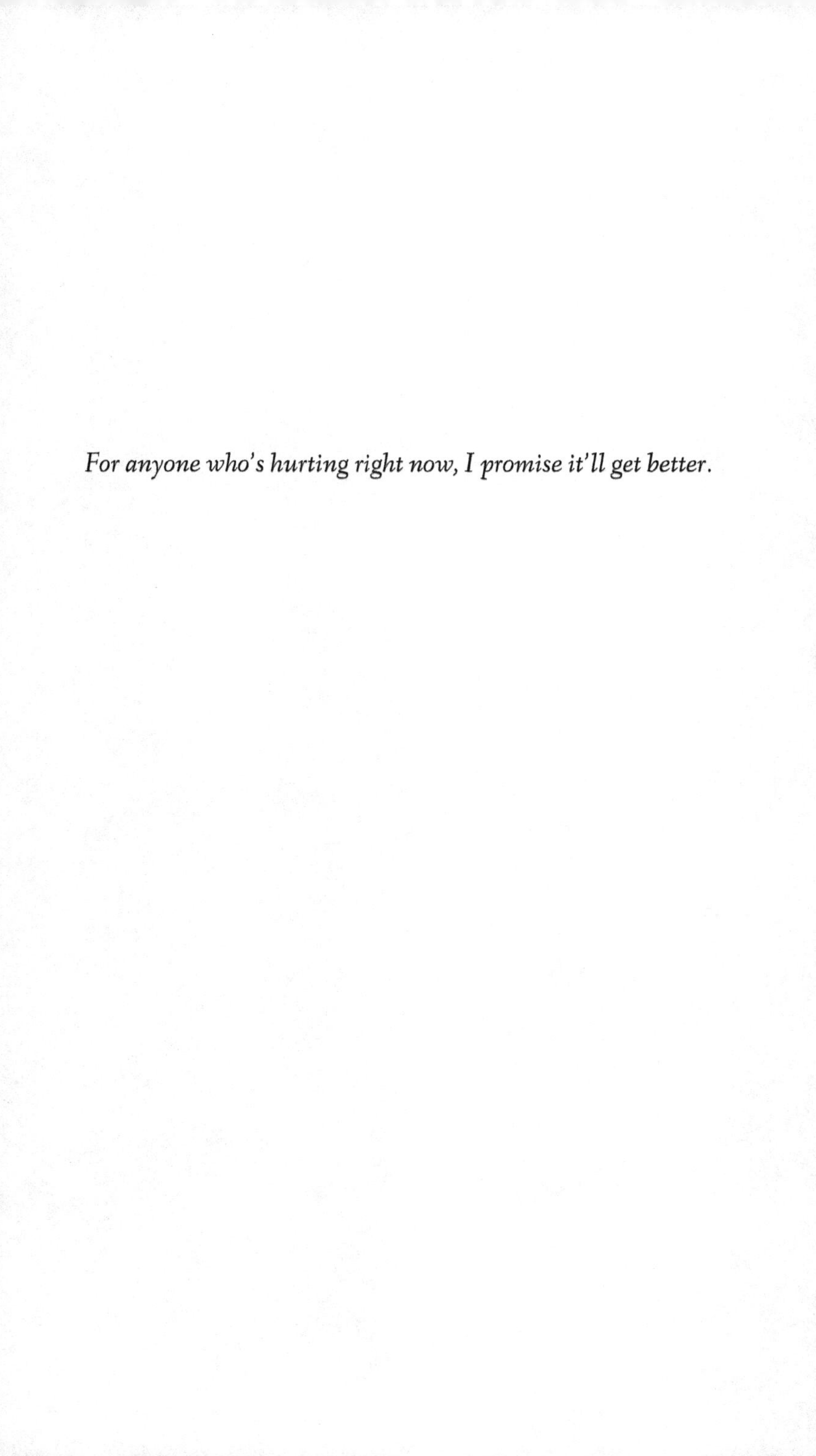

For anyone who's hurting right now, I promise it'll get better.

Her Tortured Beasts

4

E.P. Bali

Prologue

Savage

Lord Huron – The Night We Met

8 years ago

It was hailing the night I met Xander. Pieces as big as my fist crash down on my back, denting the cars, cracking the windows. Big enough to knock a weaker beast out, if it landed on just the right spot. It makes me grin though, to feel the violence of the Wild Mother, barrelling into Scythe and me. Her sound is like drums in my ears, her ice-like fists pounding into my back.

It doesn't hinder me as I swing the body of the roo, a federal agent, into the garbage disposal at our local tip. Making friends with the feds is on Scythe's list of things to do, but until then, we get rid of whoever's game enough to trace us.

The machine roars like an angry monster as it takes my gift, happily chomping away.

"I like this methy," I call to Scythe, standing watch on the top of a pile of rubbish behind me, his arms crossed, his cold shark eyes on the road.

"Method," he corrects.

"Yeah."

It's only when we're about to leave that Scythe holds up a hand. *"Engine,"* he says into my mind. *"An expensive one."*

That's strange. Frowning, the two of us lie on our bellies and peer over a pile of trash to the road that runs through the centre of the tip. Scythe is right, it's a motherfucking Rolls Royce rolling up fine and dandy along the road.

"What's a car like that doing in a place like this?" I ask, scratching my chin. Scythe made me shave this morning.

"See if there are any markings on the vehicle," my brother replies. *"And keep quiet."*

I make my muscles into stone and hold my breath as we watch the shiny black car travel right past us. Red brake lights gleam, but the rest of it is unmarked.

"Real wealth doesn't announce itself," Scythe says. *"No insignia. Illegal tint, and I bet the coppers know not to pull them over. Look!'*

Two males get out of the Rolls Royce on the far side, pulling a slumped person between them. Smoke billows out of the open door; the person remaining is smoking inside.

There's a thump before the two males hurry back inside the car. Scythe gives me a look as they drive off, and the slumped person, no more than a big black lump, lies there, unmoving.

"Is he dead?" I ask. "Why didn't they use the machine like we did?"

"They're not like us," Scythe says, not moving his eyes off the unconscious guy as hail pounds onto him. There's a movement, and the guy rolls flat onto his back with his arms and legs outstretched in an I-don't-want-to-live sort of way. He's got to be around my age, just taller, by the look of his smooth, pale skin and lean body.

"Let's go take a look," I urge. The guy's head flops over to the left. "Let's—" Two things have made my heart freeze and my guts jerk upwards.

Number One: The guy's eyelids are sunken, with blood seeping out from under them, where the sockets are empty.

Number Two: On the right side of his neck glows a skull with five curling beams of light.

And then Scythe and I are running. Without talking, without thinking. Because all we know is that we've just met our third bond-brother. There are five swirly swirls on our mating mark, so we'd guessed that we might have up to five mates. We crouch over him and I give his side a bit of a poke.

"Leave me," the guy moans. "Fucking leave."

"No chance," I say happily over the sound of the hail. "Who took your eyes, dude, because what the actual fuck?" I get the sudden intrusive thought to find two rounds of hail and pop them in to replace his missing eyeballs. You're supposed to put ice on injuries after all.

Scythe gives me a sharp look.

I roll my eyes. "Well, now we've got to find the person and take *their* eyes out. But I've never done that before and I don't think I can do it with my teeth, so it might be a finger job, right?" I grab his shoulders and shake it. "Speak up! You're my new brother!"

The boy makes a choked sort of sound, like a gurgle or a sob. Some blood seeps out of his eyes, trickling down his temple.

"Shit, sorry!" I lean in, and just like a good mother wolf cleaning her cub, I lick at the blood coming from under his lids.

The boy screams, shoving me away and turning towards Scythe.

I turn to the side and gag, wiping out my mouth because there's some foul magic or something on my tongue now. "Urgh!" I cry. "Scythe! Urgh!"

"Serves you right," my shark brother admonishes, throwing a black leather square at me. "Come on, let's get him out of here."

I catch the thing as Scythe puts his arms under the guy and

hoists him up, carrying him like a bride. The thought makes me snicker. Scythe says, "Check his wallet."

Suddenly I want a wallet too. I open it up and poke through it as we hurry the fuck out of there. His driver's licence is the first thing I see, and I squint at it before pouting. I hold it up to Scythe. I can only tell that he's got his P plates because of the red strip across the top, but I can't read the rest of it.

My brother frowns deeply. "Xander Drakos."

"Do we know him?" I ask, squinting at the photo. His eyes are green like an expensive gemstone. *Were* green.

"Yeah, Savage," Scythe says darkly, his face awfully tight. "I know the family."

"He's just a hatchling, though," I say, glancing at the unconscious boy. "He wouldn't have been involved in any of *that* sort of stuff?"

"You don't know these dragons," Scythe rumbles. "They're not regular beasts."

"Yeah," I say, brushing a wet strand of black hair off Xander's face to look at him better. "But he's our brother now." We arrive at our car and Scythe sits him in the back seat. I lean down and click his seat belt into place. "Don't worry, Xander!" I shout in his face. "You'll be right as rain, real soon!"

Xander grimaces before I shut the door and throw myself into the passenger seat.

Scythe glances at our new pack-mate. "I might know someone who can help him with his vision," he says. "It's worth asking anyway."

"I wonder who did it," I say as Scythe pulls out onto the main road.

A mumble comes from the back seat, delirious and faint, but it's definitely from Xander. "I was only trying to help."

Chapter 1

Aurelia

I'm jolted out of a troubled, heavy sleep by the sound of multiple truck doors slamming shut. My body is nothing but pain after the endless hours of travel, sprawled on the floor of this rumbling monster of a vehicle, and my bladder is close to bursting. After shock melded with fatigue, I managed to get a few hours of sleep, but chained to the side of a titanium, military grade hunting truck was like a small torture to my rattled bones. My rattled soul.

A soul that has been torn asunder by a nightmare made reality.

One of my mates has formally rejected me. While the wound on my arm has healed into a shallow red scratch, there is a deeper, darker serration within that primal place reserved for the other parts of my soul.

The part of me that was reserved for Xander Drakos is now shredded beyond repair. The regina in me lies in a pool of her own blood, her eyes barely open against the agony, her beak open under a low, aggrieved keen.

But I have no time to mourn a severed soul bond.

Because I am in enemy territory, clutching tight onto a promise.

I need to be alert. I need to be observant. Because whatever is coming for me outside of this truck is the key to my revenge. I'd sworn a solemn vow over my mother's funeral pyre: to destroy the monster who kept and abused her body for fifteen years. The monster who's a threat to every person I love.

So I scrape the aching parts of my mind out of that proverbial pool of blood and force the predator in me to come forward and bare her vicious teeth. I am the regina of the Boneweaver pack. Savage Fengari, Scythe Kharkorous and Lyle Pardalia are my mates. And though I've forbidden them to pursue me and have shut them out of my mind, they will always be with me, prowling steadily alongside my own uncertain gait.

The truck doors, on the other hand, slam open with heavy certainty, creating a new void in my reality. I crane my neck to get a look outside. The silhouette of a hulking beast forms a shadow against the night sky, and even without seeing his body, I'd know his dark, infernal presence anywhere. It tickles my deep regina instinct and I clamp down on that with all my might.

Because Ghoul is also my enemy.

A cold night wind brushes past him and rustles my long blue evening gown as the basilisk lord steps up and into the truck with ease, his weight jostling the floor like a boat on choppy water. He undoes the steel chains binding me to the wall, then hooks his arms under my armpits and hauls me up to standing.

Despite this truck being made for massive beasts, Ghoul, at seven feet, still has to stoop to be inside of it. I stare up at him, those mysterious shadows slithering around his body like dangerous, seductive snakes.

I don't miss the way he inhales the scent of my touseled hair before he steps away, flashing a bit of fang.

"You're an asshole," I mutter into his head. *"You could've made me a bit more comfortable."*

"But where would be the fun in that?" comes the emotionless reply.

A pang of anxiety hits my stomach as he grabs me by the

bicep and hauls me towards the edge of the platform, where a rowdy group of serpents hiss and jeer at my dishevelled appearance. It looks like they've all come to see the prized *prisoner*. Ghoul says, "Let's see how well you can jump, Lady Boneweaver."

I gape at the high drop before narrowing my eyes at him. The beast behind the skeleton mask gazes coldly back behind his shadows, only a flash of a red gleam showing off his eyes. I'd kicked off my stilettos a few minutes into the ride, so I'm barefoot now, and before I can think too much about it, I hike up my gown and step off the truck, landing in a crouch, the gown flaring about me in a halo. Ghoul efficiently jumps down after me, his military boots making a loud thump on the concrete. I grimace as he leans down, retakes my bicep, and forces me up to standing. The group of snakes, a mixture of dark-eyed males and females with black military uniform similar to Ghoul's, parts to let us through.

Their hisses trail me like a foul smell. As do their greedy, lecherous gazes.

Ghoul swings us around, and it's only then that I get my first look at where we are.

And all my dark suspicions are confirmed.

This building can only be described as a castle, because "mansion" is simply too small a word to encompass the dark, gothic magnificence of this dragon's lair. Beyond a perfectly clipped green lawn, black brick extends four stories tall. It stretches out on either side of a grand entrance of wide double-arched doors inlaid with precious stones. At least five turrets with pointed roofs frame the castle, stretching into the cloud-strewn night sky, giving the impression of a regal aristocrat, stern and unforgiving.

A solid gold plaque over the monstrous front doors declares it the "Drakos Family Estate" with their coat of arms: A lone dragon holding a boulder-sized diamond in its claws, its mighty head turned to the side as it roars fire in a wreath around itself.

Beneath this grand declaration stands the object of my vengeance. My enemies.

Three arrogant males. Three scaled beasts. One with eyes that glow white through the darkness.

My father is in league with the dragon king, and has been for some time. The serpent king's thin lips twitch with satisfaction at the sight of me.

"Beware!" one of the serpent males shrieks mockingly, "the *Lady Boneweaver* approaches!"

Every beast in the vicinity chuckles darkly and some asshole straight out hoots with prolonged, nasty laughter. The once sacred, secret title has become a slur. A thing worthy of a joke. Their voices coat my skin with slime that I madly want to scratch off.

Instead, I set my jaw and stare them all down as Ghoul leads me by the elbow towards my fate. A cold wind scrapes down my spine as my bare feet reach the base of the impressive golden stairs.

"Your Royal Majesties," Ghoul calls, sweeping a dramatic bow. "I present to you, the Lady Boneweaver."

More chortling comes from behind me.

I remain upright, my chin raised, staring at these awful, powerful beasts one at a time. My father, dark and wraith-like, the hollows of his eyes seeming to swallow the night around him as he takes me in with a satisfied gleam.

Flores Drakos, the dragon king and Xander's father, stands in the middle, a beast of great power and wealth who shows it in his regal stance and richly embroidered clothing and golden rings. His long, straight black hair is neatly tied back, showing high cheekbones and almost bored golden eyes. He's letting me know he's unimpressed with me. That I am beneath him.

And finally, it's with a vicious stab to the heart that I lay eyes on Xander for the first time since he officially rejected me as his mate. There is a new, terrifying darkness to him I could never have been prepared for.

He stands still as volcanic stone in that expensive suit, his hands clasped casually before him, gold rings glinting, eyes glowing as if nothing significant at all has happened. There's something infinitely dark settling around him now. Something that tells every creature in the vicinity this is a beast mad enough to sever the bond to his soul-bound regina. That this is a monster, and you should run in the opposite direction.

His neck is irrevocably bare, the sacred, celestial light of our mating mark faded into nothing.

Fresh agony of my soul twinges anew, threatening to send me falling into a catatonic stupor just like the one Minnie once had.

Except I refuse. Point blank, I refuse to succumb to this terrible wound. Because whatever Xander and these beasts think, I am here of my own free will.

They cannot break me.

Ghoul tuts as he straightens from his bow. "Looks like we'll have to teach her some manners."

"Bring her up here, General," the dragon king drones.

"With pleasure."

But it's what my father says next that gives me pause. "Make her crawl."

Here it is. A little revenge for when I burnt down the Naga mansion.

"You heard him," Ghoul says, nudging me with his elbow.

Keeping my face as expressionless as the basilisk's voice, I lower my shackled hands to the third step and begin bear crawling my way up.

My father thinks he can humiliate and degrade me with this, but he doesn't know that with each step, my mind whispers my mother's name in a reminder of my vow.

Athena. Athena. Athena Boneweaver was her name.

Twenty times I chant her name before we reach the top and I straighten, suppressing a wince at the pain in my lower spine.

The first thing I see when I raise my eyes is Xander's chest, and the shiny new bling that adorns his neck. A solid gold hunk of a metal etched with his family crest.

He looks all cosy standing there with his father. And it doesn't take a genius to figure out what it was that got him reinstated into the family.

Rejecting me. Exchanging me. His regina.

This entire thing had been *my* idea, and he'd gone and hijacked it right under my very nose. So instead of my grand plan looking mighty clever or sacrificial, he's making it look like the whole thing was his idea. That it was *his* operation that got me caught.

A flame of anger ignites in my chest.

There's no fucking way he's going to get away with this.

Chapter 2

Xander

I have dreamt of this moment for so damn long that now reality seems like the dream.

My father leads the way into our family home, straight into the majestic black and gold tiled entrance hall with the old obsidian stone dragon guards. I smile faintly at their intimidating presence and the memories I have of my child self, scrambling up their mighty bodies and perching myself on a big head, crying out to my sister to look at me.

The bittersweet scent of cinders and magic is familiar and comforting in its power. It prickles my skin, letting me know it sees me, that it recognises me. Warmth spreads through my every pore as my own power greets the ancient forces.

Tonight, after eight years of exile, I am welcomed home. Tonight, I am reinstated as heir to my family's royal seat.

For the first time in a long time, I feel *good*.

The price was supposed to be dear, but I paid it gladly and with the honour of my family behind me. I feel...more powerful than ever before. More ready to face the world as the dragon I'm supposed to be. I am forged strong by what I did, and whatever anyone thinks about it, I made myself invincible.

The only stain upon my grand return is the slithering scum my father has allowed to take up residence here. And the worst stain of all being Serpent Spawn, who just *had* to follow me home like one of Scythe's apparitions. If she hadn't burned down her own family home, she'd be far away from here. As it is, she is human capital that must not be stolen from us, and I plan to collect any and all interest from my investment.

My hand reflexively reaches for the right side of my neck, but I drop it almost immediately. It's strange not feeling Savage's chaotic energy or Scythe's cold presence in my head, and more recently, Lyle's leashed rabid power.

My eyes fall upon the golden archway that leads to the rest of the Estate and warmth like a welcoming hearth filters through my chest. My ex-brothers will be furious with me right now, even raging mad, but eventually, they will come to terms with the truth.

That I was never meant to be a part of their pack.

That I was meant to be free.

And within that freedom is true power.

Ghoul leads Serpent Spawn by the arm behind us as we turn the corner to find a group of Mace's scientists waiting with barely restrained glee.

There's eight of them, all serpents, with a steel table laden with sterile equipment, packets, and collection tubes. Every single one of the so-called team has a black serpent covenant etched for all to see on the back of their right hand.

"This couldn't wait until the morning?" my father drawls.

The lead scientist, a middle-aged bald male, immediately breaks out into a sweat, his fear perfuming the space between us. "If it pleases, Your Majesty, we have waited so very—"

"Get the initial samples done now," Mace Naga says in his ever so smooth, curated politician's voice. "And then I'm sure everyone would like to go to bed."

"Indeed," my father drones. "You'll have plenty of time with her tomorrow."

I supervise as Spawn is brought forward by the basilisk lord, her beady eyes darting around at each of the new faces and what they hold in their hands.

Each beast in the room observes her every movement as if she's a prize sow.

We all see it—the fire inside of her. Still, despite a severed mate bond. Despite being a captive and ordering her own mates not to come after her.

Lesser beasts are struck dead by a rejection of a mate bond. Strong beasts are rendered catatonic. But Spawn stares us down like a knight readying for battle.

I exhale the burning irritation through my nose.

No longer will she haunt my nightmares. No longer will I be subject to her powers, seductive or otherwise.

Ghoul shoots me a sideways glance and I swear he's gloating under that ridiculous skeleton mask. Fucking psychopath. I thought I had it bad wrangling Savage and Scythe, but this basilisk? He will have to be watched carefully.

Two scientists hurry forward with clipboards, a set of scales, and measuring tape, muttering their plans to each other.

Spawn has the audacity to put up her hand, and sets her eyes on Mace Naga. "I want surety that my *surrender*"—she glares at me—"means that my friends and mates are out of bounds. Those were the conditions." She glances at Ghoul.

"Yes, yes," my father says dismissively. "We have no need for the others."

Mace levels Spawn with an unimpressed gaze. "Let go of any idea that you are some martyr, Aurelia. Comply, and I have no need to pursue your beloved friends."

A vague statement, no doubt meant to unsettle. Sure enough, a small crease forms between her dark brows, but she turns to the scientists and nods at them as if she's in charge here.

She'll learn soon enough.

Height and weight are taken first, followed by a cutting of some of her dark hair, a clipping of her fingernail. She is made to sit down on a metal chair as they draw six vials of blood. They swab her mouth and cheek multiple times, for both saliva and DNA.

I can't fucking believe my father is entertaining this.

My dragon twitches in his slumber. He's been asleep since the bond-breaking and since I don't have any knowledge about dragon-bonds, I can only assume he's recovering from the shock of it and will come to when he is ready.

Spawn shifts in the chair, squeezing her knees together like she needs to pee. I won't have her urinating on my floor.

"That's enough," I command.

The serpent about to take fingerprints from Spawn jumps a foot into the air. Ghoul and Mace turn to look at me. The barest hint of a frown forms on Mace's pallid face, and it satisfies me to no end.

I wave a dismissive hand at the reptiles. "You're done."

They all bow and begin backing away, leaving Spawn rigid, clutching the sides of the chair.

My father turns to me, clasping me by the shoulder, and I don't ever think I'll get used to this feeling. "I took the liberty of having this made for you, my heir." The faint chink of gold sounds as he raises his other hand. I blink at the gold collar and chain for a singular moment of confusion before my instincts kick in and I reach for them.

My steps are automatic as I stride towards Spawn, and before she can complain, as she no doubt will, I sweep her tangled mane of black hair aside and clasp the golden collar around her neck, securing it with my power so it seals shut without a seam. A dragon-lock.

It makes no physical sound at all, but there's an air of finality around us like the resounding thud of the final nail in a coffin.

I hold the other end of the chain in a tight fist.

Spawn's face, upturned and pale, fixes her heinous gaze upon me. Not her, but *It*, I realise.

"What is this?" Ghoul asks, flicking at the 24-carat dragon-enforced chain with a gloved finger.

"She is *my* captive," I say, tugging on the chain.

Spawn gapes at me before she's forced to rise from the chair.

"Indeed," my father says haughtily. "Dragons of old kept chosen pets close by, and we've taken up the tradition. Sometimes, I tote my human slaves around if I have need for it."

Ghoul clucks his tongue as if this is exactly what he expected from dragons.

I can't see Mace's reaction, for I'm choosing to ignore the worm. In fact, pretending neither reptiles are here will be for the best. If the king of worms thought *he'd* be in control of this situation, he has another thing coming. The investment is here because of me. Not him.

My father makes an amused sound in his throat. "We will speak in the morning, my son."

Hearing those words from his mouth makes my chest go tight. "Of course, Father." I incline my head. "My thanks to you."

He pats me on the shoulder twice before turning around, nodding to Mace and sweeping away to his rooms.

I too turn my back upon the weevils, tugging Spawn along. She trips on her own feet before scuttling in my wake.

Not her. Not she. *It*. I must never forget that.

Chapter 3

Ghoul

The serpent king and I watch the newly reinstated heir of Drakos Estate stalk away with our prize after sending our scientists scattering.

Once the hall is emptied, with nothing but the old dragon statues to cast their sinister eyes over us, Mace turns to me. "We cannot afford the same mistakes as last time. She must be broken. That is imperative. And I want you to ensure that."

I bow low and purr, "With the *utmost* pleasure, Your Majesty."

Chapter 4

Aurelia

Whatever I imagined being held captive would be like, it was not *this*:

Being led on a Goddess-forsaken leash by a cruel and silent Xander through the hallowed halls of his monstrosity of a home.

The prodding, the poking, even the drawing of blood I could suffer through. Expected it, really. A part of me may have hoped that this is some kind of protection, something that Xander could only have thought of to keep me away from whatever horrors my father has planned for me. Except...it had been *his* father who had brought out the chain and collar, and Xander had blinked at it for a moment, as if stunned. He'd recovered quickly, of course, and the revelation that this is a private custom performed by dragons for centuries leaves a stone in the pit of my stomach.

Whatever could be said of serpent court, they'd never done anything like this. There are no more prideful, arrogant creatures than dragons.

As if this entire thing isn't already embarrassing enough *without* the collar and chain.

Xander says nothing as I follow him up a set of grand,

carpeted stairs, the glistening golden chain slack between my neck and his hand as I hurry after his long stride.

What *does* one say to the mate who rejected her so brutally? I'd asked for his help in my plan to surrender only because any obstruction from him would have stopped the entire operation. Xander might be powerful, but I also knew he'd wanted me gone from his life. That was the reason that allowed me to ask him to do this. The end result was me out of his life.

But...this result is the exact opposite.

The backs of my eyes burn and I stumble over my bare feet once again, catching myself just in time. I wrap my arms around my middle as if I can hold myself together.

Because I *will* hold myself together if it's the last fucking thing I do on this earth.

There are clues here, I must remember, both in this majestic place and the people who occupy it. Clues to fuel my revenge. Weapons I might be able to use against these creatures.

As we walk up the stairs, people appear from the shadows as if they've been waiting. Humans, by the smell of them, smartly dressed in formal black and white maid and butler attire. Two of them, a middle-aged man and woman, wait at the top of the stairs, bowing and curtseying deeply as we come to stand before them.

They both avert their eyes to the richly carpeted crimson floor.

"My Lord Xander," the man says. "It is a great pleasure to see you once again. And a greater pleasure still, to be your manservant."

"The pleasure is mine, Olly," Xander murmurs. Does he sound pensive? Is that a note of apprehension in his voice, or is that just my soul-weary, fatigued state?

"Your old rooms are freshened up and ready with all the comforts."

Olly introduces the maid, a brunette by the name of Heather, and they all ignore my irrelevant Boneweaver ass.

I can't believe Xander has both a manservant and a maid. But, of course he does. His giant egoic lord dragon ass wouldn't be complete without a set of humans waiting on him claw and tail.

They lead us down a long corridor and up yet another set of stairs. The vaulted ceiling soars high above us, the other levels wrapping around the walls mezzanine style like ribbons around a gift box. Gold glints at every opportunity. Ancient stone dragon heads sit on pillars and some in glass cases. Gems are inlaid on name plaques, portraits are ornately framed, and my bare feet trod upon plush crimson runners.

I'm barely able to keep my eyes open as we reach Xander's rooms and he has to tug at my chain to get me through his receiving room and into a large space occupied with a king bed on one side, a bathroom on the other and—

A muttered curse leaves my lips.

Because they've prepared for me.

Against the eastern wall of his room sits a square cast iron cage. The bars are thick and black, twined with gold because, of course, they couldn't help it. It's big enough to allow a person to lie down, but short enough that I would have to kneel in it. On the floor lies a folded pink blanket and two ceramic...*dog* bowls. One with water, the other with something that looks like kibble.

Next to that is a puppy pee pad.

By the Wild Mother. I gape at the thing as Heather removes a black key from her starched apron pocket and hands it to Xander.

"We won't need the training pads," Xander says with abject disgust. "I won't have it urinating on the floor."

"Apologies, my lord," Heather says quickly. "None of us were sure what condition she would be in."

Did they think I'd arrive crawling on all fours, yowling and barking? Bunch of nutters.

"I'm not going in there," I say, crinkling my nose.

With the slow, fluid movement that could only be made by a

predator, Xander turns around. Cruelty and anger drapes around his shoulders like a coat. Wisely, Heather and Olly flee the room, quiet as mice, shutting the door behind them with a definitive click.

So well trained.

So well aware of the danger of dragons.

I cross my arms and stare those glowing eyes down. "You're taking credit for my surrender and I don't appreciate it."

"Use the bathroom," Xander sneers. "You need it."

With a flick of his wrist, the golden chain snaps free of my collar, making me stumble forward. My hand flies towards the collar as the chain disappears into the gold bangle on Xander's hand. He takes out a set of metal keys and unlocks the shackles around my wrists with brusque efficiency, removing them and stepping away.

I'm as free as I can be.

But I don't move towards the bathroom. I narrow my eyes at him. "I am here of my own accord."

He doesn't miss a beat. "Yes, and that means you've signed your life away. You are subject to the rules here. Comply, or face the consequences."

I shake my head, my heart a tight fist, my throat threatening to shut entirely. But I push through it. "You—"

Xander whirls around and grabs me by the throat, shoving me right against the wall. "You will haunt me no longer," he hisses into my face. The fire in his gaze might burn me alive. "You don't get to live in my head anymore. You don't get to control me. I am free of you. Forever."

Shock slams into me harder than a slap. I had no idea I affected him that badly. That I...lived in his head, unwanted.

"I never controlled you," I choke out.

He lets me go with a snarl, striding away without another glance. I all but sag against the wall. Without another word, I hurry into the bathroom and slam the door shut behind me, pressing myself against the wood, breathing hard and squeezing my eyes shut against the pain of it all.

Taking a shaky breath, my bladder suddenly makes herself known. I blink open my eyes and rush to the toilet, planting myself on it like it'll save me.

Warm, golden bulbs highlight the most stunning bathroom I've ever been in, and despite everything, I gape at the finery of the claw-footed bathtub, the fancy black marble floor tiles, and the golden dragon head spout at the sink and shower. It's like our Animus Academy bathroom, but on steroids.

A sharp pang of homesickness strikes me without warning and I double over, putting my head between my legs and regulating my breathing like Henry would guide me to do. Minnie, Raquel, Stacey and Connor. Will they ever forgive me for this? Will my mates ever forgive me? Will they be able to *look* at me again after I regina-ordered them to stay put?

I fear the answer. I fear their wrath.

But there's nothing to be done about it, except to get off the damned pretty toilet, head over to the sink, splash icy water on my face, and steel myself for what is to come. I made the decision to be here and I will own that.

The gold collar is pretty if I look at it with a certain squint. Sabrina would have turned it into a fashion statement. Surely I can do the same.

My teeth grind themselves as I get the urge to punch the mirror into a thousand pieces. The fucking audacity. The fucking nerve of these people.

Xander might no longer see the mating mark on my neck, but he's branded himself onto me. Clutching the sides of the sink, it takes me long moments to calm myself.

When I emerge back into the bedroom, Xander is sitting in the armchair by the fireplace, a joint between his fingers in one hand and his phone in the other.

My cage door is now open. Without looking at me, Xander says in a low voice. "Get in."

I am here to play the game, so play I will. Biting my tongue, I stroll towards the cage. I have to drop to my hands and knees and crawl in and pull my gown in behind me. But once I'm sitting in there, I pull the blanket into my lap, wondering how the hell I'm supposed to sleep.

Xander rises and stalks towards the cage, swings the door shut, and locks it.

I have to clench my teeth at this feeling of utter vulnerability. I had fought the bonds of a cage for so damn long, only to crawl into one voluntarily.

It feels like absolute shite.

"The suite door is dragon-locked," he announces. "Don't bother trying to escape."

"Here by my own choice, remember?" I grumble, unfolding my new blanket and sniffing it.

Xander doesn't reply, he just flicks the black out cover shut.

I'm left in complete darkness, my only companion the sound of Xander shutting the bathroom door.

Blowing out a heavy breath, I lie down, drawing my knees up because the length of me isn't going to fit in this thing. I'm proud to say it's only a single tear that slips out.

Chapter 5

Xander

I wake up the next morning with a blaring headache. A smart rap on my door tells me Olly is waiting outside. I mentally unlock the door, and it releases its magic with a soft hum, giving silent permission for the human butler to enter.

He does so with bustling purpose, bowing as he steps inside, his heart beat like a trotting pony. "Good morning, my lord."

Pushing back my black sheet—a *much* finer sort compared to Animus Academy's cheap linens—I sit on the edge of my bed as Olly opens the heavy maroon drapes. Sharp light fills the room, and I refrain from rubbing my temples.

"There is much on the agenda today, my lord," Olly prattles. "Will it be a bath this morning, or will a shower suffice?"

A muffled snort comes from the cage against the wall. Rising to my feet, I stretch out my back. I missed my old bed, luxurious and velvet soft, but it will take some getting used to after the wooden slab that was the academy's mattress. I'd slept well after an hour of waiting for my own adrenaline to subside. The old noises of the house took a while to adjust to—the creaking, the wood settling, the low hum of other heartbeats—and worst of all, the sound of Spawn tossing and turning and huffing.

"I don't want to waste any time," I say to Olly, who is now holding out my towel in one hand and a tablet in the other. "Email me my agenda and do that every morning from now on."

I don't miss the curious glance Olly runs down my bare torso, his human pupils dilating with instinctual awe. He hasn't seen me since I was fifteen, when I was more like a string bean. I'm a man grown now, and I know what difference that will make in this household.

"Apologies, my lord." Olly bows again. "And your father has requested family breakfast this morning."

Well, that's certainly new. Olly smiles at me awkwardly as I take the fluffy white towel from him.

"I will brief you after you are refreshed, my lord." His brown simple human eyes slide towards the cage. "And should I take your...pet outside for the loo?"

Irritation sweeps through me like a sneeze. "No. It'll use the bathroom after me."

Another noise emits from the cage, but I ignore it, and wisely, so does Olly.

After brushing my teeth and showering, I check in with my dragon. He's still out like a light, in the same position as before, curled in on himself, a crease between his black brows. Smoke suddenly fills the bathroom, and the automatic air vents turn on, sucking up my anger.

Upon my return, Heather has appeared and replaced the sheets on my bed. Olly has laid out my clothes, and Heather is presently opening a small closet, hidden in the wood panelling in the corner of the room. She takes out a plain, floor length black dress. It's a simply made cotton and spandex blend with a round neck and wrist-length sleeves. In her other hand, she holds a pair of black ballet flats.

I frown and finally turn to look at the covered cage against the wall of the room. With a huff, I lean down and flip up the front flap of the blackout material.

Spawn is already sitting in its cage, glaring at me with bleary blue eyes, her inky hair like a tangled bird's nest, the blue gown from last night like a deflated balloon around her. Her scent strikes me across the nose, sour sweat over her natural, heady scent.

It shouldn't affect me the same way it used to. I sniff delicately, checking for the difference. Sweet, feminine, but not maddening. Not dangerous. Not even pleasing.

"Brush your hair," I snap as I unlock the cage door, "And shower. I won't have you embarrassing me with a foul appearance or smell."

"Of course," she mutters. "We can't have that."

Only *she* could be locked in a crate all night and still have so much attitude left. She crawls out and accepts the clothes Heather gives her. The maid ushers her into the bathroom with a wrinkled nose, as if Spawn is a mud-splattered dog that just trotted in from outside.

I don't know what I expected to feel when I formally broke the mating bond. But the vision of the mating mark fading from her neck was nothing but sheer and utter relief. Something inside of me has definitely eased. Calmed. Soothed.

Freedom is a fresh, cool breeze through my body, and as Olly holds up a black business shirt for me to wear, I allow myself a tiny smile.

Fifteen minutes later, Heather and Spawn exit my bathroom. Her hair is thankfully brushed and tied back from her face, and that black dress—

I huff in irritation. Heather has chosen the wrong size because the material wantonly clings to Spawn's snake-curves before it falls to the floor. The round neck shows her collarbones before cupping her breasts like two delicate hands.

She looks sort of grey behind her olive skin. But I've forgotten something—that's not my problem anymore. None of this is my problem at all. There's a whole team of serpents who are being paid to be interested in her bodily health.

So I simply extract the dragon chain from the gold bangle around my wrist and flick it in her direction. Under dragon telekinesis, it clips itself to the collar.

She flinches from the pressure but averts her eyes, choosing to scowl at the floor instead.

Hatred curls my lip as I look upon her. "Not a single word at breakfast, or I *will* muzzle and gag you."

Her slender jaw clenches under her own malice as those blue jewels glitter in annoyance. But she says nothing.

* * *

Breakfast is being served in the lesser dining room this morning. It's my father's—*our* less formal dining area that we reserve just for close family. So no serpents or other unwanted residents of the estate will be joining us.

Nerves bounce in my stomach as I anticipate who will meet me there. I impatiently pull Spawn along behind me, then completely forget about her as I reach the set of golden doors that will lead me to the one thing I've spent years yearning for.

No more secret visits to Sissy or the hatchlings. No more sneaking about at night. I am allowed to be here. Allowed to greet my family as one of them.

Voices trickle through the small open gap between the doors. The excited, high pitch of my niece and nephew, and the deeper, more reserved feminine voice of—

"Mother?" The word slips out of my mouth as I step into the room. It sounds disbelieving even to me. Golden morning light fills the space, as intended by the architecture. It could be heaven, for all I know of it, to see my entire family, my entire world, sitting at that dining table.

"Uncle Xander! Uncle Xander!" shriek both hatchlings, their

napkins tumbling to the floor as they hurtle towards me at full speed.

"Hello," I chuckle, reaching down to ruffle their dark locks as they cling to my legs, peering up at me with wide eyes and grinning faces.

"Mother says you're going to be here all the time now!" Emmerson shouts, fist pumping the air.

"We can play in the backyard!" Delilah squeals, pressing her cheek to my leg and squeezing her eyes shut.

"Come back here, you two." Sissy's voice is low and disapproving where she sits on the far side of the long dining table. She doesn't look at me as the hatchlings obediently run back to their seats, but I can't think on that now as I focus on the person whose very memory has the strength to make my bones shatter.

The person I've not seen since the fateful day I left this house.

Adjacent to the hatchlings, rising from her seat at the end of the table, is my mother.

She looks more frail than the last time I saw her. Her long, graceful figure is adorned in a heavy velvet green dress that seems to weigh down her ballerina's frame. Her face is pale white with perfectly applied makeup, the blush doing the heavy lifting to brighten her appearance.

"Xander!" Mother chimes. Her hands sweep outward immediately, welcoming me in. Welcoming me home. Something in my chest explodes in a shower of gold as I stride towards her and take her into my arms.

She rests her head on my chest, holding me tightly as I hold her back, kissing the top of her dark hair, the length of it neatly coiled into a bun at the nape of her neck.

"How I have missed you," she sighs.

I swallow. "I've missed you too."

A vibration courses through her body.

"Are you cold?" I ask, drawing back to feel her forehead with the back of my fingers.

"Always worrying over me," she smiles indulgently. "My handsome boy."

"He's not a boy," comes a deep voice from over my shoulder. "And your doting will spoil him yet again."

The spark in my mother's green eyes fades just a hint and she averts her gaze down. I'd shared those eyes with her once. Her hand takes mine as she guides me to the seat adjacent to hers.

"Good morning, Father," I say mildly.

"Good morning, Heir," he says formally, sweeping his long burgundy jacket aside as he takes a seat at the head of the table.

I also take mine, but not before snapping my wrist to retract the golden chain from Spawn. I jerk my chin at the right-hand corner of the room. "Sit over there."

Chapter 6

Aurelia

Suppressing a mad scowl after Xander greets his family, I slope towards the corner of the room he indicates, dutifully sitting cross-legged on the floor.

Somehow, this is far worse than being simply locked up in a cold, dark dungeon like I imagined. They didn't subject Sabrina to this sort of treatment, from what we gathered from her story when she'd been kidnapped and brought here. I suppose the Boneweaver is a special case.

Here by fucking choice, and I feel like I need to keep reminding everyone of that fact.

Sighing under my breath, I survey the table with great interest. This is Xander's family. The people he tore my soul open for.

His Royal Majesty, King Flores Drakos, sits stiff-backed in his gilded chair, his acerbic scent of smoke and burnt things lingering in the air from his entrance. I've met him before, once at my tribunal for Halfeather's murder, and a second time when they came to the academy and tried to take Lyle to prison. Even if I hadn't seen him those times, being king of dragon court, his photo is everywhere. On the news, on the TV, on social media.

An imposing, handsome man in his early fifties, he has long, straight, jet black hair like Xander's, almond-shaped bright golden eyes, and perfect, pale skin. He's dressed impeccably in a black shirt and slacks, with the long burgundy overcoat decorated in gold embroidery. He eats his breakfast of bacon and eggs with sharp, impatient strokes.

What on earth made a dragon like him stand in league with my father? What drew him to plot alongside Serpent Court? This is one of the things I have to find out.

The other two adults at the table I am even more curious about, having never seen or heard hide nor tail of them. I had no idea Xander had a sister, as neither Savage nor Scythe had ever mentioned her, but I can only presume that's who the young lady sitting with the children is. She's a stunning, delicate young woman, in her late-twenties, her long black hair worn straight down her back, a clip of gold and rubies keeping it off her face. Her slender frame is covered in a powder blue sundress trimmed with lace and on her feet are matching designer kitten heels. Next to her sits a little boy and girl, no more than eight, cherub-like faces sneaking side-eyed looks at me as they eat their breakfasts. They are dressed in formal clothing, a white lace dress and yellow vest for the girl, and a three-piece blue suit and shorts for the boy. Both wear long white socks up to their knees, and shining gold buckled black shoes.

Sitting at the end of the table, with her back towards me, is a wisp of an older woman. While she's tall and well-boned, she has barely any muscle on her frame, and moves with the delicate cadence of a person with little energy. My avian power stirs, curious, wanting to explore, to help.

"Uncle Xander!" cries the little boy. "My bacon looks like a snake!" He holds up his fork, a length of bacon hanging off the end as he wiggles it.

For the first time since I've known him, Xander smiles where he sits opposite the boy, his pale pink lips curving into a genuine expression of joy. "So it does, Emmerson. A good thing that snakes are perfect for eating." Xander spears his own bacon with a fork and wolfs it down with relish.

"Do not play with your food, my sweet," says Lady Drakos in a delicate, hoarse voice. Emmerson expertly cuts into his portion, eating it as if carefully taught.

Something in my heart bleeds a little, because it hits me then.

That Xander's mother is the only mother my pack has—*had* left. And Xander's sister is the only sibling left. None of us— Savage, Scythe and Lyle—have a family outside of our mates. It's just what we have in this room.

And by formally rejecting me, he'd not only denied me of himself, but...*this*. The happiness that comes with giggling children, the warm embrace of a doting mother, the padded barb of a sister's teasing jibe.

I sway where I sit, suddenly faint, my vision blurry.

"Woof woof," coos a little bird-like voice. "Woof woof, come eat this!"

Blinking hard, I try to focus on the sounds of the room. It's the little girl beckoning to me this time, holding up an entire boiled egg between small fingers.

"She has a name, Delilah," Xander's sister chides. She turns to me. "Aurelia. Or Lia, right?"

I stare at the polite young woman with the golden eyes.

"Do *not* use its name, Sissy," Xander says more harshly than I expect.

"We have to call her *something*," she mutters.

"What was that, Selena?" Lord Drakos asks in a low voice.

"Nothing, Father," she replies quickly.

"That's what I thought."

I clench my fists in my lap to prevent myself from launching at the king dragon. What a rude motherfucker. Selena is a pretty name. A name for the woman I might have called a sister.

"I call her woof woof!" Delilah says enthusiastically. "We've never had one before." She explains to me, and I understand they've never been allowed a dog or a pet. No doubt another stupid Drakos family rule.

Human servants move discreetly in and out of the room, serving Xander his coffee and each of the many dishes they have available. A maid leans down from a respectful distance and asks Xander a question, to which he gives a curt nod. After a moment, she returns with yet another porcelain dog bowl and places it on a mat next to me.

I glance at the bowl and find some dog kibble mixed with pieces of cold cut meats. Clenching my jaw so hard it hurts, I turn my face away from it and remain seated for the rest of the breakfast service. The family eats quietly, with the children making small comments or complaints until the servants collect their plates.

"Bring the biodata folder for the heir," Flores announces to an older butler waiting obediently to the side. The man leaves and returns a moment later with a folder leaden with a neat stack of paper.

"What is this?" Xander asks mildly as the butler places it before him where his plate was only a moment before.

"Potential females," Flores says haughtily. "For you to select a wife from."

My stomach twists. I barely stop my mouth from dropping open.

Xander shows no sign of any emotion, however, as he simply opens the folder and starts leafing through the laminated pages, reading with great care. Minnie would appreciate the organisation of the folder like that. I don't.

It's not even twenty-four hours since he's formally rejected me and he's stuck right into it! Only dragons would be capable of something so callous.

"The meetings will begin tomorrow night," Flores states evenly. "Starting with the garden soiree your mother and I have planned. They are all keen to meet you."

Oh, I'm fucking sure they are.

I can't help but notice that this entire time, Lady Drakos has remained silent, merely sipping at her cup of oolong tea as she calmly surveys Xander with a daydreamy sort of expression.

I can't imagine what she sees.

The only other beast I've met who rejected a mate bond was Titus Clawson when he rejected Minnie, and he didn't look affected by the rejection at all. Titus is a psychopath for sure, and whatever Xander was before, he seems to be one now.

Perhaps a rejection can turn a person into a psychopath? Does Xander have no feelings at all about denying his soul? Does his dragon have *nothing* to say about what he's done?

I don't even want to admit how much that hurts. How much Xander's dragon had come to me in times of need. Given me jewellery, spoken words that had filled me with forbidden longing.

And to think that's all simply...gone. For good.

A bone-deep weariness clings to me like a giant hand pressing me into the floor and threatening to send my anima deep under to a dangerous place, and I don't think it's something I'll ever be able to shake off. Minnie, after her catatonic state, said as much to me. That a severing of the soul bond is a pain that never fades. You only get better at dealing with it.

I must have let out a louder sigh than I thought, because suddenly, all eyes flick to me.

"And now it begins," says Flores Drakos with a cold smile.

"What exactly?" Xander asks, looking up from the folder.

"The testing. Mace doesn't care for it, but I do. I want to see exactly what the Boneweaver can do. Take her down to the team. They have work to do."

It's funny that dread does not coil through me at Flores' cold words. This is what I'd expected, after all. Not this sit-in-the-corner-dog-bowl-business. So it's almost with relief that I rise from my spot as Xander comes to hook his magic golden chain to my collar.

"Bye, woof woof!" the two hatchlings cry. "Bye!"

I turn and manage to get in a wave before I'm tugged out the door.

Ten minutes later, I'm being led into the Drakos entrance hall, where the team of sharp-eyed serpents anxiously wait in their nasty, starched lab coats.

"We're happy to take it from here, Lord Drakos," a bald serpent says, stepping forward and holding his hand out expectantly.

"Oh you're *happy*, are you?" Xander sneers, making no move to hand over the chain. I stare in surprise at the sheer venom in his tone. "It is *my* prisoner. *I* will oversee the study."

I'm under zero illusions that Xander might be doing this under some altruistic need to protect me. The tightness of his shoulders, the arrogance of his stance and loathing in the shape of his mouth, tell me this is a territorial, possessive, dragon asserting his authority.

If I'm not mistaken, the returned Drakos heir will be at his worst around these potential threats to his home. I know because it's something I would do in his position.

"O-Of course," the scientist replies, inclining his head and hiding the flash of fear over his face as he remembers who he's dealing with.

A beast cold enough to not only reject, but betray his regina.

The scientists lead us out of the entrance hall and through corridors, into a side passageway that slopes underground. I'm suddenly reminded of Animus Academy as a magical hiss sounds and flames splutter to life in the wall sconces to our left and right. The stones of the walls and floor are a complete matte black, allowing the threads of gold woven through them to be easily seen by firelight.

It also makes for a blinding contrast as we eventually turn into the completely white room fronted with rhino-proof glass that still smells of fresh paint.

My heart skips a beat. Okay, *a few* unhealthy beats as I lay eyes on the obviously newly built testing facility. There are three rows of chairs in front of the glass wall, and no less than five computers next to them.

A place like this filled my nightmares as a teenager. Had always been at the back of my mind, flashing like a warning siren. The entire reason I had to keep my secret like my life depended on it. The reason I'd had to run away from my mates in the first place.

Now the very man who'd warned me about this happening is subjecting me to it. My father is nowhere to be seen, but here I am, willingly walking into my wildest nightmare. Perhaps I have more control over my destiny than I gave myself credit for.

I don't regret finding my mates. Not now, not ever. And I don't regret protecting my friends either, especially not after what happened to Sabrina. No one else will ever suffer for my father's want for me.

This was my choice, *is* still my choice, and at least, I can hold on to that as my heart thunders in my ears.

Her name was Athena Boneweaver and she will get her revenge.

"We will recommence the sampling protocol," the bald, middle-aged serpent, apparently the leader of this team, says. "Miss Boneweaver, sit on this table."

Well, at least someone around here is using my name. The whole 'It' thing Xander and his dad have going is already starting to get on my nerves. Xander snaps his wrist with the usual amount of irritation, and the cold chain roughly snaps off my neck, retracting back into his gold bangle.

Exhaling through my nose, I oblige the scientist and stride into the room and towards the table like I'm not terrified out of my feathers. Even through my new dress, the steel is cold against my ass as I sit on it, but it's nothing compared to the cold that captures my heart as five tall figures in black military uniform stalk in and seat themselves on the other side of the glass as if ready for a show.

Five skeleton masks cover the lower halves of their faces, and the fifth, the biggest of them, has pulled his mask up all the way to cover his entire face. I feel Ghoul's eyes on me as a scientist jabs a needle into the inside of my elbow and takes another vial of blood. Xander, on the other hand, has the audacity to be seated behind Ghoul, concentrating on his phone, the glow of the screen illuminating his scowling lips.

I tear my eyes off all the bastards as the serpents in lab coats bustle around me, no doubt feeling very important as they commence this highly lucrative research. I wonder what their paper will be titled.

"So what's next?" I ask, noticing, for the first time the scientists are wearing name tags. "Solomon?" He's ordering people around with the importance of the head honcho.

He's surprised that I've spoken to him directly, faint brows rising. "We've taken samples from your human vehicle, now we want to sample your other forms."

Ice spreads through my veins. Of course they do. "Right," I say stiffly. "Which is first?"

"I am aware you prefer your eagle form," Solomon says, hazel eyes boring into mine. He has a burst blood vessel in his left eye. I wonder if it's from stress. "And we have a list of the beasts you can shift into. But your paternal blood is a king cobra. We'd like to see that first."

I won't lie, it bothers me that they already seem to know so much. Who told them what they know? Was it my father? I suppose it could have been any of the serpent guards at the school. Or students. Perhaps even Xander himself has told them all he knows.

Swallowing down the bile now creeping up my throat, I pretend the serpent generals are not suddenly leaning forward in their seats and nod, sliding back onto the table so my legs are straight in front of me.

Rolling the tension out of my shoulders, I shift, my world suddenly falling into darkness as my dress falls in and around me. I don't hate my serpent form. On the contrary, it's always interesting to be in a form that has no arms and legs. I'm one long band of powerful muscle, fast moving and fanged, the vibrations of the world humming in my brain. As I slither out of my dress and into the bright white of the room, I even get a little kick out of the fact that everyone's attention is suddenly and completely fixed on me and my big reveal. I rear up, stretching out my upper spine and finding a satisfying height as I'm suddenly aware of the hood on either side of my head and the forked tongue that instinctively slides out.

The air tastes like metal, plastic, and serpent. Then there's male sweat and my own blood in the vials on the bench outside. It smells like greed and excitement. I feel every boot and shoe tapping on the stone floor.

Someone takes a picture, and my head snaps towards it, my tongue snaking out again. Pens scratch on clipboards and Solomon steps forward with a tiny, covered container I recognise immediately.

"We'll need to milk your venom, Aurelia," he says, slowly and clearly. "Please extend your fangs."

While his words are polite, his tone is an order, and the ancient instinct in me responds to the threat, my fangs unfolding from their hiding place as a low *hissss* fills the air.

No one misses the large figure that rises to his considerable height outside. The serpents in the room stiffen as Ghoul stalks into our space full of languid, predatorial authority, his shadows licking around him like black flames.

"Move aside, I'll do it." That deep, commanding timbre vibrates along my scales in the most dangerous way.

"My Lord Basilisk—"

"She could bite you, and then what?" Ghoul says playfully, wagging his finger like he's talking to a favoured, but errant, child. "I can't have a dead viper. We need you for a while longer yet, Solly Polly."

He turns to me.

"Come here, little cobra." Ghoul pulls up the bottom half of his mask, exposing the bronze skin around his mouth and drawn white fangs over a crazed smile. "Little *snakelet*."

Curse my snake form because she willingly, *eagerly* slides over to her basilisk mate.

Chapter 7

Ghoul

Nothing in the land of the living or the dead could have prepared me for the vision of my regina as she assumed her cobra form.

Sheer, utter, *majestic* perfection.

Something more than me pulled me to my feet and forced my limbs to move towards her. It's in a state of ecstasy that I watch her scaled body slither keenly towards me, fangs bared in a latent threat.

"See?" I gloat, tossing a smirk at the team. "She recognises my authority."

She hisses in annoyance and I grin wider, bringing up a shadow-covered hand to enclose around her neck. Her scales are cool and smooth, and the mating mark hidden under my shadows burns at the contact.

"That's it, little snakelet," I say, unable to help myself. "Hiss at me all you want, as long as you give me that sweet, sweet poison." I turn towards Solomon and beckon with my first two fingers. The chief tiger snake passes me the clear cylindrical container, covered with a soft white cap. "Ready?" I stroke a thumb down her slender neck and lean down to whisper, "Give me everything, like a good girl."

She hisses and strikes. I meet her just in time with the milking container. Her jaws open around it, sharp fangs piercing the plastic, and all that beautiful, dangerous venom squirts out. I watch in rapture, my eyes wide, tears gathering behind them. My focus is on her, only her as she expels the powerful liquid into the jar.

"Such a good snakelet," I coo. *You are perfect*, I say into my own head.

She fills the jar twice more than a cobra has any right to before the flow stops, and it's with great pride that I prise her jaws off.

I had intended to keep my thoughts to myself, but the snakelet slithers like a piece of delicious silk into my mind.

"You're even crazier than Savage," she says.

Her voice is like a balm to the rotten crevices within my skull. "Savage?" I muse. *"That little puppy dog isn't crazy at all."*

Mace is right about many things. But the one thing we agree on the most is that serpents *are* the superior species. And now, I practically have the snakelet all to myself.

Chapter 8

Scythe

As the morning sun rises over Animus Academy, Marduk and I stare at the bodies of the five dead guards, lying sprawled on the grass before us.

"It could've been worse," Marduk says, exhaling a puff of smoke from his joint into the blood-stained air, before offering it to me.

I decline it with a shake of my head.

Even with the protections made from my regina's tears that keep the hallucinations away, I might have been driven mad by the knowledge that my regina has stolen away from me. Of her *commanding* my brothers and me not to follow her.

I had no choice but to sink into my psychopathic shark.

Ice cold, calculating, and in no need for the calming effect of an alpha-grade joint.

"Marduk?" Minnie's voice shrieks across the school grounds like a javelin. "*Marduk!*"

The Caspian tiger is already striding towards the little tigress, suddenly protective and alert. "Regina," he says attentively.

I turn to watch a furious Minnie jogging towards us, in a

purple tracksuit, pink curls wild from a sleepless night. Yeti strides behind her, his pale face tight and unhappy.

"Where is Lia?" Minnie demands, pointing angrily at us both, one at a time. "And where is Savage? Raquel is saying he *killed* school guards last night! Someone better tell me what the Goddess-damned plan is before I lose my shit completely!" Minnie's aura pulses a faint red-tinged orange as she plants her tiny fists on her hips.

Marduk reaches for his regina, but Minnie slaps his hand away before looking to me. The tiger makes an affronted sound in his throat, but Minnie isn't giving him the time of day. She tries not to look at the mangled bodies behind me, blinking sudden tears away as she does what many beasts cannot: stares me dead in the eye. "Scythe?" she swallows. "Where is she?"

"Minnie." I say flatly. "Did my regina ever give you any indication of her plans?"

She blinks, the question unexpected. Her eyes search the air in thought, but then her face becomes stormy, and she raises a finger at me. "*You* left."

Behind the cold, a faint pain threatens to pierce my heart. I deserve that. Deserve to feel the full brunt of that agony. But not now.

"I know," I say. "But I have returned for her. And she surrendered to the enemy. She has been taken."

Minnie appraises me and seems to understand that human Scythe has been put away.

She nods carefully before pinching her nose. "I had no bloody idea. She never let anything on. After you left, she, well..." She crosses her arms. "She was in a state. Understandably. But none of us could have guessed she'd give herself up." For the first time, I hear Minnie growl in her throat. "And with Xander's help, no less. Goddess, I want to *kill* that dragon! He saw what it did to me when Titus—" Infinite pain flashes across her face. "He fucking saw!"

Yeti places a hand on her shoulder as tears stream down Minnie's face and she angrily wipes them away with her sleeve.

All I can do is watch the three mates huddle together as that fresh wound within me burns like hellfire. My shark thrashes and I crack my neck to relieve the tension. Marduk turns from comforting his mate to glance at me warily.

What Marduk has with his regina is denied to me. I am unable to comfort Aurelia, unable to serve her and kiss her tears away. No doubt she is shaken from the severing. No doubt she is raging from the betrayal.

And I am forbidden to go to her.

Ice cold thoughts filter through my mind. Plans. Projections. Deaths that are needed. Blows that need to be made.

"And where is Savage?" Minnie sniffs. "She wouldn't want him to be acting like this." She jerks her chin to the bodies behind me.

"It's time for a meeting." Even to me, my voice sounds like death.

* * *

We hear Savage well before we enter the underground rocky cavern. It's the same one Lyle had previously used to cage us, what seems like a lifetime ago now. My wolf brother rages within the central electrified cage, the sizzle of electricity and scent of burnt wolf's flesh saturating the air.

Minnie rushes into the cavern after me, before a gasp stops her dead. "He's half-shifted?"

Marduk and Yeti protectively flank their regina as she wanders forward in horrified awe.

I, too, survey my brother, except a sadistic smile twitches at my lips. It pleases me that his love for our regina is on full display in this maddened form.

Savage remains in his half-wolf form from last night, a rare and terrible state I've never seen in an animalia. His head is entirely wolf, black tufts extending down his neck and stopping at the bloody skin of his human chest. His upper arms are human, but more fur starts at his forearms before ending in his large, human hands. The same for his calves and feet. He's torn off his formal evening clothes, leaving him unrestricted to blast powerful punches to the rock wall at the back of the cage. His growls and snarls fill the cavern, echoing around us in a cacophony of rage. He's been going all night.

It's a joy to see.

"Where is Mr Pardalia?" Minnie asks quietly.

"With the headmistress," Marduk says quickly, passing me a look. "Meditating, perhaps."

I'm doubtful of that. Once she'd seen the regina order written in phoenix flame, Celeste had advised Lyle, Savage and me to separate ourselves. As mates of the same pack with our regina taken, we are likely to descend into a feral hunt, urging each other on in the most animalistic way.

Savage had not taken kindly to any of it.

Minnie tentatively says his name.

My brother whirls around, baring his canines. "They have my regina!" he roars in a nightmarish primitive voice. Goosebumps erupt all over me.

Minnie flinches, but bravely steps forward and says in that gentle voice women use on pups. "I know." Yeti and Marduk shadow her every movement. I step up next to Yeti, watching closely.

"They have my regina!" Savage roars again.

Minnie's patience is apparently short-lived because she shouts back, "Yeah, and all of this—" She angrily waves her arms to indicate Savage's body. "Is. Not. *Helping!*"

Savage's jaws snap shut for a moment as he considers her. His hazel eyes are wild and feral.

"Pull yourself together, Savage!" Minnie continues shouting. "Because you're not going to get her back acting the fool!"

Savage claws at his face, howling into the cavern ceiling. He falls to his knees, a whine escaping through sharp, sharp teeth. "I miss her," he says softly, dropping to lie on his side in the fetal position. "I need her."

"So do I," Minnie huffs, stepping forward to crouch a safe distance from the steel bars. "But we can't be feral and half-shifting and all that nonsense when we've got to use our thinking human brains, right?"

"She left me," Savage whines. "Left us, Min. Why would she do that?"

A growl rumbles in my own chest. We have enemies to kill, torture, maim. We have allies to build. Bridges to burn.

Savage reflexively raises his wolf's head to growl back at me. Minnie snaps her fingers to get his attention. "Less of that."

A regina-command truly only works on a regina's pack, but it does make the rest of us pay attention. Marduk and Yeti suddenly straighten.

"Can you shift back?" Minnie urges. "You're going to scare people like this."

"Good," Savage says, dragging himself off the floor and to his feet. With what appears to be great effort, he sighs, before his wolf head shrinks and loses its fur. My brother's handsome human face appears, hazel eyes glimmering with rage and malice. He finds my gaze and holds it. "Let them be scared."

"Are you ready to work, brother?" I ask.

Savage snarls viciously in reply.

Chapter 9

Aurelia

G houl steadies me on the steel table with one hand as he plucks out a white feather from my skin with the other.

"Keep going and I won't have any bloody left," I say tightly into his head. I already have a bald patch under my wing as it is. Cockatoo feels like my millionth shift. They ran me through every form they could think of, starting with the snakes, then the birds, taking a feather from each form for their records.

In case anyone doubted it, plucking feathers from the root fucking hurts.

It seems to me like they want a sample of *everything* I am able to give. To study if there is any difference to regular animalia samples, I suppose. I have to give them credit for being thorough.

"Mammals tomorrow," Solomon announces, securing the jar holding the white feather. "Back to human form now, if you please, Miss Boneweaver."

Sure, do you want fries with that?

I have to focus to shift back into my human body. In truth, I've never shifted this much in such a short period of time, and shifting fatigue is definitely a thing. I imagine the shift and it happens slowly. My wings elongate into arms, the feathers disappearing, my twiggy legs extending into calves and toes, and my beak retracting back into my face.

Concentrating so hard, it's only right at the end of my shift that I realise Ghoul is still holding me.

"Get off me, reptile," I say, tiredly wiggling my naked body against his massive form.

"Careful, I might get excited," Ghoul drawls, unceremoniously setting me onto the floor. I snatch up my dress from the table, quickly shoving it over my head and covering my body. The maid, Heather, had given me neither a bra nor knickers—I guess *pets* don't need to wear any.

"Up on the table again," Solomon says. "Dress goes up." One of the other scientists wheels in a small machine, and I crane my neck to see what it is.

"Develop some class, serpent," Xander sneers, suddenly at the door, throwing a towel over my lower half. "Or I'll force it down your worm throat."

"You *do* obsess about worms, don't you?" Ghoul says mildly from my other side. "Is it because of the tiny one between your legs?"

Xander's lids lower over his glowing orbs, giving Ghoul a droll look before striding back to the viewing area behind the glass. Everyone knows the old wives' tales about dragons and their massive dicks. I've never actually gotten a look at Xander's dick, so I don't know if they're true.

I register a sizzling magical phoenix's presence with a jolt to the stomach.

"Ah, I thought I smelled eunuch," Ghoul drawls, glancing over his shoulder.

I'm so surprised that I miss the opportunity to lunge for the newcomer's throat.

Next time.

Damien Agnis wears his signature white suit and shirt, which does nothing good for the new, faintly green pallor to his skin. Though if Ghoul's surprising new title for him is anything to go by, I guess it explains that. His hair is the same, crimson curls piled around his head and his white glasses frame golden eyes that hungrily take me in. He holds a black box, the handle clutched tight in one pale fist.

It's then that I notice the wand to the ultrasound machine Solomon is waving at me. "Lie down, Miss Boneweaver."

My mind flashes back to a medical room I visited not long ago. My mother lying small and helpless on the bed. An ultrasound machine had sat in the corner of that room, too.

Terror floods my throat. My veins. My heart.

"No!" I shriek, mouth twisting in disgust as I move to lunge off the steel table. "Get the fuck away from me!"

Ghoul casually steps to the side, blocking my exit with his body. "Nuh-uh, snakelet."

"I thought we'd run into this little issue," Damien Agnis says lightly.

I clutch the sides of the table in sweaty fists and glare at the phoenix lord, wishing I could burn him into something more rudimentary than ash. "Why are *you* even here?"

Damien sets the black box on the edge of the table, unlatching twin locks at the top. "I had a specialist cage made," he says all too proudly. "Courtesy of the Lady Crocodylus. Marvellous woman."

The Collector?

My irritation turns into alarm as Damien pulls out a glass cage, because inside of it bounces four coloured balls of fluff.

"Henry!" I gasp. "Gertie?"

The nimpins chitter and squeak in their confinement, their liquid black eyes wide in fear as they gather at the glass, squashing themselves against it as if they're trying to get to me.

"Don't think I did not notice just how precious these creatures were to you and your friends," Damien explains, holding the cage up and tapping his nail against it as if it's a fish tank. "See this lever on top?" He points to a red knob next to the handle. "One twist and it'll send carbon monoxide gas into the chamber, which—"

Ghoul makes an exaggerated choking sound in his throat. Rage and fear pool in my stomach. This. Fucking. Bastard.

"Miss Boneweaver is powerful, in case anyone has forgotten," Damien says meaningfully to the scientists. "And she is only in steel shackles."

"She is here voluntarily!" Solomon says irritably.

"Yes, but not everything we do here *will* be voluntary." Damien says it so quickly, so casually, that it sends a chill down my spine. "She will be more compliant given the threat to these small creatures."

Suddenly, I see the males around me in a different light. Nothing they do to me here is an 'option' any more.

Swallowing, I lie back down on the table and arrange the towel to cover the space between my legs. I pull my dress up, exposing my lower abdomen. "Make it quick," I grit out.

"It is just to check the condition of your ovaries and uterus so we can—"

"I know exactly what you're doing," I snap. "As I said, make it quick."

Damien steps up so he can get a better look, and all I can do is stare at the ceiling as I try to calm my breathing.

Everyone leans forward to stare at the screen of the ultrasound machine, as if they're all so very keen to take a look at my insides. Nausea roils in my stomach and I clutch the sides of the steel table so hard it becomes sweaty under my palms.

Solomon presses firmly just inside my right hip bone. "How many times did you do this to my mother?" I ask to the ceiling. "How many times before she became unresponsive?"

From the side of my eye, the scientists move uncomfortably. Someone clears their throat. There are no women in this room. Only males, only animuses. I wonder if she was scared. If she knew what the future had in store for her and her daughter.

"Try to relax," Solomon gruffs. "You are thankfully young. There should be no issues with our work."

"Unethical work," I say. "Illegal work."

"Voluntary work," Ghoul says. "Important work."

I glance at him, where he looms over me from my left. He never knew about my mother's imprisonment, but that doesn't matter, because he's here overseeing mine now. I hope he can see the death in my eyes. I hope he can see that I will kill my father for all of this.

Chapter 10

Xander

After that complete farce of a scientific research study that lasted all day, I'm in a foul mood. Made fouler still by the fact that I had to watch Ghoul fondle Spawn the entire time.

It was the most disgusting thing I'd ever seen. Now, it's thankfully quiet as I tug it along behind me and up to the ground floor, probably moping over the miniature fluffballs trapped in Damien's cage.

Nimpins are utterly useless creatures. Barely a mouthful of bones that would probably come up as a hairball anyway. I don't know why Lyle even bothered with them to start with. The animas just treated them like Tamagotchis, and the animuses were undeterred by them. Complete idiocy, if you ask me.

Drakos Estate is expecting guests this evening. It's the biggest event of the season and my much-anticipated debut back into dragon society. Dragons are flying in from other states, even some from overseas, for the sole reason of greeting me, and I'm not going to have any of these worms screw it up for my family. I've ordered them to stay underground until sunrise and threatened them with a crispy hanging. The scientists are all keen to study the samples and data they've gathered just now anyway, so I'm certain they'll stay put. Mace Naga has also, unsurprisingly, made himself scarce. No doubt he's worried about some retaliation from Savage and Lyle and is securing his closest family members. Savage enjoys taking hostages on a good day, and he no doubt has his eye on Charlotte Naga and her remaining mate as his first victims. I don't think the Spawn knows about her Uncle Ben's death and I'm not going to be the one to tell her.

I rub the back of my neck in irritation as I check in with my dragon. Still. He's completely still except for the slow and steady breathing inflating his ribs. He looks exactly the same, and no matter how much I prod him, he doesn't make so much as a snort.

Further irritation claws at my gut. I can't even fly to release any pent-up rage.

The chain linked to the bangle on my wrist tugs violently. I throw a glance over my shoulder in time to see Spawn stumble and right itself.

"Too fast," it mutters.

I continue walking as if it hadn't spoken, exhaling through my nose. I need to focus on this afternoon. My family's reputation relies on everything going perfectly.

We reach my father's study high on the topmost floor, inside one of the turrets overlooking the front lawn. Just by turning his head, he can see who enters via the main gates. It's why I'd always entered from the north whenever I'd paid secret visits to my sister and the hatchlings.

He sits at his desk of mountain ash, facing the door, his head bowed over the moleskin folder of anima biodata. Though he no doubt heard me approach from the base of the stairwell, I respectfully rap my knuckles on the open door.

"My heir," he says, eyes flicking up. "Come and sit."

I stride in, quickly taking the gold and red velvet chair opposite the desk. Spawn stands awkwardly beside me. It's a wonder no one ever taught it manners.

Without taking my eyes off my father, I tug on the chain and snap, "Kneel."

From the side of my eye, Spawn huffs and gets onto its knees next to my chair with as much fuss as possible.

"It will learn," Father says, eyeing it with interest.

"We should use the obsidian shackles for tonight's event."

He waves a dismissive, bejewelled hand, the afternoon light making the many gold rings flash. "Our guests will want to see what we can do. I want them to enjoy it."

"There will be other entertainment," I say carefully. "Surely we do not need to parade it about."

He cuts me a sharp look, telling me I've overstepped. "That is entirely the point. They are all very interested. Particularly, Lord and Lady Hellfire from Melbourne." He removes one of the pages from the folder, sliding it across the fine wood. "I want you to consider Miss Francesca carefully. She's a good candidate."

I take the page, glancing at the tiny headshot stapled to the top right corner. "I thought so too," I murmur. She's a very attractive young lady. Blonde, tall at six feet, with dark eyes and a straight, fine nose. Her lips are curved into a coy smile, as if she's trying to seduce me through the camera lens. "And there was another candidate who caught my eye. Miss Nadine Chen."

"That would be my next preference," Father says, leaning back in his chair and steepling his fingers. "Both of good breeding. Both fertile. Both sound of mind."

"And well educated," I say slowly, ignoring that last. "The Chens are well connected."

"And her parents will return to Shanghai, convenient for us. There will be less...issues after the marriage."

Issues. Like the ones we had with Sissy.

Father closes the folder. "Your new clothes have been delivered. Wear the family crest tonight."

"Yes, Father." It amazes me how quickly I've assumed the old rules and manners. Then again, they'd been drilled into me fiercely from the cradle.

Father folds his hands in his lap as he studies me. I meet him eye for eye, keeping my heart rate steady by controlling my breathing. I do not move except to blink at the normal rate. I do not swallow, clench my fists, nor scratch that itch on my temple. My back is rod straight. My protections are sound.

My father is a beast in his prime, though there are fine lines under his eyes now, and at the corners of his mouth. It had been, after all, his own age in mind when he offered me to return to the family Estate. Emmerson was a hatchling still and there was no one else to inherit. Worse still, there were fewer dragons being born than ever before.

Finally, he nods, ending the challenge between us. "I will see you in two hours hence."

And with that, I am dismissed.

I tug on the chain, signalling Spawn to get off the carpet where it had no doubt been listening to every word. I incline my head to my father and head out the door, running through the stats of the ladies in the biodata folder. They'll all be present tonight with their parents, some of them secretly wishing we make a mess of things. Many of them will be curious about who I've become. I've barely been in the public eye since I left the estate, and whatever they've heard of me is likely from gossip. These, and a million other things, run through my mind as I head back to my room.

When we get there, Olly and Heather are already bustling about, readying all my things for tonight. I unhook the gold chain from Spawn.

"Bathe it," I order Heather. "Make sure it looks presentable for our guests. Don't spray anything. They'll want to scent her."

Spawn makes a disgruntled noise before allowing Heather to tug her into the bathroom.

Chapter 11

Aurelia

A nest of dragons from around the country are waiting downstairs and I'm being prepared like a pork roast, ready for their consumption.

Heather prods me into the bathtub, filling it with a fragrant oil and bubble bath combo. The thought of her doing the same to Xander at some stage is the only thing that gets me through the next hour. She scrubs me until I'm pink, even getting a nail brush and scrubbing at my finger and toe nails. She then tries to brush my teeth for me, and I have half a mind to let her, but instead, I put on a haughty tone and snatch the brush out of her hand. "Heather, need I remind you that I'm not *actually* a pet but a grown-ass woman?"

She looks affronted for a moment before muttering something under her breath and occupying herself with rubbing a scent-free moisturiser into my back and arms.

I shove on a new dress—a black wrap-around style satin that's simple but surprisingly elegant—before I'm ushered out into the room where Xander stalks past me in only incredibly low-slung trousers. It takes everything in me not to look, because I know it'll trigger the agony that lies at the edge of all things.

Instead, I have to sit in the corner and stay silent through the ordeal of Heather straightening my hair, smoothing my baby hairs and flyaways with a serum of some sort that Xander probably uses. The efficient manner in which she sets my hair into a long length down my back tells me she's been instructed to style me in exactly this way.

There is something about this that I find extremely disturbing.

I still can't believe Xander made me sit through that meeting with his father. Arranging a marriage like this is just embarrassing for all of us. Worse still is the fact that those young women are all going to be here tonight. Looking at him. Waiting for him to cast their eye on them.

There's no doubt in my mind that Xander Drakos will be considered a good match and—

It's at this point in my musing that said Xander Drakos strides out of the bathroom, buttoning the cuffs of his black jacket sleeves.

That crucial tear in my soul bleeds anew.

He's devastating. And in more ways than one.

Xander is wearing a three-piece tuxedo, the jacket and pants a midnight black, his vest the same colour. His hair is loose and silken down his back, perhaps to conceal the new small wireless earpieces. He's forgone his usual black dagger earring for a small black stud and removed his black nose ring. At the centre of his chest, he wears his family's golden crest, and the look is complete with gold waist and collar chains.

"You'll walk behind me at all times," Xander says flatly, keeping his eyes straight ahead as he snaps his wrist, that gold chain snaking upwards and clicking into my collar like a magnet. "No less than five paces."

"I'm supposed to be counting that?" I ask faintly.

"You never were all that bright."

"Apparently," I say darkly.

Xander glances over his shoulder, probably finding it strange that I've agreed with him. The truth of it is that my stomach is still roiling after the ultrasound with the scientists. Everything else, I could handle. The continued plucking of my feathers, the ordeal of Ghoul *milking* me, but that one thing has thrown me entirely. I rub my arms, despite the warm spring night, not caring who sees me acting like prey.

Xander begins walking before I can actually vomit on this nice carpet, and I'm forced to steady myself. Maids and butlers hurry about, all headed to either the back garden, where the event will be held, or what I'm assuming is the kitchen or wine cellar. Faint music floats up from outside. A very real string quartet, if I'm not mistaken.

Xander leads me down the stairs where we find his parents, both richly dressed in a long black velvet gown and a black and gold three-piece tuxedo, respectively.

Flores turns around to eye us, first looking me up and down, then his son. "It is time," he says, the gold thread embroidery on his cuffs glinting under the warm lights of the candelabra high above us. "Wait here a moment. I will introduce you." Flores turns to Xander's mother, who had been gazing at Xander with fixed, glassy eyes and a faint smile. "Come, Esteè." He tugs on her hand, placing it in the crook of his left elbow, before turning them both around.

Feeling Lady Drakos' presence, my avian power stirs once again.

"Don't get any ideas tonight." Xander's voice pulls me back to the present. There's a faint clapping outside. The boom of King Flores' voice and Xander's glowing eyes are fixed on the open doors. "Don't speak unless spoken to. Even then, don't prattle on unnecessarily. Don't trip or fall. Don't stare."

"Anything else?" I ask with exaggerated politeness.

"Don't cry. Don't get angry. Don't use your powers or try anything stupid. Lord Agnis is outside with the nimpins."

The fucking nerve.

"Is it true, what Ghoul said?" I ask, trying to distract myself. "About him being a...eunuch? Or was that just a catch-phrase?"

Xander's cheek perks up with the hint of a smirk. "It's true."

My stomach jumps. "Why? Who?"

"It was Lyle, funnily enough. For Celeste's sake."

Shock winds through me. My Lyle? Castrating phoenixes? Since he let his beast out of his shackles, I can believe him doing just about anything murderous or torturous, but this is something I hadn't expected. The only reason I can imagine him doing such a drastic thing would be because...

Nausea rolls up my throat once again and my hand flies to my sternum. I must make a sound because Xander half turns in irritation before King Flores loudly announces his son's name.

The butler at the door bows and extends his arm. Xander walks forward.

So careful is his stalk, so very practised is the set of his shoulders, the swing of his arms. Xander has been waiting for this moment for many years, and despite the bond-breaking, despite the betrayal of it, something inside of me doesn't want to ruin this for him. It's complete insanity, but as we step onto the deck outside, my anima keens a mournful, broken hymn.

I have to hand it to them, the Drakos' sure know how to throw a party. The back garden is stunningly dressed with sweeping bands of twinkling lights on either side of a long runway that looks like it was put here just for this event.

How long, exactly, had Xander been plotting for his return?

A round of polite applause greets us, along with the collection of scattered beasts. Although they're all dressed in glistening and expensive black tie, you can't mistake these creatures for anything other than dragons. Massive jewels set in yellow and white gold sit around necks, wrists and fingers, some even embedded into clothes, hair and shoes. Nothing gaudy, of course, only extremely wealthy people showing off their finest to their rivals. But it's the sheer power in the air. A magnificent yet brutal *burn* that singes the nostrils. My heart rate kicks up on instinct and my anima raises her own mighty head, surveying the potential enemies.

Suddenly, I'm confused as to why *I'm* here. Surely Xander and King Flores would have preferred he make his debut solo? Why string me along like a prize calf to ruin the dramatic effect of the returned heir?

Eyes with gold, silver and emerald irises greedily rake down my form. I'm the pauper of the evening, with not a single jewel on me, not even an earring.

Far at the back of things, at the edge of the shadows, stands Damien Agnis, looking even peakier by the contrast of his black tuxedo. In his left hand he holds the glass cage with my poor nimpins, all of whom sit depressed at the floor, huddled together. When the phoenix catches my eye, he raises a finger and taps the side of his nose, as if we have some cute little secret between us.

I cut away from his poisoned gaze, tampering down the mixture of rage and nausea that fills me. All of that to ensure I wouldn't *do* anything tonight.

Xander stops at the end of the platform, and I stop just in time to leave those decreed five steps as the applause dies down.

Arrogance drips off his stance, and power ripples around him like the unfurling of two dark wings. Goosebumps erupt all over my body, and from the ever so slight shift in his audience, they feel it too.

"Good evening," Xander drawls, his deep voice having no trouble reaching out around the entire garden and creating a buzz over my own skin. "I'd like to thank my parents for welcoming my return to the family. I am happy to be back." Xander bows towards his parents, standing at the head of the crowd, while there's a smattering of polite clapping.

Me? I just stand there awkwardly, trying not to look like the royal fool with a collar and leash around her throat.

"And thank you all for coming to celebrate with us tonight. I look forward to meeting you all and reintroducing myself." I can tell he's smirking as he glances around because more than a few of the ladies, young and old, give coy smiles of their own.

Flirtatious bastard.

The music strikes up again, and I cast my own eye about as Xander steps off the platform and heads into the crowd. I hurry to follow, and dragons surge forward to be the first to greet him, extending hands and smiles.

It's then that I see why I've been brought along. Once they've had their fill of the prodigal son, the dragons start eyeing me more closely. Flores wasn't kidding when he said they're very interested. Though they keep a respectful distance, their eyes are positively aglow with curiosity. Taller than other beasts, even the women reaching over six feet, I feel like a *thing* being inspected by threatening, alien beings.

When I made my debut at The Jewel of the Jungle with Scythe, I'd felt like a prize. They'd dressed me up as a jewel of their own and I'd felt, for the first time in my life, like something precious. And here, I realise that I still am.

I'm still a jewel. A status symbol. The other dragons might have the biggest emeralds and rubies, the biggest hunks of gold that find their value in their scarcity, but Xander has the biggest jewel in his treasure trove. The Last Boneweaver.

"My daughter," comes a deep, feminine voice that drags my attention back to the hand Xander is currently kissing. "You might remember her from your youth. Miss Nadine Chen."

"Of course." Xander's deep, seductive drawl stirs something in my lower belly. "You have blossomed into adulthood, my lady."

I could vomit. I *should* vomit right on the backs of his expensive black shoes as Xander straightens and stares into the eyes of a porcelain-skinned young woman with almond eyes and cropped black hair. "Will you come and see the new fairy lights we've had installed?"

"Call me Nadine, please," she purrs in return.

Quite suddenly, the crowd parts for them as Nadine places a hand on Xander's offered arm and they stroll away.

They're *taking a turn* about the garden as if they're courting. I seethe internally, trying not to show it to the dragons staring at me, settling on clenching my teeth instead. He's completely shoving this in my face as I watch him lean down to murmur something in her ear.

Heat claws at my insides as the urge to singe the both of them almost gets the better of me.

"Oh!" Nadine abruptly pipes when we are a good distance from the crowd. "Your new pet!" She half turns to stare rudely at me. "Can it do tricks?"

Xander takes a beat to turn, telling me he's annoyed with the subject choice. "I suppose." He keeps his voice bored. "Serpent Spawn, show Nadine what you can do."

I raise my chin. "What would you like to see?"

Nadine grins excitedly, stepping close to Xander and hooking her arm into his, all flirty and shit. "Can you really shift into *any* creature?"

"Any I've been in contact with."

"What about insects?"

I scoff in disgust. "They're not animals, are they, Nadine?"

"Watch your attitude," Xander snaps.

I glare at him.

He smirks with a sudden thought. "Nadine, think of the most embarrassing creature."

Nadine's smile turns devious. "A rat."

They're quite intelligent creatures, but a reptile like her wouldn't know that. I smile wildly, suddenly realising I can turn this lemon into lemonade. I reach for the ribbon secured at my left ribcage, and before either of them can do anything, untie it and open both sides of the wrap dress at the same time, exposing my entirely naked body underneath.

It's not *my* fault they denied me underwear, is it?

Nadine makes a tiny sound of surprise while Xander goes gargoyle-still. I smile, letting the dress slide off my shoulders and allowing them to see me for a moment before I shift into the creature of choice.

My height drops rapidly towards the ground, and the world

suddenly becomes huge, Xander and Nadine becoming mono-lithic beings as I drop onto all fours onto the manicured grass. Interestingly, the gold collar shrinks with me, and that gold chain leading to Xander's wrist becomes as thin as a necklace. I scuttle forward at speed, heading right for Nadine's expensive black stilettos.

The dragoness bleats like a goat, but as I reach her toe, Xander flicks his telekinetic fingers, sending me tumbling backwards into the grass.

It was worth the scream.

Nadine clears her throat. "Well, that wasn't as exciting as I imagined. Let's carry on, shall we?"

"Of course, Nadine. And Spawn? Do not shift back."

Cursing out loud so it comes out as a hopefully scary chitter, I'm forced to leave my dress behind as I rush to follow them, in case Xander thinks he can start dragging me across the lawn.

By the time we return to the bustle of the main soiree, I'm fully out of breath and exhausted. Xander purposefully lapped the gardens in what I'm sure was the longest way possible.

The string quartet isn't loud enough to smother the laughs as we return and the party sees us. And if I wasn't intimidated by the near seven-foot dragons before, I sure am now. Their shoes are far too close to my head for my liking, their laughs far too loud, and the fact that I can see up their noses doesn't help soften the blow.

Savage would find that little fact hilarious. A pang of darkness shoots through me as I remember he's not here for me to tell him in the first place.

Xander finally stops and I stand on the lawn on my tiny paws, my nose twitching madly as I pant to catch my breath and stop myself from crying. He kisses Nadine's hand and she thanks him for the *wonderful personal time*. But she's quickly replaced by another doting set of parents nudging forward a pretty blonde. Xander kisses her hand too, before looking around.

"Who would like to take the Boneweaver?"

The voice that quickly answers surprises me. "I'll take her."

Everyone turns to look at Sissy, striding forward with a wine glass in one hand. The energy in the space abruptly changes, and I notice the other dragons discreetly angling themselves away from her, like she's infested with something.

"Thank you, Selena," Xander says formally, unhooking the gold bangle from his hand. Selena holds out her own and allows her brother to clasp the bangle around her slender wrist.

She looks down at me, her face holding no trace of emotion. "Come along then, Lady Boneweaver."

Chapter 12

Xander

Four Seasons (Summer)— Vivaldi

"May I be frank with you, Lord Drakos?" Francesca Hellfire says as we walk into the knee-waist hedge maze my mother loves. The night wind suddenly feels cold against my face.

"Of course, Francesca," I say, attempting to sound like a pleasant sort of person.

She glances at me, her tanned features beautiful under the twinkling lamplights spaced periodically outside the maze. "I've never met anyone who's rejected their mate before. My mother is worried it makes you a sociopath."

I huff a laugh. "I'm not a sociopath. I care greatly for my family. I feel pain when they do. I feel great love for them."

She stares at me with sharp grey eyes. "Truly?"

"I've met my share of sociopaths," I say, patting her small hand resting in the crook of my arm. "I'm not one of them."

"Well, that's only one of the things that has me questioning this match."

While I appreciate her frankness, her manner leaves a bit to be desired. She can be taught that, I suppose. "What else has made your list?"

She doesn't miss a beat. "Your eyes," she says. "Are they an issue?"

A fiery whip of irritation snakes into my gut, but I push it aside. "No. In fact, some would say they are an advantage."

She nods slowly, as if considering this. As if she's testing whether I'm lying or not. Again, I have to push that whip aside.

"And your berserker genes, when was the last time you had an episode?"

I stop and turn to look at her. "Your research has been thorough, Francesca. I'm sure you make a great lawyer."

She tosses her length of blonde hair over her shoulder. "I'd like to think I am. I've had glowing reports from my seniors. I hope to make partner soon."

"Why consider the match, Francesca?"

Her eyes search my face, lingering at my mouth. "They say you are the most powerful dragon in the country."

"That remains to be tested."

She says seriously, "I think you are."

And her opinion matters why? I throw her a smile and turn around, offering her my arm. We start walking once again.

"And the Boneweaver?"

Insipid woman. "She is my captive and none of your concern."

"If she will be sleeping in our room, she is my concern."

Only the fact that Francesca's family holds massive shares in the gold and cadmium mines up north stops me from tossing her out of the estate. "She is barely a concern to me," I scoff. "The only reason I agree to tote her around is because—"

"Because what?" She's ogling me again, searching for falsehood. Frankly, it's insulting.

"Because a lot of thieves and deviants have their eye on her, and I cannot let them get their hands on her."

"She's *that* valuable?" Jealousy mars the statement.

"To certain people," I reassure her. "Not me."

"Like Scythe Kharkorous and Savage Fengari."

My jaw clenches of its own accord, and I have to consciously relax it to answer. "Sure."

"Your ex-mates. The criminals."

When I get back inside, I'm torching this woman's biodata sheet, if I don't torch her first. "What is your current relationship with them, exactly?"

"You overstep, Francesca."

She snaps her mouth shut over her next sentence and purses her lips. Finally.

The crickets chirp in the night, and under my music, the rhythmic sound settles me. We finish our lap and head back towards Francesca's parents, her mother rushing forward with her arms out as if to save her daughter from the evil dragon. "How was your walk, darling?"

Francesca leaves my arm to grasp her mother's. "The garden is lovely, but it doesn't hold a flame to ours."

The heat in my orbital bones makes me sure that my eyes flash. Francesca's mother stiffens, then forces a smile. "I'm sure the maze is top tier, darling. The Drakos Estate is the biggest in the southern hemisphere!"

"Is it?" Francesca frowns.

"Ah, that wasn't a part of your research, then?" I smile.

She smiles back at me, missing the jibe completely. "Thank you for a lovely evening, Xander. I hope you remember me tomorrow." I never gave her permission to use my first name. She extends her hand. "I'm sure you need to attend to your other guests."

As gracefully as my irritation allows, I kiss her skin and bow, leaving them to their drinks and gossip.

A fucking smoke is actually what I need. Ignoring everyone else, and waving away a butler with a tray of canapes, I head for the castle. The string quartet plays Vivaldi, contrasting nicely with the Mongolian rock in my ears. I can't believe that dragoness had the nerve to ask about my...condition. Do people have no sense anymore? No sense of self-preservation? Even Aurelia—

I stop myself right there, shaking my head to clear that heinous thought as I enter the warmth of the castle.

But the scent of scum fills my nose, and I turn abruptly to see Lady Hyena and a retinue of three male hyenas walking down from the stairs that lead to my father's office.

What the hell was my father doing inviting her to the estate?

The old lady passes, eyeing me with glimmering coal-black eyes. Suddenly, something in her gaze shifts. Some recognition.

She tilts her head back and cackles.

I stare at her blankly, waiting for her to finish her stupidity. The males cross their arms and look anywhere but me.

"Oh, nasty dragon," she says, wiping the corner of her eye with a black lace handkerchief. "You've gone and cursed yourself for life." She laughs again, taking hold of her cane and hobbling towards the front door.

Something dark creeps through my being and I check on my dragon. He remains catatonic. I clench my teeth and carry on to my room.

Chapter 13

Aurelia

"So that's interesting."

I look up at Selena, as I scuttle in her wake, as she blessedly strolls away from the main party. She glances down at me, bringing out a black material that I realise is my dress. "Oh, you can shift back now."

With surprise, I glance behind us, realising she's brought me around a corner where the bushes will conceal human me.

Selena respectfully turns around, clearly intending to give me privacy. My brows are still raised once I'm in human form, wrapping the dress back in place around my body and tying the strings.

I cast her a sideways look. "What's interesting?"

Xander's sister turns around. She's a few inches taller than me, slender like a sapling under her rich black gown, with almond-shaped golden eyes that search mine as she raises her hand to indicate the chain. "He let me have you. He doesn't believe you're a real threat to me. That you would try to seek revenge after what he did."

I have to cast my eyes down to the dark grass at my feet, and I'm not sure if it's shame or grief that makes the backs of my eyes burn. Perhaps both. "I would never think to hurt you. Even after...everything."

"I believe that," she says gently. There's a moment of soft silence between us before she clears her throat. "Walk with me. That seems to be the thing one does at garden parties."

She turns, and keeping the chain slack, begins to stroll back onto the lit path. "You don't have these soirees often?"

She hums as if this is troubling. "This is actually our first since the twins were born."

"How old are they?"

"They just turned eight, thank the Wild Goddess."

We come to an intersection in the path and she turns left. As she walks next to me, the giant ruby set in gold around her neck shimmers like it has magic. Is it some kind of protection charm? It's stunning over the glittery sweetheart neckline of her gown. Suddenly, I realise I've not yet met her mate. Where *is* the father of her children? But instead, I ask, "You believe in the Wild Goddess?"

"Everybody believes in something." She casts me a look. "What do you believe in, Aurelia?"

Only one word resonates in my heart. Through my entire body. I only believe in one thing now.

"I'm sorry," Selena says, turning down another intersection. "Let us talk of more pleasant things. At Drakos Estate, we pride ourselves on being as self-sustaining as possible. We have a small herd of goats and cows who give us milk, a crop of vegetables, and here"—she gestures to a shadowy enclosure and I stop short —"are our chickens. They give us a great supply of eggs."

It's a huge coop with a knee-height, wooden enclosure around it, giving the birds plenty of space to roam. Chickens cluck low and softly in their sleep within the coop, but outside, a couple of white-feathered silkies roam. But one of them is black. And staring right at me through bejewelled leather goggles on is—

"Oh, we have a new rooster," Selena laughs under her

breath. "I wonder if he has an eyesight problem. The twins will love him."

My heart suddenly rockets in its rhythm. I want to cry. I want to jump in there and pull Eugene into my arms and kiss him.

A friend. I'm not alone.

How the hell did Eugene get here? He must've snuck into the convoy somehow, because at the academy, I'd left him in Minnie's room after we left for the ball.

As if he knows he's undercover, Eugene casually looks away, pecking at the dirt for no reason. I clutch at my stomach, swallowing hard before my tears betray us completely. I wonder if Xander knows he's here.

"Birds," Selena muses. "The ultimate survivors. The only dinosaurs to make it out of that meteor's destruction alive. It was all down to their beaks. When there was no flora and fauna left, they learned to burrow for seeds with their sharp points. That single thing kept their entire species alive."

Eugene pecks the ground again and I blink hard. Selena turns to me and under her gaze I don't feel so much like an insect.

"There they are!" a shrill voice tunnels across the lawn from where a group of dragons observes us. "Bring the Boneweaver back at once, Selena!"

Xander's sister makes an annoyed noise in her throat. "It seems our tryst has ended."

As she leads me back the way we came, I curiously observe this dragoness, who seems to live by such strict rules. Then I think of her mother. Such powerful creatures who are forced to live according to such rules. The Drakos family adheres to the Old Laws in the worst possible way, and of course, the animas take the brunt of the negative aspects.

It's Damien Agnis who bounces excitedly on the balls of his white loafers right at the front of the group of interlopers. They tower over Selena and me, mythical, golden eyes gleaming with curiosity and something more sinister.

"She's quite pretty," remarks a dark-haired older male with golden eyes, casually smoking a cigar. He's striking, with a salt and pepper beard, and distinctly familiar.

"We don't require her for prettiness," says another male quite rudely. "Just for her womb."

"Sure, but it'll make the process easier."

Multiple males in the group chuckle.

I glare at them. Disgusting brutes.

Damien beams, barely containing his excitement. "Human women can have, what, up to ten children before pregnancy becomes truly life threatening? A Boneweaver could have many more than that. My bet is on thirty."

Nausea churns through my gut. My eyes flick down to the cage in Damien's hand where the nimpins sleep all piled on top of each other as if to seek comfort. Henry sits at the top of them, like a mother hen. But his eyes are open.

I can't kill these bastards with my powers but... "Imagine talking about another animalia like they're cattle," I say breezily. "The mark of highly uncivilised creatures."

Selena makes a sound of amusement so tiny, I'm sure I'm the only one who hears it.

But my words have left no mark on the others because Damien sneers down at me like I've ruined his golden moment. "You'll be passed around each time you are ripe. Ready for the next mythic shifter's cum with the most money, funding Serpent Court's militia as you go."

"Oh," chuckles a dragoness in a very real-looking tiger's pelt covering her broad shoulders. "You are quite *ruthless*, Lord Agnis."

As I fight the urge to sucker punch him, Damien waves a flirtatious hand. "She surrendered herself willingly. She knew exactly what she was getting into." He smirks at me. "Wants it, some would say."

"Surrendered?" Selena says, glancing at me with surprise. "That wasn't the story we were told."

The older dragon with the cigar narrows his eyes at her. "Unless you're going to do your duty and have more hatchlings, Selena, I suggest you keep your mouth shut."

Suddenly, I remember where I know this old dragon from. Unbidden, my power flares out, raging, rising up within me—

"Uh, uh, uh!" Damien raises the nimpins' cage threateningly.

I take a conscious step away from them all, averting my gaze to the ground as I clench my jaw. I've never felt a murderous urge this strong. Never felt the need to tear and rip and shred and *ruin* a person.

"Did you feel that?" the dragoness with the tiger pelt says. "Remarkable!"

"Oh, we knew she had power," drawls Damien. "That's why I—"

"Are we appreciating the property, Fabian?" King Flores Drakos rounds the corner, a golden chalice of wine in hand as he coolly surveys us.

"Quite, brother," says the cigar-dragon. "There'll be an extravagant turnout at her auction." This is Xanders uncle. Otherwise known as Fabian Drakos. The dragon who'd won the auction for Scythe's fifteen-year-old virginity.

A darkness shrouds my heart. Captures it so completely I think I'm going to choke on it.

That word from before. That thing that's all I believe in now?

Vengeance.

Flores Drakos takes my leash from Sissy, and I immediately miss the young woman. Her expression is reserved as I'm passed over, and I might be imagining it, but there could have been a hint of worry in her eyes.

I'd be kidding myself if I wasn't also worried. I'd been wondering about their plans for me, because I had no doubt they'd been meticulous in deciding how to proceed with my surrender. My father has been plotting my *use* for so long that the terms of the auction have been set in stone for ages, and likely now only adjusted for inflation. Flores parades me around the garden while the other dragons ogle me.

"Raised by a serpent, such a shame," says one male, leaning down to stare at my mouth. "How was it that Mace got so lucky?"

"Oh, he's quite powerful for a serpent," Flores says. "It's how I knew."

I stay the need to stare at the dragon king. So the fact that my father was mated to a Boneweaver made him certain of his power? *That* had been his deciding factor? What, then, do they think of *my* mates?

Flores continues around the garden before bidding everyone goodnight and heading inside. Sissy appears from nowhere, trailing us.

"Are you hungry, Lia?" she says. "I don't think you had dinner."

"Keep her lean," Flores drones as my stomach rumbles. "It will be better for her fertility. In fact"—he stops and turns to his daughter, eyes flicking down her body—"you should try the same, Selena."

Sissy's cheeks turn pink just as I stop the growl in my throat. But like his words aren't completely awful, Flores continues strolling into the house. "You need your sleep in preparation for tomorrow's testing," he says, leading me up the stairs, his daughter our silent tail.

"Why? What will that entail?" I ask bravely.

"Oh, many things." I don't like the way his eyes gleam as he glances at me. We stop outside Xander's room and Flores knocks with a casual hand.

The door opens on its own accord and we find Xander sitting by the fireplace in his relieving room, smoking a joint. Perhaps his last little meeting didn't go so well.

"I'm returning your pet," Flores says. "Put it to bed."

"Yes, Father." Xander stands and holds his hand out for the chain. Flores passes it over, and like some sort of disease, I'm passed from one beast to the other.

It's hot, borderline stifling, in the room, and I'm not sure if it's a dragon thing, but none of them seem to notice.

Flores turns as if to leave, but then pauses. "Just one last thing." Flores whirls around, and before I can jump back, slashes at me with one extended claw. I cry out as pain slices across my chest and sticky blood appears in a jagged line.

I step back, staring between the dragon king and his son.

Xander does nothing. Merely blinks those glowing eyes and raises his hand to take another drag from his joint.

"You should do another to make sure," he says dryly. "I promise you, the bond is quite severed."

"I could have told you that," I scowl. Every beast can fucking feel it.

It was a test. A fucking test, and Xander passed it with flying colours.

Flores hums with scientific interest. "Very good. I bid you a goodnight." He leaves but Selena lingers in the doorway for a moment longer.

"Can I help you?" Xander sighs.

Selena's face tightens. "Not anymore." Then she too sweeps away with a rustle of her gown.

I frown at her choice of wording until Xander snaps off the chain. "Cage," he barks.

"Cunt," I retort in turn.

His shoulders tighten before he proceeds to ignore me and returns to his chair. Though the shallow cut on my chest is already healing, I'm careful to take my dress off for the night and drop it onto the carpet. After using the bathroom, I crawl back into my cage and lock the door.

Such a good pet.

Goddess, it grates at my nerves to sit there, the bars cold

against my bare back. Eventually, Xander goes to bed, flicking the blackout curtain down so I'm swallowed by darkness again.

I don't sleep like the previous night. Can't. Not after the events and words of the evening. Putting my head down on my makeshift blanket pillow doesn't help, and there's definitely something about sleeping in this foreign place that makes me uneasy.

Xander makes no noise in his bed, and I wonder if he's asleep or just pretending to be. "Did you find your wife tonight?" I mutter.

"Don't make me tape your mouth," he mutters back.

So I lie there for what seems like hours, my eyes blinking at the black material.

Until I hear it.

A faint whisper makes my heart stutter in my chest. It's breathy, faint, but definitely feminine.

Is this place haunted? I wouldn't be surprised, an old rotten place like this.

I hear it again and I sit bolt upright, almost banging my head on the top of the cage. The whisper made words. Hurried and desperate. I imagine someone with wide eyes, gripping the bars of her own cage, beseeching me. Begging me.

Don't open it.

I frown, straining my ears. But the words are no different the second time.

Don't open it.

I don't sleep at all after that, but the voice does not return.

Chapter 14

Xander

The next day, Solomon and the scientists continue to undergo their long list of tests for Snake Spawn. They have a treadmill and make it run in various forms. They test the bite strength of its jaws and the sharpness of its claws. The entire time, Ghoul watches with a fixated obsession, and during the day, we're joined by various serpent generals until they get bored and leave.

I use the time to manage the sudden endless list of requests, emails, and news reports. What I'm looking for isn't even certain. Some type of...retaliation. Some type of signal. The only news I get is that Scythe has now been sighted on land. I'd thought he'd found his peace out in the cold waters of the Pacific. To find that he's returned is disappointing, to say the least.

He couldn't withstand Spawn's lure.

No one from Animus Academy has tried to contact me, and it makes the hairs at the back of my neck stand on end. I've blocked everyone's numbers, but that never stopped males like Savage and Scythe, or even Lyle from getting to someone. There are ways and means to reach me. Get a message some way, electronic or otherwise, but I haven't heard a peep.

No threats or anything.

A quiet Scythe is a dangerous Scythe. Under my advisement, Father has doubled the estate's protections, physical and otherwise.

That night, Mother invites me for supper in her rooms with Sissy and the twins. It's my favourite part of the day because it reminds me of when we used to do the exact same thing as children. Back in our day, we'd drink Milo or tea and play board games while Father sat in the corner reading.

It pleases me to no end that they've kept up the tradition for the hatchlings. Since I'm forced to bring Spawn with me everywhere, I command it to sit in the corner of the dimly lit room.

But that doesn't last long. The hatchlings are curious and intelligent, so they scoot over to it almost immediately, bringing their books and colouring pencils along with them.

"Or-rey-lee-uh," coos Emmerson, "can you draw?" He's fascinated by her name.

"A little," Spawn says.

"She's not allowed," I snap as Emmerson hands her a blue pencil. "Pets don't read or write."

Emmerson huffs in annoyance. "Why? She has hands."

"Because I said so."

"But *why*?"

I give him a look of warning, which he returns in defiance. So I try another tactic. "Come over here and play last card with me."

"Only if *she* can play with us."

"Pets don't play games," I say.

Sissy exhales irritably where she's reading some type of smut on her e-reader on the couch opposite me.

"Can she sit by my side, then?" Emmerson narrows his eyes at me. When did I become the boring uncle?

I sigh. "Fine."

He cackles like he's won a battle and grabs Spawn by its arm and leads it from the corner towards my table. To my utter surprise and disappointment, instead of taking the armchair opposite me, Emmerson prods Spawn into the seat and perches himself on the arm. "She'll play my cards as I command."

From beside me, my mother chuckles over a goblet of her nightly medicine. "Clever hatchling," she says proudly. "He'll be winning chess against you next, Xander."

"I don't doubt it," I say wryly. "Let's get on with it, then."

"What do you do all day?" Delilah says, putting down her colouring and coming over to observe.

"Paperwork, planning," I say, looking at my cards.

"Not you, Uncle Xander," Delilah says pointedly. "Aurelia."

My jaw goes slack as I stare at the hatchlings, but no one is giving me any heed. In fact, Delilah is stroking Spawn's face as if she's fascinated.

"Soft skin," Delilah says. Then she frowns at Spawn's chest "What happened there?" She brushes her fingers across the healed scratch under its clavicle.

"I managed to hurt myself," Spawn says quietly. "It's just a scratch."

"Did you put antiseptic over it?" Delilah asks, peering at the cut. "Mum, where's the antiseptic cream?"

"She doesn't need it," I frown because I don't understand why she hasn't completely healed it.

I am ignored.

The twins are now very concerned about Spawn, fussing and grumping over the cut. Delilah finds a first aid kit and brandishes the tube of cream at me. "You do it," she says, with one hand on her hip. "She's *your* pet."

"Yeah," Emmerson nods. "Do it, Uncle Xander. Be responsible."

Spawn is fighting hard to maintain a blank expression, and I'm fighting a mad growl. Under the frowns of my niece and nephew, I reluctantly take the cream and stare at it.

"Unscrew the cap," Delilah demands. "Quick, before she dies from it."

"Here." Emmerson snatches the tube from me, unscrews the cap, and squirts out a bit on my finger.

I'm left staring at the white cream in a sort of shock.

"It goes here." Delilah points to the long slash and taps the skin above it.

Spawn goes still as Emmerson grabs my finger and leads me towards its skin. I brush the cream onto Spawn's cut. It tenses under my touch. The skin is warm and I'm forced to scent it, being so close. It takes a deep breath, moving the mounds of its breasts, the cleavage so close to my face.

I blink hard to maintain focus, gritting my teeth and sweeping the cream across the cut.

"You're no good at this, Uncle Xander," Delilah says, shaking her head in dismay. "You're not a good pet owner."

Jerked back to reality, I shake myself out of whatever haze I was in.

"I suppose not," I say too loudly.

Spawn flinches and I take out my pocket square and wipe the residual cream off my finger. Delilah pats Spawn on the shoulder. "Very good girl," she coos.

I drag the cushion next to me onto my lap. "Let's keep playing."

That night, after I put Spawn away in its crate, I take extra long in the shower.

My balls are heavy and I haven't had a release in ages. That's likely why I'm reacting like this. Spawn doesn't have the same demanding draw, and my dragon isn't even conscious to thirst after it.

I stroke my thickening length in one hand, squeezing the tip hard until a bead of pre-cum emerges.

Blue eyes flash before my mind's eye, at cock level, looking up at me, pink mouth open. Muttering a curse as I slide my hand down the base, I thud my back against the shower tiles, I instead imagine Nadine Chen on her knees before me, her mouth ready and waiting—

But Nadine's face morphs into an olive skinned, blue-eyed one. Eyes like gems that glint mischievously in the dark. Eyes that sparkle with cunning. Gritting my teeth, I pump my cock, faster and faster, imagining Spawn on her knees, taking my cock like she needs it, hungers for it. Thirstily taking me to my base, moaning and groaning—

I come, shuddering against the wall, a strangled sound tearing from my throat. Sighing as I glare at the door behind which Spawn lies, I wash my body and dry off.

It's just frustration. Just weeks of pent-up desire I needed to release. She carries no hold over me. Absolutely none.

The best thing for me to do is focus on my current matches. Matches of my choice and my choosing.

That night, I sleep perfectly well.

The next week passes quickly, with each day much the same as the last. Each night, Snake Spawn goes quietly to bed in its cage. Each morning, I flip the cover off to find it waiting, angry eyes staring me down.

I wonder how long that will last.

When Sunday comes around, I find Solomon and Ghoul arguing inside the testing room. By 'arguing', I mean to say that Solomon is trying to protest something mad Ghoul has put forward.

"We're not ready, Lord Basilisk," Solomon says before I make myself known.

"Well, I am, and that's what's relevant here. Ah!" Ghoul senses me and Spawn, turning around and clapping his hands. "We've reached the second phase of our testing," Ghoul announces. "We're all quite excited about it."

The team of scientists shifts uncomfortably. I frown at Ghoul. "Can't be anything good, then."

The hint of a fanged smile appears beneath his mask. "Follow me."

We leave the bright lights of the testing room to head back into the dark, further down the corridor. I'm not familiar with this part of the mansion. It's not an area with the books where I used to play as a child or wander as a teenager. The cobwebs have been swept away, and it still smells faintly of antiseptic wash and bleach.

Ghoul abruptly turns into a darkened room, the gleam of steel bars on the opposing wall. He takes out a ring of black keys.

The fact that he would have keys to something in my mansion could send me into a rage. I'd have to have a word with my father about this. It's completely unacceptable. Does he think he's a dragon by association?

Useless, arrogant prick.

"Hand her over, *dragon*."

"I'm not going in there," Spawn scoffs.

"We're just testing your eyesight," Ghoul shrugs. "Don't be afraid."

I release its golden collar with a sharp snap, making her stumble back a step. "Go."

Muttering something foul under its breath, it saunters past the basilisk—who inhales deeply as it passes him—until the darkness swallows its body up. Ghoul shuts the door with the air of someone way too used to imprisoning people, and locks it with a definite clunk.

"Well, that's that." Ghoul brushes his hands like it's a job well done and stops short, as if he's surprised to see me still here. Dramatic bastard is worse than Savage. "Don't you have important meetings with politicians or something?" Fangs flash again. Madder than Scythe.

"How long is it supposed to be in there for?"

"You're obsessed with her," he says with delight. "Can't stand the thought of being without her pretty blue eyes. That soft, kissable mouth. You loved toting her around just so you could look at her and get all the private time your greedy dragon *craves*."

I scowl. "No. In fact, the distance is preferred. It's been annoying having it follow me everywhere."

Ghoul smirks and it almost sends me into a rage. I control myself, stalking forward, and lean over the basilisk, bracing my arms on either side of him and staring right into those lethal, laser beam eyes. The bastard doesn't move and doesn't stop smirking.

"Fuck her eyes. And fuck her mouth. There is far better out there for me."

With that, I turn and leave, feeling more free than ever before.

* * *

At today's meeting with my father, I'm thoroughly displeased to find a worm sitting his accursed, withering behind on one of our antique chairs.

Mace Naga does not get up when I approach, instead brushing non-existent dust off his knee. "Master Xander. A pleasure."

He addresses me as a child, with that wraith voice of utter evil. I refrain from the urge to pull the second seat away from him and instead sit in it. "Mace."

My father casts a disapproving look at me before gesturing to the worm in the black duster. "The dragons got a good look at the girl. I have taken the liberty of inviting a few more interested parties to your wedding, and that will give us ample interest for the big day."

"What is the big day?"

"The Boneweaver auction," Mace says as if we are talking about a race horse and not his own loin-spawn. "Your father and I have already discussed the particulars." He gestures to a closed brown manila folder, no doubt containing the contract of use. The moment Mace told us to hunt down his daughter for execution way back at Halfeather's mansion, I knew he was a head case. And this cold, calculated way he speaks of her breeding auction is despicable at best.

"A good deal, I should think," Father says, nodding with satisfaction. "A great benefit to Serpent Court."

"Indeed," Mace says, standing. "And a great benefit to the endangered communities."

My father's lips twitching is the only giveaway that he's annoyed by the implication of some weakness on our part.

Mace inclines his head, one king to another, before leaving.

I wait until I hear Mace clear the middle of the staircase. "Was that really necessary?"

Father sits back in his chair, his irises glowing with irritation. "When did I ever give you the impression you had permission to question me?"

"I am your heir," I say reasonably. "Your politics are my politics."

"And apparently, my intelligence is not your intelligence. You have no idea who Mace Naga is."

I concentrate on the gold of his eyes. "A creature who would auction his own young."

"And that benefits us directly." His tone holds an undercurrent of fire, indicating that I'm toeing the line.

"Well, I've given it some thought, and I think Nadine Chen will be the best choice for me."

"She won't do." He waves a dismissive hand. "Francesca is the superior candidate. Her father owns the biggest law firm in the country, he has ties with the human intelligence services, and further, her genetic profile is most compatible with ours."

I close my eyes for a brief minute, remembering our ill-fated walk through the maze garden.

"Father, she is entitled. She has no manners, is outright rude in some cases—"

"All that can be changed after marriage. She will learn with time, or are you incapable of handling her?"

I clench my fists on my knees, where he can't see them. "I can"—*fucking*—"handle her. She is attractive enough, but—"

Father scoffs. "Half the males are vying for her. Young *and* old. If you don't take her, she will be snatched up by someone within the week. Her father wouldn't stand the slight, of course, but that's besides the point."

So he's already discussed it with them.

I pinch the bridge of my nose as pressure builds in my sinuses. Smoke threatens to stream out of my nostrils, and it's not going to—

The faint sizzle is the only warning I get before a band of wicked flame latches around my throat. I suppress a shout at the malicious burn that seizes me, my hand reaching for my neck before I drop it, staring at my father.

His eyes are wide with rage, his right hand upturned as the whip of flame stretches between us.

Dragon flame on human skin is a maddening sort of torture.

The scent of burning, then charring, flesh fills my nose, but still I maintain my father's stare. Agony threatens to consume me, but it manifests as only a tremble.

His voice is a scalding, draconian hiss. "Do not think you are being given *choices*, Xander." And here it is. I have been waiting for this moment. "I indulged you as a child and it ruined you. A decade with those creatures couldn't help you. You are still spoilt."

I stare at him, unblinking. Unwavering. He wants me to submit. To buckle under his power. He would enjoy it to see me cry.

Just because I know he'll hate me for it, I keep my voice low and calm. "I will marry Francesca if that is your wish, Father."

Something flashes in his eyes. Surprise. Irritation.

He lowers his hand, and the flame unwraps itself from around my throat. I remain ramrod straight in my chair.

"Leave, before the scent of you spoils my office."

I rise slowly, leisurely. Straightening to my near seven-foot height without a tremble, I turn on my heel and stalk out the door. Agony spreads through the flesh and tendons of my neck, all the way through to my trachea. I've lost feeling in some places where the nerves are damaged.

But it doesn't matter.

Because two things have happened tonight. One, it is now confirmed that my father has not forgiven me for my so-called transgression. And two:

Flores Drakos has realised that I am no longer the spoiled teenager he once knew, but a full grown, hot-blooded dragon male.

And his rival in every way.

Chapter 15

Aurelia

Even my eagle eyes can do nothing to penetrate the darkness of this prison. Nor my owl eyes. Nor any nocturnal creature I know.

It's an infinite sort of darkness in here. The kind of the dark that can swallow the spirit.

I won't let it. Not while my mother's name still sits on my tongue. Because I don't believe Ghoul for a second that they're 'testing my vision'. This will give me a chance to think.

I feel my way, one hand on the wall, the other stretched out in front of me, and find a spot of comfortable concrete.

And I sit. And wait.

Perhaps that voice I've been hearing every night won't be able to reach me here.

Chapter 16

Ghoul

7 days later

We watch Aurelia through the thermal cameras, my team and I. It's no longer Solomon's team, and I think he gets that now.

The snakelet has taken longer than others before her to start losing herself. Perhaps it's her Boneweaver spirit. Perhaps it's just her.

Isolation, after all, is not a new enemy to her.

Within the first twenty-four hours, she found the drinking water and the toilet. Between hours of quiet contemplation, she occupied herself with a singing and dancing routine that changed over the days. When she tired of that, she made up stories, speaking out loud as if to an audience.

It was on the third day that she cried.

Not a loud, angry cry like I'd expected. But a silent weeping whose only giveaway was the shaking of her shoulders and the scrunched-up brow over the hands shielding most of her face.

It may have just been the hunger in her belly that time because minutes after, she'd loudly complained about the absence of any food.

Today, she has stopped the pretence of an invisible audience and is now talking to herself. Muttering to herself. I catch a laugh now and again, but most of it sounds like nonsense.

Something about fairy bread, and then Eugene was mentioned. She whispers the names of her mates sometimes, just before she nods off to sleep. *My* name is never spoken, which makes my blood heat in irritation.

Currently, she's still in her human form, scraping elongated cobra fangs against the stone wall as if they irritate her.

Solomon checks the time on his Rolex. "She hasn't yet shifted. At all."

"She's still aware of the risk." Of rabidity. She's been in that state before, and knows coming out of it is difficult.

Aurelia hisses angrily at the wall as if the entire faults of the world lie within that black stone.

"She is not nearly desperate enough," Solomon mutters.

"Send in some game," I advise, leaning back in my chair and crossing my arms. It squeaks under my weight. "See if she's feral enough to hunt it."

"The lamb may do it."

"No," I say quickly. "The rooster."

Solomon speaks into a walkie-talkie, and within two minutes, a metal grate by the toilet silently opens. The snakelet's head whips in that direction as the thermal camera picks up a tiny figure, stepping cautiously out into the wider cell. He sniffs the air and so does the snakelet. She whispers something the camera doesn't pick up and goes onto her hands and knees to crawl along the wall.

I sit forward again, watching with interest. With hope.

The bird slowly steps along, his head bobbing before his body as is the way of poultry. The snakelet crawls faster and faster, raising her head and sniffing, before she cries out and grabs the bird. Solomon and I both squint at the screen as she buries her teeth in its neck.

My heart leaps with a profound sort of joy.

The snakelet raises her head, and the bird hops to the ground, clearly well and alive.

Disappointed, I shake my head. She'd been...*hugging* the bird, not tearing into its throat like I'd dreamt.

Solomon scoffs in disgust. "She has a strong maternal instinct. That is a good indication for breeding, His Majesty will be happy to hear. But this is not what we are after."

"No. We want her broken."

Solomon furiously types notes into the documentation system.

I sigh in annoyance. "Another week then."

Chapter 17

Aurelia

I'm sure they've forgotten about me. Perhaps the entire world has forgotten about me. And until Eugene arrived, I'd almost forgotten about me, too.

As I lie on my side, the hard stone digging into my hip, I cradle his soft body to my chest, where I can feel his heartbeat alongside mine, a constant reminder that we are real. That I am not mad. That, at some stage, someone will come for us.

Yet the dark stretches out into infinity. It's the not knowing of when. Of how long that's pressing on my brain, stewing it like water and sugar stew green apples.

I'm sleepy all the time now, dozing in and out, not sure when it's night or day. The hunger has turned into an empty, dull ache, and I feel like I'm floating in the void of nothingness.

Luckily, Eugene is here to peck me now and again, a sharp pain on the hand or cheek to remind me there are people waiting for us on the outside. His mates. My mates. Henry and the nimpins in their own, sad cage.

The hours bleed on, strange shapes appearing in the void, symbols and patterns that make no sense, until finally, my anima lets out a low, tired keen, and something appears to me.

I must be asleep and dreaming because the shape of tall pine trees comes into view, many of them, under a sea of stars against a twilight sky. I stare up at it in wonder.

Have I forgotten what the sky looks like already? But it is vast. Never ending. Ready to swallow me up.

Raw emotion surges in my stomach as I look up at the expanse. I have never been afraid of the sky before. Never been nervous at the thought of being engulfed by it.

The snap of a twig behind me makes me spin around in panic. But the person walking out of the shadows is someone I do not expect.

I've gone mad. The solitary confinement has *finally* driven me batty.

Scythe's sky-blue eyes stare at me as if he's seeing a ghost. His face crumples. "Regina?"

I let out a sob, and we are running towards each other. Me, frantic and stumbling upon the strewn twigs and leaves, him sturdy and sure as he reaches out, strong arms pulling me into his big, warm body.

By the Wild, Rabid Goddess, his scent fills my nose, my entire head, and I breathe him in like a drowning woman. May I drown in this beast forever and be swept away by his powerful current. His hands, first wrapped tight around me, now slide up my arms to my face. He tilts my head upward, forcing me to look into his severe and desperate gaze.

"You are queen of my heart," he whispers in that damaged rasp. "Queen of my soul."

He has grace enough not to say it. That first he left, then I left in retaliation. What are we but broken, damaged creatures?

"I miss you," I breathe. Missed you. Was broken by you. Then broken again by another.

His eyes soften on me, his big tattooed thumbs stroking along my cheekbones. "I love you."

My vision blurs as he presses his lips to mine. Eyelids fluttering shut, a lone tear escapes. Scythe pulls away to catch that tear with the brush of his tongue. I shiver under his mouth, clutching at his black shirt, fingers pressed against the hard muscle underneath.

"What have they done to you?" His breath tickles my face, warm and masculine. His silver hair is kissed by the light of the stars, shining even to my tear-filled vision.

Are you really here? Am *I* really here? I dare not ask it out loud because the answer might rip me apart.

"What drew you here, Aurelia?"

My name. That is my name, spoken with love by a mate. I tear my gaze away from him before I collapse into his embrace and never let go. I turn in his arms, looking around at the forest that surrounds us. Tiny golden lights twinkle amongst the trees as if they are made by magic. Somewhere nearby, water bubbles —a sweet, delicate sound. It's comforting to my empty ears. Carried on a gentle breeze are jasmine flowers and Scythe's cold, tundra scent. Safety and love. That's what I feel from here. As if the soil itself welcomes me. This can't be a *real* place?

"I can't say what drew me here," I reply. Changing the subject seems best. "This is beautiful. Did you make it for us?"

"I think we both did," he says quietly. "Our subconsciouses merged, and we made something between us."

"I love that." We'd made something beautiful together, and it was just for us. My thoughts must have drifted to Scythe in that darkness. I stare wistfully around, feeling with more than just my body. A presence whispers through air; the padding of canine feet; the shake of a lion's mane. "I feel the others here."

Hand in hand, we wander through the forever twilight, my bare feet comforted by the mossy ground, my heart warmed by his hand squeezing my own.

The forest opens up into a grassy clearing, where the open moon is reflected upon the surface of a lake. I gasp in surprise at the small pavilion standing before us, a thing of stained glass and stone. We walk up to it, getting a better look at the figures standing beneath.

At the centre of the raised platform stands two grey stone

statues, correct to the height. I hurry forwards in awe, touching their hands. Their faces. "I'm a terrible regina," I whisper.

"They would never say that of you."

"That makes it worse. You were right. About Xander...he is —" I swallow a sob. "He is lost to me."

"You could never have prevented what he did. Savage and Lyle...and I, we are angry, but I think a part of us understands."

"Wait..." I turn to stare at him, then at our surroundings. I feel as if the cotton wool inside my brain is being swept away. "You're *really* here?"

Scythe's eyes glint in the dark. "I am, Aurelia."

I let go of him, shaking my head. "No. You can't. You can't be." I need to get out of here. I need to get away from him. I surrendered myself for a reason. I cannot let him sway me from my purpose.

Scythe grips my arm firmly to get my attention. "Come here when you are lost." He swallows, an unusual note of desperation entering his rasp. "Come and see me."

Shame fills me, a great swallowing beast, mightier than anything I could turn into. "I'm sorry," I say as I tear myself away from my great white shark and find myself alone in the ever-dark once again.

Chapter 18

Lyle

Scythe abruptly snaps the neck of the serpent he'd just been holding still. Everyone in the room freezes. His eyes search something in the air over my shoulder before he strides out of the small suburban living room of the house next to Charlotte Naga's.

We've been at it for days now, against Celeste's advice, no less. But once Savage and Scythe came to see me in Celeste's office where I'd been madly pacing...that had been it. I'd taken one look at my brothers, with fire in their eyes and vengeance in their hearts, and that was all I'd needed to growl in assent to the question in Scythe's eyes.

Yes, I will do anything to get our regina back.

Yes, I will kill, castrate, or torture anyone necessary to stake our claim.

Yes, I will wreak havoc on the world if I can't get what I want.

And so here we are, in serpent territory, feral, mad, doing as much strategic harm as possible. We came here to find Charlotte Naga's large two-storey house empty. It's evident they moved out in a hurry with the children. The kitchen still had food on the table. The milk has gone off in the fridge and clothes are still on the line, now dry. Mace got them out before we arrived, passports and all.

He knows exactly what he's doing, but so do we. So we headed over to their neighbour's house and found them to be spies.

Savage, the five ex-inmate wolves and I watch Scythe leave with frowns. There's a strange energy in the air, something my human self can't feel, but my *lion* goes insane for.

"Put him with the others," I command, waving a hand over the serpent before stalking after my shark-brother.

More than one of Savage's feral wolves licks his chops before shifting. These wolves are older, harder than the ones at the Academy. They'd been in Blackwater prison before Savage blew it up and gave them the chance to escape. If they were left to their own devices, they'd dispose of the evidence the old-fashioned way and obtain a meal in one swoop. But we have other, more purposeful plans today.

Savage follows by my side, sniffing and growling in his throat. Almost fully descended into ferality, he'd torn his clothes off days ago. Clothes and Savage have never gone so well together, and in this state, on a hunt with his pack-brothers and missing his regina, he is barely human.

For myself, I fear the three-piece suit is the only tether around my body that keeps me from devolving completely. My lion stalks freely within me, but without our regina, we are *in a rage*.

Scythe stands before the front gate of the property, frozen, staring out at the sky as if fixated. I too look out at the bright blue expanse as if I can see my regina's eagle form soaring high above us, as I had so many times. How *dare* the sky look so bright when *she* is not joyous within it.

"Is it my regina?" Savage's voice is rough with ferality as he rounds me to stand before our brother. "Tell me it's her. I can feel it." He sniffs the air with a blood-covered nose, licking the wet crimson off his lips as he searches Scythe's face for some hint of what's caught his attention.

I rub at my own chest, suddenly aching with primal need of many kinds.

Scythe blinks, some moment passed, a lighthouse going out. He lays a hand on Savage's muscular shoulder. "I saw her."

The snarl that tears through me makes both brothers glance my way. "Where? How?"

"Through a psychic bond. That tells me she still has her powers. They don't have her bound in obsidian."

Likely to enable her to keep us shut out.

"I want to see her too," Savage growls, stepping up close to Scythe and getting in his face, angry he didn't get his own chance. We've all been trying every day and every night to contact our regina telepathically, but have been coming up against the strongest wall Savage has ever seen. It was completely useless.

"I have an idea," Scythe says, turning to me. "We need to head back to the academy."

There's a new gleam in his eyes, and I have no doubt it's from seeing our regina first hand. Jealousy fills my blood and my animus takes over, snarling in the great white's face. Nose to nose we stand, and Scythe returns my growl.

"Soon, Lyle," he says. "Soon."

I exhale heavily in irritation before tearing away from his unrelenting stare. "Fine."

The wolves are prowling out of the house now, ready with their cargo. Savage points at the nature strip. There, the other wolves carry the wooden pole, tied to which is the dead, bloodied body of the serpent, ready for display.

We may not have permission to rescue our regina, but we *can* slaughter our way through Mace Naga's court until he has no choice but to surrender her back to us.

Chapter 19

Xander

9 to 5 — Dolly Parton

I fold the newspaper and set it beside my empty breakfast plate.

"My lord." The family butler stands at my side, bowing over a silver tray, holding an A5 black envelope.

I would recognise that scent anywhere, in any life. My magical sight tells me Savage has left me a present in that envelope. Something nasty.

My own nasty smile grows on my lips as I take the envelope. Rising from my chair, I excuse myself and take the thing outside. Sissy casts a worried look my way, but Father merely continues reading his newspaper, and Mother sips at her usual health tonic. The thing smells disgusting, but if it helps her as my music does, she needs to keep drinking it.

I stride as far away from the parlour room as possible before impatience gets the better of me and I tear it open.

Inside are photos printed with great care on glossy photo paper. There's dried blood smeared on some of them and the remnants of a thumbprint, which I can tell is Savage's. The photos were also taken by Savage because they focus on just the right things. I hope he cleaned his phone afterward, but know full well that he didn't.

A cracked open skull here, the loop of a small bowel there. Serpents stuck on a wooden pike right on the nature strip of various suburban streets.

If my ex-brothers had learned anything from me, it was old school dramatics. The message, the threat, is clear.

You're next.

None of this had made *Animalia Today,* or any news outlet of course, and no doubt the Council of Beasts retrieval teams are stalking at a distance, taking down the bodies before any humans spot them and ring their own police. But these beasts *want* to create havoc. They want to destroy and maim. Everything in their blood is telling them to do so.

I pocket the photos before getting out my phone and doing my hourly on the various security cameras around the estate, including the closed-circuit ones. The last one makes my lip twitch in disgust. The Spawn is in its dark cell, gnawing at her own arm with two long fangs. It bleeds freely from the wound. I've been watching it daily, and until now, it hasn't done anything I'd consider mad.

With great annoyance, because I have a great many other things to do, including planning a wedding, I storm down there, where the basilisk is no doubt wreaking hell.

When I arrive, the team of reptilian scientists are indeed swarming, while the basilisk lord sits in a chair too small for him, leaning back with his hands behind his head as if he's on a beach holiday.

"You've ruined her," I snarl.

"Not yet, my lord," Solomon says in a resigned voice. "She is proving stubborn to our attempts."

"Take her out," I command.

Ghoul finally turns his head to regard me. "No." And then into my head, he says, *"She started a heat yesterday and we tried an experimental drug. It's enhanced her natural heat. Take her out now and you risk chaos in this place."*

It's annoying hearing his voice in my head. We may no longer be bond-brothers but we are still mythic shifters that have telepathy. But I have to fight fire with fire so reply in same. *"I thought you had a fetish for chaos."*

Ghoul smirks, flashing his fangs, knowing he has me. Spawn's heat scent would send all the unmated males into a frenzy. With our bond in tatters, I have no idea what effect that would have on me, but I'm guessing I would be subjected to the same heat scent as every other unmated male.

"She has the power to conceal her scent," I mentally remind him. Out loud, I say, "I don't care what drugs or games you're playing. You are not damaging my property."

"Think about it, though," Ghoul says loudly. "If she's slightly"—he pinches his fingers together—"insane, she'll be easy to breed. That's how the pros do it."

Solomon shrugs with a nod, as if he agrees. "It would be easier if she were compliant with all things. The conception ritual, for example."

I stare at them before sneering, "Oh, and that worked with Athena Boneweaver, did it?"

Solomon's neck turns red.

"I thought not."

It's then that Mace Naga, who'd been strolling down the corridor, listening to our conversation, decides to step into the light of the observation room. "I agree with the young dragon," he says, stepping beside me as if we are in league. "We won't make the same mistakes as last time, Solomon. We need her docile but not mad."

The fact that he casually talks about his wife and now his daughter in this manner is vile.

"Get her out, now," Mace says.

Ghoul hands me the key dangling on one of his gloved fingers and pipes happily into my mind. *"Go get her, young dragon. Try to cover your little hard-on while you can, but I know it's there. You've already got a semi, don't you?"*

The bastard just doesn't want to go in there while she's in heat. *"I'll enjoy the day I get to rip your fangs out."*

His deathly red eyes glow behind his mask, and the fact that he can't kill me with them probably gnaws at him.

I snatch the key out of his hand and whirl around, heading for the cell down the corridor. Exhaling a breath of rage, I push the old cast iron key into the lock.

Chapter 20

Aurelia

I have become friends with despair. I see things in the dark now. Sometimes horrible things. Sometimes wonderful things. Moments that shine brightly. A tableau that makes my gut twist. I've not tried to reach Scythe again, tempting though it became. He cannot help me here, and I won't risk distraction.

When my heat came, it was nothing but torture. Not having my mates here, my hands straying down my body in an attempt to mimic their touch. Not here, I thought desperately, it is not safe. My body has betrayed me and the sharp prick in my arm only made it worse.

Perhaps it's thoughts of Scythe that does it, or the feeling of losing control of my body, but at some point in this dark torture, something shifts within me. Something cold and ancient. The gnashing of a shark's teeth joined the cacophony of beastly voices in my head a while ago, but this time, she shoves forth, dominant and cunning. I feel it under my skin when it happens. My body drops its basal temperature, and though I feel 'warm' on the inside, I'm cold to the touch. My heart rate slows down, becoming steady, and my mind...

Well, now I know exactly what it feels like for Scythe to

descend into his shark. The crevices of my brain also become cold and deep as midnight depths. There is only smooth calculation and a dampening of my emotions and the sensation of the heat. They are still there, only buried *deep*.

I've learnt something new.

So when the door of my gaol creaks open and cool light spills in, there is no joy or relief sweeping through my veins. In fact, I barely register the pain behind my eyes at seeing light for the first time in what feels like years. I only mark the imposing silhouette as someone I once knew.

"Put your scent shield up," snaps his voice. "Right now."

My body creaks like it has aged a hundred years. "Why?"

"So that neither I nor the others have to smell your malodorous stench."

Something ancient in me registers that I am still in a biological heat. Why, then, are they letting me out?

"Keep me in here then," I reply evenly.

"I can't have you going mental," Xander snarls. "Get out. I have better things to do than argue about something this nonsensical."

Eugene nudges at my leg and I relent. Dragging myself off the floor, I rise to standing, noting the drop in my blood pressure as my head spins. Not enough water. Not enough food.

But I point blank refuse to faint. There are enemies about, and I need to be alert. With one hand upon the stone wall for support, I walk towards the dark-hearted dragon, the one whose heart beats in a cursed song.

"Wicked dragon," I whisper. "Nasty, dark, evil winged creature."

Xander blinks, those glowing whites shimmering with so many colours. I step out of my prison.

"Shields up," he hisses.

I look at him and smile. His aura pulses with slashes of black and grey and so, so much red. Like a festering, necrotic wound. "So many sins," I whisper. "So many scars."

With an angry flick of his wrist, a golden chain clicks onto the collar around my throat, and the cursed dragon strides out of the antechamber as fast as he can. I am forced to follow. "Severed, yet still bound," I whisper to Eugene, following close by my ankle. "Black heart. Black fire."

Waiting for us in the bright room of steel and plastic is something I do not expect.

"Serpent king," I hiss. "Come to see his spawn."

The king cobra stares at me from his great height, dark eyes flashing, nostrils flaring as he registers the scent that I have no desire to hide. Abruptly, like the cut of a sharp knife, he turns and leaves.

A dark, husky laugh leaves my lips.

"She is dehydrated," the cursed dragon snaps at the serpents. "Put IV hydration in her stat."

I feel death's eyes on me and turn to regard the basilisk. He is the *other* cursed one. Two peas snuggled in a pod of darkness. "Come here, snakelet," he says with a voice of ghosts and shadows. "Let's make you better."

Chapter 21

Ghoul

Though her head is downcast, her eyes remain staring forward, deep bags underscoring them. Her eyes might be full of darkness, but I know her thoughts are darker. Her raven hair is wild and loose about her face, the tight-fitting black dress hugging her sinful curves. I suppress a shiver as I feel her power.

There she is.

My dark goddess.

She has only become more dangerous than before.

I beckon to her. "Come here."

Something in her recognises me and she comes forward, unblinking and serene, taking my gloved hand without question. I lead her towards the hospital bed the team had prepared for her eventual release. Two of the scientists hurry to set up the IV.

She has not washed for three weeks and smells like it. But it only makes her delicious heat scent stronger. My shadows surround me like a shield, and the only tell of my struggle is a slight tremble in my hand.

She notices it. A tiny, malicious smile curves her lips.

"Bring food," I say faintly, unable to take my eyes off that sinful, tempting mouth.

I have been watching her on the screen for weeks now, so why does it feel like an age since I saw her? Why does it suddenly feel like I need her eyes on my skin? Need her mouth on it? My cock twitches, and my balls feel tight, begging for release. My hand twitches towards my groin.

"Control yourself, you fool," Xander's voice is like a draconian hammer in my head, and I close my eyes in irritation.

Suddenly, I am aware of the room again. Aware of the sweating team of scientists, the angry dragon and...the annoying little rooster rex parading behind me to settle himself at the snakelet's side.

"Bastard," I mutter.

"Who, me?"

I stare in surprise at the snakelet, who'd spoken so innocently in that husky voice, her blue eyes observing me with a coldness that makes me want to kiss her. She lies in repose on the hospital bed and licks her dry lips. That scent of her, like sweet darkness and summer rain, fills my sinuses.

Mace only ever hires mated serpents to be his scientists for this very reason. The others are aroused by the smell, but their thoughts will stray to their central mates or their nest. This is the only reason I do what I do next.

Which is leave.

Chapter 22

Aurelia

"**S**hut it off, you stupid girl." Xander's voice is a dragon's rumble.

"When this is so fun?" I reply in turn.

In truth, the sultry coils of lust slide through my body like sexy dancers. I haven't had all that many heats, and I'm still getting used to the sensation. That cold, calculating great white shark in me recognises that this feeling is heightened both because of the drugs and that I've been deprived of *any* sensation for so long.

Everything is hitting all at once, and the only thing keeping my own self at bay is the shark currently holding me—

"Cold," Solomon says after taking my tympanic temperature with a handheld device. "She is far too cold." He feels my forehead with the back of his hand.

Xander looks up from his phone. I think he's trying to distract himself from my scent. "Aren't serpents supposed to be cold-blooded?"

"This is no serpentine magic."

Xander stares at me and I level him a stare back. *He* looks warm. The blood under his skin thrums with delicious heat.

With great purpose, I allow the shark to recede, allowing seductive warmth to fill my body once again.

My head tilts back, my back arching as I close my eyes, feeling the full power of my desire speed through my limbs like bullet trains.

"If she's in heat now," Solomon says, wiping the sweat off his own forehead. "The king will want the event in her next cycle, which makes it three weeks. No more, so that she is ovulating for the first attempt."

"Right," Xander says tightly. But instead of his voice drawing away, like I'd imagined, the cursed dragon's voice strays closer.

"And she will require extra security due to these extra pheromones," Solomon says. "It would be wise to lock her up again."

A chair scrapes, and all that hot blood sits next to me. "My room is the most secure lodging after these dungeons. She cannot return to solitary."

Cold fluid begins to travel into my hand, where they have begun the drip. I breathe deeply, the flood of lust overcoming my thoughts. My left hand slides down my stomach and towards the apex of my thighs, where I might gain some relief—

"None of that." Xander snatches up my wrist and pins it down to the side of the bed, his skin hot. "Didn't anyone teach you any manners?"

"I'm sure you will," I purr, my eyes still closed against the too-bright lights as I register the feeling of his skin against mine.

That broken part of me wails in agony. There is no bond here as there should be. No mate to be found here as there once was. My anima screams for the other pieces of our soul.

Quite suddenly, the cotton wool that had filled my mind in sustained isolation clears like clouds parting for the sun.

"You've gotten hard for me once," I say. "Once that I know of, anyway." I'd felt it that time Damien Agnis had locked our class in a cage filled with water and we'd asked Xander to break us out. I'd picked the lock of the obsidian shackles Xander was wearing, but in order to do that in the cramped cage, I'd had to straddle his thigh.

I'd loved and hated every part of that moment. It had been the validation I'd needed. Xander didn't find me disgusting at all. It was quite the opposite.

Every heat I'd had, he'd made himself scarce, and now...he had no choice but to experience it.

"Does it affect your cursed, blackened soul?" I pant. The rest of the room quietens. "Or are you too far gone down the path to hell?"

"You're lucky I didn't kill you, Snake *Spawn*," comes the deep drawl. "Just lucky that you're more useful to everyone alive."

I hate that I desire him even now. Hate that his voice makes my stomach flutter, that it makes me want to run my fingers along his bare skin and lower still.

"They'd never let you live that down," I whisper. "They'd make your life a nightmare."

"They can try," he scoffs with flaming arrogance. "They'd never succeed."

I laugh then. A hacking rasp that *could* be taken for sexy. "Your dragon powers know when other people are lying, but do they know when you're lying to yourself?"

"Tape her mouth shut."

My eyes fly open and I immediately regret it. Cringing against the pain of the light, I choke. "What?"

"We need to feed her first," Solomon says carefully.

"This was supposed to break her, *serpent*." Xander is standing now, his voice rising. "You fools with your bloated educations and useless serpent magic have no fucking idea what you're doing."

I smile where I lie. There's a little glucose in this drip; I can tell by the new energy in my veins and it feels rather nice.

"I have half a mind to fire you and instate a new team," Xander continues angrily.

"But my lord—" Solomon starts.

"Be quiet, reptile," Xander snarls. "Your incompetence is astounding. These so-called experiments are a farce. I'll be speaking to my father about this."

The scientists blubber their protestations and explanations, but I can tell Xander is at his tether's end when he plucks the IV bag off the pole and all but snatches me off the bed. "I've had enough of this," he says loudly. "She'll be in her cage in my room, and when *I* am ready, I will bring her back."

There is no kindness in his touch, and I feel like nothing more than a bundle of clothes in his large arms as he hauls me back to his room. I take the opportunity to indulge in his fireball scent. Oh so angry. Oh so riled up.

Up many stairs, passing through many corridors, I hear the mutterings of the estate's staff. Eugene follows us at a quick pace, no doubt causing some of the stir. Xander appears to be ignoring him.

When we get back into his room, Xander kicks the door shut behind him and I giggle.

"I'm a new bride," I say breathily, sweeping my arms around me. "Brought home by her husband for their first night. Ready to be ravaged!"

Xander swears under his breath before he sends me tumbling into my cage, locking it shut with a definitive clang and hanging my IV bag off the top of the cage. Eugene speeds into the bathroom and closes the door with his beak.

But I am not deterred.

"Hot," I mumble, tugging at my dress. "So hot." I pull the annoying material off in one movement, sighing in relief as the room's cool air strokes my bare breasts and stomach. I flop onto my back.

I let my head swing to the right where Olly the butler is suddenly standing open-mouthed. I flash him a lazy-grin.

"Out!" Xander commands. "Get out! Do not return!"

Olly sprints out of the room.

"Why'd you send him away?" I say lazily, bending one knee and rubbing up my thigh. "The servants are nice to me."

"They don't understand these things," Xander snarls, pacing his room. "And I can't have you seducing my butler."

I sit up with interest. Excitement. "You think I could do that? Seduce him?"

Xander runs a hand through his hair and mutters to himself, "You could seduce a fucking tree."

Well, *that's* news to me. My brows shoot up, and when the big nasty dragon realises I heard him, he scowls and points a finger. "Don't get any ideas. I might have to shut down the estate because of you. I have a fucking wedding in a week's time." He begins pacing again.

"A wedding?" I frown. "Whose?"

He freezes before pinching the bridge of his nose. "I need to fucking fly."

"Yeah," I sigh, stroking my arms as if I see the feathers under my skin. So soft. So smooth. "That does sound nice."

"Shut up, Spawn."

"It's not my fault your voice turns me on."

He whirls around to stare at me, his face twisted in fury.

"Don't let anyone see you like this," I say sagely. "It'll ruin your reputation completely."

Xander's entire face darkens. "How many days left?"

I shrug, cupping a breast as I do, rolling my nipple under my palm. "There were no days in that place, so I don't know. I can't even tell when it started."

"Shit."

"Wait," I say, gripping one of the bars of my cage. "Is your new wife going to sleep in here with us?"

Xander's claw clenches over and over again as his gaze shifts to the bed.

"You should just breed me instead—" I clap my hand over my own cursed mouth. "Sorry, that's the heat speaking," I say, voice muffled. Dramatically, I flop back down onto my blankets, rolling until I'm face down so that I might try to smother myself. But I don't even realise that I'm arching my back and presenting my pussy to him until I'm waving my ass in the air.

I gasp and flip over and find Xander staring in pure and utter shock. He'd seen everything, no doubt, pink, dripping pussy and all.

"I can't deal with this," I choke, pulling a blanket to cover myself before throwing it back off. "This is fucked. You *rejected* me. You're keeping me in a cage."

Chapter 23

Xander

I need to get her away from me. My response to her heat is nothing more than a natural response from an unmated dragon male. Nothing more.

During her previous heats, I'd removed myself from the entire building, taking refuge in the fresh, clean air of the sky. With my dragon not on speaking terms with me, I can't even fly to get away. And if I left her, who's to say which manner of untamed beast would claim my property for himself?

Eugene has locked himself in the bathroom. How the fuck he got here is beyond me, but I'll be separating the two of them immediately. And with my upcoming wedding, every powerful and threatening beast in the state will be here to witness the union. I need to be at the top of my game to let them all know they cannot steal anything from me. That if they so much as think about it, I will slaughter them and take their gold for my own.

When I glance at Spawn, her round ass is in the air, her pussy completely unobstructed for me to see. It's flushed and pink with her heat, glistening wet and dripping with—

Stricken, I suddenly can't move, my very being frozen in time and space. Spawn makes a sexual sound and turns over. She stares at me, affronted, as if I'm the one at fault.

I fly at her cage, roaring at her between the bars. "Put your scent shield up or I will kill every last nimpin in Damien Agnis' cage with my bare fucking hands, Aurelia Boneweaver."

Her mouth drops open, but she leans forward with her eyes wide as if she's not afraid of me, but *enamoured*. "You wouldn't!"

"Do you really want to try me?" I snarl, drawing my nose away from her.

She rests back on her elbows, dropping her head back as if in great pain, baring the column of her neck and squeezing her eyes shut.

Her scent shuts off. Abruptly. Completely.

The ability to do that seems to be from the Boneweavers alone. It's a skill not even dragons have. It makes the Boneweavers the ultimate predator.

Not for the first time, I wonder how the fuck they went extinct. I exhale heavily, smoke streaming from my nose as I rise to my feet.

"You made a grave mistake," I say faintly, heading to my window and opening it wide to the night. "Everyone knows you have a powerful heat and exactly when it's expected. They'll use it against you now."

I ignore the rustle of feathers and the small black shadow under the bathroom door. My phone rings and it's my father's executive assistant.

"Lord Drakos, the Lord and Lady Hellfire and Miss Francesca are scheduled to arrive in five minutes."

"Thank you," I say before hanging up.

Opening my bedside drawer, I pick up a red velvet box that came from the family treasury this morning. A stunning ring of white gold with a rare, princess cut ruby sits inside. I pocket it. With this ring, I declare to my family, to the world, that I am my own dragon. That I am a beast with his own independent desires.

I look back at Spawn. I need to deal with this, and fast. My balls tighten, my cock straining against my pants. I can hardly go to a meeting with the Hellfires and ask Francesca to marry me with a giant tent in my pants. There is a way I can prove that I am truly free of the Spawn. A test.

Reaching out with my telepathy, I locate the basilisk lord. He's outside on the front lawn, likely smoking a joint and keeping away from Spawn.

"What do you want?" comes the reply.

"You need to satiate Serpent Spawn," I say curtly. *"She is insufferable. And I want to test my...lack of bond."*

His interest piques immediately. *"Is she asking for me?"*

I turn to look at it. Spawn sits with her face pressed between the bars, licking her lips, her eyes wide. She toys with one nipple like she can't help it.

"I want my mates," she whispers. Her hand tightens around her breast and she screws up her face, her brows drawing tight. "I need their cocks. Cock. Cock. Cock. Cock." She groans, throwing herself dramatically on the blankets and writhing around. A tear slips from one eye. "Goddess this *hurts*. Someone help me." Her hand slides down her body, her fingers slipping between her legs. Her wrist rotates.

I turn away. *"Yes. Get the fuck over here. She's half mad."*

His gloating smile is audible. *"Just the way I like her."*

Chapter 24

Aurelia

It's dark in the room, as if they think they can stifle my heat with the lack of light. But I am an eagle. A desperately horny eagle, and there is nothing on my mind except the delicious finger that twirls around my hot, aching, swollen clit.

I tell the room exactly that. I need them to know. I need everyone to know how hot and awful I feel without a cock inside of me. How desire can turn into sheer torture.

One part of me knows I'm being ridiculous writhing and sulking. That it's just the drugs they've darted me with. But I like it. It's a relief that I get to be the ridiculous one for a change.

A sharp knock on the door outside tells me someone is here, and the regina in me knows exactly who it is: a mate come to fuck me. To fill me with so much cum, I'm like a cum balloon.

"Yes," I nod, shaking my bars and baring my teeth as Xander heads to the door to open it. I watch his movements with acute precision.

He is stressed. He is horny. These things are very good for my aching pussy.

Ghoul saunters through the door, a little bag in hand. My eyes slide to the bathroom door, making sure it's closed. Immediately I hide Eugene under one of my bubble shields of invisibility.

That's the last thought I have about the rooster.

"You look tasty," I hiss. "Come and play with me."

"Oh, she is delightful like this," the basilisk says, flashing his fangs. "What the fuck have I missed?"

I run my tongue around my lips. "Get your cock out. Take advantage of me," I urge. "If you give me both cocks, I'll take them. Cross my heart." I make a little X over my right breast.

But neither of them obey.

Instead, they look at each other and something passes between them. Xander lights up a joint. With his telekinesis, he pulls the heavy drapes shut with a *swoosh*.

Now there's nothing but the cherry glow of the cigarette butt, Xander's white orbs and Ghoul's red pupils.

"Give me some of that," Ghoul says, holding his hand out. Xander passes it to him with a grim expression, and Ghoul takes a long drag of the dragon-strength weed.

Holy shit. My mouth drops open, my pussy drips under me. Ghoul exhales smoke into the air and passes the joint back. Watching the two monsters share a joint, their eyes on me and the air hazy with smoke makes goosebumps erupt all over my skin.

Ghoul strides right up to my cage and crouches to level me with a red laser beam look. "I want to taste your venom," he says. "You'll give me some."

Oh, he's taking full advantage.

"I want to see your face," I breathe, awestruck.

"Give me what I want first, pretty snakelet."

Because I have no willpower, I pout for a brief moment before opening my mouth and shifting my teeth. Fangs grow against my upper palate and I extend them out with a hiss.

"Good girl," Ghoul whispers, taking off a glove and reaching for my face. His cool fingers squeeze my cheeks together. "I've been dreaming of this."

I open my mouth wider and allow a drop of venom to fall from both fangs. Ghoul watches transfixed, his lips parted, his own fangs drawn in arousal. His mouth rushes towards mine and he sucks on my right fang, scraping his tongue across it.

I suck in a shocked, aroused breath.

"More." His voice is haggard as he swings open the cage door and grabs me out of it. I put my hands on his shoulders and he lifts me up, using his arms as a seat for my ass.

Smoke billows from behind him as he licks his lips. "More."

I open my mouth and slant it over his, letting the milky fluid of my venom stream freely downward.

Ghoul opens his mouth and *drinks*, swallowing down the venom with relish.

"Sick fuck," Xander mutters.

I stare down at the basilisk in wonder, never feeling so horny in my life. "Fuck me." I grab his masked face in both hands, staring deep into the red points of light. "Right now."

He chuckles and walks me over to the bed, laying me down before glancing at Xander.

The dragon comes to stand on the other side, the cherry glow of the joint flaring up before he exhales smoke into the air. He hands the thing to me.

"Smoke it."

"Oooh!" I say excitedly, carefully taking the thing between my thumb and index finger. Lying on my back, the joint makes pretty smoky patterns in the air. I soar it over my head like a plane, admiring the swirls it makes. "Wow!"

Xander snarls and snatches it out of my hand. "Stop that." He kneels on the bed and leans over me. I look up at him in awe, but he presses the joint to my lips. "You suck on it."

"Like a cock?" I say sweetly.

He takes the opportunity to place it further into my mouth and I'm aware of Ghoul opening up his bag on my other side.

I inhale on the joint, but cough on the smoke, turning to the side and rubbing my sore throat.

"It takes practise," Ghoul chuckles.

"Useless," Xander mutters. He places the joint in his own mouth and presses his first two fingers to my lips.

"What are you doing?" I say muffled, frowning at the hot, nasty dragon.

"I'm proving I can withstand you," Xander says between clenched teeth. "I'm proving you have no control over me."

"Yes, of course," I coo, wriggling my hips. "Let's see how well you can do."

"Then suck."

Eagerly, I open my mouth and let Xander's fingers in, swirling my tongue around. My eyes roll to the back of my head at the slightly salty taste of his flame-kissed skin.

Xander tugs his fingers out of my mouth and climbs onto the bed, pushing me in the centre of the chest so I go falling back.

"I never signed your silly contract," he says, his eyes fixed on my pussy. "What was your safe word again?"

"Fairy bread!" I say excitedly, spreading my legs.

"Right," he mutters, before pressing his wet fingers to my wet slit.

I hiss, arching my hand and reaching for his responsible wrist. "Yes!"

"You're already so swollen," he frowns. "Is this normal?"

I raise my head to stare at his fingers, gently brushing a circle around my lips. "Uh-huh. I get really wet too."

A low buzz sounds, and I turn to see Ghoul waving a purple vibrator at me. But Xander is dragging his fingers, coating them with my hot slick, driving me absolutely feral with desire. "In me," I pant, raising my hips. "In. Me."

Xander's jaw ticks, and I don't know if he's doing as well as he thinks. But he shakes his head. "Not today. Not ever."

I groan in frustration, thumping the bed with a fist. "Then give me someone who will!" I leap for Ghoul, completely catching him off guard, and we both go crashing to the floor. I shove him onto his back and he lets me, before I sit on top of him and grind against his trousers. I do a test bounce, watching my breasts jiggle.

Ghoul chuckles before grabbing me around the waist and somehow managing to stand and throwing me onto the bed.

I roll onto my stomach and present my ass into the air, fingering my pussy and sliding my fingers all the way inside. Moaning as finally something is in me, I pump my fingers in and out.

There is silence behind me. Predatorial, hungry silence.

Suddenly, the vibrator clicks on and buzzes before someone presses it to my pussy. I flinch at first, then lean into it, the pleasant buzz spreading through my labia. I cry out in approval, rubbing myself against it until I'm in a haze. Smoke billows around me and I inhale it with bliss.

A low voice murmurs by my ear. "Do you want it inside of you, snakelet?"

My heart leaps. "Yes."

"Yes, what?"

"Yes, please, Ghoul."

"Good girls get rewarded, sweetheart." The wand presses against my entrance.

I'm surprised by Xander's voice this time. "Fuck the vibrator, Spawn. Fuck yourself with it."

So I do. I push against it, angling my hips for better depth and letting it fill me up. I groan with satisfaction.

"Faster." Is it me or is his voice haggard? I look back at the dragon, his white eyes flickering different colours.

"Pretty," I murmur, staring at him as I fuck myself. He can't take his eyes away as he watches me grind and fuck the vibrator. "I want to know what they look like when you come, Xander. I want to know how pretty your eyes go when you're pumping cum into my pussy."

His lips part as he stares at me, unblinking. I have him. I know I do, and it makes me scream as I come, throwing my head back and squealing my release for them both to hear.

As I let the orgasm fade, Ghoul scrapes his fangs against my shoulder, picks me up and sets me on the floor. "Go to him." The command in his voice makes me pant as he nods at the stricken dragon.

I drop to my knees before Xander, and slide my palms up his thighs. The dragon looks down at me, his breath short and sharp. I rub my cheek against the hard seam.

"You *are* big," I murmur, pressing my lips against the straining length of him. "I want you in my mouth."

He grabs the back of my head, burying his hands in my hair and pulling a little.

"You fucking love that," Ghoul drawls from where he sits in Xander's arm chair, watching us with a grin. "You fucking love her pretty eyes looking up at you. We all imagine it, dragon. We all fantasise about her. And you're no fucking exception."

I press my lips to the steel in his pants, blinking up at him as I rub my mouth against it.

Xander sucks in a breath.

"Let her have it," Ghoul says. "Let her put her lips around your cock and let her suck you empty. You want it."

Xander snarls and seems to come back to his senses. He wrenches my head back, forcing me to look up. He leans down and his breath tickles my face as his eyes become nothing but hot, angry fire.

"Not now," he hisses over my lips. "Not ever."

Xander kisses me, hard, punishing and nasty. I let out a sound that's half a protest.

He releases me abruptly and turns around, striding for the door, his body taut with pure rage.

"Leave him," Ghoul drawls.

I turn to the basilisk.

He beckons with two fingers. "Come to daddy. I'll take care of you."

Chapter 25

Savage

The guards scatter as we stride into the dining hall of Animus Academy during late-night supper service. Every student in the hall goes still. Someone drops their plastic cup.

Maybe it's the old blood on my body? As if I was going to stop to shower! We have *no* time for showering. Their shock could also be due to the Dabu pack sauntering in behind me. The three hyena animas have a reputation, even out of prison.

I zone in on the person I want.

"*Yoohoo*, Raquel?" I call. "Get over here."

Raquel, who's sitting next to Minnie, drops their fork in shock, but stares at me, all wide-eyed and nervous. Sighing dramatically, I continue forward, while Lyle goes to speak with Theresa, standing at the buffet. Scythe steps aside to speak with the Forklift Twins who man the front door. This was his idea after all, but I'm the one who's gonna execute it.

Students stare at me as I pass, nostrils flaring as they scent the death that follows me at all times now.

I gesture at Raquel, waving for them to come to me. "Come, come, Raquel. I need to talk to you."

But it's Minnie who gets to her feet. Yeti and Marduk remain sitting on either side of her, their faces wary.

"Savage, this is in no way, shape or form, hygienic."

My brows shoot up. "I'm not worried about hygiene, Minnie."

"That much is obvious."

There's a spare plate of pancakes on the table. I grab a fistful and shove it in my mouth. Carbs are always good at a time like this.

"Hey, that was mine," Connor grumbles.

"Sorry, not sorry," I say thickly. "Anyway, Raquel?" I jerk my head at the door. "I am in need of your services."

Minnie narrows her eyes. "What for?"

"What, are you their lawyer now?"

"That's exactly what I am."

I roll my eyes. "I'm not going to hurt Raquel! And they're sworn to us anyway."

"I-It's alright, Min," Raquel says, getting to their feet. "I'm coming, Mr Fengari."

I nod enthusiastically, leading the way back out. To my surprise and annoyance, multiple chairs scrape back and my ears tell me the entire table is now following, Connor and Stacey as well. I roll my eyes at Scythe.

Raquel's eyes light up when they see the Dabu pack have come with us. The pack greets our wolf anim like they're old friends. I suppose they got along really well during our mission to the Naga House to rescue my regina's mum.

We all head out to our hidden suite, and once everyone is seated, Scythe explains his idea.

"Raquel," he says, "you are the strongest broadcaster we know."

"After me," I clarify, tearing into another pancake.

"After Savage," Scythe confirms. "But Aurelia has blocked us out of her mind. She does...not want us to be in contact with her."

Minnie bites her lip as if this upsets her. It upsets me too. More than I can even put into words. I need to do something with my hands, but I have no pancakes left. I stare at my palms, my fingernails crusted with dark red and black.

"Here," a small voice says by my elbow. It's Stacey, and the little lioness is pushing a colouring book and pencils into my hand.

I take them with a grunt, almost ripping the book as I open it and choose the black pencil. I begin frantically colouring the butterfly on the page. Black. All black.

Scythe clears his throat. "Aurelia may have blocked us out, but she may be open to others."

"But the distance!" Minnie exclaims. "Drakos Estate is *hours* away by car, isn't it?"

"I c-can probably reach," Raquel says quietly. "It's w-worth giving it a go."

"If there's trouble, you leave straight away," Marduk says. "We don't want them—"

"Right." Scythe takes out a joint and his silver lighter. "Be observant. Be careful. It'll be bad if you're detected."

Raquel inhales slowly and gets out of their seat to sit on the floor as if it's more comfortable. They look nervous. I suppose this is sort of dangerous.

"But it'll be protected by intense dragon magic, right?" Connor says from his spot on the dining table.

"That's why we are here," Hyacinth Dabu says. "We've got a little workaround to trick any protective spells." She begins to set up her cauldron, Bunsen burner, and ingredients on the dining room table. Connor and Stacey watch on with great interest as she lights it up and takes out a bit of hair from Xander's hairbrush.

"Can you put clothes on now that they've agreed to do it, Sav?" Minnie says rudely.

"What, are you offended?" I exclaim.

"Yeah, actually. You have blood on your dick, did you know?"

Marduk gasps and slaps a hand over Minnie's eyes. "Stop looking at his dick, regina!"

I cackle like a madman as Minnie tries to claw Marduk's hands off her face.

Connor throws his jacket at me. "You can keep that."

Sighing, I take the long sleeves of the jacket and tie it around my waist like an apron, leaving my ass out. "Happy?" I retort as Marduk frees Minnie and I come to sit down cross-legged opposite Raquel.

"Yes, actually," Minnie says.

"W-What should I tell her?" Raquel asks.

My chest puffs out as all the damned, bloody things I want to say fly through my brain. "Tell her I want to spank her silly, and then I'll—"

"Tell her we love her," Lyle interjects quickly. "Tell her we need her to come back."

I cross my arms and grumble. "Yeah. Yeah, that's good too."

Raquel closes their eyes and so do I.

"What's he doing?" Stacey whispers.

"He can go with Raquel," Scythe explains. "As far as he is able. Since Raquel has never been to Drakos Estate before, he can guide them there."

"Ready?" Hyacinth says, dipping a strip of cloth into the cauldron before pulling it back out all glisteny and steamy.

"Yes," Raquel says, holding out their arm.

"It's hot." Hyacinth wraps the piece around Raquel's wrist. "But it has Xander's hair inside of it, which will trick the protections into thinking you're him. You only have until it cools down to get in and out."

I nod faintly as I link my mind with the wolf anim before me. Raquel accepts my hook and together we send our telepathic power across the land, north and west, towards Drakos Estate.

"Eyes on the prize, Raquel," I say. *"Let's be quick."*

"Yes, boss."

We soar over the land and I tug Raquel along with me. Nothing of great interest lies between the academy and Drakos Estate, just empty land, so it's pretty easy to spot it from ages away. It's a big black cube of power, sort of oily and dirty feeling. It's nothing like the physical version of the place, and you wouldn't guess what lies protecting it until you've gone looking for it.

You'd have to be a loon to try to get in.

"You're on your own, now," I say softly. *"See if you can sense her. But I'll keep watch from here."*

Raquel swears under their breath, but I unhook my mind from theirs, telepathically stepping back and watching from afar. I feel the wolf anim approach the barrier of the estate and they breeze right through. I hold my breath, all my senses alert, ready for any sign to get the wolf anim back out.

But too much rides on this. I need to talk to my regina. I *need* to know she's okay. I need to know why she left me.

"Anything?" I ask Raquel, speaking out loud for the benefit of the rest of the room.

Raquel speaks softly, as if they're worried they'll wake something up. "Not yet. It feels sort of empty. Let me scope out the lower levels."

I rage to think they have my regina in an underground cell or something. But knowing these fucking dragons, they would do exactly that.

"Calm, brother," Scythe rasps in my ear. "Focus."

I nod, but it's irritating that I can't feel Raquel anymore.

"Talk to me, anim," I growl, clenching my fists to resist the urge to leap after them and feel it out for myself.

"There's nothing here," Raquel whispers, as if afraid someone will hear them. "I can feel faint movement, but it's buffered."

"Their protections are too strong," Hyacinth says.

"We knew that going in," I press. "But Aurelia—she might feel you if you're close enough."

"Aurelia," Raquel whispers, as if she's calling out. "Aurelia, can you hear me?"

I slap my knee. "I can't even feel where she could be either. It's like reaching out to a ghost."

"Don't say that," Lyle growls from what feels like far away. I growl in agreement.

Raquel calls out to my regina again. "Aurelia? Oh, here's something."

"What?" at least four voices call out at the same time.

"It's a dungeon," Raquel whispers. "I sense wolves, though. Not dragons."

A hint of warning prickles at my mind. A familiar magic. Dark and prowling low, close to the ground. It snaps at Raquel's heels. My heart leaps.

"Abort mission!" I command. "Raquel, out! Those are Lunaris wolves!"

But instead of obeying me, Raquel lets out a blood-curdling scream.

"Lunaris?" screams Minnie. "Like Ruben Lunaris?"

"Raquel, where are you?" I shout.

"Stop!" Raquel screams. "Mr Fengari, help!"

"I'm trying!" I'm panicking now. I surge towards Drakos Estate, but Scythe's cold power suddenly grasps my mind, holding it tight. "They'll get you too. Leave her."

"No!" I roar, getting onto my knees. I've never left a wolf behind. Not now, not ever. I strain towards Raquel, reaching out to try to hook them back to safety. "Raquel! Find me!"

Raquel screams again, this time in pure agony. And then their voice cuts off and I hear a thump in the room. Minnie and Stacey cry out. Sour panic fills the air.

Scythe grabs my mind in a grip like a cold current and forces me back to Animus Academy, where I open my physical eyes with a howl. I lunge for Raquel. But the wolf anim is slumped over, their eyes open and fixed in place.

Minnie's arms are around the wolf anim, and she pins me with terrified eyes. "What have you done!"

Chapter 26

Xander

Something stirs in the air, an echo of a thought. My eyes fly open and I sit up in bed.

"Raquel?" Spawn mutters in its sleep. "Raquel!" it cries, sitting up abruptly and hitting its head on the bars above. "Fuck!"

"Be quiet," I snarl.

Spawn sighs loudly, lying back down. Its heat finished a few hours ago, and I'd had to levitate its sleeping body off my bed and back into the cage. I ended up torching my sheets to ash afterward.

"Your little broadcaster friend just tried to contact you," I mutter. "They have a death wish. This place is protected to the nines. They had no chance." And yet Raquel had gotten far enough for us to sense them, which shouldn't have even been possible. Scowling, I shove the covers back and leap out of bed, finding my stride immediately.

"Get up," I command, flicking up the blackout cover of its cage and throwing her dress at her.

Spawn blinks sleepily at me, rubbing its temple as it dresses and crawls out. With a snap of my wrist, it's leashed and I'm speeding out of my room.

The castle is dead quiet just after midnight and we are but shadows charging towards the underground levels. I'd been expecting a penetration attempt long before now, and had been prepared on a number of levels. The fact Savage thought he could get anyone in here, even telepathically, makes a dark, twisted part of me smirk.

Do they even know me at all?

Whatever I felt for them before is long gone now. Especially after the chaos they're causing out in the streets. Since *Animalia Today* is no longer a reliable source of information, Father and I have sent out scouts to bring news directly from the ground. Mace is proving to be informative, but everyone knows he holds back information. He's not been the King of Serpents this long for no reason.

My enemy's enemy is my friend.

One of the first things I did in my role as heir was to bring in everyone I thought would be useful.

Including—

"My Lord Drakos," announces the massive wolf anima standing guard in the lower dungeon. Spawn makes a sound of surprise.

"Debrah Lunaris," I say. "We have an intruder."

Spawn makes a choked sound upon hearing her name as Debrah steps into the light of a wall sconce. She is a wolf regina as big as her late mate, the wolf who was head of security at Animus Academy before Savage blew him to bits at Blackwater Penitentiary.

Naturally, his regina and two pack-mates were out for blood after that.

And now they work for me.

"There's a wolf anim I don't recognise," Debrah says, scratching her shaved head. "Wasn't expecting to see us and walked right into the trap. Savage was with them, but he got away."

Spawn's breath quickens as Debrah leads us into the dark chamber she's guarding. Three shifted wolves prowl back and forth, in front of a wall fixed with two pairs of shackles. They snap their jaws at the shackles as if there's something there.

"I can't see anything," Spawn says, fear coating its voice.

"We've telepathically trapped their mind," Debrah gloats, gesturing at the shackles. "They'll be stuck here until we release them."

Smirking, I draw Spawn forwards. "Go on, use your power and see them."

A frown creases Spawn's brows as it concentrates for all it's worth. I also take a look, sending my telepathic power into the chamber.

There are a few prisoners in our telepathic prison. Some, who have been here for decades, lie slumped where they're fixed to the wall by obsidian shackles. It's a unique prison made by my great-grandfather, made to protect our family from enemies who would try to get to us and our hatchlings.

Raquel whimpers on the far side of the chamber, the slightly transparent sheen of their body reminding me we're not in the physical world. They are strapped like the rest, in an X position, tears streaming down their face. They look exactly as I remember them, a denim jacket with club and pack patches sewn on, closely buzzed hair with a face full of silver piercings. Their eyes are closed, breathing hard as if trying to control themselves.

"Release them!" Spawn cries, as it spots them. "Oh my god, Xander, you *know* Raquel. Release them right now!"

I come back into the chamber, yanking Spawn back out of the doorway.

"Your mates have been on a rampage," I sneer. "And they'll feel the consequences of that soon."

It stares at me, and the darkness that has been lurking in me comes out in full force as I get out my phone and show it the photos I've been sent. Bloody, horrible scenes of torture. Spawn gasps, covering its mouth in horror.

"That's right," I say quietly. "Savage, Scythe and Lyle have done that to Serpent Court officials." I let it sink in for a moment. "Because of you."

"I...I have to get them to stop. Get them to—"

"The only way that they'll stop is if they have you back. And that's not going to happen, is it?" The gloom of the underground corridor makes my voice seem deeper and darker. I chuckle under my breath, and even to me, it sounds evil. "And a part of your surrender was no communication with them, or I will execute those nimpins. Trust me on that. But if you think Mace Naga will stand by and watch his court bleed for you, you're not as intelligent as I gave you credit for."

Spawn covers its mouth with both hands now, muffling its sobs. I turn around and tug it back to my room.

* * *

Spawn is quiet the next morning. Its period of isolation has made it flinchy and it blinks more often than it used to. It comes with me to every appointment with my father, and the meetings with my mother and Sissy where we go over every detail of the wedding. Though it makes no sound, its heart rate remains a constant irritating trot. The gravity of the situation seems to have hit it. This is not the game it thought it would be.

I never treated this like a game.

"Here, poppet, have some cake," Mother says, gesturing to a bundt Sissy and the hatchlings made for afternoon tea.

To my great irritation, she's not talking to me.

"It doesn't eat cake, Mother."

"No thank you, Lady Drakos," Spawn says, blankly staring at the carpet where it kneels next to my chair.

"Do you enjoy keeping her on a leash?" Sissy suddenly asks, her mouth twisted.

It comes out without much thought. "Wouldn't you enjoy keeping Ragnar on one?"

She drops her spoon with a clatter.

Hurt mars her expression. "Really, Xander?"

I sigh, rubbing at my forehead. Another fucking headache coming on. "Sorry. I'm not—"

"Thinking?" she snaps. "Not feeling yourself? I wonder why."

I stop rubbing my forehead to glare at her. "You have no idea what you're talking about."

"Let's not fight," Mother says breezily. "Aurelia, dear, will you pass me my tonic?"

She is trying to *involve* Spawn in things. Offering it food, asking it to fetch this and that. It bothers me to no end, but my mother is so sweet, so fragile, that telling her to stop something she seems to enjoy feels counter-intuitive.

"Yes, Lady Drakos." Spawn rises to its feet before heading to the mantelpiece to get the silver bottle Mother's tonic is delivered in. It lingers at the mantel, apparently forgetting why it's there.

"Hurry up," I drone, sipping my own tea.

It brings the bottle back, handing it to Mother.

"Have we decided on the flower arrangement for the aisle?" Mother asks, pouring the tonic into her teacup. "Lady Hellfire has allergies; we had better cross lilies off the list."

"Francesca wants hydrangeas," Sissy says. "Do you have a preference, Xander? We need to order them tonight, otherwise the florist won't have enough time."

They could get black flowers for all I care. "No preference."

"Your vows are finalised?" Mother asks.

"Not yet. It's on my long list of things to do."

"Well, prioritise it," Sissy snaps.

I put down my cup and saucer. "Is there something wrong, Sissy?"

She purses her lips and says in a voice that is clearly the opposite of her words. "No."

"Is your dress ready?" I ask pointedly. "Mother, is yours?" Both women avoid looking at me, and suddenly, the energy changes in the room. "What is it?"

Sissy turns to regard me, her face stony. "I'm not to attend the wedding."

A fiery spear shoots through my chest. "What?"

"Father has decreed it. The Hellfires requested it. Me and the hatchlings will stay in our rooms."

Slowly, I rise to my feet, leashing my composure with a band of metal. "Did he care to mention why?"

"Don't start an argument, dear," Mother says softly. "This is not the time."

"This is just the right time, Mother. Sissy, what was the reason?"

Sissy swallows, and I suddenly want to tear the world apart. "They said it would be bad luck."

Violence threatens to tear from my body, and I'm out the door a heartbeat later, Spawn stumbling along behind me.

"Xander!" Mother cries. "Xander, no!"

I pause outside, hating to hear the fear and anguish in my mother's voice, directed not for me, but *at* me.

Sissy comes rushing out and grips my elbow, turning me around to look at her. "Don't," she says, her eyes shining. "Please. Do not cause a fuss over me." She swallows again. "Yet another time."

I frown, the backs of my eyes burning. I take her face in my palms to speak to her fiercely. "You deserve respect, Selena. *Respect*. You deserve fuss. And I will always be here to stand up for you."

She pulls away from my palms, casting her eyes down. "I'm the older sister. I'm supposed to be protecting *you*."

"We've been through this before," I sigh. "It is my right and privilege to care for you. And now that I'm here, I can do that better. This is part of the reason I came back, after all."

Sissy stares at me in horror, stepping away from me with a horrified expression, as if I'm some terrible monster. "Do *not* use me as the reason you're here." She takes another step back and all I can do is stare while my stomach sinks. "Do *not* use me as the reason you did something horrible to *this*"—she points to Spawn standing as far as the leash will allow, staring pale-faced at us—"poor girl. You did the most heinous thing, Xander. Do you even know what *you've* become?" She points a shaking finger at me and I stumble a step back as if she's shot me. "You're the same as Ragnar. Don't you see that? What you did is almost the *exact same thing* my husband did to me."

All violence, all rage, suddenly *poofs* out of my body as my sister turns her back on me and slams the drawing-room door shut in my face. I blink at the door. I blink again.

Chapter 27

Aurelia

My heart pounds as I stare at the closed drawing-room door. Xander is still as a statue, in shock, I think at the words of his sister. One breath passes, then another before he seems to recover and turns away from the door, silently heading down the corridor.

Hurrying to keep up, I stare at the stony set of his shoulders.

Selena's husband. What had happened between her and the children's father? Something so awful that the Hellfire family thought she and the children were *bad luck?* It should make me profoundly happy that finally someone gave Xander a piece of their mind, but instead, I feel sick.

Xander reaches his room and unlocks the door. With a snap, I'm free of the gold chain, and telekinesis shoves me through the door. It shuts between us, leaving me in the quiet of his room. Cold footsteps sound on the carpet outside before they fade away completely.

I suddenly feel extremely alone.

Eugene is my only comfort, hidden in a bubble shield by my side. Xander, despite his advanced hearing likely alerting him, has not mentioned it.

In fact, the dragon made no mention of anything that had

happened during my heat yesterday, as if we're pretending it didn't even happen. I'm completely fine with that game since I made a complete fool of myself, slobbering all over him like a thirsty, feral creature.

Lyle said this was all because I have five mates and my regina instincts push my heat times five. It doesn't make me feel any better right now, of course, especially since they've planned for the auction around my heat.

And then there's Raquel. Poor Raquel, who'd likely been told to try to contact me and is now captured in the Drakos dungeon. They must be terrified. An idea strikes me, and I hurry to my cage and pull down the blackout flap.

Xander is in a state, and will likely leave to gather his thoughts for a while. I no doubt have some time up my sleeve. I settle myself in a sitting position in the cage and close my eyes, protecting myself with a bubble of invisibility, then reaching out with my telepathy. Remembering the way to the dungeons from last night, I follow the same path carefully in case a wandering Flores Drakos or someone just as bad detects me.

But this late in the afternoon, I sense no one other than a stray maid rushing down the corridor with an armful of laundry, and I make it underground with no fuss.

There's a wolf at the door, resting with her head on its paws, but I breeze easily past her. Beyond is the darkness of the stone chamber.

There, hanging against the wall in that X position, with their head slumped, is my Raquel. My heart squeezes in pain as I surge towards them.

"Raquel," I hiss. *"Can you hear me?"*

My friend is still where they hang, and if I couldn't see their chest expanding with breath, I would have panicked.

I call their name again.

Raquel flinches, but their eyes are squeezed tightly shut as if in pain. It would be uncomfortable to be separated from your body by force, the pieces of you straining to return to each other like two magnets held tightly by invisible hands.

"It's okay," I whisper. *"I'm going to try to get you out somehow. I'm so fucking sorry. No one was meant to get hurt because of me."*

"Everything is a mess, Lia," Raquel breathes. "A fucking mess."

My insides turn cold as I register the broken words.

"Well, well, well," comes a female sneer from behind me. "If it isn't the Boneweaver bitch."

I whirl around and realise I'd somehow dropped my invisibility shield in my shock at Raquel's words. As soon as I do, though, I'm grabbed by a telekinetic fist and shoved violently backward into the wall.

Crying out, I lash back, pulling my mind away from the grip of this wolf. But a second wolf joins the forces holding me, then a third. I scream in frustration. Metal encloses around my mind, holding me fixed in place with ancient draconian forces far stronger than me.

"I'm going to kill you," she snarls, and I can almost feel her breath on my face. "A mate for a mate."

"I didn't kill your mate," I choke.

She bares her teeth, growling deep in her throat. "No, but Savage Fengari did, and you are his regina."

I'm slammed against the wall so hard my physical body crumples where I still sit in my cage in Xander's room. Stars break across my vision as my entire body seizes under the force.

Shit, Aurelia. Think.

But the hold on me is beyond anything I've experienced before.

"All they'll find of you is your cold body," Ruben's regina whispers into my mind. "That's the price of taking my mate from me."

Honestly, I kind of understand.

Until the pain starts. I try not to scream, I really do, but having your mind prised apart via telepathic forces feels like hot scissors digging in and cutting you apart.

"That's right," one of the wolves rasps in sick fascination. "Scream like our mate couldn't."

I get to take a breath in, and in that moment, I hear a whimper that must be Raquel. The pain starts up again, a grating, cutting sensation that might very well drive me mad after my isolation.

It's too much. Altogether, all of this is too much.

My anima rears up and roars, a thunderous sound that echoes all around us. The three wolves are thrown off me. One of them whines and I snarl against the wall, daring them to come closer.

Xander strolls into the dungeon. "Return," he orders me. "And you don't get to leave your cage for the next week."

I flee, only sparing a glance at Raquel, whose head is now raised, red-rimmed eyes staring at me in desperation and horror. As I rush back to my physical body on all fours, I know the terrible truth. I can't risk coming back down here. They would have done worse than kill me. There would have been nothing left of my mind if I'd not telekinetically thrown them off.

That would leave them to do what they wanted to my body. Just like they did to my mother.

Chapter 28

Xander

In the week that follows, I am blessedly free of Spawn. Wedding preparations continue with great success, and I only have to deal with the moping Boneweaver in the evenings when I let it out to shower. It's quiet, maybe slightly reduced to ferality since the fright with the Lunaris wolves. Serves it right for attempting to free Raquel.

The twins have been asking daily for Spawn, Delilah going so far as to cry and stomp her feet at not being able to check on the chest wound. It's the first time I've denied them something, and it feels like shit to not be the perfect, doting uncle. Sissy just stares at me with her arms crossed, and refuses to engage in conversation. I don't push the matter, knowing that after my wedding, things will change for the better.

The afternoon of the wedding comes quickly, and I efficiently get ready in my room. Olly glances at me with worry as he fixes my bow tie. "Eyes down, butler," I snarl.

He flinches before kneeling to give my shoes a final polish. I turn and check myself in the mirror.

I've never looked finer.

The most expensive tux money could buy, coupled with the most precious gold and jewels from our horde, made an outfit worthy of the heir to one of the most wealthy dragon families in the country. No one really knew who was the wealthiest. After all, we all kept our treasuries secret, allowing rumour and gossip to fuel the eternal debate.

The biggest issue had been what to do with Spawn during the ceremony. It couldn't be left unattended with so many beasts in the estate, and I hardly wanted to see it while marrying my new fiancée.

A knock at the door brings the solution. Olly opens it and my father steps inside, looking regal in a tuxedo and blood red rose pinned to his lapel. He hands another to Olly, who fixes the flower to my own lapel.

"Hmm," Father says, surveying Spawn where it sits in its cage. "Out you come, little Boneweaver." He waves his hand and the cage door swings open.

It crawls out and gets to its feet, spine cracking and popping as it adjusts to being upright. I take the bangle off my wrist and hand it to my father. He smiles as he slips it on and flicks his wrist to let out the chain. It clicks into place.

"Let's try a tiger," he says, as if speaking to a sweet child. "Can you do that, pet?"

Spawn inhales as if annoyed before shifting. When it drops onto all fours, it is paws that hit the carpet.

"Amazing," Father murmurs, reaching out to pet it on its big, furry head. It's even bigger than Minnie, who's a sizable tigress. "The unique orange and black pattern is similar to other tigers, but it's the eyes that give her away."

Blue. Always those fucking ethereal sapphires that glint like they know something you don't. Like there are secrets Boneweavers know that other beasts can never hope to understand. Even now, silent and depressed, its eyes gleam with vicious intent.

"I've had her other forms in mind too," Father says. "It'll be a nice surprise for our guests."

"Are the Hellfires here yet?" I ask, checking the backyard camera feed on my phone. "The guests have started to arrive."

Father doesn't take his eyes off Spawn as he speaks. "Just now. The bride is settled in her suite, making final preparations. She is resplendent. I'm glad we chose her instead of Nadine. The Chens are not happy they've been overlooked but they'll get over it in time."

I haven't seen Francesca since the night I offered her the ring a week ago, and she was happy enough then even though I didn't get on one knee. Drakos dragons never kneel for anyone.

A great fuss was made over wedding preparations, but Father had made a point to *not* get her everything she wanted. It is a Drakos wedding after all, and she is marrying into *my* household.

My collar suddenly irritates me as I head downstairs, nodding at the incoming guests. Mother stands at the entrance doors, greeting them all, her arm on a maid's for stability. I frown at the sight of her. Beautiful in a gown of magenta, she's thinner than a dragon of her age should be, more quiet than a lady of the Drakos household should be. I tug at my collar again, glancing around.

"Need a smoke, Xander?" comes a voice from behind me. It's my Uncle Fabian, handsome in a tux and red rose. He is a forever-bachelor, taking only lovers but no actual mate as far as anyone knows. "There's no shame in pre-wedding jitters. We can sneak away for a moment." His gold irises gleam with mischief.

"No thank you, Uncle," I say, clapping him on the arm. "I'd prefer to be sober for this. We're about to start."

He nods and goes to find his place at the aisle as my groomsman as the last guests wander into the back garden.

I tug at my collar yet again as my mother approaches me. "Take a seat, Mother," I say. "You look tired."

"Oh," she beams weakly at me. "I am always tired, Xander. A side effect of old age, I'm afraid."

"You are hardly old," I say, stroking her cheek with the back of my index finger. "You're still a spring hatchling."

She takes my hand and kisses the back of it, looking up at me. "I want you to be happy, Xander. Are you sure this is really what you want?"

"Of course it is," I say softly. "We're all together now."

Her smile turns sad. "*Is* that the most important thing?"

I step away from her, that darkness in me rearing its head. "Take your seat, Mother."

She turns away, nodding, a maid rushing forwards to assist her. I wait a beat, looking around the hallowed halls of my forefathers. I share their blood, and yet I've never felt more set apart from them. But doing my duty, marrying and having hatchlings would surely make them proud. They all did it and I am honoured to continue the tradition. Rubbing my temple, I stride towards the open doors of the back of the castle, and through to where the aisle is set up in the back garden.

It's going to rain this evening, with clouds already gathering in the eastern sky. The guests are seated in near twenty rows of black and gold seats, casting a wary eye on the rich and influential people around them. I nod at the lesser guests, distant family, friends, and business partners. Near the front, I stop to shake hands with the human Prime Minister and some of his senators, as well as the regent of each major court: the avian queen, the feline king, the wolf queen and Mace Naga, sitting at the end of one row, looking smug. An impartial tiger stands at the front of the wedding as celebrant and I shake his hand.

It sours my mood further.

The last time I saw this particular tiger was at Aurelia's farcical wedding to Halfeather. He's the celebrant of choice amongst the elites of our kind. Mostly because he turns a blind eye to our...more unsavoury Old Laws.

I turn and survey the crowd. They all stare back at me curiously, especially the Hellfire family. They are small, as most dragon families are these days, but she has at least one aunt and uncle, and her cousins have two hatchlings between them.

An unfamiliar, heavy scraping sound from the entrance hall makes me frown. I recognise my father's steps, but—

Unbidden, a chill runs down my spine. The people closest to the door turn around and gape.

Because on the golden leash, my father drags a fully grown great white shark anima behind him.

Whispers and gasps break out amongst the crowd and the celebrant lets out a long-suffering sigh. Father has a smirk on his face, his chin held high as he drags Aurelia behind him, the heavy body of the shark pulling up the carpet behind her. Servants rush forward and straighten the carpet as he goes, so he doesn't ruin the entire aisle.

Mother turns around to see what all the fuss is about, and her hand flies to her mouth as she audibly gasps.

Has he forgotten there are *humans* here? Shit. I exchange a look with Rebecca, our publicist, sitting in the second row, and her face is pale as a sheet as she stares at the display.

Father gets to the altar, where I give him a blank look.

"The fucking Prime Minister is here, Father," I growl into his head.

"Watch your fucking tone," he replies just the same. *"They'll all love it after what Scythe Kharkorous has done to the serpent court."*

I risk a glance at Mace, and sure enough, there is a fell sort of gleam in those sociopathic black eyes as he looks upon his daughter as she's dragged up to me, gills uselessly expanding and contracting as she tries to gain breath.

"It'll die without water. The ceremony will go for too long," I murmur as Father comes to stand next to me. We both look down at her.

"Oh, she'll be fine for a bit. She's a Boneweaver, remember?"

A few in the crowd shift uncomfortably. I know this is a

show of power for my father. Probably something he's been fantasising about since she arrived.

But great white sharks suffocate without water. Even Boneweavers need oxygen to live.

"Father, I don't think—"

His eyes flash, and I shut my mouth, knowing I'll pay for this later.

"Boneweaver," Father says in a voice everyone can hear. "Shift into your human form."

No doubt desperate for air and hungering for water, she has no choice but to obey. My ears pick up the crunch of her cartilage, the scrape of her skin, and when she crouches there, in human form, she wheezes, sucking in air so loudly that the entire room can hear the struggle. The skin of her side is red and bleeds from being dragged. Eyes watering, she looks accusingly up at me.

I look away, and with the knowledge that everyone is watching us, I keep a smooth, unemotional face.

"When the shark king hears about this," Father says into my mind. *"He won't know what to do with himself."*

There's nothing I can say to that, so I remain silent until the pianist strikes up Wagner's March and everyone gets to their feet. I would have preferred Pachelbel's *Cannon in D*, but my father insisted on tradition.

My bride appears at the flowered archway, beautiful in a dragon's wedding gown. It's linen woven with gold, strong enough to take the weight of the diamonds and rubies that stud the bodice and full skirts. A gold and ruby diadem, loaned from the Drakos treasury, sits atop her head, and a veil of jewelled silk trails down her back in a long seven-foot train.

Francesca's eyes widen when she steps up to the altar and sees Aurelia crouching naked by my father's knee. Lord Hellfire raises his brows but says nothing as he hands his daughter to me. My bride's eyes flick to mine, but all I do is take her hands like we're supposed to.

My headache suddenly returns with a vengeance.

The celebrant begins the usual speech about love and tradition as the two of us stand there and I pretend to listen. My head pounds a murderous beat along to Spawn's laboured breathing inside my skull. A bead of sweat runs down Francesca's spine. My father shifts impatiently behind me. The entire room breathes. Lungs expanding, throats swallowing. The birds in the trees at the edge of the estate chirp a raucous call. I should have taken up Uncle Fabian's offer of that smoke.

Spawn sniffs.

I want it all to fucking stop.

And then Francesa begins speaking her vows, dragging my attention to her powdered face. "Under the Wild Goddess, I bind myself in holy matrimony to you, Xander Flores Drakos. I vow to honour, serve, and obey you until my last day upon this earth." She places the gold wedding band on my finger.

Does she mean it?

When it's my turn, I say, "Under the Wild Goddess, I bind myself in holy matrimony to you, Francesca Nolene Dorothy Hellfire. I vow to love, honour, and cherish you until my last day upon this—"

It's right at that moment my dragon decides to awaken with an earth-trembling roar. His mighty jaws open wide, white glowing eyes terrible and raging.

"You have no authority over me!" he roars, low and guttural.

"I have the only authority!" I scream back.

He stares me down, smoke streaming from his nostrils in a dangerous volume, fogging up my brain. *"You thought there were no consequences for what you did?"* he snarls, making my very skull rattle. *"You thought you could violate the most ancient laws of our kind?"* He prowls closer to me, putting his massive face in mine, but I clench my jaw and stand my ground. *"The only thing more cruel than a curse from the Wild Goddess is a curse writ by a dragon."*

"You will obey me," I snarl. *"I am your master."*

He ignores me completely, eyes flashing red to black, before pressing his mighty forehead against mine. *"You will know all the times we have loved her, and may they torment you for the rest of your cursed, miserable days."*

A broken scream fills the air, and it takes me a moment to realise it's mine.

Chapter 29

Aurelia

Something changes in the air as Xander cuts himself off and promptly collapses onto the ground with a heavy thud.

Lady Drakos cries out, lunging towards her son as Francesca steps back, her mouth dropping open, looking towards her own parents for some explanation.

The dragon king does not move at all, which means that when I reflexively reach out a hand towards his son, I can't move any further due to my leash. I shouldn't even try, being bare ass naked and still recovering from near suffocation. I think that entire traumatising episode may have killed more than a few of my brain cells because I'm fluffy-brained as I stare in shock at Xander's collapsed form.

Lady Drakos and the celebrant shake Xander, and servants rush forward to assist.

"Move over. Let me see him." Lady Hyena's voice sounds like a firecracker through the mutter of concerned and affronted dragons. It's a surprise because I didn't even realise she was here. We all turn to see her hobbling up to the altar, using her black cane to swat away the human butler trying to roll Xander over. She huffs darkly under her breath, leaning on her cane, both hands propped one on top of the other, and she stares down at the supine dragon heir as if reading him. "Natural consequence." A dry sniff. "He'll be fine." She looks out at the crowd. "Best to get on with it, eh?"

Flores gives a very dragon-like snort that I'm convinced only I hear before he saunters forward.

Old, dark eyes catch mine on her way out. A hint of knowing. A hint of amusement. I meet her gaze steadily. Just because I'm naked doesn't mean I can't give a fucking nasty glare.

But what does she know? Does Xander's collapsing have something to do with his severed bond to me?

I watch Xander carefully as Flores steps up to the altar, which means I'm the only person except Lady Drakos who sees the king dragon's whip of fire lash at Xander's neck. He flinches before his eyes begin to open and crescent moons of white light are shown to me. Xander frowns, and different colours flicker through his eyes until they settle on a deep and terrifying black. Obsidian smoke streams from Xander's nose as his eyes open all the way. It's then I notice one of his earphones has dropped out and is lying on the crimson rug.

Without even thinking, I lurch forwards and grab the earphone, shoving it into his ear.

Xander blinks rapidly, the black eyes shifting colours backwards through the spectrum until we reach yellow, then lastly white.

A sigh of relief breezes past my lips before Xander's eyes widen and he leaps to his feet.

"Apologies," he says, helping his mother up. I scuttle backwards, away from the eyes and behind Flores. "I suppose that's what I get for eating too much this morning. Shall we continue?" He holds an expectant hand out to Francesca, who by this time has retreated all the way to the side of her parents, standing with her, clutching each other's arms.

The dragoness plasters a very fake smile upon her bridal-pink glossy lips and nods. "Of course, Xander."

I scowl at her doll-like features. A perfect, stunning creature that would have many a beast drooling. She sweeps back up to the altar, taking Xander's offered hand. The celebrant hands Xander the bride's massive ruby ring again and he puts it onto her finger without so much as another word.

The celebrant finishes the ceremony as if nothing happened, and I feel like I'm the only one who knows we'd been moments from disaster.

Damn my conscience. I should have let his bloody berserker genes, or whatever Savage called them, out into the open so everyone could see what a monster this dragon is.

Scratch that thought; he'd probably come for me first. Those black eyes were actually terrifying to see.

A hiss of pain drags me back to the present, just in time to see two coils of flame fastened around both Xander's and Francesca's arms where they're grasping each other at the wrists.

The scent of burning flesh fills the air as the bride and groom stare into each other's eyes. Sweat freely drops from Francesca's neck as the morbid hand-fastening is displayed to everyone until Xander smiles at her and they both drop their powers, flames going out with a puff.

Xander's left hand reaches for Francesca's burnt one, her forced smile almost breaking as Xander hovers his palm over the inflamed flesh and the angry red burn smooths itself away, healed. She quickly does the same to him and I have to look away.

Something in my periphery catches my attention and I find Lady Drakos, seated in her front-row seat, not looking at her son, but me, her expression infinitely sad, her golden eyes glistening. Her shoulders move on a sigh, but she holds my gaze.

I'm sorry, she seems to say.

A polite, subdued round of applause lets us both know the ceremony is done and Lady Drakos tears her eyes off mine and rises to her feet as Xander and Francesca smile at their audience and make their way down the aisle, hand in fucking hand.

* * *

"Does she have to be here?" Francesca asks rudely, the corners of her mouth turned down as she tries not to look at me. "I feel as if she's staring at me."

"Pardon?" Xander seems distracted as he undoes his tie. But he's been distracted all night. As if only half his mind is in the present in the room.

After a subdued reception and dinner, in which I had to crouch by Flores Drakos' knee the entire time—at least I was hidden by the table—we've returned to Xander's room for the night. All three of us. A happy family.

My skin hurts, my temples ache, and the lights are burning my eyes. A jittery sensation has taken over my body and I have to hold my hands together to stop their trembling. From where I stand at the cage door, finally clothed in my black dress uniform, I say, "The Old Laws dictate that the bride should return to her natal home for instruction after the wedding. She's supposed to return the next day." That's what happened after my wedding to Halfeather.

"Maybe for *your* kind," Francesca retorts. "But not for ours. Send it away, husband."

"Get into your cage," Xander says without looking at me. "Pull the covers down."

I crawl into my cage as slowly as possible and pet a waiting Eugene. A venom captures my heart as I turn around and catch sight of the married couple.

"Will you help me with this?" Francesca's voice purrs.

"Of course."

Nausea roils in my stomach as Xander helps her unlace her corset and extracts her veil from her high-set bun. Quickly, I flick down my blackout covering, but that doesn't remove the sound of fabric or the low voices. Just when I think I'll need to sink my fangs into my own arm, Xander says absently, "I need a shower."

The sound of him moving into the bathroom follows, and Francesca is left alone in the room.

Well, not completely alone, and I'm really glad she has no privacy. Eugene and I creep up to the bars, up to the crack in the covering and we peer at the dragon bride with interest. She sits on the bed in her sheer white slip, the glow of her phone illuminating the fact that she's chewing a fingernail.

That's a bad habit.

I sigh and curl up on the blankets with Eugene, and we wait in awful anticipation as Xander returns after his shower. I hold my breath, but instead of getting into bed—

"I need to speak with my father," Xander says tersely. "I'll be back shortly."

"What, right now?" Francesca protests. "Can't it wait?"

"No," Xander says firmly, already making his way to the door.

"You can't do that!" she cries. "This is our wedding night! We have to consummate the marriage."

"Later, Francesca," Xander sighs irritably.

She makes an affronted noise. "My father will hear about this!"

"You speak with your father about having sex?" Xander says in a bored voice.

The door clicks shut before she can reply.

I exchange a happy grin with Eugene. "Don't worry," I call out through the coverings. "He hates everyone, not just you."

Francesca makes a rude sound before storming into the bathroom.

This night, when I dream, it's not like the other times when my serpentine magic draws upon the memories of my mates. This time, it has the feeling of something that's being given to me.

Chapter 30

Xander

10 years ago

There was a storm the night my mating mark appeared. The type of storm that sends rain lashing at the windowpanes, the glass trembling under the force of the thunder. Lightning illuminates my room, creating long shadows. I sit bolt upright, rubbing at my chest as a strange sensation glimmers within it.

That's when my body starts burning.

It's not my skin that feels agony, nor a superficial sensation that makes me grimace. It's a visceral, deep-seated fire that consumes my body, the sheer force of it ripping a scream from my throat.

I tear the covers off and my feet hit the floor, running, *running* away from the pain, running towards the feral pull I've felt since I was a child.

Towards the open sky.

Light and heat erupt from me, licks of flame dissipating off my arms, legs, hair. I reach the flight tower of Drakos Estate, and as my dragonfathers before me, I open my mouth and let out a cry.

Only it's not the cry of a human boy that leaves me, but a cavernous, guttural roar that rivals the sound of the thunder and pounding rain. My body changes, gaining colossal size, muscle and tendons ripping through my shoulder blades and elongating into something I've obsessed about since I saw my father shift for the first time at four years of age.

My powerful body unfurls in the way of newborn dragons, my head rising to meet the sky, my wings stretching out to feel the wind. Huge claws grip the dragon perch that runs around the perimeter of the open tower.

I am nothing but lethal magnificence.

Something in my mind explodes at the same time that I do. With one bend of my knees and a powerful thrust, I'm in the sky, the rain but light fingers upon my thick hide, my wings catching the current of the air, keeping my enormous body aloft.

Master of the sky, of the wind, as the land becomes insignificant below me. I snap my jaws, feeling the powerful bite force, the need to rip and tear and shred. My vision turns red and I wheel around, searching for the enemy. My power spans outwards, new and volcanic.

Beating my wings, I propel through the air. Soon, I will face my enemies. Soon—

I'm aware of someone shouting in the far distance. "He's heading towards the town!"

Then something huge slams into me, tackling my body in thin air. I bite and kick and roar my fury, but the bigger beast proves stronger and more skilled. Grasped in his claws, sharp tips dig into my sides as I thrash, we spear towards the grass.

I'm shocked enough to shift back, shrinking smaller and smaller until I am insignificant.

But no less deadly.

Back on my feet, I cry into the oncoming rain, swinging my arms, looking for my enemy. People rush about; someone cries my name. My feet are lifted off the ground and I shout in frustration, my arms wheeling. I'm thrown into the castle's entrance hall, slammed against something soft.

We land on the tiles with a thump.

"Sweet baby dragon, down by the sea..."

A soft singing falls into my ear, warm arms encircle me, and despite the madness, the need for blood, the lullaby soothes my body and it relaxes along with my mind.

"Mother?" I whisper.

Her mouth forms a smile as she sings softly into my ear. *"Sweet baby dragon, down by the sea. He frolics in the waves, happy as can be..."*

I smile up at her and she stops singing. "Better, my love?"

"He is a grown beast now." Father wrenches me up to standing by the bicep. Water drips from his long hair onto my shoulder, his naked body towering over me. "And he'll act like it."

I slam a fist into his neck so fast he stumbles back from the shock. But he's ready for the next jab, catching it easily in a big fist. I rain punches and kicks upon him, fully aware of what I'm doing and revelling in the feeling of the fight. As if I was meant to do this. As if this was my life's purpose and mission. To fight. To kill.

"The song, Mother!" my sister shouts. "The music!"

"Enough of this!"

Two things slam onto the sides of my head and loud sounds make me grimace. But they also stop me in my tracks.

Headphones cushion my ears where the music plays from, my father holding the player in one hand.

I look up at him, his handsome face taut. "You have your mother's genes," he snarls, grabbing me again. He calls over his shoulder, "Assemble the family. We may get a prophecy tonight."

* * *

A little less than an hour later, my uncle, mother, and my older sister meet me in the throne room. It's deep underground where the walls are made of rock, and the throne itself sits on a high dais of ancient stone, inset with jewels. It's a place for formal occasions and celebrations, and thus today, I will get to stand on the dais in a place of great pride. I wear a loose black robe of my father's, with trim of gold and silver thread tied closed at my waist. The headphones still play music in my ears, but I've turned it right down to a soft classical number, and that killing rage has settled to burning embers at the back of my mind.

I stare at myself in the reflection of a small hand mirror, checking my neck. A skull with five curling beams erupting from it. I wonder what it means. *Who* it means. What anima was destined to be mine and only mine.

Behind my smiling mother and sister, I can hear as my father welcomes a foreign presence into our private domain.

A feminine voice greets, "Your Majesty."

"Lady Agnis," Father says formally. "I thought Damien Agnis was a male phoenix."

"You sent for the best, Your Majesty. Damien is my cousin. I am Celeste Agnis."

There's a slight pause whereby my father is no doubt looking the female up and down. She will get no apology for the lateness of the hour, nor the continued storm, because in this household, to serve a dragon is to serve the Wild Gods no less. Finally, Father says, "Please, come in. It is a happy evening for us. My own mark never appeared."

"Indeed?" she says. "Hopefully, the bonding plane bears luck for your son."

The door opens, and my father leads in a slender red-headed woman in her late thirties, sharp golden eyes revealing what she is.

"Xander, meet Celeste Agnis," Father says.

I reach a hand out to her, but she chuckles under her breath and does not take it, indicating the dais behind me. "Please, let us save it for the reading."

Heat floods my cheeks and I quickly take up my position

upon the dais, as does the Lady Phoenix. She smiles softly, studying me with great interest as my father lights the flames upon the pillars on either side of us.

"A great honour has been bestowed upon us tonight," he booms, voice echoing through the cavern. "A dragon has become grown. My son, the heir to the Drakos throne, will find his soul-bound mate in this lifetime. He will carry our family name. He will bear many children. He brings us pride tonight. Begin, Lady Phoenix."

Celeste Agnis inhales, her hands clasped at her waist. "How do you feel, Xander?"

I blink, rapidly checking for anything abnormal. "Very well, thank you. I think."

She smiles kindly. "Such manners."

"Oh yes," drawls Father. "He is well trained."

Lady Agnis inclines her head at Father before turning back to me. She holds out her hand.

The weight of the universe and my entire destiny lies in those hands. I reach out, feeling my ancestors who had done the same before me in the wake of the movement.

Her palm is hot when I take it, and ancient fires light up her irises.

I gasp.

She intones in a deep melodic voice, "Five black hearts are calling. Five black hearts are wanting. It is five who cry a dark and lonely song, calling for their queen. W—" She inhales and blinks as if coming back to the present. "Dragon," she says with a small smile. "Dragon."

The room is silent—dead silent as we all register the words.

"Queen?" I finally say. "Why does it refer to a-a queen?"

"It seems," Celeste says slowly, eyes flicking over to my father looming behind me. "That you have a regina."

My mouth drops open in surprise. "So I have a pack of five," I breathe in wonder. "I am one of five who serve an anima."

"Get out," Father snaps. "Get *out*."

Celeste stiffens, but I see she has great sense because she quickly bows and steps off the dais, heading right out of the throne room. Only when the door closes behind her does my father begin pacing, muttering to us. "She was wrong. We should have had Lord Agnis read for you. It cannot be true. How can it be true. A regina? For my son?" He stops to rake his eyes down my body, as if looking for some defect. His eyes snap to my mother and he points to her. "This is from your side. No son of *mine* would be slave to a *regina.*" He spits out the word like it's filthy, which I think is a bit dramatic.

Having a regina wouldn't be *that* bad, would it? I've always wanted a brother anyway. Having four would be challenging, but there's nothing I can't handle. Father taught me that.

But then a snide voice enters my mind. *How can you be dragon king if your destiny is to serve a queen?*

I look to my father, who is now staring at me as if I'm someone else. "It is of no consequence to us what the bonding plane presents. Dragons decide their own destinies, we always have. We will continue as if this never happened. Is that understood?" He looks to my mother and sister in challenge. They rapidly nod, eyes wide in fear.

"Xander?" he snaps, eyes burning into mine.

Lost in my own thoughts, I snap to attention. "Dragons make their own destinies, Father. I will not be hindered by *any* beast. Male or female."

He nods before turning around in a swish of silk and cotton. But even as I say the words, my hand reaches up and brushes the warm skin that contains the mark only I can see. Music rings through my ears but I can still hear Celeste's deep melody:

It's five who cry a dark and lonely song...

Chapter 31

Xander

I stride to my parents' rooms, tying back my hair into a knot as I do. I've just had a shower, but I'm already covered in a sheen of sweat, my mind racing, my heart still pumping.

My dragon rages within me—pulling at my seams, clawing at my insides, shredding at the sane parts of me. I clutch at my chest, commanding him to stop, but he's unwavering in his pursuit of destroying me.

My mind flashes back to the hyena witch, cackling at me the other night. Somehow, she'd known this was coming. Her nasty words echo in my mind like a funeral chant.

I send out a shaky spear of a request towards my father. He obliges with resignation. When I get to the deep green double doors, embellished with the golden pattern of our house sigil, I raise a hand to stroke the raised wing of the dragon.

The door swing opens of its own accord, revealing my father sitting in his receiving room, a glass of whiskey in hand.

"I thought you would be deep...in conversation with your new wife by now."

Grimacing as I step inside, I shut the door behind me with my power. "There are other matters on my mind," I grit out, running a hand through my hair.

The mad energy within me is like a storm of fire and it makes me pace from one end of the room to the other. "My dragon is driving me mad. He's angry like I've never seen him before."

"Did you expect to gain sympathy from me?" Father sounds bored. "The consequences of your actions are yours to suffer alone."

I pause to stare at him. He flatly meets my stare, the glow of the fireplace casting half his visage in harsh orange. I'd done what *he'd* asked of me. This has all been for our family. "When I fell, my earphone was pulled out of my ear. It could have been a disaster. I could have—"

"If you had done, I would have killed you where you stood." He pauses to take a sip from his glass, the picture of male arrogance. "It's such a shame you took after your mother's family. If you had taken after mine, it would be a different matter entirely. You'd be a completely different person. Likely, you would be rex of some pretty, obedient animas and I would have no concerns."

Suppressing the oncoming groan takes colossal effort. Why did I ever think my father would give me advice? I have no one else to ask, that's fucking why. There's no one left to confide in. Scythe always had something wise to say, whatever the issue was. But fuck him. I glare at the gilded walls of his receiving room. "Where is Mother?"

Father levels me a look and I shake my head as I remember. After I was exiled, my parents chose the traditional route of sleeping. They both have their own suites, only seeking each other out when they feel the need. Mother has her maids who look after her, Father gets his...privacy.

My feet increase speed of their own accord, and I want to tear my clothes off. Hell, I want to rip my dragon out of my own head. "I don't know how to fix this. How do I fix this?"

"Fly it off. We must speak of more important matters. Your plans have changed for tomorrow. The Hellfires will have to wait for their breakfast appointment. You will need to attend the meeting with the other region leaders. The last time was delayed because of the little Boneweaver's heat. Can you handle it?"

"Is it necessary, Father?"

A log cracks and both of us look at it as he continues. "It is imperative that we do not leave the estate without a male. It will be a good chance to...introduce yourself."

Reintroduce myself, he means. "Of course."

"After your little display during your nuptials, you'll have to make a strong impression. Clearly, nothing I taught you as a child has stuck." He sips again, boot swinging in the air. "You'll have to take the pet with you."

"That makes a strong statement?" I ask dully. There's a portrait of himself above the mantel. Shirtless, in his prime, our tribal tattoo rippling down the muscles of his left arm. I remember when I'd had mine done. It had been the morning after my first shift. So proud, I'd been then to share the same markings as my father.

"If the only thing she's wearing is our collar, it definitely makes a statement."

Pinching the bridge of my nose as my dragon roars in my head again, I nod. "Right. Right. Property and all."

"Yes, you must be on high alert. They will test you. Do not embarrass me and this family."

My stomach twists. "Of course, Father." I'm ready to slash my claws through the stone wall of this very room. "I won't let you down."

He makes a sound I can barely hear, which is just as well because it was probably rude.

I bid goodnight to Father, feeling worse than before. Swinging a hard left to the closest window, I open it and jump right out, shifting as I do.

Bones grow massive as I fall, wings explode out of my

shoulder blades, and all I know is the deep-seated burning release that feels even better than coming. Finally. *Finally*.

But where before my dragon stretched happily after a shift, tonight, every drop of rain only increases my irritation. Every beat of my wings fans the fire of this never-ending rage.

They can probably hear my roars in the closest town.

Chapter 32

Ghoul

"You look excited," says the General Death Adder in great disgust as he takes the wheel of our Serpent Court Jeep.

I chuckle under my breath as I fasten my seatbelt.

Crime lord meetings are sort of like family reunions. There's food, jealousy, posturing, lively arguments, and someone occasionally loses a body part. I don't have a family after all, so it's all in good fun and I quite look forward to them.

This one in particular, I've been counting down the days on a special colour-coded calendar on my phone. There are apps for these things.

We arrive at The Jewel of the Jungle in style, as Serpent Court always does, under a pleasant spring sun, the scent of venom and roses in the air. Our noble king is guarded by two generals in his Rolls Royce, one Jeep at the front with me and Mamba and the second Jeep at the back with two other generals.

A family trip. I even packed extra towels.

I leap out of our car, beating Adder to Mace's door so I can open it. The shorter general flashes a dark look my way and I grin with my fangs.

Mace extracts himself from the car, unfurling to his full

height a few inches below me. Today he wears a deep emerald green trench coat over his black shirt and slacks. An unusual bit of colour for a spot of celebration.

"Right on time, Your Majesty," I pipe. "Ten minutes late."

He nods absently, his mind on important matters. Some of the others are already here, parking their vehicles, their guards smoking out the front. In daylight, The Jewel loses its glamour only a little bit. After all, it's who's sitting inside that makes the place what it is.

Mace lopes inside with three of the others. I stay outside, monitoring who's coming in by lighting a cigarette and leaning against the wall by the entrance. I flash my fangs at a couple of hyena grunts who scatter away as I approach and take up their spots.

Mentally, I count everyone off. The Clawsons are already here, and I'm kicking myself because I didn't get to see Titus debut his new hardware. But that's okay, there's plenty more fun to be had. Lady Hyena arrived first to ward the area, as she always does, paranoid little thing. The falcons are present by the smell of metal in the air because they're always loaded with the best weapons, useless as their power is.

The screech of a Ferrari makes me grin, and it's not long before the Collector sashays in on leopard skin with two muscled roos flanking her. She pauses before me and I tap my cigarette so ash lands just shy of those expensive, heeled boots.

"Careful, Lord Basilisk," she coos, "or I'll make you pay for it."

I offer her a cigarette straight from the packet and she takes one, allowing me to light it. She takes a drag and exhales smoke towards my face.

"I would never pay for it," I say. "I like free samples. Short on cash, you see."

She grins, shaking her head on her way inside as if she finds me amusing. I *am* fairly funny, but not everyone can see it.

Then finally, the moment we've all been waiting for. The

purr of a new Rolls Royce fills my ears, and I wait in anticipation for the doors to open and close in the carpark.

I frown, because a pair of footsteps, one booted and one bare, pad down the path to us.

They appear around the corner—just the two of them because no dragon needs bodyguards.

My being goes still. Because it's something I do not expect.

And rarely does something happen that I have not expected.

Xander, his power roiling like black flames about him, leads Aurelia Boneweaver, naked as the day she was born, her hands crossed over her breasts to hide them, the mounds deliciously pushed up. Her cheeks are pink, her blue eyes sparkling with humiliation, and she must be thanking her lucky stars for her own grooming choices because black curls of hair hide her pubic area from the view of every shadow-hearted beast here.

If I hadn't seen her naked a few times—including her heat when she was greedy for my cock in her mouth, a moment that will go down in history for me—I might have ended up on the ground before The Jewel. She has a body made by the Wild Goddess, perfect for a beast's tongue and teeth. Perfect for a monster's dark hands.

There's a new golden collar around her neck that gleams like the sun. This one is studded with two sapphires, and between them is a single sentence, emblazoned in black, so it's easy to see from a distance: PROPERTY OF DRAKOS ESTATE. Old blood crusts the edges of it because they've seared it into her skin.

Cursed dragon bastard.

Likely, a statement of power after his little meltdown at the wedding. And boy oh boy, is it working.

Mace is not going to like this.

"Ah, it's the Lady Boneweaver," I muse.

"You look like you belong in a theme park," Xander snarls, his power sizzling like a barbeque just over his skin.

Ooh, he's in a mood. A permanent one, by the looks of it. I can't wait to see what fun this makes.

"Fancy that!" I say in mock interest. "You'd give an oven a run for its money, mate. Useful on a winter's night, I bet." I take a long drag from my cigarette.

Mamba snickers next to me and I grin at him.

"I wondered why you looked familiar," Xander drawls at him, brushing microscopic lint from his shoulder. "Your son made amusing noises as he died."

In the blink of an eye, General Mamba lunges towards the nasty dragon. Luckily, I'm faster and I manage to intercept. The serpent general slams into my considerable bicep.

"Now, now, children," I say reasonably. "Today we come together and put our differences aside. Let the big scary dragon through. We can play later."

Xander pretends none of the last thirty seconds happened and saunters on inside, his pet trailing miserably behind him. I watch her perfect, round, bare ass leave me.

Mamba glares at me from behind his mask. "You should have let me at him, Ghoul. I deserve blood for my son."

"And you'll get it," I say, placing my ciggie between his lips. "You just have to wait a little longer, that's all."

I decide it's best to leave him outside to calm down, but I head inside, eager to see the show on its way.

Chapter 33

Aurelia

I'd enjoyed being watched the first time I entered The Jewel of the Jungle. Hell, I'd even enjoyed being seen naked that one time when I'd had no spare clothes and I'd landed at that human service station.

But this type of entrance is something from a nightmare. It's humiliating and degrading—everything it's intended to be. My feet hurt from being denied shoes, and the skin of my neck is in rotten agony. Before dawn this morning, Xander had replaced my collar so quickly that I'd barely had time to protest before my screams of agony forced me to my knees.

He'd watched me writhe with no expression before commanding that I get into the car.

It takes everything in me to keep a straight, stone-like expression, because the only thing worse than being naked in this place is being naked and clearly distraught.

Is it worse than being dragged up the aisle in my shark form, suffocating in long miserable seconds? I can't even say. Every bad thing that's happened during my stay at Drakos Estate has blended together in one giant mass of tar, sitting at the bottom of my gut, trying to pull me under.

My anima hides her face under her wing, whining in pain at

the memory of our ex-mate burning our new, thicker collar onto our skin. Since his wedding, Xander has been even quieter than before, his power not pulsing, but *thrashing*. It feels like it would only take one small push and he'd burn everyone to high hell.

We walk on the edge of a knife, he and I.

So many things in common.

But it's made him a prickly, nasty thing. And clearly murderous, judging by that display outside. A young serpent had died because he and a few others had kidnapped me. Had been about to start torturing me, too, if it weren't for the nasty dragon that came in and killed all of them except Natalia, whom they'd then spent days torturing until I'd called Ghoul and organised her escape.

The fact that Xander was rubbing it in his father's face showed just how far gone he was. Just how different he was from the the dream I'd seen: the boy who'd seen his mating group mark for the first time and jumped for joy.

I try to keep in Xander's shadow as we walk in, but it looks like we're the last to the table, so everyone sees us. My one saving grace in this situation is Eugene, protected and invisible in a shield bubble of mine. He sticks close to my ankles, his silken feathers brushing the side of my leg to let me know that he's here with me. That I'm not alone and there is one person on my side.

Drinks are already being poured in the main room, where tables have been pushed together to make a bigger one.

There is only one seat left.

And there is also a person missing from this criminal underworld meeting. Only one of my mates is here—Ghoul stalks behind me, simmering with excited energy. If I didn't know better, I'd say that nasty thing is looking forward to this.

Scythe is the only crime lord of the state not present, and I'm guessing it's from a lack of invitation.

Though my anima whines, I'm glad my great white shark, wolf and lion are not here. It would be a greater torture for them to see me like this and not be able to do anything.

As Xander takes the final seat, I take my mark from the other attendants and stand next to Xander's chair, using the tall back of it to cover as much of my body as possible. Even then, it doesn't stop the leering. Each crime lord has three to four guards standing behind them, all massive don't-mess-with-me type animuses. Xander is the only lord with no retinue.

One of the two other animas in the room catches my eye with a smirk.

"Property of Drakos Estate," drawls the Collector, looking fashionable in a twenties bowl hat and off-the-shoulder black dress. She holds her cigarette so delicately between the fingers of her propped-up hand. "Well, well, well. That collar looks like it chafes, Lady Boneweaver."

Amused chuckles surround me and I try to meet them eye to eye, I really do. But it's so fucking hard when I'm being put in this humiliating position. Heat floods my cheeks and the backs of my eyes burn as they laugh at me and my naked body.

Damn Xander Drakos. Damn Flores Drakos and his whole fucking lineage. Someone on the far left of the table shifts and a glint of metal catches my eye. When I see who it is, I stare.

And stare again.

Because sitting next to his father, Tiberius Clawson, is Minnie's ex-mate, the dark-haired, black-eyed brute called Titus. And they weren't kidding when they said I'd broken his jaw when he'd held me captive in his mouth that one time. He *has* no lower jaw now, not one made of flesh, anyway. It's been replaced with some ingenious avian healing craft made purely of steel, including his lower teeth.

The overall effect is terrifying.

"Fetch me a glass, Spawn," Xander says, his voice strangely low. "Double whiskey. Neat."

The breath freezes in my lungs as Xander flicks his wrist, separating me from my leash. Suddenly, I'm left cold and bereft as everyone watches me with great interest. I raise my chin and finally work up the courage to lower my arms from my tits as I walk towards the bar all the way at the other side of the table. Somebody audibly smacks their lips, and another noticeably adjusts himself in his seat, but I put on my best resting bitch face and ignore them, keeping my eyes on the whiskey glass and bottle I need. The only thing keeping me from bursting into tears is Eugene's warm presence at my calf. He pecks me once, to let me know we have to concentrate. I listen to him, knowing this is sage advice.

It's not until I've poured the drink and turned back around that I see Ghoul casually stalking past Titus. The basilisk sneers, "I like the cyborg look." Quick as an adder, he gives the gleaming metal a little flick with his fingers. The metal *pings* like a bell.

Titus reacts instantly, shoving back his chair and lunging at the basilisk with a snarl. Tiberius and the feline on the other side of Titus grab him, holding him back as Ghoul hisses, flashing his fangs before cackling with mirth.

Lady Hyena thumps her black cane on the ground in a way that tells me it's heavier than it looks and metal at the base. "If we're all quite done, shall we begin?"

Everyone settles down, with Titus shoving off his father and sitting back in his chair. I let out a slow breath as I set Xander's glass on a coaster on the table and he flicks his wrist to chain me up again.

"Start with our great white shark issue," the Collector says, wineglass in hand, cigarette dangling between those same fingers. "What are we going to do about that, Your Majesty?"

All eyes move to the serpent king, whose gaze I've been avoiding this entire time. His presence is like a shadowy cloud— that *could* be Ghoul's shadows snaking around him where he guards to the right of the king's chair, but my father has his own sort of corrupt darkness that eats at the very air. I also know he enjoys the fact that the table will be hanging onto his every word.

"It will be taken care of," Mace says. "Tiberius and I will be working on a solution that I will not state here." His eyes flick to mine, the implication clear. I could snitch on any plans laid out in this room.

"That's right," Tiberius says. "Blood for blood."

A chill trickles down my spine. Scythe killed Caius Clawson, Titus' brother, in this very same place.

And there is vengeance in the eyes of both Clawsons.

"Why has it not been taken care of already?" the Collector asks, tapping her cigarette over an ashtray.

I have to give it to her. Woman's got a strong pair of ovaries to push at both the Nagas and the Clawsons.

"We needed more information," Mace says evenly. "Scythe Kharkorous is devious. He plans well in advance."

"We need other options for the Council's marine seat," Lady Hyena says. "Are there more controllable candidates we might hook in?"

"He's got a bunch of them locked up in that mental hospital of his," Tiberius Clawson says casually. "We could take our pick from there." Tiberius turns to Xander. "*You* could get a patient list, Lord Drakos."

Xander has lit a joint and is mid-drag when he's asked. He exhales slowly, making Tiberius wait. The smoke dissipates into the centre of the table. "Sure, but it will cost you."

Tiberius narrows his eyes, dark brows knitting together. "How do we even know you're on our side?"

To everyone's surprise, it's Mace Naga who speaks up. "Xander has made his allegiance clear." He gestures to me with a lazy hand.

"Once a turncoat, always a turncoat," Titus snarls. "He could be a double agent for all we know."

"Ha!" Lady Hyena slams a fist on his table. "You should know what a severed mate looks like, Titus. They are cursed. No trickery can hide a hate like that."

Oh, I don't know, my father for one? There's a bunch of psychopaths at this table who would murder their regina in cold blood. But everyone turns to stare at Xander and I know they see it.

"Oh yeah?" Titus says. "Then dance for us, Boneweaver. Bend over and show me your pussy. Let everyone see where Scythe Kharkorous was putting it every night until you were taken from him." He learns forward, black eyes sparkling like beetle shells. "Bend. Over."

No one says anything until the combined telekinesis of multiple felines turns my body around. I gasp, not prepared to be manhandled. My shields are down and I didn't even realise. Fuck.

"Enough," Xander snarls. "The Snake Spawn is property of the Drakos Estate, the last time I checked. Not the Clawson...house."

"Weak as fuck," Titus spits.

Xander snorts. "Did you give your jaw a little funeral after they couldn't put it back on?"

Titus doesn't miss a beat. "Have you started planning for your mother's funeral? I hear she doesn't have long."

Pain blooming in my foot is the only warning Eugene can give me.

Some mad thought, or perhaps his berserker genes must possess him, because Xander apparently loses his shit. Quicker than anyone can realise what's happening, Xander reaches up to his ears and takes both earphones out.

Instantly, his eyes are consumed by a black so void-like it makes me freeze. He opens his mouth and roars, the sound of a full-grown dragon leaving his throat, making the glasses rattle on the wood. He lunges across the table at Titus and I careen over the table's edge after him, that golden chain forcing me to scramble over the table to avoid choking myself.

Whatever telekinetic powers are being used on him, Xander is completely undeterred as a whip of fire circles the table, turning into a ring of blazing crimson flames around us.

Screams fill the air. Chairs fall to the floor.

"His eyes!" the Collector shouts, diving under the table as Xander punches Titus in his metal jaw.

"Get out!" someone else cries as Titus jabs Xander with his own punch.

But Xander's berserker genes make him so impossibly quick that he's nothing more than a blur as he gives Titus an undercut that violently snaps his head back. Tiberius comes at us from the left, but Xander is already on him and they tussle on the ground. Two serpent generals jump on Xander's back and I'm jostled left and right.

In the mess, somebody grabs a fistful of my ass and I shriek, turning around to see Titus, who lashes his hand around my throat. "You don't need a throat to breed, Boneweaver bitch."

Put it in capital letters and it could be my new title.

Xander roars and everyone goes flying—

Until one of the falcons whips out his handgun and shoots three times at Xander's chest. The dragon dodges them all, ducking to the side. I go swinging to the ground, scraping my knee and I double over, grunting in pain. A bullet catches one of the serpent generals in the stomach instead and he goes down. I'm yanked forwards once again, this time landing on my ass. Xander is snarling in the face of the shooter, breaking his hand and snapping his neck like it's made of wood.

"How do we stop him!" someone cries. There are people running around but I can't make head nor tail of them. I'm pretty sure the serpents have fled.

I yank hard on the chain, because I'm sick of being dragged around like this. Xander roars, turning on me.

"Where are his earphones?" I scream. "Get his earphones!"

Xander leaps on me, his face contorted into an expression of rage, shoving me back onto the ground.

But I've seen all the rage he has to offer me already. I'm no longer afraid of his anger, nor his betrayal. With his body heavy on my own, I do the only thing that's left to do and cover his mouth with mine.

The dragon stills in shock, magma solidified into stone. His lips are firm until I take the opportunity to prise them open and slip my tongue inside.

His mouth softens. Xander moans, meeting my tongue with his.

Encouraged, I bury my hands in his hair, pushing the long length of it back as I suck on his lower lip.

"His earphones!" I telepath to whoever the fuck is left in this place.

Xander growls as if the telepathic waves have distracted him, and he goes to lift away from me. But I arch my naked body up into his and his hand finds my neck, squeezing possessively as he tongues my mouth. I moan into him, our tongues dancing in a dangerous, seductive tango. I've waited so long to kiss Xander, thought about it during class, imagined what the taste of him would be like while I was tangled with my other mates.

The reality is nothing like I'd imagined.

His power is darker and more foreboding than the others, wrapping around me as if he wants to drag my soul to hell with his. His body might be a furnace, but his mouth is like the inside of a volcano, demanding and greedy. He tastes like fire on my tongue, the pressure of ancient volcanic rock and the scent of flowing molten lava. A rumbling sound courses through his chest and into mine, and that hand clutching my neck slides to cup my breast. His thumb runs across the taut bud of my nipple and I moan into his mouth again.

"Earphones," drawls a voice from somewhere above us. They clatter to the floor on my right and I break off the kiss to grab them.

Xander's mouth moves to savour my cheek, then my neck as I snatch up the two black pieces of plastic. The dragon toys with my nipple as he licks my neck, growling and scraping his teeth against my skin.

It feels so dangerously good that I worry I'll miss it.

But it can't be helped. I move Xander's hair aside and put

one earphone in, followed by the other, hoping beyond hope that his music will automatically take up the previous track.

I know something has changed when Xander goes still again. This time, when he lifts his head, his eyes are starlight white.

There's a moment then. Hot, disastrous, and smoky between us. When time seems to lose its place and neither of us understands quite what just happened. I see it then. In another time and place, where we're not enemies. Where he could have worshipped me. When I would have freely loved him.

The moment shatters when he jumps off me with a strangled sound of disbelief. My collar is yanked, my skin burns, and I leap to my feet.

"What the fuck happened?" Xander says, his head lowered in a predatory stance as he turns to survey the room through the smoke. The table still on fire, the broken chairs, the blood splattered on the floor and the two dead bodies. One serpent, one falcon.

"You don't remember?" I ask.

Xander exhales, more black smoke joins the mix.

A slow clapping sounds from our right.

Ghoul is leaning against the wall nearby, one foot casually braced on the wall behind him and a joint dangling from one hand. "Nicely done, sweetheart," he says mildly to Xander. "I always knew you had it in you."

Chapter 34

Ghoul

We're driving into town with the Naga convoy when a little snakelet tangles herself in my brain.
"Are you there?"

"Here, there, everywhere," I reply smugly.

The dragon has her in the back of a truck on the way back, so she knows he can't tell she's communicating. He wasn't happy with his own display. Fuming and near-mad when he left actually, which is sad because it was such a brilliant show. Pyrotechnics, sparklers and everything. By the time I tossed Transformer Titus and the rest of the stragglers out, I'd returned to find the snakelet using covert manoeuvres.

"I need you to find Scythe, Savage, or Lyle and send them a message."

That could be fun. *"It's going to cost you."*

She sighs heavily. *"What do you want?"*

Blank cheque? It's my lucky day. *"You'll give me your venom whenever I ask for it. Straight into my mouth."*

There's silence on the other end as her brain contemplates this. Maybe remembering the first time I drank from her.

"You sicko. Why do you want that?"

"Because I am a sicko. And...I love the taste of your poison."

I can fucking feel her getting wet at that. *"Fine. You have a deal. Now, when you find them, tell them I want them to stop the rampage. To stop the killing. To stop the harm. Tell them it'll only cause more death. I don't want that."*

My cock hardens at the thought until I realise I have to concentrate. *"It's not really a good message. What makes you think they'll understand?"*

"Just tell them, damn it! They're plotting against him and he needs to know."

"Oh, he knows."

More silence comes. *"Please."*

I grin, because she doesn't know I'd do anything for another taste of her. *"You still owe me for Natalia. Don't think I've forgotten."* I shut the connection and settle into my seat.

* * *

It's dark by the time we halt our convoy in the expensive restaurant on the outskirts of the city. It's serpent-owned, of course, because Mace won't risk eating at any place other than one of his own. And when you deal with poison for a living, you get paranoid about it.

I open the glass door and two generals head inside, scouting the scene first. Only after I get a head nod does Mace get out of the car and head inside.

The Collector waits for him in there, her people taking up three tables with all the textbooks, notebooks, and documentation they've brought with them. I head back to the car and haul out two plastic tubs labelled *Frank Ulman scientific documentation no. 1* and *no. 2*. I head back inside and hand over the tubs to the scientists. They eagerly snatch them up, practically hard with excitement as they start going through them.

Signalling to two lesser serpent guards, I head back outside and into the night, heading back to the Jeep. The other generals drive off with their vehicles to park them in hidden locations nearby, while I take the third Jeep and drive out to the carpark around the back.

Only then do I let my body become shadow and become one with the night. Travelling by shadow is quick and easy. I get to scout through the air and no one is any the wiser.

It also makes spying on people easy as pie.

The naughty boys are not so hard to find tonight. When you leave a trail of blood behind you, it's easy for predators to sniff you out.

And Savage hardly washes these days, which makes it easier still. Following my nose, I hunt the wolf to the top of a five-story apartment block. It has a pool and barbeque area, where the leftovers of a beast's dinner lie, large bones and tomato sauce packets. Loitering in one of the tall trees overlooking the house, I get a good look at him.

He's naked, as expected, his tanned skin easily visible through the shadows of the roof where he sits with his legs dangling over the edge, his head resting against a solar panel.

There's a forlorn look on his haggard face and he casts his eye up to the moon, frowning like he's in deep thought.

His mouth moves like he's whispering something and I strain my ears to hear if he's finally gone mad and started talking himself.

"I miss cuddling you," Savage whispers. "Why won't you come back to me? Lyle's hugs aren't nearly as good."

Such a sad, pathetic puppy.

I chuckle to myself. Savage goes still as he senses me, and I roll my eyes before allowing myself to be known.

Lion and shark feel my presence, and sure enough, the sweep of a heavy glass door opening tells me both beasts have arrived.

I turn into shadow again, soaring over the gap between us and become corporeal as I land on the fake grass by the pool. Savage leaps to standing and saunters over, frowning at me. Lyle and Scythe are both behind him and the rippling fluorescent blue of the pool makes them glow like the dead.

"You missed the party," I say. "Don't worry, I brought cake." I throw my little present at Savage and he catches it. "That's hers."

"That's not hers, you sick fuck!" Savage cries, waving the charred toe in the air like a baton.

"Oh yeah, you're right, it's not," I chuckle. "Wait, are you sure? I must have gotten them mixed up. Shit. So many missing limbs these days." It's actually from one of the serpents who got shot and I took it as a souvenir, but they don't need to know that.

"What do you want, Ghoul?" Scythe asks, hands in his pockets to tell me he doesn't find me threatening. Brave shark.

"Anyway," I say as Savage throws the toe into the pool where it lands with a little plop. "*She* sent me to tell you that she wants you to stop your murder bender."

Lyle narrows his eyes at me, stepping forward. "You're lying. She could have told us herself."

I take off my glove and hold up my fingers where some dried blood is there for all to see. It's hers, scraped off the floor from when she'd grazed her knee. "She doesn't want to talk to you."

Savage punches the brick wall to his right, and Lyle snarls.

But it's Scythe, the cold-hearted bastard, who makes my heart pound. He takes a step forward, and with a deathly seriousness that makes the back of my neck prickle, he speaks in that slow, measured rasp. "Tell her she doesn't get to choose what happens."

"Yeah, she has to be here for her to regina-order us," Savage says like a lost puppy. "Otherwise it doesn't count. Also, we need Raquel back."

"Don't know of a Raquel."

Savage drops his head back and groans.

"The Drakos family has a wolf anim telepathically hostage," Lyle explains. "Their body is at the academy, but their mind is stuck here. We need them back or it could kill them."

"Dark magic," I muse. Just my style. "Well, that'll cost you," I say reasonably, hooking my thumbs in my belt.

"Coming here without my regina is going to cost you," Scythe says. It's so funny that he looks so much like the snakelet when she went cold. I wonder how well this is working for him.

"What of the traitor?" Savage pipes, baring his teeth at me.

My chuckle is dark, thinking back on what I'd seen today. "Oh, he's having a good old time, that's for sure. He's—"

I should have seen the attack coming from a mile away, but honestly, these three males are perhaps the only creatures in existence to jump me unexpectedly.

Savage sinks his canines in my leg, while Scythe's teeth find my neck. The lion grabs me around the torso from behind, aiming to take me to the ground.

"You guys are nuts," I say, grinning with my fangs as we soar through the air and land with a gigantic splash in the pool. There's only one thing left to do: shift.

Chapter 35

Savage

Wrestling with Ghoul is like wrestling with a big old boulder, until he has to go all snakey and shift.

We crash into the pool with a big splash, white bubbles all around us, a mess of beastly limbs, and the bastard suddenly expands. The three of us brothers shoot away from each other as we've all got one part of his body, which is now ten times as long.

None of us let go.

Nope, we're all feral and manic from missing our regina. Plus, I've had ten whole lamb shanks for dinner two hours ago and am ready to rumble. I'm hanging onto what is a suddenly massive trunk of reptile muscle, covered in large jet-black scales.

I get the sudden urge to climb on and ride him like a bull, with one hand in the air, and see how long I can stay on. Except nobody ever told me that basilisks thrash more madly than bulls.

I'm whipped through the water and slammed into the concrete side of the pool. Even underwater, it blows the wind from my lungs and I have to kick upwards, choking on water and air. I scramble out of the pool and whirl around, holding my side and getting my lungs back as I watch.

I've never seen Ghoul in his shifted form before. In fact, I think few people have. He's easily the size of Xander, only his body is slimmer and has no wings. They could be brothers, though, with how similar they look.

Anger and jealousy roll through me like a storm and that has me even more confused.

As similar as they are, Ghoul has giant needle-like fangs filling his mouth, so he can't even close it properly. Water splashes high into the air as he whips his body this way and that, and I see why. Red peppers the water where Scythe, in his shark form, has taken a chunk out of Ghoul's ass. Tail, I mean.

"Hey, snaggletooth!" I shout.

The basilisk's head whips towards me.

"Close your eyes!" Lyle screams.

I slap my hands over my eyes. "I thought we said he might not be able to get us!"

"Do you want to test it out right now?" Lyle shouts back as he runs around the other side of the snake.

This is going to be hard. Why hasn't someone taken this guy's eyes out yet? Xander's dad might be up for it.

I decide that since I can't see, jumping in his direction might be best. I run up and leap, opening my eyes at the last minute to see where I am. The basilisk is still thrashing in the pool, sending water everywhere, but he takes up so much of the space that I land right on him. I dig my fingers into his shining scales and realise too late that he's bloody slippery. My fingers slide as I scramble onto his back, making me dig my fingers and toes into his scales.

Ghoul makes a terrible sound, a mix between a hiss and roar as I run up the length of his long body.

Something has his head focused in front of him and away from me. And then I see Lyle off to my left, both his hands angled at Ghoul's head, forcing him to stay put with telekinesis.

I whoop with excitement as I make it to the part of his body that's rearing upwards. Scythe's fin emerges next to me and I feel a wave of his power crash into Ghoul, making him shudder beneath me like he's cold.

Because I'm so very clever, I climb up Ghoul's neck, ready to grab his head. If I can just sink my teeth into a soft part—that'll be the best part of the day. Grab an eyeball and I'd deserve a medal.

Hand over hand, I climb him like a tree, using my feet anchored on the edges of his scales. It cuts into my skin but I don't fucking care. It'll be all worth it.

He's trembling, straining against Lyle's hold as I reach the top of his head. "Hello, snakey," I snarl, before shifting my teeth into their canine form and sinking my teeth into the scales on his cheek.

Ghoul roars, immediately fighting off Lyle's hold and violently tossing his head.

My body goes flying and I shout dramatically, wheeling my arms through the air. Lyle catches me though, like he always does, his grip around my body in mid-air before he dumps me on the fake grass. I land on my ass, but I'm up in half a second, my head spinning as my world tilts sideways.

Ghoul's blood taints the air now, and I grin as I take a few steps forward and see Scythe and Lyle coordinating an attack. Scythe has leapt from the water and has taken a bloody bite out of another part of Ghoul's body as Lyle throws his hands in a sweeping motion, roaring his anger.

The basilisk's head snaps sideways like an invisible giant is trying to break it. He roars an awful sound that hurts my ears, and I cackle as Lyle rolls both shark and basilisk out of the pool and onto the land in front of me. I take a running leap for the snake's tail. It's strong and thick, but nothing I can't handle as I tackle it with both hands, wrapping myself around it like a tree before shifting into a wolf and ripping into his flesh.

This time, Ghoul shifts and I get sucked across the concrete as he shrinks. By the end, I'm holding onto his bare calves, my teeth sunken into the top of his right foot.

"Urgh," I say, turning around and sitting on his legs so he can't move. "I'm not into that with you."

Scythe has his naked human forearm pressed against Ghoul's throat, while Lyle is behind him, legs wrapped around Ghoul's torso, his forearm pressed firmly against the basilisk's eyes. I've never seen a beast move so well in a three-piece suit, but he *is* my bond-brother.

Ghoul sighs and goes limp, dropping his arms in submission.

"As regina," Scythe says, "Aurelia has the right to execute you. But mark my words, I will be the one to hold you down before she slits your throat. Same for Xander. You tell him that."

Ghoul gives a wet cough. "Yeah. I'll tell him."

Chapter 36

Aurelia

Francesca's mouth twists in distaste when we arrive at dinner. Still naked, I kneel in my usual corner of the formal dining room. Xander has stopped talking to me completely. He doesn't look at me, nor communicates in any way. It's like I don't even exist. The children were already in bed by the time we returned from the long drive and servants told us to come to dinner.

Xander had cleaned himself up, changing his bloodstained clothes while Heather fussed over my tangled hair and grazed knees. The dragon murmured choice words to her, likely about keeping me unclothed as some sort of punishment for what I'd done.

Which was save him from disaster. You're welcome? *Some* beasts would pay a lot of money to get a kiss from me, and here he is getting one for free.

The scowl on my face is a permanent fixture now, especially as I have to walk around the castle with tits and ass out. Eugene, thankfully, was waiting by the new truck when I'd left The Jewel and he follows by my ankle once again, hidden from the monsters of the world. I wish I could do the same.

Flores is particularly smug in the one second I glance at him, but Selena and Lady Drakos go still in shock.

Selena's mouth opens.

"One word, Selena," the dragon king says, "and I return the children to Ragnar."

My blood heats with rage. Where *is* this fucker called Ragnar?

Selena blinks furiously into her plate, and just when I think that's that, she grits out between clenched teeth. "This. Is. Wrong." She glares at her father. "You know it is. To show her there like that. And around the house!" She turns to Lady Drakos, her eyes beseeching. "Mother? Say something."

The Lady Drakos sways in her seat as if she's about to faint. I'm alarmed enough that I send a burst of healing towards her, hoping it'll be enough to keep her upright.

"You would not understand the world of animuses," Flores says, baring his teeth at his daughter. "This is a language that carves out respect with the underworld lords. This is a language they understand." He gestures to me. "I trust it went well, Xander."

"They were...amused," Xander murmurs, sitting back in his seat in arrogant repose. That aura of darkness has only increased around him and even his father seems to be sensing that. Francesca subtly leans away from him where she sits in the chair adjacent to the king.

"I don't care what *they* think," Selena hisses.

"Sissy, stop," Xander snaps, glaring at her. She looks at him like he's betrayed her. "I'm trying to help you."

"Oh, is *that* what you've been doing?" she hisses with great venom.

Xander glowers at her while Flores levels his daughter a dangerous look. "You know where to go."

"I refuse."

I'm proud of Selena. In the short time I've known her, those tiny attempts to stand up for herself have never really led to anything. Perhaps she's sensing that it's time for something with more gusto.

Except then Flores snaps out his wrist and a whip of fire latches itself around her delicate throat. Selena lets out a choked scream before he drags her to the floor, the sound of sizzling skin and her choking filling my ears.

I hug myself, knowing this situation couldn't get any worse, that I'm useless against the forces of both Xander and his father.

Lady Drakos slides off her chair sideways, collapsing to the carpet right in front of me. I cry out, reaching for her shoulder and rolling her into the recovery position onto her side.

"Don't touch her!" Xander roars and flies at me, shoving me backwards so I slam into the wall with a thud. Xander crouches over his mother. "Father, I think Selena gets the message."

Flores' nostrils are flaring, his gaze cold and harsh as he continues his assault over his daughter, now lying prone and unmoving on the carpet for a moment longer, before his whip goes out in a puff of black smoke.

I huddle in the corner, my arms wrapped around myself, shaken by one of the worst days I've ever had.

"Take her to the tower," Flores remarks to the servants. "Release her at dawn."

I watch as a male and female servant hurry forward and scoop Selena off the floor and take her away.

A foul scent lingers in the air, and it smells of misogyny.

"Xander?" comes a weak voice. Lady Drakos is stirring where she still lies on the carpet. "I feel so tired."

"It's alright, Mother," Xander says through gritted teeth. "The servants will take you to your room."

A wheelchair is rushed in and Xander carefully lifts and places his mother in it. Lady Drakos is an unhealthy shade of grey, and I remember what Titus said earlier today.

But her illness makes no sense. Her dragon lineage should protect her from almost every common ailment, including old age, and she's only in her fifties. Non-specific tiredness just isn't a thing. It makes the healer in me want to problem solve this.

I glance back up at the table where Xander, Flores and Francesca have resumed eating.

My mouth twists in disgust as I realise that through the entire ordeal, Francesca stayed silent. I stare at her with suspicion and wonder if all dragon families are like this, and this is simply the type of dinner she's used to.

"This meal is lovely," Francesca says breezily, her posture ramrod straight. "My compliments to the chef, Your Majesty."

"Call me Flores, please." He gives her an indulgent smile.

Dinner ends and we head back to our rooms, the air solemn and silent. There are no evening drawing room games tonight. No children to take my mind off the darkness steadily gnawing at my insides.

Later that night, when I've crawled into my cage and huddled against Eugene, Xander leaves the room. Storms out, in fact.

"I'm going to fly," he says over his shoulder.

"Let me come with you!" Francesca coos. "I'd love to fly with you."

"No." He slams the door in her face.

From between the crack in the black fabric, I watch as Francesca clenches both fists and purses her lips. Finally, she stomps her foot and opens the door, slipping out.

Suddenly, the walls of the cage push in on me, crowding me in. The black bars are like teeth, the blankets like needles. It feels like a tomb. I rub my arms from a chill that has nothing to do with the night.

Tears stream and I let them, closing my eyes as the silence presses on me and the day's events flash through my mind. I don't know how I feel, but I know I have to get out of this fucking cage.

I grip the metal bars, tugging on them. "I want out," I sob. "I want to go home."

Eugene clucks next to me, but I push him away. "Get the key, Eugene," I sob. "Get the key, please."

Eugene is out of the cage like a lightning bolt, leaving the blackout fabric swinging in his wake. I'm openly sobbing now. From the physical pain of the various injuries I'd suffered tonight —I'd healed all the superficial ones, but Xander had dragged me from table, around the room to the floor, and I ache like I've been beaten bloody. The humiliation of the day, followed by missing my mates and the confusion of Xander's mouth on mine. His mouth on my skin.

Then the ordeal at dinner. Selena is all alone in a tower somewhere, burnt and bleeding. And Flores threatening to take away the hatchlings?

A clank draws my attention to the cage door where Eugene is trying to fit the keys into the cage with his beak.

With a cry, I take them from him, fumbling with the lock for three unending seconds before I manage to catch the lock and it clicks open.

I scramble out of there like a monster is chasing me.

There is a monster chasing me: my own fucking decisions. The consequences are catching up, hard and fast.

Panting, straining for breath, I stare around the room. I'm weary, weak as Lady Drakos, and dizzy on my feet. I make my way over to the bed, sitting down on the maroon duvet. Damn the velvet softness of it compared to my cage floor. I've not had a solid night's sleep since I arrived here and I feel every second of that missing now. I swallow, looking over my shoulder at the thick plush blankets and soft, fluffy pillows.

Just a moment's reprieve. That's all I need. Minnie always said that a solid night's sleep always makes things look better.

I lie down and the mattress feels like a cloud against my sore bones, the sheets like silk against my skin.

Somewhere out there, in the space around me, that terri- fied female voice whispers for the hundredth time: *Don't open it.*

Sinking into sleep feels like being buried. And I welcome it with open arms.

Chapter 37

Xander

8 years ago

"What's wrong, Sissy?" I ask.

Selena sighs, but it's a feeble thing. "Nothing, Xander. Let's talk of happy things."

I frown at her, sniffing the air and scanning her body for some physical ailment. "Like what? Everything is boring since you married and left me. There is no one left to talk of intelligent things."

Her lips twitch and she rubs her stomach. Then, in a soft as down voice says, "Like...Ragnar and I are having a baby." Her golden eyes glisten as she looks at me hopefully.

"What?" I breathe. "Wild Goddess!"

I reach for her and she pulls me into her arms, though I'm already taller than she is so I rest my cheek against her temple. "I'm so happy for you, Sissy. But...why don't you look happy?"

"I am. Oh Xander, I am. I just worry, you know?" She reaches up to swipe at a tear.

"I think that's normal—" I freeze because I've just seen the skin of her wrist.

Three finger-shaped bruises mar her skin like three marks of doom. I grab the offending wrist, an emotion I've never felt steadily growing within me.

"What is this?" My voice sounds like the scrape of a heavy boot.

"It's nothing." Selena pulls her wrist away, frowning at me. "It'll fade to nothing by tomorrow."

But this rage inside me will not. "Who did that? Was it one of the servants? I will flay him. Or her."

Selena pulls down her long sleeve to hide the bruise. "It's literally just an accident. No harm, no foul. Drop it, Xander."

"Anyone who touches my sister deserves a slow death, Sissy. Don't forget that. Ragnar would know that too."

She rolls her eyes and swings around to loop her arm through mine. "As I said before, let's talk of happy things."

Chapter 38

Xander

Hands of Gold — Peter Hollens

Flying used to give me a sense of peace. Now, there is only agony. When I leave Francesca in our marital bed and set into the night, she's not happy with me, protesting and demanding things, but I can't fucking care about that when there's a constant rage in my mind.

We'd said our vows, burned and healed each other in the sacred ways of our ancestors, and that would just have to be enough for now.

I head up to the family dragon launch pad. It's the highest balcony of the castle, a massive open-air turret made exactly for the perch of one dragon with space for them to spread their wings and launch off the castle from a height, directly into the sky.

It's raining tonight when I get in there, a cooling drizzle that is like a balm to my hot skin. I rip off my pants, toss them aside, and shift.

Expanding under violent energy feels good, and stretching out my wings feels even better. I was a creature born to fly, born to tear through the wind and let my majesty be known to all beneath me.

And yet I want to tear apart the very sky. I want to sink my claws into the world and shred it to pieces. My dragon toys with my mind like it's his personal Rubix Cube, flashing through fragments of foreign images, sounds and smells on a near constant basis. They are from other times and places, maybe even from other worlds.

Sometimes they are images of death, sometimes many bodies, writhing together in a rhythm I'll never understand.

He roars in my mind as he relives these moments. Pure furore. Pure pain. Pure yearning. It's agonising and irritating all in one.

But this is *my* price to pay for what I did. And by the Wild Gods, I will pay it with joy. I fly hard and fast, high into the sky until the air is so thin there's no oxygen for my lungs. At this point, I plummet, tucking my wings in and making my nose a spear, keeping my eyes open so I can see the expanse of the darkness as I fall through it.

But even the roar of the air past my ears and the oxygen deprivation can't drown out the living nightmare in my head.

Only one thing had done that today.

Swearing bloody murder, I head back to the estate, rearing up and backflapping to slow my speed so I don't go crashing into my family home. I extend my claws out, finding a perch on the massive black stone bar that runs the circumference of the platform. Shifting into my human form, I wait until I've shrunk down to my human height before stepping off and striding to the stairs at the centre of the tower.

The rain beats harder still deep into the night, drumming away even the sound of Mozart in my ears. I don't bother with my pants, leaving them there for the servants to pick up on their morning sweep. There's a towel rack as I exit, and I dry myself off before marching back into the castle proper, naked. The sound of the rain penetrates all the way inside, and I'm thankful for that thunderous, regular hum.

It makes me want to kill something just a little less.

My bedroom is dark when I enter it, rubbing my temples to try to dispel the images of a bloody sword fight flashing through my mind's eye. Although everyone looks different, I recognise them all, and I know the tall blond man who took a killing blow for his brother was me.

Exhaling black smoke, I close the door behind me, surveying the pitch-black room. Francesca is fast asleep on her side of the bed, the sheet tucked right up to her chin and Spawn's cage is covered for the night as usual. Rain beats on the double window panes, which have been left open, suiting me just fine. Beads of rain water trickle down the window, their reflection making a pattern across the bed. Hoping I don't wake her up, I slip under the sheets.

My head pounds in time with the pulse of my cock, the need for release, long built up within me. With one hand covering my eyes, I allow my right hand to wander where it pleases, down the hard plane of my abdomen and lower, to that insatiable beast between my thighs that has been aching all day. My balls feel heavy, calling me to empty them.

I crack open my eyes just enough to see the shapely mound that is the anima next to me.

My wife.

A scream pierces my skull and the fractal vision of a bloody chase blinds me for a moment. I don't realise that I've reached for her until I feel smooth, luxurious skin. Closing my eyes so I don't have to look at her face, I run my hand down her shoulder.

She makes a small, sleepy noise that might be endearing if I didn't dislike her personality so much. Francesca sighs, the scent of arousal perfuming the air as she turns towards me.

At least she can't say that I'm not doing my husbandly duties. For all I know, she'll take every detail of this back to her father. Her arousal is so strong that it consumes my sinuses, leaving no other scent, no other thought in there. It drags me deeper into my own need and my hands sweep away her long tresses, finding her face and tilting it up towards mine. I capture her lips, the taste of her heady and sweet. So fucking sweet.

She gasps into my mouth.

And it does something so primal to me. A growl tears from my throat, greed and desire taking me over completely. Her *scent* —gods, her scent is everything, and my dragon sways in approval. I sweep the sheet off her, sliding my hand down the curve of a delicious waist, down a smooth thigh and lower to the back of her knee. With another growl, I hike her leg over my hip, my cock painful and hard as obsidian stone.

"I need you," I mutter. "Fuck, I need you."

She whimpers, her own primal desires making her writhe, making her skin slide over my naked skin, leaving me panting and half-mad. My cock twitches and catches her between the legs, the head sinking into moisture.

She hisses and so do I, making me slide my hips, greedily wanting to be coated in that sweet wetness. I palm her breast and she arches into me, moaning wantonly. The scent of her wet pussy makes me drunk and I suddenly can't think of anything else except what that would feel like inside of my mouth and on my tongue and on my entire face. I want to cover my whole body in that sweetness.

"I need to taste you," I say hoarsely, sliding down her body, tasting her skin as I go. The centre of her chest, a line down her body. The taste of her is almost orgasmic, like a buffet of every perfect taste in the world. It gets better the lower I go and I covetously grip her hips as I find my lips tickled by a tuft of soft curls.

I took her for a Brazilian type of woman, but it doesn't fucking matter, not when it's ambrosia, not when I crave it like I crave the fucking sky.

She cries out when my lips kiss the line where her labia meet. I stroke my tongue down her centre, lapping up the beads of her heady juices as I do. Sliding my tongue between her lips, I groan deep in my throat as that nectar slides into my mouth, simultaneously heating me up and cooling my brain. The cerebral relief I feel is unmatched as I lave into her pussy, exploring the delicate skin like a skilled explorer. A flick of her clit makes her cry out, hands reaching into my hair and tugging in just the way I like. My lips find her clit and I suck on it gently, and happily find a flood of the heady slick in my mouth. I reach down and stroke myself as I savour this delicacy, feeling my hard shaft respond to the pleasure in my mouth.

I squeeze the base almost cruelly hard, milking my cock and feeling its veins bulge. Precum coats the broad head and I imagine the flutter of my tongue of her most sensitive spot, grinning as I feel her writhe and almost choke on a moan. I'm relentless, wanting to feel more of the unexpected pleasure, pumping my shaft hard and fast as if I was in her.

Release gathers at the base of me, rumbling like a volcano ready to explode. I work my cock as I work her clit and she comes first, screaming and crying, her back almost lifting off the bed completely before she pants, yanking on my hair so hard it hurts in the best way. Pressure hits a breaking point in my own body and I sit up, tilting my head back and moaning into the sky as I let go weeks of release onto her body, milking out every laboured millilitre of my seed. I inhale a sweet breath and exhale a relieved one before flopping down on the bed.

Lazily, I rub my cum into her skin, letting my scent claim her, letting my seed soak into her skin.

Silence.

There is blissful silence in my head.

And for the first time in an age, I go soundly to sleep.

* * *

I wake to a soft, warm body wrapped next to mine. She smells like me and my release and that makes the dragon in me snort in lazy contentment. My mind is calm, near serene, the feeling so unexpected and so delightful that I actually smile. It's a vague thought in the back of my mind. Could it be that fucking another dragon is the only thing that placates my own? Perhaps I should take Francesca out flying like she'd asked. We could probably work out how to fuck in mid-air and that would bring back my joy for flight again. Keeping my eyes closed against the cruel light of day, I run my hands up that interesting curve of her waist, then higher up, dragging the pads of my fingers up her arm, across her collarbone and—

Find a thick hunk of metal encompassing her neck.

My very world tilts sideways as my limbs throw my body to the other side of the bed and Aurelia stares at me, wide-eyed and panting, as shocked as I am.

Olly knocks on the door before opening it, revealing himself and Heather in the doorway.

Spawn's off the bed as fast as a rabbit, scrambling back into her cage and shutting the door as if she'd been in there the entire night.

Chapter 39

Aurelia

The pretending that didn't happen game is probably the best one ever invented. And everyone plays it with me. It serves us well this morning as, just as I tuck myself under the blankets next to Eugene, Heather opens my blackout curtain with a cute flick and I pretend to look out blearily at them as if I've just woken up.

I *have* just woken up, but it was rudely...after it had been somewhat cosy and soft. Xander has that sort of dangerous masculine scent that drives me to do wild things—letting him think I was Francesca notwithstanding.

Heather lets me out and I hurl myself into the bathroom, jumping in the shower and rubbing myself with the soap she silently hands me. It's halfway through my aggressive scrubbing that I realise its scent-neutralising soap.

I can't imagine the disaster that would result if I walked around the castle with the scent of Xander's cum all over me. His father might get a kick out of it, but Francesca?

She'd likely roast me alive.

Once I'm out and Xander has had his turn, I self-consciously tug the sleeves of my dress in place and turn around to accept the leash.

But he's not standing anywhere near me.

"Not today," Xander says, sneering not at me but at the door. "Today it stays in its cage."

I bet he can't look at me because he'll be turned on again... but I can't go back to that cage. I just...can't.

"Please," I grit out, hating myself for the tremble in my voice. "Don't put me back in there."

"Get inside your cage, Spawn." His voice is pure cold, hard malice. The complete opposite to the gentle moans that had filled my ears like a lullaby last night.

Heather tries to usher me into the cage, but I stand my ground as heat and anger rise within me. Eugene presses his invisible self against my leg.

"You know, I didn't see it before," I say with disgust. "But until I saw you sit by and do absolutely *nothing* while your sister was hurt by that monster you call your father—" Xander's massive shoulders stiffen. "You're not a monster at all, Xander Drakos. You're worse. You're a fucking coward."

His telekinesis shoves me backwards and I hit the bars at the top of the cage door. Pain explodes across my back and I fold forward, allowing myself to be stuffed inside the cage like a roast turkey.

The cage door slams shut and locks itself before Xander and the human servants leave. I cover my mouth to hold back the sobs, screwing my eyes shut to try to control myself. That bastard would be able to hear me all the way down the corridor and I don't want to give him the satisfaction.

Instead, I hold it together all of thirty seconds before that cry of frustration that had been building up in me since yesterday morning finally lets itself out. I scream at the bars, shaking them until I think my arms are going to come out of their sockets.

Eugene flaps his wings in protest, brushing cold air over my face and squawking his alarm.

"I can't fucking do this, Eugene," I sob, covering my face as he climbs into my lap and I thud down onto my ass, holding him close. "The humiliation of it. The rest of it I was ready for, but toting me out in front of those awful creatures…" I shake my head. Back and forth. Back and forth. "He's truly a different person now. So, *so* much worse than before. He didn't even feel sorry about trapping Raquel." Leaning back into bars behind me, I let the tears flow.

Worse still, I'm confused about last night. When I'd woken to a movement next to me, it had hardly felt real. I was tired, in pain and miserable, just woken from one of his memories as a teenager. And then he'd reached for me with soft hands and I'd crumbled.

Crumbled like an old, weatherbeaten statue, too fragile to hold itself together any more. I missed my mates and that heinous soul-wound had ached a little less by the masculine touch. Shame fills me now, the memory of how it felt on my skin, my mouth, my pussy.

I whimper and immediately get angry at myself.

"Fuck this," I say. "What if we just went home?"

Eugene lets out a sad cluck as if he wholeheartedly agrees.

"But we can't," I explain. "We're here to protect our friends. To keep my father's fangs away from those I love. And Damien will probably kill Henry and the nimpins in retaliation. Flores will kill Raquel. We'll have to figure out a way to rescue them."

Eugene lets out an angry sound at that.

I mumble to Eugene for a few minutes before I see a shadow flicker under the door. My immediate thought is of Ghoul, but I scratch that as the larger shadow is accompanied by a smaller one, then another.

There's a giggle at the door as the whoosh of the dragon-lock deactivates. It slams open and the two hatchlings charge through the door.

"We're on a mission, Lia!" Emmerson skids to a stop in front of my cage just as his sister and Selena quickly enter. The dragoness shuts the door behind them and I sit up, suddenly on alert.

Selena is pale this morning, no doubt from an awful night in the tower she was locked in. She's freshly showered and scrubbed clean, and nothing would look out of place except for the faint red mark around her neck that only my eagle eyes can see. There is also a dark gleam in her eye as she sets sights upon my cage.

"Lia is in a cage!" Emmerson chuckles. "Why are you in a cage, Lia?"

"Yeah, why are you in a cage?" Delilah parrots. Then she wrinkles her nose. "It's way too small for you."

"People don't belong in cages," Selena says quietly.

I regard her carefully. "Or towers."

Her eyes sparkle.

"But it looks kinda fun," Emmerson says, getting on his hands and knees to peer inside. "Maybe we can do a sleepover?"

"No," I say quickly. "This is not for kids."

"Then who's it for?"

I glance at Selena. "How did you guys get in here?"

A rare smile twitches at her lips. "A little loophole in Xander's magic. He never wants harm to come to the kids, so his magic will let them in anywhere he's locked."

"Uncle Xander loves us," Delilah nods.

"Heaps," Emmerson says, raising a finger and touching the lock of the cage. Silently, and without protest, the door opens on its hinge. He reaches in and strokes Eugene, clucking softly under his breath.

"Let's find some clothes, shall we?" Selena says.

I stare at the open door, at the children, at Selena. "Are you sure this is a good idea?"

"Xander and Father will be at a long meeting this morning," Selena says, and her voice is curiously sad. "We have at least three hours' free time."

"Free time!" The hatchlings cheer, fists in the air.

Eugene squawks with excitement, wiggling free of my vise-like hold and running out of the cage.

Selena, seemingly able to see the hidden doors in the room, finds the tiny cupboard that houses my two dresses and hands one to me. Delilah insists on helping me get dressed, tugging the hem of my dress in place and pulling my sleeves down for me. Emerson insists on brushing my hair and I sit through the ordeal, hiding my grimaces.

When Delilah starts looking for my leash, Selena gently explains that people don't wear leashes.

"Then why does Uncle Xander lead her on a leash every day?" Delilah puts her hands on her hips.

"Uncle Xander is wrong to do that," Selena says calmly, "But we'll talk about it later. Let's go see Grandmother. No doubt she's waiting for us."

Eugene and I are ushered out the door, fully ashamed to admit that it feels very much abnormal without my leash.

Have I gotten used to it so quickly?

Rubbing at my neck, I follow the scampering hatchlings down to the main hall and through to a part of the castle I've never been in before. The sounds of clanking, water running, and porcelain scraping on wood tell me what it is before we round the corner.

Lady Drakos sits on a stool at the long wooden kitchen bench, cutting up walnuts on a chopping board with a small paring knife.

When she sees us, she beams—as best as she can—and holds her arms out. The hatchlings run towards her for hugs before she casts her eye at us adults. "It'll be a fig and walnut cake this morning," she says in that hushed, weak voice. "And a cheese and bacon loaf."

My mouth immediately starts watering. They've not been starving me, exactly, but the food has been simple and unseasoned. Prison-fare.

"That sounds lovely, Mother," Selena says, immediately heading to the ingredients piled onto the table.

I step forwards tentatively. "Are the chefs not in today?"

"We like to cook once a month," Lady Drakos says. "It's more satisfying to eat something you've prepared together."

The backs of my eyes burn.

"Come," Selena says, beckoning to the children. "Wash your hands and let's measure out this flour."

It takes a moment to realise that she's also beckoning to me. As Lady Drakos continues to chop the walnuts, I head over to the other side of the kitchen and wash my hands too. The kids put on frilled tartan aprons with little dragons embroidered on them. They look hand sewn with love and well-worn, and I wonder how long it took Lady Drakos to make them.

Emmerson reaches into a drawer and whips out a neatly folded stack of white clothes. He unfolds one and plonks the material on his head, grinning at me.

"Chef's hats!" he says with excitement. "Everyone gets one!"

He then proceeds to hand one out to his grandmother, then his mother and Delilah. Xander's niece looks from her hat to me. "We only have four," she says quietly. "For today, you can have mine." Shyly, she hands it to me.

The backs of my eyes prickle again and I have to swallow before I say, "I can't take yours, Delilah."

She pouts a little before unfolding it and gently putting it on my head. I have to bend down to oblige her, but she gets it on and tugs it into place. "Uncle Xander says sharing is an important thing for a little dragon to learn. Otherwise, when we get older, we might become too possessive."

I feel Selena observing me. Her eyes flick down to the band of etched gold on my throat, but I pretend not to notice.

"Well, that's kind of you," I say, trying not to sound bitter about her uncle not following his own advice. "Thank you."

Selena and Lady Drakos take great care to include me in their family baking. Emmerson ends up with self-raising flour all over his face, after which time we have to refer to him as 'the ghost dragon' or he won't listen to instructions.

"Will the ghost dragon now roll the dough?" Selena asks formally. "Delilah, you can only eat one raw. No more or you'll get a tummy ache."

"Grandma said sally-mona is only for humans," Delilah says, popping an entire raw dough ball into her mouth. "I'm not human."

Eugene lets out an indignant squawk. "Eugene is correct," I say. "There was no *salmonella* in those eggs anyway."

Emmerson stops licking the wooden spoon. "You can tell?"

"Avians can tell bad eggs from good ones."

"So handy," Selena murmurs, peering into the oven.

Before long, the air smells like fresh baked bread, melted cheese, and crispy bacon. Combined with the joyous laughter of the children and the fact that every time Delilah is embarrassed by something, she hides her face in my side, I am, objectively, in heaven.

For the first time since I arrived here, I manage to forget the pain of the skin melded to the metal around my neck. I forget I'm a captive animal.

"Your hatchlings are a delight," I murmur to Selena as I dry the wet dish Emmerson carefully hands to me.

"They are a blessing." She smiles wistfully before she turns serious. "They came into the world under the worst circumstances." She swallows. "But we prevailed."

I blink at this unexpected revelation. "I'm sorry, I didn't know. I'm glad everything is better now." A small frown appears between her fine brows. She opens her mouth to say something but clearly decides against it.

"It's close to twelve," Lady Drakos says, running a knife around the edge of the pan with the cheese and bacon loaf. "We'd better start plating up for lunch. Aurelia, darling, will you pass me my health potion from the cupboard there?"

My heart squeezes at her term of endearment. "Of course."

"And would you be so kind as to pour a glass of orange juice for me?"

"It would be my pleasure, Lady Drakos."

She beams at me and I feel as if the sun has come out from between the clouds.

I turn around, head to the small cupboard, and open it to find it stocked with rows of familiar emerald glass bottles, long-necked with a round body. They all bear a black label with *Lady Drakos* and nothing else. Taking one out, I carefully place it on the bench and allow my power to investigate it. Giving myself more time, I move slowly, heading next to the drawer with glass-ware, then the large, industrial steel fridge further away.

Avian healers typically don't prepare potions. Our domain is healing the body directly, and that was the way I was taught when I trained after high school.

Potions and tonics are the domain of hyena witches.

The mixture is a cloudy one, and I can tell it's been lightly strained for final preparation. Tiny herbs float around the brown liquid, forming a slight sediment. But there are more than mere herbs in there. It has the suppressing feel of a sedative; but not of the sleeping variety. Frowning, I take my time as I unstopper the cork and pour some into the glass of orange juice.

Turning around, I present it to Lady Drakos, who smiles as she accepts the glass. There is a look in her eye. Some glint that I barely understand. I take the potion bottle back to the cupboard and place it back inside. Staring at the entire stock.

I know I've taken too long when Selena coughs politely and I close the cupboard, guilt twisting my stomach.

Emmerson pushes a plate of the fresh, gooey bread in front of me, eating his own warm piece with a happy, sloppy grin.

"Take as much as you want," Selena says, glancing at her watch. "Then we'd better get you back to your room."

"Right," I say, taking a piece of the bacon and cheese loaf, the mozzarella stretching between the pieces in the most delicious way. "Lucky that meeting they had lasted so long."

I can feel it when the energy of the room changes. Lady Drakos goes rigid, and she sets her glass down on the table. The hand she rests on her lap trembles as she turns to look at me and there is something in her expression I cannot, *dare* not, read. "I'm so very sorry, Aurelia."

Chapter 40

Scythe

It's near dawn that I wake up, tangled between Savage and Lyle like pups in a litter. I shove Savage's leg off and he mumbles as he wakes.

"Cheese...yum."

Lyle leaps out of bed and immediately begins pacing the room like a...well, like a lion, the same way he has done every morning since our regina was taken.

"She sent us a good memory," Lyle grits out. "Likely to subdue us."

"But how did she send it?" Savage asks, getting up to look out the window. "We've been trying to make contact for weeks."

"Somehow she established a connection outside of the estate," I say. "Likely when she left for the meeting with the crime lords."

"But why would Xander have taken her?"

I can think of a number of reasons, and every single one threatens to wrench me out of my cold state. Our reports of the fateful meeting have been scant, to say the least. It had been a tight-knit group that attended.

"We need to talk to one of the other crime lords," I say. "But which one to choose? They all have reasons to want us dead."

"The Collector?" Savage asks.

"Cunning enough to give me half-truths," I muse. "No, we'll see the falcons."

"Did you see her, though?" Savage asks wistfully, still looking out of the window as if he'll see his regina walking up the academy driveway. "She felt happy, for a little while."

"She was in pain, too," Lyle mutters. "They've collared her. She's trying to convince us otherwise, but I know better."

I sift through the memory of my regina in the Drakos kitchen. I have not seen Lady Drakos nor Selena in person for many years now, and even then it was from afar. They were kept well out of the media.

"The hatchlings have grown," Savage muses. "Has it really been that long?"

"Lady Drakos looks older than I expected," Lyle says. "What was that potion she was taking?"

"Yeah!" Savage says with interest. "What *was* that?"

My shark and I go still as we hone in on the memory of it. Because we know exactly what that potion is, and I think my regina has figured it out too.

Chapter 11

Aurelia

It takes me a little while to find out what Lady Drakos was apologising for. The next morning when Heather flips open my coverings, there is the tense, bustling energy of an event in the air. It's like the morning of Xander's wedding, but worse.

Xander still doesn't look at me, or talk to me. Instead, he instructs Heather not to give me clothes once again. When I'd returned to my cage yesterday, I'd taken my dress off and hidden it under my blankets so I could cover myself better for bed. Luckily this morning, I'd remembered to take it off before the covers came up.

I stand naked before Olly, Heather and Xander, but this time when he clips his leash onto my collar, he does it by hand.

Silently, he leads me downstairs, Eugene's wing skimming my ankle to let me know he's there.

It has the feel of one of those bank heist movies where the high security clearance banker has a suitcase of something valuable handcuffed to his hand to make a bank drop.

Something *so* precious it needs to be locked up.

Xander leads me to the underground facility where Ghoul, Solomon, and the scientific team wait.

To my great dissatisfaction, today, Mace Naga, Damien Agnis and Flores Drakos are also present. Whatever they think of my nudity is kept to themselves. In fact, everyone is quiet and deadly serious. There are no throwaway jokes or smiles. Even Ghoul has nothing to offer me as I cross the threshold into the lab with the steel table.

"Lie down, Miss Boneweaver," Solomon says gravely.

"What are you going to do today?" I say, moving towards the table as slowly as I can. With the way the table is set up, my feet are facing the viewing window where everyone sits. It's an awkward way to lie, especially with my father sitting right there. I perch on the side of it and Eugene flaps up next to me.

"Today we document your condition," Solomon says. "Please lie down."

My heart pounds and I break into a sweat. Reluctantly, I swing my legs up, careful to keep them pressed together as I rest my head on the steel.

"The time is oh-nine-hundred," Solomon dictates, and two serpents document by hand and on laptop. "On November the first." He peers into my eyes. "Condition of the subject, Aurelia Naga-Boneweaver, is as follows. Forehead: unmarked, both eyebrows present, both eyes are present, irises are cornflower blue, sclera are white with small broken capillaries bilaterally. Bluish bags under eyes. Nose, unmarked—" He squints. "Ruler, please. Oh yes, two millimetre pimple right side of nostril." To my great dismay, they go on in detail about the condition of my body, down to tiny hairs and blemishes, even beauty marks. They'd done something similar on my first day, but not in *this* much detail. He briefly mentions my nipples, which is bad enough, but it's not until he gets to my lower stomach that I start to panic.

"You'll need to open, Aurelia."

My eyes snap towards Ghoul, who has silently watched on this entire time, towering over me like a shadowy giant, no sign of the beast who'd fucked me senseless just weeks ago. "But everyone will see."

"That's the point," Solomon declares without emotion. "But if it makes you feel better, Lord Ghoul will temporarily block the sight."

"Thanks," I say dryly.

Ghoul casually strides towards the end of the table before crossing his arms. I thought he'd face away from me, but of course the bastard wants to see.

I pull my heels up before flopping my knees out. Solomon whacks on gloves before spreading me open with two fingers. He's gentle enough, but it's fucking torture regardless. My toes and fingers curl in disgust. Eugene is sitting by my head, still invisible, and he presses his warm body against my cheek.

It occurs to me then—what they're doing. The same thing the owner of furniture would do when listing an item for sale online. Documenting that all my parts are present.

That darkness consumes me. The one that's cold, deep, and black. The one with dangerous gnashing teeth and the eyes that see just a little more.

My feelings get pushed out and away as I sink into the cold.

Solomon is quick, as if he doesn't want to do this either. "Virginity is not preserved. Vulval anatomy presents as normal and unmarked."

Normal Aurelia would have snapped her legs shut and glared at the men present. Cold, great white shark Aurelia closes them slowly. Solomon documents the condition of my legs and feet before they draw blood from me. Next, one of their eagles scan my internal organs and they document every one of those as well.

My greatest fear, the one that as thirteen-year-old had me waking up in the middle of the night thrashing and screaming, is going to happen tonight.

The auction.

The key stakeholders are here and their guests will arrive this evening.

I wonder if it will be like what I saw of Scythe's virginity auction. I'll have to tell him all about it when I see him next. I also wonder what sage advice he'd give me if he were here.

'Let them know you're not prey,' or perhaps 'Don't let them play with your mind.'

"An auction of monsters," I muse out loud in a cold, deadpan voice.

"The worst," Ghoul agrees, still standing over me and blocking the view of the onlookers.

"To breed the Boneweaver," I continue.

Solomon glances at me uncomfortably. "She's gone cold again. We should consider the obsidian shackles."

Mace Naga gets to his feet. "Obsidian for tonight, after Lady Hyena has completed her spell."

If I couldn't protect myself from my own mates, someone needs to do it for me.

"Even with the obsidian," Mace continues, "she won't be compliant for the first."

The grin that spreads across my lips shows teeth that have shifted into needle sharp points. One of the scientists gasps and Solomon stumbles a step back. "Dear Goddess."

"I will be a compliant Boneweaver." My voice is jeering and dark—something from a nightmare. Because if I'm forced to live in a nightmare, the smartest thing to do is become a nightmare myself.

I gnash my teeth. The horrified look on Damien Agnis' face is truly satisfying as he stumbles into the lab, holding up his box of nimpins. He exclaims, "You must be compliant or I will kill all the nimpins!"

My grin does not falter. "But if you kill them, you have nothing else to use against me."

Xander finally speaks, his eyes sharp, his stance rigid. "We have Raquel, Spawn."

"Are my eyes familiar, cursed dragon?" I leer at him. "Do they scare you?"

"Why would you ever scare me?" he snaps.

"Only the frightened reject a mate bond," I reply smoothly. "Only the frightened *rage* so hard. Only the frightened curse themselves." My chuckle is dark and ever-cold. I am a poet. A prophet. My mates would be proud.

Xander pushes Ghoul aside and gets in my face, his own expression fierce, nostrils flaring, eyes flashing. "Then let me ask you this: how long can you stay in this state before the hallucinations appear? How long before you become haunted and demons follow you?"

I laugh in his face. "I am already haunted, cursed-one. I am already mad. The ghosts will be my friends and we will dance a mad dance as we watch you burn in black fire and cold blood." I tilt my head back and cackle again, only vaguely aware that my great white shark is a crazy bitch.

That suits me just fine.

"Gag her," Damien Agnis says, distaste twisting his mouth. "I don't want to hear any more of its talk."

I point at him. "Spine-less *and* sperm-less. What's next for the phoenix lord?"

"Lord Basilisk," Mace snaps, his coldness rivalling mine.

My gaze turns upon him, my eyes flashing with menace as I meet his malicious eyes. "Regina-killer," I hiss, just before a ball of thick shadows is shoved into my mouth.

The sensation is all at once strange and amusing. Ghoul's shadows taste sweet on my tongue. Soft like velvet, powerful like a midnight storm.

My laugh is muffled around the gag of shadows and it makes the beasts all leave one by one, until the only persons left are Xander Drakos, the cursed one, Ghoul, the lord of the dead, and Eugene, my loyal poultry companion.

"It's another long drive," Ghoul says, taking both my wrists in his hands and pulling me up and off the steel table. His voice is quiet, but still emotionless. "Don't do anything stupid while you are like this."

But I can't do anything stupid because like this, I'm clever. I respond with a hum as Xander hooks my leash back in place. I stare at them both from beneath my lashes, allowing my loose hair to slide down and frame my face.

Xander exhales through his nose. "You'll walk in front of me."

I chuckle knowingly.

Ghoul seems to be of the same mind as I lead the way out, high priestess of the cold deep. "Scared she'll attack you from behind?" he jeers. "Or are you obsessing over her ass again?"

Xander makes a rude sound, but says nothing.

We head straight outside to the waiting fleet of cars and the army of serpents with drawn automatic rifles.

All this for me? Why, what fun.

"*Stay behind,*" I warn Eugene. "*Where we go is no place for you.*"

I feel his reticence, but he is a good rooster and obeys me.

The drive is long and boring. It gives me time to think, I suppose. Time to disseminate. Time to calculate. I do not know what human Aurelia expected from this surrender to the enemy.

The cold saves me from turning rabid like I did once long before. Though I suppose, in some way, the cold is a shark's version of rabidity. Because how else could I cope with what I've done?

With what is about to happen?

You made this choice, I say to myself. *Lady Boneweaver sacrifices for her friends. Sacrifices her skin. Her womb. Her honour. Because tonight, great beasts fight to purchase us. And where once before they used their claws and fangs, tonight, they will use the modern world's form of power: money.*

I sigh, long and low. Eventually, when I close my eyes, I dream of my mates. But it's not a pleasant dream, because Savage, Scythe and Lyle are covered head to toe in blood.

* * *

The truck rumbles to a stop exactly five hours later, and I can tell, even through the thick walls of this vehicle, that we're in the city. The buzzing energy of humans, animalia and their Saturday night shenanigans vibrates along my skin and hair.

Except it's not only the buzz of a city at large, is it?

The doors unlock and swing soundlessly open, revealing Ghoul standing there with a lit cigarette in his mouth. Outside wait twice as many guards as usual.

"All this fanfare," I say innocently, as Ghoul steps into the truck, making it sway side to side. "Who could it be for?"

His shadows are out in full force tonight, making him look like a true entity of the night, barely a limb visible, the edges of darkness twitching expectantly around him like a nightmarish aura. "For me, of course, snakelet," he says, bending down to unlock both sets of steel shackles from where they're anchored to the wall of the truck. "They all want a piece of *this*." He gestures to himself in a dramatic sweeping motion.

My anima also wants a piece of that. But she's a nutcase like the rest of her mates, so my shark ignores her.

I'm brought up to standing, and as we reach the edge of the truck, I get to see I have a special guard of honour where we're parked at the loading dock of a looming, dark building. Serpents line a path on either side, holding automatic rifles on their chests. All seven generals are present, and at the end, Mace Naga, Flores Drakos, and Xander stand like the father, the son, and the holy ghost.

I chuckle at my own joke as Ghoul steps off the truck and hoists me down. That makes me Mary. They expect me to birth the saviours of their species.

Dance music drums in a nearby club and I know it can't be where I'm headed.

People with the amount of money required tonight, the

animalia and human elite, don't listen to dance music before they make a purchase.

"They listen to the screams of the innocent," I mutter.

The serpent militia closest glance warily at me as Ghoul leads me by the elbow. They close in behind us, cutting off any hope of escape.

"So cosy," Ghoul says. "Just one big, happy family."

The three evil beasts part, revealing something that makes me raise my brows.

"How medieval," I muse. "How barbaric."

Because standing before me on ancient wheels is a man-sized birdcage of obsidian and cast iron. The bars are set into a heavy obsidian base, reaching upwards like begging hands until they meet at the top. Along the bars and on the floor, brutal metal spikes are set at intervals, leaving only a small clear space within.

The person who stands in it would be poked by spikes on every part of their body. Unable to move lest they risk being pierced. A total prisoner.

Flores blinks at Ghoul in a bored way as we come to stand in front of them. "You were told to gag her, General."

"Apologies, Your Majesty," Ghoul chuckles. "Used to giving orders, not following 'em." He gestures to someone behind us and metal passes hands. "Open up, snakelet."

I eye the ball gag with distaste before opening my mouth. I feel like every damn beast in the vicinity is watching me as Ghoul places the metal ball between my teeth and tightly fastens the straps at the back of my head. The creek of old hinges tells me someone has opened the wheeled cage and I'm being turned around and led to the metal steps built into the platform.

Eyeing the metal spikes, I gingerly climb in, Ghoul's gloved hand under one of mine. His shadows slide up my forearm in a forbidden caress before he lets me go, and I step over two spikes and into the cage's centre, making myself as small as possible. Even then, multiple spikes scrape my bare skin on the way in. But it's not until the door clicks shut that I truly feel the danger of it. Spikes press into the space between my breasts, multiple on my abdomen, two on my kidneys, three on my spine, and two on each thigh and calf. I grimace as the cage begins to roll and one of the spikes draws blood from the motion. Luckily the thing is electronic, with Ghoul remotely driving it with the device in his hands. We head up a ramp into the building in the wake of the two dragons and king cobra.

The corridors are thankfully wide as I'm wheeled through, the serpents forming a procession around me. We finally head into a room, fancy red walls with crimson patterned carpet that reminds me of a casino. It's bare of anything except a gilded mirror and a lacquered wooden table.

"Get her in there," Mace Naga says, standing just outside the threshold. "Guard her with your lives. We begin in one hour."

My cage wheels itself in, stopping right in the middle of the room when the door closes behind us.

I stand stiff, tightly clutching the bars in both hands as Ghoul and Xander prowl around me, staring. Appraising.

Xander sighs. "She doesn't look good. Why has no one brushed her hair?" He looks around like Heather might pop out of the woodwork, but of course, there are no maids here. "There are bags under her eyes."

"And what's this?" Ghoul picks up a bottle of clear liquid that sloshes around like oil with a bronze sheen. He shakes it, chuckling as if the sparkling of it amuses him.

"That's for her skin," comes a female voice from one of the soldiers. "It needs to be rubbed in. Looks good under the down-lights on stage."

I am a jewel, after all.

"Here, I'll do it," says one of the other generals, stepping forward and eagerly removing his gloves.

"No, you'll get your scent all over her," Ghoul snaps, pock-eting the oil.

Xander steps up behind my cage, reaches between the bars and expertly runs a brush through my hair, holding the strands close to my head when he hits resistance. He mutters darkly under his breath and I'm suddenly reminded of Lyle and how much he loved to wash and brush my hair for me. It was one of the ways he showed me he cared.

There is no one to care for me here. Only enemies.

The cold threatens to slip as a burning behind my eyes takes over all things. My throat closes up and my breathing quickens as the ball gag makes saliva flood my mouth. Ghoul notices straight away and reaches up to unbuckle the gag. A shadow reaches out, fingerlike but gentle, and wipes at the corner of my mouth.

At that point, a sharp knock comes at the door and the soldiers part as it's opened. To my surprise, King Flores leads Lady Hyena, and behind him, Fabian Drakos.

"Uncle." Xander shakes hands with him, and suddenly, I forget why I'm here. The entire room fades away underneath the shaking of those two hands. This is Xander's family. His people. This betrayal not only belongs to me, but Scythe as well.

And I can't handle that.

Hot, hot, hot, my body turns, cold icicles morphing into licks of flame. Time passes around me like sludge as Lady Hyena circles my cage, sprinkling something as she goes. Magic to prevent outside influences from reaching me while my magic is put out. Finally, she makes a satisfied noise, but I barely notice it. When everyone else leaves, Xander changes my silver shackles for obsidian magic-dampeners.

All I see are those powerful glowing eyes flashing in surprise at the temperature of my skin. "You fucking coward," I hiss. "How *dare* you shake hands with *him*. The one who hurt Scythe."

A crease forms between Xander's brows. "What?"

He doesn't know.

The obsidian stone hums as it cuts off my power, taking all the anger and heat and funnelling it away. Even so, I'm still livid.

"Scythe never told you who won the auction for his virginity?" My shackles are in place, and Xander steps away from me. I stare him down, hard and brutal. "How could you not have known?"

Ghoul reaches up and shoves the ball gag back into my mouth.

When I can see him again, Xander is acting like I'd said nothing, looking at a pocket watch. "Ten minutes!" he barks. "And then we move out."

The serpents all flinch at the volcanic boom behind his voice.

Chapter 12

Xander

"There he is!" My father holds out an arm as I come into view of the open entrance doors where he's pouring wine for a human politician. "My heir."

"Good evening, sir," I say, shaking the human's hand. We've really descended into the gutter, inviting them here. I doubt the old geezer has enough money to compete with the other elite beasts. It's all for show and networking anyway.

After as many handshaking and pleasantries as the darkness in me can tolerate, I slip away into the quiet and get out my phone.

Scythe had only given Savage and me whatever information we'd needed to do our work. He'd given us a list of names, people he'd directly seen to be involved in the skin trade. I had just assumed that included whichever creature had purchased him first.

Serpent Spawn is likely trying to unsettle me. Turn me against my family. But something about her particular kind of rage is flagging something in the back of my mind. There's no way to verify the transaction, of course. The auctions are kept confidential and any electronic data is stripped and scrambled.

The only way to verify it would be to ask any person who was present or...

A gong sounds, soft but commanding, alerting the audience it's time to find their seats and any bidders to assume their positions. Sighing, I head back down the corridor, hanging back from the crowd until they've all entered the auditorium. The light is dim, almost too dark for the humans to see, and somebody's wife trips over her own train. The Mozart that plays over the speakers adds to the illusion of this being some certified, elitist event.

They might have money, but at the end of the day, these people are all trash. Dirt beneath a dragon's feet, and my father would agree. We're just here to take their money.

Just over one hundred of the country's elite sit on the plush chairs to observe, and the richest, nastiest of them saunter down to the front, where the first five rows of seats are set up with electronic auction buttons. A more recent invention, to create a curated bidding experience. If they're going to spend millions tonight, they might as well do it in style.

As the attendants get ready to close the doors, I stride through them into the auditorium.

Food and drink flow, and white-coated waiters run back and forth with bottles of the most expensive Scottish whiskey, Cuban cigars, and Colombian cocaine.

I head past all of these bottom dwellers right to the front where the real money is: ancient houses, century-old trust funds, vaults full of gold bars. Damien Agnis sits in his white suit right at the front, his finger tapping against his wine glass like he's rearing to bid. To his right lounges The Collector, in a sparkling magenta gown, cigar in hand like she hasn't a care in the world, when everyone knows she's just as keen as Damien to win this auction.

Behind them sits Mace Naga and my father, conversing over their crystal tumblers. On the other side of the aisle in the first row sit some interstate tigers, arrogance and poise dripping off every ruby and diamond-encrusted finger. Behind them sits Francesca and her parents, no doubt judging every part of the evening. In the fourth row from the stage sit a line of staff from various houses, overseen by Drakos administrative staff. These represent the anonymous bidders of the evening. Beasts and humans, who want their faces and business kept private from the rest. I can only guess who they are, but I don't care so much. All I know is that they had to pay a healthy deposit just to have their staff sit here.

Just in front of them sits Uncle Fabian. I take a seat next to him and he smirks at me before looking back at the stage. He's clearly excited, like the rest of them, their hearts all pounding in that annoying, pitter-patter rhythm excited people have. It grates at my ear drums before my attention is dragged to the stage where the auctioneer we imported from the UK strolls onto the stage to a round of applause.

"Good evening, ladies and gentlemen! Flores Drakos and his Estate presents to you a premier event, the likes of which you've never seen." He bounces on shiny heels. "For tonight, we have something extra special."

There's another round of applause and someone hoots at the back. If I could have rolled my eyes, I would have.

"Ladies and gentlemen!" he says with dramatic gusto. "The combined powers of Drakos Estate and Naga House present to you the last known Boneweaver in existence."

They roll her out then. This time, without the electronics, because Mace just *had* to get four of his generals pulling the ancient thing with ropes like a roman carriage.

Uncle Fabian chuckles softly in his chair before leaning forward to look. I too observe the stage as numerous gasps resound through the audience. For some of them, this is their first live look at her.

Aurelia stands naked before us all, the points of the cage making indentations all over her flesh and curves. Her raven hair is darker than obsidian, trailing to the small of her back, small strands framing her face. Ghoul's ball gag is clenched between two rows of white teeth, her face the picture of such violent aggression that it makes the hairs on my neck stand on end.

She glares out at us. Challenges us. Those blue irises like the brightest sapphires from the deepest parts of the Earth. I don't realise I'm leaning forward in my seat until the auctioneer's voice brings me back to reality.

"Female Boneweaver anima, twenty years old. Unbred. Pristine condition. Estimated ovulation less than a week away!" The auctioneer turns to look at her, shaking his head and smiling like he can't believe it.

"So much spirit left in those mythical blue eyes! So much *fire*. We are living in privileged times indeed!"

He assumes a formal position at his lectern and bows to the bidders on the left and right. "Bidding will commence at eight million USD. Who would like to begin? My! Lady Crocodylus, you are looking fine tonight indeed."

The Collector tilts her head back and laughs before shrugging. "Ladies first," she says flirtatiously before pressing one of her buttons. "Eight point five."

"Do I have a nine in the room?"

Damien Agnis excitedly enters the bidding, exuberantly pressing on his console. According to our intel, he's had his sperm frozen for some years, meaning Lyle's old castration trick didn't work as well as we thought.

"Ten and a half, ladies and gentlemen, ten and a half million dollars."

"Twelve, dammit!" Lady Crocodylus shouts, poking her button with gusto.

Four of the anonymous bidders and the Collector go at it for a bit, eventually bringing us up to eighteen.

At that point, Damien bows out with a shake of his head and a fist smashing into his table. The bidding goes up by two hundred-thousands before The Collector starts grimacing.

It's at that point that Uncle Fabian presses one of his buttons. A giant red twenty flashes in the screen above us and people clap. The Collector whips her head around and gapes at him before crossing her arms and chewing on her lip in thought.

Something in me shifts then. Something made of magma and smoke. Blue flame and steam.

I hadn't intended to interfere with this whole farce. But this is different. This is personal. No fucking dragon will outbid me for my property.

Whipping my phone out, I text the Drakos administrators.

A second later, another bid flashes on the screen.

"Ladies and gentlemen," the auctioneer exclaims excitedly, "we have an anonymous bidder entering the game at twenty-one million!"

Mutters break out and everyone looks about as if they can figure out who it is. We're not taking phone bids tonight. While they may have a representative at the bidding chairs, all parties must be physically present. It was part of the exclusivity of the whole affair.

My father glances at me, frowning as if he's wondering who it is too. We had ten approved bidders tonight, and he doesn't like surprises.

Uncle Fabian chuckles as if this is good fun before pressing his button with a flourish.

"Twenty-two!"

I send another message.

"Twenty-three to anonymous bidder six!" cries the auction-eer. "What'll it be, Lord Fabian?"

"Twenty-four, of course," Uncle Fabian replies, ever so smooth.

Discreetly, my fingers fly across my phone screen.

"Twenty-five from Anonymous Six! Come on, Lord Fabian, I know you've got it in you."

My uncle taps his knee in thought. "I'm out." He puts up his palms.

Now it's my turn for my heart to pitter-patter. I glare at the stage.

"Ladies and gentlemen," the auctioneer says, mopping his forehead with a black kerchief. "I believe now is the time for any more surprise bids!" The room is pin-drop silent. Everyone looks around the room, but the screen doesn't flash again.

Draconic satisfaction winds through my insides, greedy and golden.

"Ladies and gentlemen, Drakos Estate, Naga House..." He bows towards my father and Mace Naga. "Tonight has been the highlight of my career. I thank you." He smashes his gavel. "*Sold* for twenty-five million dollars to Anonymous Bidder Six."

A raucous applause ensues, and for some blasted reason that has everything to do with power, I fold my arms and smirk.

Chapter 13

Lyle

We stand at the ruins of The Lily Institute around Scythe, who crouches down, crushing a piece of rubble with his fingers. Darkness coils around his entire being. Violence curls around all three of us.

The entire complex has been destroyed. The casualties are in the hundreds, the injured being carted out on stretchers by more ambulances and healing eagles than I can count. It wasn't fire that destroyed Scythe's pride and joy, nor water.

The humans put it down to an earthquake. But we know better.

It was telekinesis.

They had ripped the place apart with sheer force alone.

It's Beak who brings us the picture, tentative, unsure as he steps through the rubble. He's covered in blood that's not his, healing as many patients as he can in rapid succession. Saving the innocent lives affected by this horror.

"What is it?" Savage growls.

Beak holds it out to me as I stand closest to him. I take it, turning it over because he's been trying to hide it from passersby.

When I lay eyes on the photos, on my regina, naked in that

medieval cage, gagged and enraged, my entire universe crumbles around me, just like The Lily Institute.

This had been a distraction. They had used the innocents inside The Lily Institute to keep us from interrupting the auction of my regina.

The roar in my head rattles the bones of my skull.

Chapter 44

Aurelia

I'm wheeled off the bright stage with confusion roiling in my belly. The bidding had gone as expected, but I'd not anticipated so many anonymous bidders. I don't remember any from Scythe's auction, and it unsettled me not knowing which parties wanted a piece of me.

It's dark as Ghoul flexes his fingers over the controls and wheels me behind the stage to a different room. He then leans into the cage and takes the ball gag out. I lick my dry lips, making him stare.

"Like what you see, basilisk lord?" I purr.

He flashes a fang at me before hopping down, violently jostling the cage. I swear under my breath as those awful spikes puncture my skin.

"Close ranks," Ghoul snaps. "We can't hand over the goods until money is exchanged. Until then, guard her with your lives, because if anything happens to her, that's what I'm taking from you." For the first time since the start of this whole event, he leaves my side.

The serpent militia closes in around me, facing outward with their guns. Immediately, they begin gossiping.

"We'll find out who it was soon enough," says a loud voice. "Settle down."

One of the guards lowers her hood and I'm surprised to see a familiar face. It's Natalia, a serpent I'd grown up with. I'd also released her when Scythe, Savage and Xander held her captive for days. For all intents and purposes, she's still my enemy.

"I bet you're enjoying this," I say, gesturing to myself.

Natalia shrugs, though her face bears no emotion. "A little."

It's fair. Her friends are dead because of me. Sure, they'd kidnapped me first and attempted to torture me before Xander came and off'ed them, but they're still dead.

"Do the terms include her getting pregnant?" asks another female voice, hooded, so I can't see her face.

"Wait, so this auction wasn't to keep her?" asks one.

"No, you idiots," Natalia says. "It's just for the duration of her heat. The whole point of it is so they can use her to repopulate the dying species. Why do you think Damien Agnis was so excited?"

More murmurs.

"That much money for a week is insane."

"Well, if they get her pregnant, she'll be out of action for nine months," Natalia says. "So really, they've paid for nine months."

I blink dryly at her, my insides burning like they've been scraped with sandpaper down to the quick.

I'd asked for this. I'd signed up for this. I only have myself to blame.

A commotion outside stops my thoughts in their tracks.

"The beast that comes through that door is the man who'll be attempting to impregnate her," one of the generals says, hoisting his gun up more securely. "Look alive, lads. Here comes a wealthy bastard."

Except when the door slams open and the sounds of Damien Agnis and The Collector shouting become deafening, it's Xander who stalks through it.

I sigh, the tension in me suddenly whooshing out. "Well, who is it, then?" I ask impatiently.

"It's *him*!" Damien answers my question, storming in behind Xander. "You fucking cheat!"

Xander freezes mid-step. Except it's less of a freeze and more of a predator's stillness. He swivels around on his heel and steps towards Damien. They're both tall, being mythic shifter males, but Damien is two inches shorter than Xander's near seven feet. As a result, when Xander steps chest to chest with Damien, he's looking down into the phoenix lord's upturned face.

The old bird goes as pale as his white blazer.

Everyone in the room goes deathly silent as Xander snarls in the softest, most lethal of voices, "Call me that again, phoenix swine, and I'll finish Lyle Pardalia's hack job."

Xander talking nasty to me is one thing, but Xander talking nasty to Damien Agnis is like music to my sore ears.

"Hear, hear," I say, slapping my bars.

Natalia and several of the serpents give me sidelong looks that tell me I must be mad. Other beasts have entered the room behind them—Flores, Mace Naga, the auctioneer, and some of the other bidders, their faces a combination of anger and surprise.

"See that?" Xander snarls, pointing at my gold collar. "That means I can do whatever the fuck I want. And if I paid for it, I fucking own it."

I have to stop my mouth from gaping open. Xander was the winning bidder.

The auctioneer shrugs. "Unprecedented, perhaps, but there are no rules against it."

Flores is looking at his son like he wants to strangle him. I suppose he will, when they get home. They won't make any money this way. The auctioneer shepherds the rest of the beasts back out, leaving Xander and a lingering Mace Naga.

"There will be consequences for this," Mace says quietly. "I have my money, so I'm settled. But the others..."

"Like you said, Mace," Xander drawls, not looking at him, but striding towards me. "You have your money. I'm leaving." The serpents part, and Xander gestures in annoyance with a hand. The door creaks open.

"Out." It's a raw command.

He doesn't have to tell me twice.

"Aw, just when I was getting used to it, too," I say, gently extracting myself from between the various spikes and stepping out onto the first step.

Xander snarls at me, flicking his wrist as that golden chain snaps into place at my collar again. With another wave of his hands, both sets of shackles fall off.

I sigh in relief before he turns around and yanks me forwards. I go stumbling after him, the serpents all blinking in shock at the sight.

Allowing myself to ascend out of the cold of my great white, my emotions come back like the crashing of cymbals.

What exactly does he intend to do with the thing he purchased for twenty-five million? And what the hell? I knew he had money, but *this* kind of money?

"You're *rich*, rich," I say.

That gets a reaction out of him. He stops and whips around, glaring down at me with those white eyes.

"I'm Xander fucking Drakos," he says, before turning back around and continuing on.

Some of the uncertainty and confusion lifts then. This is an ego thing. A dragon-sized ego thing.

Someone isn't in control of his dragon.

Xander whips around for a second time and I realise with a gasp that I've said that last part out loud. He points a finger at me, his mouth pressed into a hard line. "Don't fucking start me, Spawn." He turns back around and I jump at this new shiny opportunity.

"Well, you paid twenty-five mil for me. I suppose you can call me what you like for a little while."

Black smoke filters through the air as we get outside and I'm amused by the difference in the way I'm leaving the building compared to how I went in. Does my father not care anymore now that he's got his money?

That stings a little, I'll admit.

"What song were you listening to while you were bidding for me?" I chirp, padding after his long strides through the concrete car park. "Candy Shop?"

He makes a very dragon-like snort, and smug as a bug, I smirk into the night air. "What if someone steals me out here?" I muse. "There's not as much protection."

Black smoke streams out of Xander and the voice that comes out of him is loud, guttural, and deep. "They can fucking try. No one would dare. And if they did, they'd be dead before they hit the ground."

"Are you sure?" I prod.

The air suddenly smells like cinders, and my smirk grows wider. If I'd known triggering Xander's possessive dragon instincts would be this much fun, I'd have done it a long time ago. Apparently, making a large purchase is a trigger of his.

"Do you spend this much money every weekend?" I inquire sweetly. "Should I feel special? Oh!" I gasp with sudden realisation. "Will I go into your vault now? Safe with all the other gold bars and diadems? Will I get to sleep on a bed of gold coins?" I hum for a moment, looking around us, but the space is silent. Everyone is probably still gossiping back inside. "Or is all your stuff plated and not *real* gold because—"

Xander whirls around and grabs me by my neck. My own hands fly up as he presses his nose against mine. "Nothing of mine is *plated*," he snarls in disgust. "Nothing of mine is cheap. Everything I own is precious. Is treasure."

I chuckle. "Including me?"

"Yes."

Abruptly, he lets me go and I'm left reeling with his words.

"That was a Freudian slip," he says tightly as we get to the car. To my surprise, it's a fancy bottle-blue sports car. The type that looks sleek, expensive, and powerful. I suppose this is what he drives when he's not transporting me. He opens the driver's side door and gestures like he wants me to get inside.

"Oh, I'm driving?" I say with a giddy sort of excitement. "Okay! It's been a while, but no worries."

He growls with irritation. "No, you're not. You're getting into the passenger seat from this side."

I make a face at the chain. "Just undo it."

"No." His nostrils flare.

"What? That's silly."

Xander just stands there, glowing eyes staring unblinking at me, black smoke streaming from his nostrils like toxic gas. His shoulders move up and down in great strain.

"You don't want to separate the chain," I say, working this out like a quadratic equation. "You don't want to be separated... from me?"

Still, he says nothing, simply heaving and glaring like there's a war going on in his head.

Glad to fucking see it.

I press my lips together to suppress the grin of amusement and oblige him, crawling into the driver's seat for longer than is necessary, so all he can see of me are the two round globes of my ass bouncing and shaking before I stretch one leg over into the passenger side and then the other.

Once we're both in, Xander Drakos, silent and fuming, drives his *precious* prize and treasure back to the Estate.

* * *

The pre-dawn light spreads across the horizon by the time we get back to the estate and I crack an eyelid open to see it before shutting it again and pretending to sleep.

"I know you're awake," Xander mutters after he turns the engine of the sports car off. He tugs on the chain a little and I bite down on the hiss of pain that comes from the wound where it's melded into my skin.

He huffs in annoyance, but to my surprise, I feel his hot hands under my thighs and behind my shoulder blades. I keep my eyes firmly shut and my mouth open a little for good effect, and he somehow manoeuvres me across the gearbox and outside, into his arms.

Xander clutches onto me like he thinks someone is about to snatch me away.

Light footsteps sound on the steps outside.

"What happened?" comes Selena's voice. "Why is she here?"

"I won't talk about it," Xander mutters, taking the steps two at a time. "Get out of my way."

"Alright." She sounds concerned and slightly disturbed, but we quickly leave her behind. I just get to see her call to Eugene and scoop him up before I lose sight of them both.

Before we know it, he's kicking the door shut, and just when I think he's going to put me in my cage, he opens the bathroom door.

I stir then, blinking my eyes open against the golden heat lights.

"What are you doing?"

"Washing the stink off you," he mutters, his movements determined as he sets me down and bustles about. "You smell of other beasts and metal."

Blinking blearily around, I stand bereft as Xander rolls up his sleeves. He fills the tub with water, testing it with his fingers first and filling it with bubble bath. He reaches for me, a stern, no-nonsense look on his face that I've never seen before. Before I can stop him, he picks me up and gently lowers me into the tub.

I hiss at the sudden heat.

Xander freezes my descent. "Is it too hot?" he asks quickly, testing the water with the hand curled around my thigh.

"No. But you're acting weird."

His jaw clenches, but continues to lower me into the tub.

The hot water engulfs me like a perfect hug. He picks up my left arm and begins rubbing a wash cloth along it. "Don't ask questions."

"Why?" I say sleepily, reaching for the cloth.

He slaps my hand away. "I must be the one to clean you."

There's a knock at the door. "My lord, we can do that," comes Heather's voice.

Olly and Heather pop into view, concern and alarm clear on their faces.

"Out!" Xander roars, leaping to his feet. "Out!"

Their faces morph into comical levels of terror before they both make a run for it and Xander slams the door shut so hard it vibrates

"This must be a dragon thing," I say quietly. "Is it?"

"It's the treasure haze," Xander says through clenched teeth as he scrubs at my other arm. "I can't stop it."

"But I'm a person," I say slowly. The term is vaguely familiar, but in this context, it makes no sense. "Not like jewels or something."

"It works the same," Xander says, plunging his hand into the water and reaching for my foot. He brings it out of the water and begins meticulously cleaning each toe. "I must clean you thoroughly before I set you in your place."

"I've never seen you like this," I say, watching him inspecting the space between my big toe and the next.

"It's temporary," Xander says, carefully placing my foot back into the water and starting on the other. "Don't get used to it."

It's not until he's finished with my lower limbs and reaching under the water that I see the problem.

"Oh no."

"What?" he says, alarmed. "Are you unwell?" Xander leans toward my face and sniffs before making a growling sound. "You are fine." Then he begins washing my thighs beneath the water.

The sensation is so nice, so soothing compared to Heather's

brusque movements, that I close my eyes and sigh. "I mean, yeah, I think so."

The washcloth moves up to the apex of my thighs. "Shit," he says. "I can't stop."

My eyes fly open. "Pardon?"

Xander's hand spreads my thighs open, and the washcloth runs over my clit. "Spawn, I can't fucking stop."

I hiss, arching my back. "Okay, wait. Here." I try to ease my hand between his and the washcloth. But his hand is hot, large, and covers mine completely, eventually sweeping it to the side. He keeps rubbing between my legs like something mechanical.

He swears again as his hand keeps moving up and down over my core, that washcloth and the warm water creating the sort of friction that could drive a woman mad.

"Oh god," I pant. "I— We—

"I—" Xander groans. "Shit—"

My eyes roll to the back of my head, and try as I might to fight it, the orgasm takes me. A gasp turns into a loud moan and I can't help but close my eyes and arch into it like I've been craving all week. He keeps rubbing and I lose myself completely to his hand, the steam, the warmth.

"Did you just—" Xander is panting, sweat beading on his forehead, his jaw clenching.

"Yeah, sorry," I mutter, embarrassed, trying to sit up again. "It's just been a while and—"

"It's my fucking fault," he mutters. "All my fucking—" He begins washing my abdomen, but his hands become gentle and he frowns deeply. "These never healed properly."

The change in topic is jarring, but I register he's talking about the scars my father made on my stomach. Celeste's phoenix tears had taken them almost all away, but they still left faint red lines diagonally across my skin.

"They're healed," I say, cringing at the sensation of the cloth rubbing along the tissue. "Just not—"

"That hurts you," he mutters, before discarding the cloth and continuing with just his hands. Hot skin caresses mine with a gentleness that is confusing.

I can only stare at him when he gets up to my rib cage and to my breasts. Without missing a beat, his hands move over the mounds and cup them. My body welcomes his touch, and honestly, I feel like I've been waiting my whole life to feel this. To experience this.

It eases that primitive wound at my core.

Xander holds both my breasts, frowning and rubbing his thumbs over my nipples. "Everything has to be clean," he says firmly. "Everything."

"Yeah, I know," I sigh, curling my toes in pleasure. "You said that already. Do that again."

"This?" he says, rubbing his thumb over the tops of both nipples at the same time. I gasp, arching my back as the sensation connects to my clit.

It's exactly then that I understand Xander is not himself. I immediately feel ashamed.

"Um, *ow*. That hurts," I say in mock pain.

He immediately moves his hands away and I totally miss them.

"Face," he announces, grabbing a new cloth and a fresh bowl of water. He gently washes my forehead and I keep my eyes open the entire time, studying his expression for clues of what exactly is going through his mind.

"Xander," I say sadly.

"Yes?" he says with that concentrating frown still fixed as he sweeps the cloth under my nose.

"You're good at this."

His brow smoothes over, as if he's relieved. "Thank you."

Chapter 45

Xander

I know this is wrong. I know this isn't just bad, but the worst thing I could be doing right now, but by all the Wild Gods, I can't stop it.

The need to inspect and clean all of her, to ensure she's unmarked, healthy and safe, is fucking overwhelming and all-consuming. I'm mad, I know it, and there's nothing I can do except to keep going.

She came under my touch. So easily and so freely, that I stared, fascinated at my new possession. All mine, only mine, safe in my room, in my arms, for no one to touch and hold and stroke but me.

Mine.

Mine

All mine.

Her orgasms are all mine. Her mouth is all mine. Her touch is all mine, too.

I shake my head to try to clear the treasure haze, but it won't relent for days. All I can do is concentrate on the important tasks. Once I'm done cleaning her, I gather her up in a towel and dry all of her parts.

When we get to that sweetly scented spot between her legs, I can't help but look up at her as I dry her.

Her lips part, and she wets them in anticipation of the pleasure.

She likes this. It feels good to her.

So I do it more. She liked my mouth on it that previous time too; I remember that clearly.

Her stomach grumbles and I jerk backwards, remembering that this treasure requires sustenance.

I send a thought message to Olly and demand he bring a tray to the door and then leave. I also tell him to rope off the entire wing so that no one enters and disturbs me. I must be left to covet my treasure alone. If anyone approaches my domain without warning, I will burn them alive, then burn their ashes.

After I make sure she's entirely dry, I carry her out of the bathroom and to the bed. I'll also need to sleep soon, and that means she must be with me at that time so I can guard her in my sleep.

Carefully placing her under the covers, I tuck her in, making sure she's warm and safe. Then I take off my dirty clothes, put them in a neat pile on the floor and climb under with her.

She doesn't protest when I gather her up in my arms and hold the length of her against the length of me. All parts must touch for safety reasons. I will not stand for another beast to come here and mate with her. The thought of someone else mating with my treasure makes me growl with rage.

My treasure sighs sleepily and I pat her for comfort.

"Do not fear my jewel," I say softly into her clean hair. The hair *I* cleaned. "No one will touch you. No one will take you."

"Oh dear," she says sleepily. "I think we're going to get in trouble for this. Correction, I think *I'm* going to get in trouble for this."

Anger spikes within me. "The only beast in trouble will be the person who tries to get inside this room."

* * *

Three hours later, an enemy tries to enter my domain. I leap out of bed, taking my treasure with me as I rage towards the antechamber door.

"Who is it?" I roar, nostrils flaring as I sense another dragon. A usurper. A villain.

My treasure, my jewel, protests against my chest.

"It's Francesca," comes the pert reply. "I demand to have a discussion with you."

Growling, I set my jewel on her feet and push her behind me so she cannot be seen by this interloper. Cracking the door open, I peer out.

Angry eyes flick down my body. "Where is she?"

"Who?" I narrow my eyes at her.

"That *whore* you purchased last night without my permission."

She cannot mean my treasure.

"Filth!" I spit, my power flaring in lethal concentration around me, making the threat clear. "Remove yourself at once."

Her mouth drops open as another dragon rapidly moves towards us. Kin, this time; she stands a respectful distance away as she addresses the interloper.

"Get away from him, Francesca. It's the treasure haze. He's not thinking properly."

"Oh, he's certainly thinking properly!" Francesca cries, stomping her foot. She glares at me, white steam leaving her nose. "I had hoped you'd enter the treasure haze for *me*, but apparently I wasn't enough." She points an angry, gold-tipped acrylic nail at me. "Damn you, Xander Drakos!"

"I was already damned before you came along. Get out of here before I kill you."

"I am your fire-sworn *wife*," she hisses, eyes flashing, her entire human body trembling with anger.

I recoil from the word, bile rising up my throat. Wrong. That word is all wrong. But the dragon in me recognises that we have, in fact, made a vow to this dragoness. Killing her is not an option. So, without another word, I slam the door in her face.

My treasure stares at me and I stare back in wonder. Brilliant blue eyes glint with many emotions I cannot decipher. I reach out and stroke her soft cheek. "Pretty," I murmur.

Her mouth drops open. "I don't think you meant to say that."

My frown is deep and profound. "Why not?"

"You're not yourself."

I gather her into my arms. "I must brush your teeth."

She makes an affronted sound. "This is normal, my jewel," I say reasonably. "I must care for you when you need it."

"I'm not dirty. You scrubbed me for all you were worth last night."

I grow pensive at the memory of said scrubbing, rubbing and...the pretty noises she made. "I am pleased you came for me."

She swears under her breath as I sit her on the edge of the washbasin.

"Open," I command, squeezing toothpaste onto her allocated brush. "You must be good and accept this is your life now."

She protests, but I begin brushing her teeth and she's forced to make nonsensical sounds and roll her eyes at me.

Her mouth is a fascinating thing and I take great pains to scrub each tooth until she begins to gag.

I allow her to spit into the sink.

"When this is over," she says, wiping the side of her mouth with a towel. "You can't blame me for any of it. And you can't talk to the other dragons that way."

Growling my dissent, I plonk her into the tub on her feet, climbing in after her. "No dragons may access my treasure. I don't care who they are." I turn on the shower, stepping under the stream to wash myself.

"What about your father?"

My power spans out like in a flare like the sun.

"Hot, hot, hot!" She attempts to flee the tub as the water heats up, but I pull her back and immediately withdraw my magic. "Apologies, my jewel. Do not speak of other males before me."

She splutters under the shower head before placing her small hands on my chest and pushing away.

"How long does this go on for?" she says, wiping water from her eyes. "Days? Or is it weeks?"

I quickly soap myself while she's distracted. "To what are you referring?"

"This!" She gestures to me, glaring.

"Shit," I say. "I forgot about the food. It was on the doorstep." I send Olly another message to bring us more. "I must feed you."

"Are you ignoring my question?"

Taking her by the shoulders, I arrange us so we have swapped places and take the bar of soap. "I do not wish to hurt your skin, just a quick wash."

"You can't touch me between the legs anymore," she says, eyes hard as she tries to glare. Instead, it's adorable. "Or here." She indicates her breasts, the nipples pebbled from the cool air.

"Why? I cannot leave those unattended." Sometimes jewels don't know what's best for them. "Every part must be polished until it glistens."

"I'm a person, not a gemstone!"

"No, you are something better." I rub the soap on my hands and set it aside, gently washing her breasts with my hands.

She groans. "Please, Goddess, this can't be right."

"Why does it feel right, then?" I growl, sweeping my palms over her nipples. I am overcome with desire so strong it drives everything else from my mind. I lean down and capture her nipple in my mouth.

"I must take care of you in every way," I murmur around her sweet, sensitive flesh. "I must treasure you."

I drop to my knees, hooking her knee over my shoulder. "And this part is telling me that it needs me." I dive between her legs, my mouth covering her sex. She cries out, yanking at my wet hair with one hand and bracing her other hand on the shower tile.

Sometimes polishing must be done with a mouth and tongue. I drag my tongue over her, listening to every movement and sound of her body because it feeds me. Her inner lips are dessert to my tongue and I savour them, slowly, completely. My lips find that swollen bud right at the top, a beacon to her pleasure. I suck gently, and she bucks into my mouth, crying out. I grin into her secret place, working that bud until her muscles clench around me.

I slide my hand up her inner thigh, and when I coat my fingers in her juices, she jerks.

"In here," I say, because she must understand how important this is. "I must attend to this."

"This is too much," she says. "We can't."

I remove my mouth and my hands, letting go of her completely so I can study her face and body. "Is it not good, my jewel? You appear to be enjoying this."

"Yes, but—" she says, her lips parting as she pants. I give her pussy a long, slow lick. "Oh Goddess, don't stop."

Happily, I seize her again, devouring her pussy with my mouth while stroking her entrance with a finger. She whimpers some number of pleases and Goddesses, and for some reason 'help,' so I do help her and breach her centre.

She cries out and I send my finger deeper. I'm met with a gush of fluids that I lap up immediately, licking faster and faster at her clit. She moans and I stroke her inside, a slow, lazy rhythm that makes her muscles loose. I have to hold her up as she whimpers. Grinning into her pussy, I work my pretty jewel, massaging her, licking and tasting until she screams, coming completely undone and all but collapsing onto my face.

My own cock is hard and pulsing, begging for release, but I must ensure my most precious treasure is attended to first.

"Good jewel," I say, hauling her into my arms and stepping out of the shower. "Very well done."

"Me or you?" she says, eyes drooping.

Something primal in me roars with satisfaction. A job well done. A treasure well cared for. Smiling, I set her down and dry her off thoroughly, before taking her back to bed. Our food is here, so I quickly retrieve the two trays. There is no one outside when I open the door, but there is a request for communication from another dragon.

"You have three days, Xander," my father drawls into my head. *"Three days until you face the consequences. Be ready."*

A challenge for *my* jewel? For *my* property?

The roar in my head is terrifying, and it shakes the room around me.

Chapter 16

Lyle

Scythe is not coping.

I see it in the evening as I watch him walk out of the ocean, glistening under the crescent moon. His gait is a prowl, his head bent in a predatory fashion, looking so shark-like that I suppress a shiver. He makes a beeline for me and I don't move, don't give way to his fury as he grabs my biceps in a terrifying grip that says he wants to massacre an entire lineage.

"I *need* her back." His voice is dark and malicious.

"I know," I snarl.

He gets into my face, furious, demanding my full attention. "You don't understand. I fucking need her, Lyle."

I close my eyes against the pain. The pain in his voice. The pain in my own heart. My ache for her grows day by day.

"The Clawsons need to die," he says. "I will remove them from existence with my bare fucking hands. They will have no lineage. Their ancestors will weep."

It's rare that I need to remind Scythe of his duties. Inhaling through my nose to subdue my own lion, I shake my head. "You promised Marduk. Titus belongs to Minnie, as does his death."

Scythe snarls, pushing away from me with a violent movement and turning his face towards the stars. "Where is Savage?"

"Tearing someone apart, I think." Casting an eye down the empty beach, my brow furrows as I put out a thought.

"*Leave me alone,*" comes the wolfish reply. His mouth may or may not be full of blood.

"*We return to the academy,*" Scythe tells him. "*We must discuss this with Marduk. He will know the best place to hit first.*"

"We're sure it's the Clawsons who did this?" I ask tentatively. "It's not some red herring, or bait?"

Scythe slowly shakes his head. "There were at least twenty felines used in this attack. The Clawsons were the leaders. Likely the feline king as well. They will all die for this."

I grimace. Ablo Obon had always been a friendly acquaintance of mine. Going up against him will be a sad day. But for what they did...what he was a part of? He deserves death. The death toll from The Lily Institute is profound. Thousands of flowers have already been laid at the shattered doors of the institute. It was pure luck that the assassin twins had been visiting Sabrina and gotten her out when their instincts had fired off.

But so many innocents had been unlucky.

"It's time to make them pay." I reassure my brother that I will always be on his side.

Scythe turns to me. "But will she forgive us for it?"

My mouth quirks up at the thought of my regina, with her fierce eyes and soft mouth. "She has a kind heart, but a thirst for revenge. I have a feeling she would approve."

Scythe nods, meeting my gaze as if he needs it. "I wonder what she's thinking right now. I wonder if they're caring for her properly."

My jaw clenches until I hear a crack. "Don't let your mind go there, Scythe. You'll go mad. Properly this time."

A muscle in his jaw pulses. "I can't stop thinking about it. I can't stop—" His hand goes over his right pec. "This agony I feel. It's like nothing I've experienced before. She needs to know what I feel for her."

Vulnerable Scythe feels dangerous. "She will know." I try to use a reassuring voice, but in truth, my mind has gone to the same places. "I think everyone will understand how much we love her soon enough."

"And Xander." Scythe's tone changes completely. Thunder booms in the distance and I eye my brother warily as the tide seems to change, seems to become furious. "He will know what his betrayal means to me too."

Chapter 47

Xander

8 years ago

Whoever these people are, they keep bothering me.

"I keep telling you to fuck off and you keep not listening," I snarl at the new, forever darkness that plagues me.

The wolf, from his scent, pats me on the head. "Calm down, brother. You need to listen to us."

I shove away from him. "Stop calling me that. I don't know you."

"Well, it's not my fault you can't see the mating mark!" he exclaims. "But I can see yours, mate, and I promise you, I'm your brother!"

"It's not possible," I snarl, waving off the hand I feel coming.

"Xander." This voice belongs to the shark. He smells of brine and darkness and I quieten to listen to his damaged voice. "Do you want to see again?"

The burn in my eye sockets hasn't gone away. Despite my dragon healing, despite the weeks that have passed, there is a permanent fiery buzz inside my head that makes me—

"I want to die," I say firmly. The shark says nothing. Blessedly, neither does the wolf. I sigh. "Okay, fine, I don't actually want to die, but I'll probably be killed soon enough. How many blind beasts do you know that live until old age? I'm a dead beast walking."

"I know one," Scythe says. "But you'll have to trust us enough to help you."

"Why *are* you helping me?"

The wolf sighs loudly, and I hear him dramatically move away. The shark, however, goes still. There's a knock in my mind, a request for communication I've only ever received from other dragons.

I frown, letting it in. *"You're our bond-brother, Xander."* The shark's voice is in my mind now. *"I know it may be hard to believe, but for some reason only the Wild Goddess knows, you share our mating mark."*

"You believe in the Wild Goddess?" I grumble.

"Everyone believes in something. And I also believe you can see again... I have a friend who might be able to teach you."

"Who?" I ask suspiciously.

The shark moves closer to me, and for some reason, I don't get the urge to cringe away. "His name is Eko. He's a Greenland shark who sees with magic."

Chapter 18

Aurelia

Three days.

For three confusing, heavenly, agonising days, Xander takes care of his *jewel*, as he now calls me. It's him—haughty, arrogant, predatory Xander—and yet *not*. It's as if all inhibition, all the parts he'd lost to hate and anger have returned to him. That perhaps I've gotten a glimpse of the person he might have been if whatever awful thing that had happened to him never did.

I had never asked Minnie about it because it was a sensitive topic, but my anima still calls for him. I'd thought it was a broken, lonely call into the dark, never to be returned. A wound that would never heal. Just as sad as the story of the last Kauai bird. The last of his species calling to a mate who didn't exist.

And yet, in these three days, the call *is* returned. My soul no longer calls into a void. Wherever I turn, he's there, earnest, serious in his invented duty to me. How can a broken heart deny itself that medicine? How can a broken bone decline healing?

It can't.

Xander feeds me, keeps me warm, strokes my hair, whispers pretty things. I watch him as closely as he watches me, looking for any sign of the end of this treasure haze, as it's called. I had no idea what that would look like, but in a far corner of my mind, a quarantined corner meant to keep me safe and sane, I know it will be ugly.

At dawn on the fourth day, I find out what that looks like.

Xander wakes up. Slowly, with that predatory grace only monstrous animals possess, he walks naked to the window and opens it.

I recognise this immediately because at no stage during the three days did he leave my skin or open the window. So I too slowly get up and a sense of self-preservation moves me to the other side of the room.

When he speaks, his voice has the deathly seriousness of a man about to lose his mind and is trying hard to stop that rhinoceros' charge. "I want you out of my sight. I never want to see you again."

A chill breaks out along my bones.

I blink at his form. Utter naked perfection, gilded in sunlight that could inspire ancient Greek sculptors.

Whatever crucial thing in me that broke the day he formally rejected me, doesn't break again. It shatters into fine dust. And it makes me feel worse than before. There's an eternal cold inside my heart, one that has nothing to do with my great white shark form.

Silently, I turn around and press on the wall panel that contains my two dresses. It opens and I shove one over my head. Quiet as a mouse, I escape through the front door, closing it behind me.

Despite my racing heart, I feel lifeless. Guilt and shame hover at the edges of me, like hungry serpents ready to tear my throat to shreds. I don't even know where I'm going, I just duck under the new ropes that cordon off the wing and head down the grand stairs.

But they all know. They're all waiting.

Flores, Francesca, Lady Drakos, Selena, and a whole bunch of servants are assembled in the entrance hall.

"There she is," Francesca hisses as I clear the final step. "Seize her."

Flores flicks his wrist and a gold chain snaps towards me directly from his hand, latching onto my collar with brutal force.

I stumble backwards before he heaves his arm and I go flying towards the floor. I break my fall just in time, my palms slapping on the cold tiles with a loud snap of flesh. Flores yanks again and I'm dragged across the ground towards them. My hands fly up to the chain, pain blasting through my neck as the melded flesh tears anew. I end up on my back, sliding over the tiles until I land before them.

Flores and Francesca's upside-down forms stare at me. The dragon king shakes his head in dismay while his daughter-in-law crosses her arms and glares.

"You've ruined this family," she hisses.

"Hardly my fault," I mutter.

"You're right," Flores says, and I blink up at him at this unexpected response, with hardly any energy or motivation to get off the floor. "This is hardly your fault too." He gestures to Francesca.

The smug dragoness shows me her phone and a news report with the headline:

LILY INSTITUTE DEVASTATION— Hundreds of patients
left homeless after 'freak' accident.

Below it is a photo of the crumbling remains of the biggest mental health hospital in the country. If I could sink any lower into the floor I would. That had been Scythe's pride and joy. His life's work. And because of the auction, because of the greed of these bastards, they'd destroyed something important and beautiful.

Steps sound from behind me. I lift my head just enough to see that at the top of the stairs stands the dragon heir, in a fresh black suit and shirt. His face is grim, his jaw clenched.

"I'm ready," he says.

"You are not," Flores sneers.

I don't know what happens to Xander after that. What the consequences of his purchase of me are. All I know is, after the scientists check me over in their lab, I'm taken back to Flores Drakos' room, where my cage has been moved.

And that night, as I lie curled as small as I can in the corner of the cage of the grand room, I hear Flores fucking someone who is definitely not his wife.

It's not until I hear him say her name that a trickle of disgust makes its way through the numbness.

"Francesca," Flores moans.

Chapter 49

Xander

Blood Upon the Snow — Hozier & Bear McCreary

There is no coming back from this shame. The shame I've caused my family, the shame I've entombed around myself. And sitting in my father's office, opposite him and my new fire-sworn wife, I'm half convinced they're going to kick me out again.

I watch them dully. Emotionless. There is nothing in me anymore. No anger. No fury or rage or irritation.

Something in me died four nights ago. That's the only explanation for what came after.

"For three days," my father states, "I've been asking myself the same inane question." He narrows his eyes at me. "What demon possessed my heir the night of the auction? Was it a plot against me? Against the family? Some elaborate, long-planned revenge?" He shrugs. "But no, I almost immediately ruled that out because you couldn't be so intelligent nor so stupid as to construct a plan so obvious and dim-witted as that."

I don't miss the way Francesca's lips twitch. No doubt she's plotting her own revenge.

Father leans forward, clasping his hands upon his desk. "I've decided it was your mother's genes at play. The berserker gene transformed into an evolved form of insanity."

He could very well be right. Not much is known about the berserker dragons as they were all hunted and put down. My mother was saved that fate by her beauty and the fact that my father claimed her and promised to keep her controlled. The council at the time accepted that and let them live their lives as long as the terms were fulfilled.

"However, your temporary insanity has put us into a dire position," my father says frankly. "More than one wealthy beast is out for our family's blood. By all rights, I should remove you as my heir."

I sense there is a 'but' coming.

"Luckily," my father continues, "the newest member of our family has proven to be of sound mind."

Francesca smiles at my father, a pleased, ugly expression as she says, "The only solution is to keep you shackled."

At one time, hearing this might have sent me into a rage. Might have sent me destroying this room and the people in it. But today, the sound of my Uncle Fabian and Ragnar stepping into the office from behind me makes me feel nothing but cold.

I don't even turn to look at them as they each take a wrist of mine and secure it with an obsidian shackle.

Immediately, my vision blinks out, along with any trace of fire and my powers as a dragon.

A blind man might as well be a dead man.

Francesca inhales sharply. She's never seen me without my glowing eyes, and unfortunately for everyone who has to lay eyes upon me, empty and scarred eye sockets are a fucking ugly sight.

Luckily, my hearing picks up the slack and I'm able to get to my feet without falling over like the fool that I am.

"Anything else, Father?"

"You are not to leave the house unless I say so. You are not to communicate with anyone outside the house. I will confiscate your phone and all electronics."

Less than dead, then. For once, I wish I had Scythe's ability to go cold, or Savage's ability to go unhinged.

Instead, I am left with nothing at all. A fire that has been put out. All that is left is smoke.

"Very well," I say. "I will await further instruction."

"You do that," Francesca huffs.

Chapter 50

Aurelia

If I thought there was nothing worse than being chained to Xander, I was wrong. Being chained to his father is much worse.

Luckily, I'm too numb to really feel it when his hand slides down my ass for the first time in his office. Or when I'm told to kneel on the floor by his seat the entire time he has his meetings. Some of them are in person, some of them are on screen. The first meeting is with Fabian Drakos, and the fucker runs his thumb along my bottom lip with great interest, then tugs experimentally on my hair before taking his seat.

They talk of things I don't even hear, because there's a ringing in my ears that makes hearing anything impossible.

Or caring about anything.

The next meeting is with Ragnar Firewing, the father of Selena's children, and I barely pay attention to that too. In some weird power play between the two dragons, Ragnar requests to touch my breasts. Flores declines with an arrogant drawl.

I fall asleep after that, my head bowing as Flores speaks figures and plans with people on his computer screen. It's not until the evening when Francesca arrives, standing primly before me, that I'm forced to wake up.

Because she yanks me up by the hair. I grunt, getting my feet under me just in time before she slaps my face, hard. I choke on my own spit before she slaps me on the other side for good measure.

"Whore," she hisses. "You reek of him." She paces the room, huffing and puffing, her face pink and shoulders heaving.

Flores chuckles. "Get it out of your system, my love, but leave some for tonight."

Francesca points at me. "You might have escaped this week," she spits. "But the first beast to take you won't have as much class as us. You will be expected to *perform*." She addresses Flores now. "Why don't we just strap her down and inseminate her with your chosen ally? We could make a healthy sum if we do it now. Her heat is due any time now and it would placate everybody."

Flores nods. "Great minds, Francesca. I've already put the plans in place for a private auction. The Collector will not pass up the chance."

"Nor will Lord Agnis," Francesca nods. "He's especially impatient."

"As am I," Flores murmurs. "Let us go to dinner."

"Not with her," the dragoness sneers. "She only gets dog food from now on."

The next three days are the same. I sit by Flores Drakos' knee in his office, and when he doesn't tote me around, I'm locked in my cage in his room, forced to hear him loudly fuck Francesca every night.

I understand pretty quickly that he's trying to get her pregnant. It has to be the only reason he hasn't tried with me.

I don't see Xander or any of the other family members. They only feed me tiny brown kibble in my dog bowl, and on the second day, I'm lightheaded and desperate enough to try some. It's actually not bad, and if I squint a certain way, it tastes like Vegemite.

The worst part is that I'm not allowed to use his bathroom.

The servants, a new set of humans who don't talk to me, actually take me outside three times a day. None of them want to do the job the old-fashioned way, so they all end up sneaking me into the servant's toilet in their quarters under the castle.

Got to count your blessings where you get them.

Finally, on a day that I think might be the fourth, Flores tells his butler he's going out for the day for an important business meeting.

I assume the business is me, but they don't take me and he tells everyone to keep me in my cage. After he leaves, I sigh in great annoyance because my back is starting to hurt from being cooped up in there. The numerous servants all look around sort of sheepishly.

"It's the children, miss," one says quietly. "They're asking for you. Daily. Miss Selena was hoping you could come down to the garden for a bit now that His Majesty is out."

The butler hisses in shock. "You can't do that! He'll have our heads!"

"Miss Selena will take the blame," she says quickly. "She said so herself."

My voice emerges as a croak from disuse, but the thought of sun on my skin and the sight of the open sky sparks a light in me. "Let's go then."

* * *

Lady Drakos sits in a chair, arranging flower pots on a trestle table. Her hair is tied in a chignon and she wears white long sleeves protecting her arms from the warm sunlight. "Aurelia, darling!" she says with delight. "There you are!"

Eugene rushes at me, squawking loudly, as his bedazzled goggles reflect the sun and he peers at me to check if I'm okay. I catch him in my arms with a pained grimace and he pecks at me affectionately.

"I'm glad to see you all," I say quietly, letting Eugene down. He presses himself against my leg.

"Are you alright?" Selena asks worriedly, getting up from her crouch and lifting her sun hat to get a better look at me. Then she pinches her nose. "Stupid question. I'm sorry."

I rub my tummy where there's now a constant, empty sort of burn. "There aren't any snacks around here, are there?"

Selena jumps as if she's remembered. "Oh yes, of course. I'll send for some right away." She rushes off to speak with one of the maids waiting nearby. I almost smile at the thought of real food.

"Lia!" Emmerson cries. The twins are crouched amongst a line of strawberry bushes, broad-brimmed hats covering their inky hair and in matching yellow overalls and gumboots. "Where have you been? Look at this massive strawberry!"

I all but jump over to the little boy and the basket of fruit he carries. He holds up the biggest one for my inspection, and I squint at it with great importance. "Can I have it?"

Emmerson giggles. "Yeah, but we have to wash it— Hey!"

I've snatched it from his gloved hand and shoved the entire thing into my mouth before he can finish his sentence.

"You might choke!" Delilah cries, rushing over and wiping her dirty hands on her overalls.

The hairs on the backs of my arms stand on end as I swallow the strawberry. I rub at my skin, glancing up at the sky.

"Have another!" Emmerson says, wiping off a second strawberry. "This time, chew carefully or you'll choke."

I take it from him with a forced smile, chomping on half of it and using my teeth like a normal person. "It tastes so good. Are you guys adding sugar to the soil or something?"

Emmerson makes a face, his cheeks a pink from the sun. "They're sort of sour, actually. Mother is preparing cream for us to eat them with!"

Delilah licks her lips and nods, showing me her basket laden with crimson cherries.

As I lean in to inspect her haul, a chill runs down my spine and I straighten to glance around us again.

A barely perceptible boom, sort of like an aeroplane, rumbles over us.

"What's that sound?" I say, wiping juice from my chin.

Eugene promptly keels over, falling flat on his face. Delilah and I lunge for him with a cry.

Emmerson frowns at the bird before looking around and scanning the sky. "Yeah, I heard it—" He quietens before he shouts, "Look!"

It happens so quickly.

I turn around to see a massive, fast-moving shadow in the sky.

Selena's scream shoots across the grass. Both children set off running towards their mother. But the back lawn is so expansive, so huge, that when the mighty cloud-coloured dragon swoops down, none of us are close enough to stop it from snatching up Delilah in his car-sized claws.

The scream that tears out of Delilah's throat is enough to curdle my blood.

And set it on fire.

My bare feet are pounding over the grass as I tear my dress off and shift into my favoured form. My wedge-tail eagle wings pump hard and with relish after so long cramped inside my body.

A dragon might be faster than an eagle in open air, but they're also heavy, and the effort it takes him to heave himself up into the sky after such a low swoop is massive. He's slow and I catch up within seconds.

In the back of my mind, I wonder why neither Lady Drakos nor Selena have shifted, but I don't dwell on it. Lashing out with my telekinesis, I try to drag Delilah out from the dragon's claws.

Delilah screams again, punching at the claws entrapping her. "Let me go!" But those claws only squeeze her small body tighter and she squeals in pain.

My mind scrambles. I've never been faced with a dragon before. Never thought of how I'd bring one down. But a phantom Savage's voice appears in my head. *Get him in the soft parts, regina.*

But eagle claws are no match for a dragon's hide. The dragon wheels around, heading out of Drakos Estate. I need to act fast.

I blast through his natural protections with a ferocious cry, seizing his heart in my mind like I've seen Scythe do. Those powerful chambers shudder under my grip and the dragon falters in mid-air. I squeeze tighter and his wings tremble.

I hold that massive heart with all my might, squeezing, *squeezing.*

And then he stops moving completely and his eyes close as he falls from the sky. His claw opens up and Delilah goes tumbling out of his hold.

I let the dragon's heart go and nose dive for Delilah, who's shrieking in terror as she plummets, her two plaits streaming upwards. She reaches a hand out for me and my claws close around her forearm. Completely taking on her weight, I madly beat my wings, whipping out my telekinesis to keep us both aloft.

We're so high off the ground that Drakos Estate looks tiny beneath us. I descend rapidly, letting Delilah's weight pull us down and sweeping my wings to regulate our speed.

A heaving choked sound comes from somewhere in the distance, followed by a thump, and I know that the white dragon has fallen outside the estate somewhere. I turn around to look and see a bomb-sized dust cloud and a massive body scrambling to take flight once again. This time, away from us.

I'd been too distracted on the way up, but entering the estate from the top, I feel it when we pass through the aerial protections of Drakos Estate. It has a dome just like the one at Animus Academy. How, then, did this enemy dragon get through?

I glance behind us again, and the dragon is speeding away into the distance.

It's not until we're in line with the lower turrets of the castle that I sigh in relief, my heart banging against my ribs. Delilah sobs beneath me, clutching onto my legs like the lifeline they are.

Selena, along with about a dozen servants, sprint towards us. "Oh, Wild Goddess!" Selena cries. When we're low enough that Delilah's legs skim the grass, she tumbles out of my grip and straightens before breaking into a sprint. I land on the grass and watch the little girl safe in her mother's arms. They both sob, clutching on to each other.

My heart pounds with adrenaline, my wings wanting to take flight again. That had been close. Way too close. Who the hell was trying to steal Drakos hatchlings? It had to be in some kind of retaliation for the events of the past weeks.

After a moment, Selena wipes her eyes and catches mine. "If it weren't for you, Lia, he would've taken her! He would've taken her!"

I stand there in eagle form, panting, staring at them at all.

In my furore, my question comes out in a scream, directed at Selena via telepathy. *"Why didn't you shift?"*

She blinks at me.

"Selena, why didn't you shift?"

In the quietest voice, she says. "I'm not permitted to."

I stare at her in a mixture of horror and disbelief.

A shadow appears to the side and I look up to see Xander's towering form, standing frozen in shock, staring at me with empty eye sockets and obsidian shackles.

Chapter 51

Xander

Creep — Radiohead

I thought I knew all the agonies a person could suffer.

But I was so incredibly wrong.

Because listening from a high window as my niece was being stolen by another dragon, while I was pathetically helpless to stop it, is a new level of pain. My power had been taken away from me, and with it, my autonomy. My authority.

For seemingly eternal moments, I listen to the aftermath. Spawn remains in eagle form, mahogany feathers rustling in the breeze as adrenaline courses through her body and she remains alert for further enemies. Her lungs inflate with air, her beak remains slightly open as her breath sucks in and out.

And somehow, I can just tell that those blue eyes are accusingly staring me down.

You did nothing, she's thinking. *It was me who saved her.*

While Emmerson is secured inside, Delilah remains in my sister's arms, where she's being squeezed hard but doesn't care as she sniffs and blubbers her misery.

"Get inside," I command my sister. The pale dragon might have fled, but there was still a chance he could return.

Sissy's head snaps up at my words like she's suddenly remembered we're still out in the open and she bundles Delilah up and hurries inside. I hardly know why I do it—habit, perhaps—but I flick my wrist and that old golden chain finds its place on Spawn's collar.

Without another word, I head inside after Sissy and Delilah.

The protections around Drakos Estate are ancient, fortified monthly by my father and again by me when I arrived. There's no way any dragon could have silently breached the area at all, let alone without me knowing. There is only one explanation.

My sister hurries Delilah towards the kitchen, where Emmerson is nervously waiting. I, however, head downstairs, towards the dungeons.

Spawn has to shift to keep up with my stride, but to my surprise, she chooses her wolf form of midnight fur. Some far away part of me recognises she must be thinking about Savage, but at the forefront of my mind is a single need.

My business shoes hit the flagstones of the dungeon floor, because I'm not bothering to hide that I'm coming.

As expected, neither Ghoul or any of the other serpent generals are anywhere to be heard. There are only the scientists typing on their computers, processing files and samples. Solomon and a few others stop their chatter.

"My lord," Solomon says, getting to his feet. "We weren't expecting—"

I may not have my power. I may not have physical vision, but I have everything else. I stride right up to him, and my hands take the sides of his face and snap it hard to the side.

The rest of them try to run, but a growling wolf at the door blocks their path. I'm on them in an instant, and one by one, they fall, their heads twisted at odd angles.

It doesn't take me long to find lengths of rope in a storage closet. Once I've tied them all up, I fetch one of the heavy-duty trolleys the scientists use for transporting equipment.

Working without my power is annoying, but I can manage just fine. There is more than one way to skin a snake.

There's a bit of fuss and bother going up the stairs with the trolley, but I manage it in the end, carrying it most of the way. Through it all, I feel Spawn's eyes on me.

When I get up to the open turret that is our launching pad, I arrange my bounty carefully and in the traditional manner. First, by tying the rope around their necks and securing the other end of the rope to metal stakes cemented into the stone just for this purpose. Finally, I throw their bodies over the ramparts, where they dangle for all to see.

Where, to a good pair of eyes, they'll be visible for a great distance.

I inhale the afternoon air, deeply and thoroughly. Behind me, Spawn does the same. I angle my face towards the sky, where I know it must shine bright blue. The warmth of the sun doesn't reach my darkest places. Perhaps it never will.

Her heart beats behind me. A little fast, but steady. No fear comes from her. Unlike me, her power is free for all to feel if she chooses. Right now, it sways around her like a tree in the wind. She is, no doubt, conflicted. She has never taken on a dragon before and come out the victor. Very few beasts can claim such a fact.

From one of those dark, lost places within me, the words come out between clenched teeth. "Thank you."

Chapter 52

Ghoul

Deep in our brand-new underground facility, I have the head of the Serrated Serpent between my fingers. He's a death adder, and I'm one of the few he permits to milk him.

Us generals all milk each other.

"What are you smiling about, Lord Basilisk?" Charlotte Naga asks me from where she's writing the labels for our contributions.

"Things not meant for a lady's ears," I say smoothly, observing the volume of the milky liquid. "All done."

I release the old adder, and he slithers away for his turn in the shedding cave.

"I've often wondered what goes on in your mind," Charlotte says a little tightly as I hand her the container.

"Death," I say simply.

Her entire body flinches at that. I don't particularly care if she's forgiven me for executing her mate, Ben, but that flinch tells me she's still affected by it. She can't really complain, can she? Not when her brother was the one who ordered it. Not when her mate helped the snakelet.

"They say that you see them," Charlotte says quietly, marking off something on her list. "The dead."

"I'm not a shark," I say, beckoning to the next general to slither forth.

"So you don't?" Charlotte presses.

I take the Adder by his serpentine face. He bares his fangs and I angle the container under him. Only after he pierces the plastic, I reply, "I didn't say that."

At that point, Mace Naga walks into the clinical room. "What is the status of the venom stores?"

"We're getting there," Charlotte says, consulting her list. "Since we tripled the venom tax, we're well on our way—"

"That's not what I want to hear, Charlotte," Mace says tersely. "I want the numbers. Have we replenished the stock that was destroyed or not?"

"Not yet," Charlotte says quickly.

"Well, perhaps—" He stops short, frowning and pushing up one heavy sleeve. Before our eyes, five of the black tattoos on his skin fade into nothing. Uh-oh. "Pull up surveillance of Drakos Estate."

I get out my phone and message the two serpents we have hidden in the trees outside the dragon's lair. It takes a few minutes for the photos to come through.

What I see makes my heart race. I show the king.

"That's the entire team," I say with surprise.

Mace stiffens, and for the first time, he runs a hand through his hair.

"He figured it out immediately," I say quietly. Of course he did. Xander is far too clever.

"He can't have spoken to Flores yet," Mace says, quickly pulling out his phone. "I'll get to him first." He leaves the room, dialling the dragon king's number as he goes.

"Such a shame," I say conversationally to the room. "I really enjoyed my time there."

Chapter 53

Xander

Four Seasons (Winter) — Vivaldi

There are few joys left to me in this world, but one of them is the piano. Both of us children were trained on the piano, violin and flute since we could walk, and even though the piano has called to me little of late, I'm compelled to it now. My fingers skim across the keys, finding familiar and comforting chords that ease into my chest and soothe the sharpness inside of me.

The best part of it is that I don't even need to see to enjoy it. I don't even need my earphones in either. I can just be free to listen and feel the vibrations in the air. Let the waves of it crest and plunge into my ears in a rhythm that's mine alone.

It's here that my father finds me when he storms through the castle, a light-footed Francesca in tow. Two cosy peas in a pod. Perhaps she's the son he wished he had.

Father's heat slams into the room like a sledgehammer, dangerously vibrating the air around me. "You don't know what you've done!" He stops a distance from the piano. My fingers never falter upon the keys.

His chest heaves with rage, his power licking furiously

around him. But I answer him simply, not taking my focus off the keys. "I did what I had to do. Those worms would've tried to kill us in our sleep as soon as they had the chance."

His chest rumbles. "That was our entire fertility team."

"Mace's team," I correct. "And they betrayed us."

"You have no proof. If you hadn't broken your bond, I would have suspected *you* for this and cut out your cursed heart. Mace was not involved."

Those words hover between us, my fingers trailing off gentle notes before I answer quietly. "You know it wasn't me, but someone did let that dragon in."

"Mace thinks it was the wolves."

Ruben's lot. "It wouldn't be in their best interests to betray me."

"Nor Mace's!" he roars. "You are a fool and completely useless. The damage control itself!" He takes a step toward me. "Perhaps I should not have listened to Mace when he told me to take you back." With that, he whirls around and storms out.

Shock makes my fingers trip over the keys. Mace. Fucking. Naga.

Francesca hovers for a moment. "This entire thing is your fault. That dragon wanted revenge for things *you* did. No one else but *you*."

I continue playing as if they'd never come in. According to our database of records, the only dragons that pale in this country were Chen dragons. No doubt Nadine's family felt slighted by my choosing of Francesca over her and wanted to assert their dominance. But to parlay with a serpent to gain entry was something no one expected. I knew Mace was cunning, but this is a game of a new level.

Five minutes later, I hear the roar of Father's lungs as he coasts above the castle, crying out his anger and challenge to the world.

He patrols for hours, no doubt plotting his revenge against

the Chens. We hear him every so often, fortifying the protections and roaring into the dark.

Eventually, I put my earphones back in and pay a visit to my sister and mother in their nightly drawing room. To my surprise, I can hear Spawn's eagle's breath from the corner. I'd left her with them, but had not expected her to remain in this form. The twins and Eugene have formed a nest of pillows and cuddle next to her, apparently finding comfort there.

Spawn is more shaken than I anticipated. Occasionally, her feathers tremble.

"Are you alright, Sissy?" I ask.

Selena lets out a long-suffering sigh from where she's cocooned in a blanket on the couch. "We're fine, Xander. Thanks to Lia."

That stings, but I swallow it down. "Mother?"

"I am well, my son," she says, sipping from a sherry glass, which tells me she's not, in fact, well. She rarely drinks alcohol, yet her voice is louder today, her breath less laboured. "Xander," she continues, and I turn to her keenly. "You should attend to your wife. I have a feeling she's shaken by the events of today as well."

The disappointment may have been clear in my body language because I can practically hear my mother give an uncharacteristic scowl. "You must attend to your duties. I fear she has not been happy."

"Of course, Mother," I say dutifully. "I will see how I can help her." But I don't leave. I stand there, lamely for a moment. Just...listening.

Emmerson coos to Spawn, stroking her feathers. Spawn exhales a long breath, her heart suddenly kicking up its tempo like the climax of a song. She swallows, then shifts as Delilah feeds her something. Cake, from the scent.

Suddenly, I realise from the silence that Selena is watching me. So is my mother.

"Xander," Selena murmurs.

"I'm going," I reassure her.

Feeling like I'm being dismissed from the drawing room, I leave without protest, shutting the door behind me. Something makes me pause outside the door.

Sometimes being without my sight feels akin to being lonely. I *am* missing a crucial part of me, so it only makes sense, I suppose. Inside the drawing room, Selena pours Mother another drink and Emmerson giggles at something.

Spawn makes a small bird sound that makes both hatchlings giggle. My heart clenches. That treasure haze is long gone, but something is making me linger by the door. I wish I knew why I was given this misfortune. Why I had to be the sole dragon bound to a Boneweaver.

Why I was the only one who'd had the gall to sever it. And why, at every turn, I was led further down the path to misery. I lean against the wall next to the door, listening to my family.

I'd done everything I could to return to them, so why does it still feel like I'm still utterly alone?

* * *

When Francesca returns to my room that night, I'm waiting for her in my chair by the fireplace.

Her bare feet slap against the stones before she tries to quietly open the door. "I thought you'd be asleep," she says upon seeing me.

When I catch a whiff of her, that scent of my sire and his cum, I feel nothing. No spark of anger. No boom of fury. There is only dull emptiness. There is only the dark.

My voice sounds like it's cut from cardboard. "I couldn't do anything today. Because of the shackles."

She pauses at the threshold to the bedroom, watching me for signs of violence. She swallows. "Well, it was supposed to be a punishment. Perhaps now you'll understand what I'm going through."

Through the dull shadows of my mind, a flicker of orange flame lights up a silhouette of dry, bare branches. I set my whiskey glass down. "I hope you don't mean that witnessing the kidnap of my niece was intended as a punishment for me."

She takes a step back from me and swallows again. Despite her fear, her tinny voice remains sharp. "I permit them to come off."

I remain silent.

Francesca clears her throat. "We are leaving in the morning. It's high time we visit my parents at their holiday home. They wish to see me before they return to Melbourne."

"I'm guessing you planned this with my father already."

"You'd be correct."

"Was that before or after you fucked him?"

She's silent with shock. I don't know why, because she's done nothing to hide it tonight. Or any other night.

"When you would not consummate the marriage, he offered...and I accepted."

I snort. "Don't think this will somehow protect you. He will use you for your body, and then when he tires of the novelty, he'll return to the arms of one of his favoured mistresses. That's how it's always been."

Her voice twists with fury. "You have no right to speak of such things! Not after what you did!"

I rise to my feet. "Where is the key?"

She reaches for the fine chain around her neck and pulls out the key from between her breasts. When she throws it, I snatch it out of the air and unlock the shackles, placing them carefully on the table.

My power returns like a tired candle spluttering back to life. I have to funnel my magic up and into my empty eye sockets. It pools there for a second, creating new eyeballs as my eyelids pop over them. I see white light first before that fades away and the darkened room comes into view, aglow with only the light from the embers of the fireplace.

Francesca stands frowning and defensive before me, a fist holding the edges of her robe together.

But I'm distracted by something over her shoulder.

I catch a glimpse of myself in the gilded mirror on the opposite wall. Suddenly, I don't know the man who stares back at me. Perhaps I never knew him. Unbidden, my hand reaches up to touch the skin under my right eye. The fine scars made by my father's claws. The old ache pulses within my sockets. Sometimes I still get phantom pains, but most days I don't notice them.

"He should have ended it that day, you know," I say faintly. "No one would have stopped it. But it wasn't *enough* for him. The pain he inflicts is always calculated. And he thought it would be a slow, agonising death that lasted years. That was his...hope."

Then Scythe and Savage had found me lying hopelessly in the rain. And they changed everything. Scythe introduced me to Eko, and the Greenland shark had taught me how to see. I'd been a useless student at first, but eventually, under the patience of both sharks, I'd learned.

I never knew beasts could be patient like that. That males could be gentle and understanding of the nuances of a teenager in pain.

Then years later I find out that he is mate to Aurelia's mother. That knowledge had shaken me, that night on the beach when Athena Boneweaver had died in Eko's arms.

My mentor, the beast who had given me the greatest gift also had a regina. And he'd grieved for her loss like he loved her.

"He did what he thought was right at the time," Francesca says through gritted teeth. "It was his right as a father."

I'd almost forgotten she's still standing there. So she'd heard the story of my eyes being taken, likely from gossip, because none of the servants had reported her asking the question in her detailed interrogation of them.

"It's also the responsibility of a father to protect his offspring," I say in that dead voice.

"Do not speak ill of him when he took you back in," she says, lip curling in contempt. "He didn't *have* to take you back."

And the price he'd asked was for me to curse myself. My dragon unfurls his wings, snorting in distaste. With my power back, he glares at me, and those fragments of memories from times long past flicker through my mind once again.

Torment. That's all it wants from me. Except a dead man feels nothing.

I turn away and head to the entrance of the suite.

"Where are you going?" she demands.

"I'm going to patrol our lands," I say. "I'll be ready to leave at dawn, as you asked."

Chapter 54

Xander

8 years ago

The beach is cold and I clutch the sides of my jacket together as I stumble over a soft mound of sand.

"Fuck!" I cry.

"Here, let me—"

"No!" I violently wave off the wolf's arm, except the movement unbalances me and I go crashing in the opposite direction. Scythe catches me and firmly sets me back upright.

I scowl into the night air.

I'm learning, slowly, the difference between the sounds of night and day. Time moves excruciatingly slowly right now, and all I have for input are the sounds and smells around me.

I suppose it's just lucky that Father didn't take my ear drums. He probably could have, except the eyes had felt like the worse torment at the time.

"Just a little further," Scythe says in that broken voice of his. That's the three of us. Three, broken boys. All of us fucked up in some way. Savage's was a little more hidden than mine, but all he had to do was start speaking and you could see it.

Even now, he bounds before me, kicking up sand with a completely mad hooting.

The ocean feels loud in my ears above the crazy wolf's laughter. I'd never noticed how it seemed to crash. Each droplet making it's own noise until it became a cacophony. An orchestra with no conductor.

Gulls call out to my left, the wind tugs at my hair and something in the ocean stirs.

"What's the moon like?" I ask quietly.

"Round," Savage says.

"Beautiful," Scythe says. "A hunter's moon. Here he comes."

I strain my ears for all they're worth, trying to sort through the sounds like a sieve. Everything is just loud. Then, the movement of wet sand, the press of heavy, broad feet. Someone with lungs much bigger than mine takes a breath.

"Scythe Kharkorous has brought me a friend," comes the husky voice. It's deep and coming from high up. This is a big animus.

"Eko, this is Xander, the young man I was telling you about."

Eko's big body steps before me. He smells fresh and briny. He takes my face in one wet hand, turning it side to side. I suppress a cringe at being inspected. "You are not broken, dragon," he says. "You are not injured." My stomach tightens. "You are steel waiting to be re-forged."

I swallow through a thick throat.

"Are you willing to bathe in fire?"

My nostrils flare as I suppress the sudden burn where my eyes should be. "Yes."

"Are you willing to cast aside everything that you are, to learn to see what others do not?"

I pause at that. Everything that I am? "My father has already taken everything that I was. I am nothing right now. No one."

He makes a deep sound, a whisper of a chuckle. "Dragons do not lose themselves so easily, Xander *Drakos*. A fish may lose himself in the ocean, but a dragon does not lose himself in the sky."

The thought of flight makes my head spin. The thought of never doing it again makes me want to vomit. To my great embarrassment a sob darts like a thief out of my lips.

Eko puts a hand on my shoulder and to my surprise I find it reassuring. "You have not lost your heart," he says gently. "That is good. You will need it."

Chapter 55

Aurelia

I know Xander and Francesca have left the estate because Flores orders me to dress and takes me down to breakfast this morning.

Their places are blessedly empty and the twins are quiet as they eat—except to demand that I sit next to them. Eugene is also absent, as Flores won't allow him at the table, Selena has been keeping him tucked in the nursery during meal times.

Despite Francesca being gone, Flores is in a good mood and allows me to take a spot at the table for the first time. Is it his way of saying thank you for rescuing Delilah? Surely not.

I take my seat between the twins. Emmerson gives me a chipolata and most of the wilted spinach off his plate. I smile at him and scoop up the entire wad of spinach, shoving it into my mouth.

The little dragon grins at me before turning his face down to his food. A hand approaches me from my left and I turn to see Lady Drakos' delicate, veined hand reaching out to pat my own. She smiles at me, and I notice her mythical eyes have a new sort of sparkle.

"Will you be a dear and fetch my tonic, Aurelia?" she asks.

A slender trolley sits by the window behind me, her day's three bottles sitting expectantly on top.

"Of course, Lady Drakos," I say quietly. "With your juice again?"

She nods and I take her cup to the trolley.

"I hope Xander and Francesca have a productive trip," Flores says as the butler pours black coffee into his mug.

"Indeed," Lady Drakos replies. "Francesca's parents will be most pleased to spend time with their daughter."

Something in my chest squeezes at the words.

I'd been someone's daughter once.

Blinking hard, I take my time at the trolley, gazing out the windows as I stirred the mixture in the glass, before turning back around and returning the cup to Lady Drakos.

"Hopefully they'll have good news on the way soon," Flores says mildly.

I almost keel over as I make my way back to my chair.

"Does that mean we'll have cousins?" Delilah says, frowning. "I hope Uncle Xander doesn't forget about us."

Flores chuckles. "I'm sure he won't forget you, but hatchlings of rare breeds are important for the community, are they not, Aurelia?"

Luckily, I've seated myself this time. "Certainly," I say tightly.

Selena glances at me with unmistakable worry.

"Hopefully we'll expect good news from you too, Aurelia," Flores finishes.

I stare at my plate, darkness swirling in my stomach. Without Mace's scientists, what are the dragon king's plans? What are Mace's plans?

I'm suddenly highly aware of the fact that Xander is *not* here.

We eat in silence for fifteen more minutes, and I don't miss the look of warning Selena throws my way.

"Well, we must be on our way," Flores says, pushing his chair back. He gestures to me. "Come along, Aurelia."

Lady Drakos and Selena have gone very quiet. I avoid looking at them both, silently pushing my chair back and going around the table towards Flores. With the flick of his wrist, any illusion of a normal family breakfast is gone, and I'm leashed once again.

We head outside to a Rolls Royce with its engine already running.

There's not a serpent in sight, of course. No Ghoul, flashing his fangs at me with a snarky greeting. There are only Lunaris wolves, staring me down with hard, unforgiving eyes.

Raquel has been in the back of my mind, still trapped down there in the dark. Minnie and Stacey are probably beside themselves, but at least I know they'll be looking after our wolf anim's body.

As chilling as this is, nothing makes a fell tingle crawl down my spine like the moment Flores Drakos opens the back door of the Rolls Royce and smiles at me.

With my jaw clenching back my fear, I head inside, scooting all the way into the other side so he sits as far from me as possible. Two wolves, a male and Ruben's regina, get into the front seats and we're off down towards the gate.

Long drives are a killer. It would just be easier to ride on dragon back, and I don't know why Flores doesn't choose this option. Scythe always rode Xander to get from Animus Academy into the city, and while it was a little uncomfortable, it was much more efficient than sitting in a car for so many agonising hours.

Flores puts his headphones in and gets out a laptop, busy for most of the time. I don't get any such luxuries and am forced to look out at the sunburnt countryside until I eventually nod off.

By the time we reach our destination, my hands are numb from sitting on them, my eyes are wet at the corners, and my mouth is as dry as the Australian outback. My nerves are shot through.

And the entire time, the dragon king sat on his phone or laptop, ignoring me. I think a part of him enjoys the fact that my fear perfumes the car. That my heart is beating so loudly all three beasts can hear it. I don't attempt conversation, nor ask any questions. I won't give him that satisfaction.

For the first time, our destination is not in the city, but a property in a regional area, where the soil is red and the scattering of visible grass is crispy. Located practically in the middle of nowhere, we come to a gate topped with barbed wire, manned by four shirtless beasts with rifles resting on their shoulders.

The wolf in the passenger seat gets out to talk to them, the gate is quickly opened, and we're waved through to a long, newly sealed road. It's a ten-minute drive down the deserted, private road, with nothing but dry land on either side. Eventually, the empty land becomes decorated with more barbed wire, and when I spot what's on the other side, I immediately know who owns this land.

A human-made river snakes along my right, and sunbaking along its bank is a long line of crocodiles. Huge, leathery-skinned reptiles, their powerful jaws slightly open as they warm themselves.

On my left, a mansion comes into view; it's a white rendered brick palatial residence that reminds me of a delicate swan. There are wings that sweep out from the central building, tall and sloping roofs on the fourth storey. It's clean and brand spanking new.

It makes it all worse to know this property has come from blood money. From the buying and selling of rare creatures. I'd seen enough from Scythe's memories of the Collector to know that. She's been doing this for over a decade and is very good at her job.

The car stops directly before the entrance, where the square door is already open on one of the fancy hinges that operate on a swivel from the middle of the door. Flores gets out of the car and I scramble to follow before the chain yanks on my collar.

"Welcome, Your Majesty!" The Collector's silken feminine voice dances out of the house, and I straighten to see her gliding forth in a flowy green dress with long draping sleeves. Beside her, a servant carries a tray of crystal tumblers.

"Lady Crocodylus," Flores says, stalking forward to greet her.

"Come in, come in, Your Majesty!"

We follow her into the house, where the air conditioner is on full blast and something sickly sweet perfumes the air.

"Will you stay the night?" The Collector says, gesturing to the servant.

Flores accepts his glass of lemonade. "I'd prefer a timely exchange."

"Understandable."

The Collector whips out her phone and calls someone I can only imagine to be her personal banker. Sure enough, she approves for 'the previously discussed sum' to be deposited into The Drakos trust account.

Flores answers his own phone when it rings. When he hangs up, he takes off the bangle around his wrist and hands it to the Collector. She accepts it with a silken smile.

As easily as swapping Pokémon cards, the deal is done.

"Lovely!" the Collector says, admiring her new bangle. "Shall we go on a tour? I wanted to show Aurelia what I have here."

"I'm afraid I must return home," Flores says, clapping his hands with finality. He's reluctant to leave the estate for longer than necessary with no one to protect the hatchlings. "I hope to hear some happy news soon." He turns to me, his eyes raking down my body. "Behave yourself."

"She will," The Collector coos.

Flores is gone faster than I would like. Somehow, without anyone from Drakos Estate accompanying me, I feel...alone. This is unfamiliar territory and The Collector studies me, tapping a long red acrylic fingernail on her chin. "Let me show you my pets, Aurelia dear. My family is rather large!"

We head back outside, the dust of the Drakos car barely settled before The Collector climbs into the driver's side of an open-roof Jeep and ushers me into the passenger seat. A couple of her shirtless guards discreetly get into the back, and as I scent them, I realise they are roo shifters.

We don't see them in the cities. They prefer to stay away from human populations and live out in regional and rural environments. It also explains the guns, because their only power is the ability to jump extremely high like they've got springs on their feet. So I've heard, anyway.

The Collector drives deeper into her property, where the artificial river continues behind that tall barbed-wire fence. Wind blows through my hair so hard I have to gather it up into a fist to keep it from becoming a nest. The sun beats down on us, and eventually, she comes to a stop, pointing at something in the river.

We climb out and she grins, gesturing to the water where I see them. A row of perhaps twenty crocs, deep in the water, the only visible parts of them being their eyes. I let out a shiver.

"They're all mine," she says proudly. "All purchased through my business. We have strict regulations on their cages, of course; wouldn't want them all getting out." She nudges me with her elbow as if this is a joke.

We stand there quietly for a moment, sweat trickling down my spine. If she's trying to scare me, it's hardly working. I'd just shift into a bird. The crocodiles stare at us in a way that's unnerving, and it takes me a second to realise these are no regular animals.

I suppress a choke.

"You finally got it," she murmurs almost intimately, running a hand through her bob. "Most of them are near rabid, but they listen to my commands. I've trained them to do so."

A red flag goes up in my mind and an inkling makes my

phoenix power rise to the top. My vision changes as the bonding plane becomes visible, twinkling strings stretching out from the closest crocs. I track them to their origin. One croc animus, larger than the others, eyes us with hard intelligence. Four strings lead from him. Three to crocs close around him and one—

I stare at The Collector and the bond coming from the centre of her chest. She's keeping her rex and her other mates prisoner here. What a psycho. I shake the disgust out of my head and the celestial bonds disappear.

The Collector moves closer to me and the scent of floral perfume, mixed with her own salty sweat, fills my nose. I detest it. I detest her and everything she stands for.

Her breath is sour as she whispers in my ear.

"The easiest way to break a woman?" She points to the army of males she's created. "I will let them all have you. One at a time, against your will. I don't know how many it will take. Fifty? One hundred? But eventually, you will submit to me. Eventually, you won't even care what I do to you."

A chill shoots down my spine. "You're plain evil."

Her breath tickles my ear. "You will understand, Aurelia. Soon enough, you will understand why I need you so much. No one knows the real reason. Not even Flores. Not even the Lady Hyena. Not even your beloved Scythe Kharkorous. No one knows what *I* have that *no* one else does."

I see it now. A feeling snakes between my bones, settling in my marrow. A destiny. A certainty.

I will meet my end here.

Chapter 56

Aurelia

My hands tremble at dinner that night, alone in my allocated room. It's bare, with a regular, single bed with a white lacy duvet and cotton sheets. There are no windows, and the door is made of metal. I feel cold as I sit at the small table. It too is steel and bolted to the ground.

It feels more like a prison here than it did at Drakos Estate. I try to assess my options, but my mind is fuzzy like soft drink shaken up in a can. It almost feels like someone else is captive in this cell. Like someone else feels cold inside and numb on the outside.

The only upside is that, despite tasting like ash in my mouth, the food is well made. A classic roast chicken and potatoes and a fresh side salad of cucumbers and rocket. I have orange juice and some pills that smell like vitamins. She's not going to kill me by starving me, at least.

Sometime in the evening, the lights go off and I get the message that I need to sleep. I use the bathroom in the dark and climb into bed, huddling under the bleached sheets.

I can't bear to close my eyes. I want them to stay open. I want to be alert when she comes for me. I need to think of a way out of this.

Kicking myself that I didn't try to think of escape sooner, I recount the events of the day, thinking of the number of times I could have shifted and flown away. But flight would have been impossible. Here, there are beasts with guns in every room and I'd been escorted everywhere with gun-toting animuses. They're a whole different sort of threat that needs careful consideration. It only takes one person with good aim to catch me in the wing and send me down.

Dread, hard and dense sitting in my gut, doesn't allow me to sleep at all.

* * *

The next morning, she makes me wait.

I'm not given any food through the slot in the door, and straining my ears reveals nothing on the other side.

Hours tick by and I pace the length of the room to keep busy. I've been in isolation before, so I'm familiar with this. But Solomon and the other scientists had never said openly cruel things to me. Had never threatened me so thoroughly.

And something about the Collector tells me she's not one for empty threats. She has a plan, and she's going to execute it.

By what I estimate is the evening time, the lock at the door jangles open. I stand to attention, my heart pounding as she saunters through the door.

I wonder if I should attack her now and get it done with. Launch myself at her and—but no less than six guards enter the room immediately after her, surrounding us both with their weapons drawn.

"Don't bother," she says carefully, examining me from top to toe. "They'd make it hurt."

I can only blink at her, my coiled muscles needing to be told to soften. The scent of the males crowds me in, filling my head and making me dizzy. I huff to hide my anxiety. "So what's the plan for today?"

She shows me her teeth. Today she wears a yellow lace dress that ties at the breast. It's oddly cheery for her. I'm still wearing my black dress from the estate. It needs to be washed, but she hasn't given me anything else and I refuse to ask.

"I want to show you something."

Oh, there's more to see. "Great," I say stiffly.

She throws me a knowing smile before I'm escorted out of the room and down a corridor, deeper into the house. The cell is on ground level, and I'm not surprised when she leads me to an elevator that descends several floors.

As I stand there, surrounded by metal and guards, listening to the mechanical whirr, I'm reminded of Halfeather mansion and another dungeon that was kept underground.

I'd met my mates in such a dungeon; I shouldn't be afraid.

Except, a voice reminds me, your mates are monsters of their own kind. Monsters are kept in dungeons.

The Collector is mysteriously excited as the elevator comes to a stop and pings. They slide open to reveal a brightly lit corridor of all white, with a row of steel doors. Apparently, the dark isn't her style. She leads us out, her energy positively giddy, her gait near bouncy, and I wonder what on earth could have a bloodthirsty person like her so damn excited.

We come to a stop by a door and one of the guards unlocks it with a heavy set of keys.

"Do not fear," the Collector reassures me, a little breathless, her pupils dilated. "He's not the violent sort."

It swings open, revealing a complete darkness. But the soldiers take no heed and march right in, sweeping me along with them.

When the door closes behind us, we're entombed in the dark. My heart pounds in my ears as I strain to see what type of monster of pride and joy she keeps here.

A warm glow expands from a dimmer. It's a small globe set in the corner as an afterthought, but its light reveals something I never, not in my wildest dreams, expected.

The beast lies on his side, amongst strewn hay, motionless, bereft, his hooves bent to the side. A pelt of silver glimmers under the meagre light. A long, powerful horn extends from his forehead. It has its own glow, dimmed, I think, from—

I can't breathe. I can't blink. I can't tear my eyes away from the horror I see before me. This creature of light and beauty... Someone had hurt it.

On its rump is a blackened mark, circular, festering with necrosis.

The Collector sighs wistfully.

"You have a unicorn." My voice sounds far away. "You keep him in the dark."

"You can make many Boneweavers, Aurelia," she replies in a dreamy voice. "But this is a male. He cannot make more of himself."

She turns to regard me and my response. I tear my eyes away to meet her gaze in grave disbelief.

"He's not been forthcoming about what his order's powers are," she continues. "As you can see, I cannot risk trying to convince him. That wound hasn't healed, which leads me to believe he's ill. You will need to heal it. You've healed mythical creatures before."

She means a particular basilisk, who'd also lain in a dark dungeon all alone.

"He needs to see the moon. The sun. That's why he is ill!" That mockery of light in the corner is hardly a replacement.

But the demon before me is shaking her head. "I cannot allow it. With great difficulty, I claimed him. I will *not* risk discovery."

My mouth twists in utter contempt. Selfish creature of the gutter.

"Don't you see it, Aurelia?" she presses. "Who wouldn't want the seed of a unicorn? The most majestic creature in existence. It would be an honour to carry his offspring. *You* would be greatly honoured."

Except nausea is twisting in my stomach, along with an insidious feeling that extends its wings in protest. I look back at the unicorn. "Of course I'll try to help him," I say softly. "May I go forward?"

"You may not touch him," she says sharply.

I flinch at the sudden change in tone.

"I know what you can do. You may not touch him. You may heal him from a distance. Go and stand there." She points to a spot next to a guard on the unicorn's other side.

I have every desire to destroy the person who did this.

"What made the wound?" I ask between gritted teeth.

The Collector hovers near me before crossing her arms. "A cattle prod."

My eyes near boggle out of their sockets in morbid disbelief. "You didn't!"

"Do as you are told or I will have you shot in the leg."

I huff in disgust before crouching down to look at his face better. His eyes are closed, long silver lashes sweeping downward. I wonder what colour his eyes are. His mane reminds me of Scythe, and my heart pangs for a moment before I realise the strands of hair emit their own gentle glow.

I shake my head. *Magnificent.*

"Who are you?"

I inhale sharply from the shock. His voice is like a moonbeam on an open field. It's somehow dark and light at the same time. *"My name is Aurelia."*

"You are like me."

I want to smile at the joke of that. *"I could never be."*

"I've never met a humble Boneweaver." Dry amusement marks his tone.

My body freezes as his words hit home. I'm almost terrified to ask. *"You've met other Boneweavers?"*

His eyes blink open. The Collector gasps.

It's irises of the lightest purple that greet me. Appraise me.

Like lavender under the sun. *"Many of them,"* he says. *"Are there none left here?"*

My throat is suddenly tight. *"I don't think so. I'm alone. But...what do you mean by 'here' exactly?"*

He blinks at me, and for a moment, he seems infinitely sad. *"Unicorns travel between worlds, Aurelia. But promise me you'll not tell her that."*

My heart pounds and I place a hand over it. *"I will take it to my grave."*

"What is he saying?" The Collector asks with a voice like a knife. "He's speaking to you, I know it!"

I cast her an annoyed look and find her expression full of jealousy. "He's saying it hurts. He's saying he needs the moon and an open field."

She waves her hand, irritated. The roo next to me moves, and suddenly, the end of a gun is pressed against my shoulder.

I close my eyes in dismay before sending my power out, lingering at the edges of this magnificent creature. "May I?" I ask out loud. "I'm sorry, I don't know your name."

He blinks once with certainty and I allow my lips a ghost of a smile before I push my power towards that awful wound. My avian power practically rushes at it, eager to help, eager to please. The tissue above has to be sheared off to allow the newer flesh beneath to proliferate. My power sloughs at the rotten skin, urging it to leave, urging white blood cells to pool over the bacteria. It hurts him, I know it does, but the creature doesn't move as he closes his eyes once again.

His scent is mild, as if all his power has retracted into himself to preserve his strength. But his scent is like nothing I've ever experienced. It's wild and powerful, like a thousand horses galloping over a plain, but also sweet and sensual, like a lover's caress. It would have been enough to enamour me, was I not already fated to be regina to five others. No wonder The Collector is besotted and obsessed worse than any dragon in a treasure haze.

Sweat trickles down my spine, and I waver on the spot a little as my power funnels itself into him. His body seems to gobble it up, a never-ending stream of hunger. Frowning, I withdraw, glancing at my captor.

"I'll need to come back. The wound is deep."

She nods curtly from where she watches me, before turning on her heel and leading the way out.

I rise to my feet, casting another sad glance at him.

"*Lorian*," he says softly. "*Let everyone know that my name was Lorian.*"

I turn to stare at him. He thinks he'll die here. He thinks this is the end of him, and perhaps it is.

Something rises up out of the abyss at the centre of me. Something massive. Something heavy and hard, made of fire and claws and a roar that could shake mountains.

With a push of a gun into my spine, I follow The Collector out of the cell, back into the cold white lights of the corridor.

Only when the door is closed do I turn to her. Slowly, and with great purpose, I take a single step towards her. Guns swivel towards my body, too many to count. I no longer care.

"I want you to know something," I hiss, my eyes filling with tears of rage, but I don't blink, fixing my gaze on the crocodile with terrible, violent focus. My voice trembles, but not with fear. "I will *not* break. Not here. Not ever. Torture me, rape me, leave me to be forgotten in the dark, but know that I will never, not in this life, nor in any other. *Break. For. You.*"

She's silent as she marks me, her eyes also unblinking, her focus pinpoint. I know she realises I'm right. Perhaps she expected it from the last fucking Boneweaver. Perhaps she thinks she'll enjoy the challenge.

Something changes in her eyes then. Some decision made.

"Very well, Aurelia." Her voice holds a note of quiet resignation. "Very well."

Chapter 57

Xander

Daylight — David Kushner

The Hellfire's beachfront holiday house is nice enough, and for once, Francesca is happy. Her parents are nervous around me, but I hardly care about that.

She's hiding something from me. There's a spot of darkness around her that catches my eye in every annoying moment. She's not pregnant—I'm quick to hear rudimentary heartbeats in pregnant women and I've been checking for it daily.

I'm asked to go to the beach this morning and I've said no for the last two days, so I oblige them. Lord Hellfire and I sit under the cabana, he with the day's newspaper and me with my tablet. His daughter and Lady Hellfire walk along the beach where the tide meets the water, likely talking about me, but I don't care enough to listen.

My screen captures my full attention as I read reports I obtained from hacking into the Animus Academy databases. I've been slowly making my way through Aurelia's medical reports from when she first arrived at the academy, and now Lyle's notes from when he first counselled her.

He really didn't like her at the beginning. That much is

obvious from the curt, short notes. I just don't know when exactly that changed.

Student appears distressed at the mention of her father.

Was it then? When he realised she was afraid of her father? Or later, when she'd taken a lioness form. Did he love her because he'd seen her as a feline?

The attached pictures are from her student ID card, and there's more from the journalists at the courthouse before her trial.

She appears grey in them, her face first surprised, then grim, her mouth a straight line as Lyle escorts her inside. I wonder what she was thinking in those moments. We now know she was hardly plotting anything because they absolutely thrashed her at the trial. She had little to no cunning with that.

And then came the nimpins who'd executed their little attack precisely enough to allow her to escape...but only to a hidden part of the school.

When she'd gotten herself kidnapped by the serpent scum, I'd come upon them about to cut her open. If I hadn't arrived, if I hadn't been there, they would have succeeded in their plan to maim her.

She'd been powerless to stop them.

There are more photos from the place she lived before the academy. I've seen these before, but they look different to me now. It's sort of depressing to look at the Two-Minute Noodle packet on the counter and the clear hole in the ceiling.

I swipe back to photos from the trial. Those jewels she wears. The earrings, that necklace...

She looks different now. Compared to these photos. Drakos Estate has changed her and not for the better.

"You're obsessed with her!"

My head whips up and I realise Francesca is standing behind me, reading over my shoulder, and I was so engrossed in what I was reading that I didn't even notice.

"What?" I snap, shutting off the screen, furious at myself. "Don't be ridiculous."

"You are!" she screams, pointing at me. "Every time I see you, you're staring at her, and the worst part of it is that you don't even realise it!"

I shake my head. "You're mistaken, Francesca. She is merely a pawn."

"Darling," Lord Hellfire says in a soothing voice. "He totes her around in a collar and chain. He made her *bleed*. Of course he could only hate her."

She narrows her eyes at me until they are slits. "Only a man so obsessed with a woman could hate her *that* much." Francesca's sun-reddened face glares at me for a moment longer before she beckons to her parents. "Let's go."

Francesca storms away with her mother in tow, but Lord Hellfire perches on the side of his beach chair, facing me. His voice is quiet as he says. "Sometimes feelings take time to grow, Xander. Just give her a chance. You'll see there's so much more to her than what's on the surface."

I turn to stare at him. He blanches under my gaze until his words register and I blink like a normal person. "Thank you, Lord Hellfire."

He nods and trails after his family, leaving me alone with the waves surging and the harsh sun on the sand hurting my eyes. I pull down my sunglasses and tilt my head back, letting the heat of the day sink further into my skin.

Scythe had fought his attraction to her for the longest. She'd even been scared of him at the start, just like the rest. When did that change? When did she decide he would no longer hurt her, and more importantly, when did *he* decide that?

Chapter 58

Aurelia

I'm surprised when they don't take me back down to see Lorian the next day. The Collector seemed so obsessed with him that I assumed she wanted him fixed as quickly as possible.

Instead, I'm kept in my own cell for the next three days.

Perhaps she's jealous of me talking to him. Perhaps she's punishing me for my tirade. Perhaps she's planning something.

Even so, they feed me well. The meat is good, the vegetables perfectly cooked, the juice cold. I eat the vitamins that come in the little paper cup.

On the third day, a collared anima comes into the room and takes my blood. Oddly, guards don't follow her into my room; they remain outside. I regard the woman carefully. What type of anima would they feel safe leaving alone with me? She's slender and pale-skinned with reddish-brown hair and a distinct port-wine birthmark on the side of her neck.

She stares at me in challenge, almost as if she's daring me to make a comment about it. But I could care less about birthmarks. Instead I stare at the metal around her throat. Unlike mine, hers reads with only an ID number. I glare at it.

I scratch at my own collar as she brings out a vacutainer and blood-collecting vials.

"Nice," I say drolly. "The scientists at Drakos House only ever used a needle and syringe. So old school."

Her eyes flick up to me before she goes about her business, placing a tourniquet above the inside of my elbow.

I suppose they're checking for ovulation. I'm not sure if my heat will even come on being so far from any mates for this long. It was coming to the right time, however. No doubt, The Collector is keeping track on a whiteboard somewhere.

"You should be more careful."

I'm surprised by the harsh scratching of her voice and raise my brows. "And why's that?"

"She is merciless."

It's cold water down my spine. She finishes up quickly, and before I can ask her what she means, the guards whisk her out. But as she leaves, her scent whirls before me and my brows shoot up in recognition.

The next day, I get to find out what she meant. They come to get me in the evening. My nails are bitten down to the quick by then, my lips peeling from where I've been tugging at the fine skin. There is a listlessness to my limbs and a heaviness over my chest.

The worst part of is, I know they won't kill me. I know they'll stop just short. That's a new kind of mental torture.

Waiting for death I might have handled well. But *this?* This makes my anima thrash and snarl within me. She fights. Goddess, she fights it when they unlock my door and five guards enter with their guns first.

There is a single moment here, when I am surrounded by their hardened faces, the tang of metal in my nose, and I wonder what would happen if I shifted. If I fought them, tried to kill them. How many could I take down in the minutes before their gunfire would render me useless?

A shot to either leg would do it. They would have me on the floor.

Fight would only delay the inevitable.

So I raise my chin and walk out with them.

You will not break me, I remind myself. *Not in this life or in any other. Athena Boneweaver was her name. Lorian is his name. My mates love me, and I love them.*

I'm escorted to the ground level,

We walk past a number of beautiful rooms, but I don't really see any of them. Eventually, we come to a room lit with natural sunlight streaming through white curtains, a round plush rug and a single electric medical bed in the middle.

The Collector stands with Flores Drakos, waiting for me. Both are fresh-faced with smiles, as if some good news has come their way. The Collector wears an elegant dress, tightly fitted and starch white.

As if she tries to portray with clothes someone she's not. As if she can hide the jealous, greedy monster that lurks within. More covetous than a dragon, more cunning than a snake.

"Good evening, Aurelia," she says slowly.

In my head comes the distant sound of knocking.

A feeling like old and dead things winds its way about my heart. I've only felt like this one other time: when the sounds and smells around me faded to nothing and my vision tunnelled; Scythe had told me my mother was still alive.

I glance at Flores, and to my dismay, he has a strange look in his eye and his face is slightly flushed. My gaze flicks to the bed. *He* doesn't intend to sire a hatchling from me, does he?

"I'm not in heat," I blurt out.

"We know," Flores drawls.

"But there is still a matter outstanding," The Collector says. What matter? What is still outstanding? "Pop up here, like a good girl."

It's nicer than the steel one I've been used to at Drakos

Estate. This has thick foam padding, a crisp white sheet, and a large, soft pillow.

Someone nudges me with their gun from behind, and I walk towards the bed. I miss Eugene's presence. I even miss Ghoul's overlordship over my scientific proceedings.

This path I must walk alone.

When I sit on the bed, the mattress doesn't let out a sad exhale of air like the Animus Academy medical beds. She paid a lot of money for this.

She paid a lot of money for me.

Flores gestures for me to lie down, and reluctantly, I do, resting my hands on my stomach as I try to control my breathing.

The Collector heads over to a cabinet and rummages within it. Flores comes to my side and sighs over me, looking me over from head to foot. "I knew, Aurelia, that it would come to this eventually. There was too much fire in your eyes, and we need you..." He rests a palm on my right thigh.

Broken. That's what they'd said.

My heart gives an arrhythmic thump before kicking up into a hammering beat. I flick my gaze between him and The Collector, who's still searching through the cabinet.

"Hold still now," Flores instructs with clinical coldness. "It'll be a bit of a shock." And with the strength only afforded to the order of dragons, he grasps my right thigh in both hands and tears the limb clean in two.

The scream wrenches from my throat with a violence I've never experienced. Shock drives me into a block of dry ice. My mind seizes. On and on, my scream rips through the air. My blood saturates the sheets.

The Collector lunges forward with a cattle prod and strikes me in the cheek. "Shift!" she roars. Pain explodes through my face.

Everything turns black.

My anima screeches forth and takes over, shifting into the only thing it can think of to save us.

Chapter 59

Savage

Something rumbles through the air—wild, dark, desperate. My head snaps up from my notebook. "Did you feel that?" I say, squinting up at the sky. A sinister feeling settles in my stomach. It makes my eyes blink hard. If I'd been in my wolf form, my hackles would have been raised. Something bad has happened. Panic strikes my chest and I whip around, looking for my brothers.

"I did," Scythe says quietly, coming to stand next to me.

"So did I," Lyle grits out, putting a hand on my shoulder.

Chapter 60

Ghoul

On the planes of shadow and smoke, something vibrates through the darkness. The hairs all over my body stand on end.

It whispers of heinous things.

I press a fang into my lip hard enough to draw blood.

Chapter 61

Xander

It's at the Hellfire family dining table that the wave of power vibrates the table, making the cutlery dance on the starched cloth.

To my magical eyes, a familiar sizzling energy of red and black spreads through the air. A breaking. A severing. Whoever it came from is a powerful beast.

"What is it?" Francesca says, placing her hand on the table in surprise.

I swallow my mouthful of dry turkey, and without looking up, confirm, "The beginning of the end, no doubt."

She exchanges a worried look with her parents.

Chapter 62

Scythe

It slithers over my skin, this ominous feeling. Something is wrong and I cannot reach out to my regina to check on her. My great white no longer wants to be cold. He wants to be hot. He wants to feel water boil around him. He wants for it to burn off his skin until there's nothing left but a skeletal being who will tear apart the world with the sharp points of his own bones.

Lyle leads us to the office of Animus Academy's headmistress. Asking for help from the phoenix irks me. I should be able to fix this on my own, but Aurelia's silence is making that impossible. As it is, after we'd torched their two warehouses and fifteen boxing gyms, the Clawsons have gone into hiding, making them also impossible to find. Everything is working against us right now.

Celeste answers the door in a dressing gown and slippers. "Forgive me," she says, rubbing her forehead and stepping back to let us in. "I'm not feeling my best."

"What is it?" Lyle says, and despite the heavy growl, his concern is clear.

"Damien's preserved seed didn't take," she says, taking a seat at her desk. "But there is also something else in the bonding planes..." She gives me a pointed look. "Xander's betrayal has left a lasting darkness. Titus left a stink, to be sure, but a bond-rejection by a dragon carries a particular kind of distasteful fracture. It's like a wound."

"We'll fix that when we kill him," Savage says, plonking himself on the floor against the door as if to guard it.

"I didn't know you would feel that," Lyle says, tugging at his collar out of habit. "What are the implications of this?"

"All beasts can feel it to some extent," she replies, crossing her arms. "It leaves everyone feeling unsettled."

"There is something more," I press. "Something that just shook the very air. Did you feel it?"

Celeste's face goes from pale to grey. "I've never felt something like that before."

"It was her," Savage says, his voice breaking on that last word. "My regina. I know it. We can't even sense where she is, otherwise I'd already be there."

"Can you find her?" Lyle asks. "We wouldn't ask if it were not imperative, but we don't think she's at Drakos Estate any longer."

Celeste nods. She doesn't say what we all know. That they've had a second, silent auction. That the winning bid could not have been Xander this time. "Give me one moment," she says faintly.

It's with a grimace that she shuts her eyes and us three brothers hone in on her person with an acute observance. Her aura pulses a murky colour that reflects her state of mind and body, a pulse of fire still glowing at her core. Her power suddenly flares around her as she sends it out, licking flames reaching into the ether before they go out of my psychic sight.

"Anything?" Savage asks impatiently, leaping up from the floor and coming next to me to lean across the table and stare at the headmistress.

Lyle shushes him.

Celeste's pallid cheeks turn pink, then bloom red with effort. "It's strange..."

"What's strange?" we all say at once.

Her jaw clenches before she opens her eyes. They glint an ethereal gold, but the expression on her face makes my insides bleed.

"She's gone to a place I cannot follow."

Savage roars and whirls around, wrenches the door open off its hinge, and storms out. "How many!" he screams outside. "How many do we have to kill to get her back!"

My great white demands my attention as I too turn on my heel and stalk out of Celeste's office. "We know the candidates," I say evenly, staring out the window. "We know who has the money. We just track them down one by one. And I know just where to start."

Lyle has gentle words with Celeste before joining us in heading to the elevator. "If she's shutting out even the phoenixes, she still has substantial power. She can't be too badly hurt or injured."

"You don't know her power then," Savage says, shoving at Lyle.

Lyle shoves him back into the elevator wall, making it shudder violently. "I know her power. I remember how she endured her father's attacks and walked around like nothing was happening. Hid it from us." He grinds his teeth at the memory.

Savage slams his fist against the elevator wall as it opens it to let us out. The emergency alarm sounds and we continue back to the Animus dorm.

Instead of going back up to our rooms however, I stop at the rec room, where I find Connor sitting pale faced with a group of lions. With only one look from me he strides over, his face drawn.

I rest a hand on his shoulder and he looks at me alarmed. "I know about the call you received three days ago and the offer that was made to you."

He opens his mouth but I shake my head. "You're not in trouble. Have you come to a decision?"

Connor tugs nervously at his long black mane and I note his aura of clear, sky blue. He's not happy about it, and there's no betrayal in his heart. "Yes. I want to do it."

"If you needed the money, I would give it to you, but you would be sworn to me."

Connor nods, his dark eyes considering this. "I would like to remain a free agent, if you don't mind. And if this will help my grandfather and potentially Aurelia, then I want to. To be honest, I've been expecting it for a while now."

I nod gravely. "You're braver than me, Connor."

He looks alarmed as I wave Lyle over. "Hand him the contract."

Connor pulls out a stapled booklet, complete with council seals from his satchel and smoothes it over, staring at it before handing it to Lyle.

I don't have to look at it to know why Lyle's brows shoot upward. It's an official contract of 'employment' stating that in exchange for a large sum of money and freedom from the academy, Connor will participate in the scientific research of his anima. He is a rare beast after all.

I get out my phone and dial it.

"Scythe," purrs The Collector. "Always *such* a pleasure to hear your sweet voice."

* * *

Five hours later, Lyle drives us through the barbed-wire gates of the crocodile sanctuary The Collector calls home. She gets plenty of money from the state government for 'conservation' but it's much in the same way Frank Ulman got funding for his park of horrors. Lyle's fists tighten on the wheel as he lays eyes on the barbed wire cages and finds them all too familiar. Connor's eyes stare unblinking around his new home. The saltwater in the man-made rivers calls to me, as does the wild call of the other predators, and I find I can't tear my eyes off the glistening surface.

"She's been here," Savage says with his head out the window. "I can feel it, but I can't tell if she's still here or not."

I agree with him and it makes my eyes dart around the air, trying to sense the timing of her arrival or departure. She'll have scent masking on—potentially all of her shields—to hide from us and others. All reports say they've kept obsidian off her this whole time. It was the only way to make sure we'd not come to get her.

We pull to a stop outside the front of her white swan-like dwelling and Savage and I are out of the car before the engine is even off.

I can't sense Xander, but a dragon has lingered here. Flores, perhaps, but not his son. Thank the Goddess, because it may have driven me mad if I'd also sensed him.

The four of us are at the wide closed door and pounding on it in three heartbeats. Two females pull it open, roo shifters, by their scents, and in gossamer dresses so sheer it leaves nothing to the imagination. They bow as they stand aside.

"Mr Kharkorous," the first says quietly. "Mr Fengari, Mr Pardalia. Connor. Please be welcome."

"Thanks," Savage says loudly. He showered, for once, if only at the thought that he might get a glimpse of his regina. Lyle wears a white dress shirt and slacks, and I'm in my usual black shirt and pants, despite this heat. Connor wears his usual stilettos as well as black denim cut-offs and a flowered blouse.

It would do me well to swim in cold, cold brine, but my mind is fixed on my regina. "She's in her throne room, I imagine," I say to the girl.

"Please follow me," is all she replies. "Connor, please follow my colleague."

Connor gives us a final nod before setting his suitcase on the floor and wheeling it after the roo anima. I wonder if I will ever see him again.

The first roo turns around and, with her rear in almost full view, leads us to The Collector. Savage makes an *are-you-serious?* face at the girl's back, but we all know Lady Crocodylus is very purposeful in her reception of us.

In her taunting of us.

We are led to a drawing room, which she has styled with a long emerald carpet, leading to a large, elaborate green and gold throne. She looks ridiculous sitting in it, but she tries her best with her cigarette and the bare legs draped over the armrest.

She's also in lingerie.

As we enter, nothing but three murderous predators on a hunt, her flirtatious smile widens before she draws on her cigarette. I lead the way, and despite stopping at a fair distance away, she holds out her hand, tipped in long gold nails.

"Your Majesty," she purrs.

She's the only one who calls me that. I might hold the marine seat at the council, but the title was never cold enough for what I am.

"My lady," I say formally, ignoring her hand by crossing my hands over my belt buckle. "We are pleased you accepted our request for a meeting."

"I am also quite pleased," she purrs, rising from her seat and revealing how sheer her crimson babydoll nightie is.

Savage lets out a sound of irritation, looking around the room with impatience. There is a fish tank by the wall, bubbling away under a UV light. Seaweed and artificial rocks along with a miniature castle line the bottom, making it look full. I wonder if one of her 'collectables' lies sleeping in there. Some rare aquatic creature.

"Forgive me for my dress. I wasn't expecting you so late."

"It is of no consequence to us. We have a regina," Lyle says dismissively.

"Of course, of course." She doesn't miss a beat, waving her

hand to the servants behind us. "We will discuss matters now, of course. You must be hungry, no? I am, of course, well versed in the needs of alpha males such as yourselves."

Revulsion scores through me at her overt flirtation.

Savage cracks his neck as servants hurry forth, carrying an entire table laden with a roast dinner and...sushi. There is raw steak for Savage and two whole roast ducks with plum sauce for Lyle.

She's done her research.

"I'm not hungry, Collector," Savage announces.

Her eyes flick down the length of Savage's body, his bare torso with the tattoo of the snarling wolf's head. "Please call me Katerina, Savage. I am most happy you didn't decide to dress for me. Word on the street is that you've been quite a busy feral boy."

Chairs are brought out for us and The Collector sits down, bringing up her bare legs to rest on the edge of the chair as if to show them to us. "Please, eat while we talk."

Lyle and I sit, but Savage chooses to pace the room behind us."I want my regina," he says.

Katerina's eyes flare with something for a moment. As a crocodile, her aura is hard to read. She's naturally protected by her Triassic skin, from both physical harm and being read. But I'm strong enough to see a flash of bright, venomous green.

Jealousy, then.

"We are aware," I say, picking up my chopsticks and selecting several pieces of sushi, "that Aurelia has been sold at auction."

Savage prowls to the fish tank in the corner, bending down and all but pressing his nose to the glass.

"Don't break it, Sav," Lyle warns.

"I won't," he says irritably.

The Collector laughs for a beat too long. "Come here, Savage. I told them to only warm up the steak so it was just to your preference. Or are fries more to your liking?"

Savage turns around and frowns at his allocated plate. "No games. Answer question."

Katerina licks her lips and tucks her short black hair behind her ear. "Well, I've heard much the same. Though *leased* would be a more accurate word."

"You were at the first auction," Lyle says. "You cannot deny that you've seen the other bidders."

She takes another drag from her cigarette, her gaze hovering between us. She knows something and is withholding it.

A movement at the corner of my eye makes me snap my brother's name. Savage quickly removes his hand from where it was wrist-deep inside the water. He gives me a sheepish smile as he wipes his hand on his shorts.

"Thought I saw something."

"Really?" the Collector says. "If you want to take a bite out of something in there, you are most welcome to, my love."

Savage frowns at her. "Do you know who has Aurelia, or are you wasting our fucking time?"

"Manners," she chides, blowing smoke in his direction. "If you want information, you know my price." Her eyes slide meaningfully to me.

The desire to imbed my chopsticks into her eye sockets almost gets the better of me. Lyle seems to register this because he leans forward.

"Scythe is a mated male, Katerina. He cannot."

"Not fully mated, from what I can sense," she narrows her eyes at me in thought. "That is my price. If you cannot meet my demands, you do not get information, full stop."

For Aurelia, I would do anything, including whore myself, if she would ask it. But she would *not* ask this of me, and she would rage if she heard of it.

"You will not compromise for another?" Lyle says. "What about another great white?"

I look at him sharply and he shrugs at me.

"Are they all...like you?" she purrs at me.

Further revulsion almost makes me stop chewing, but I doggedly swallow my bite of salmon sashimi. "Aurelia is insistent that we keep away from her...business." I sit back in my chair and cross a leg over the other knee. She keenly follows my every movement, her pupils dilating. "However, I cannot and will not allow her to be bred. Do you understand me, Katerina?"

She visibly swallows.

"Any beast involved in hurting her will find themselves on their back with Savage's canines four inches into their small bowel," I continue.

"I like the taste of acid," Savage says, licking his chops. "It fits my mood right now."

"Do we make ourselves clear?" I ask.

She smiles and says in a sing-song voice, "You come here, you make threats. You try to seduce me..." she chuckles. "You forget that I have my own leverage."

"And what is that?" Lyle asks, sitting back in his chair too.

"I'm the only one on her side," she purrs. "I would *never* hurt that poor girl."

Chapter 63

Aurelia

It had been completely out of my control.

I'd known for weeks that my anima was trying to claw her way back into control of my consciousness as she had once done. We needed protection from the increasingly maddening consequences of the decisions I'd made.

And she was not happy that we'd left our mates.

So when Flores Drakos, with all the sheer power the Wild Goddess had given dragon-kind, had broken my femur and torn my leg clean off, my anima had shifted into the only creature that could save us.

One of the few creatures on the planet who could re-grow an entire limb.

My anima holds me in a tight grip now, as we lie on the rocky floor as a star-shaped being, a form so alien, so new.

I'd never shifted into something without a head before, and the only reason I even knew I could was from a trip to the city aquarium in grade two. There was a shallow petting-pool for us tiny kids to feel the sea urchins and starfishes under the water. I'd giggled and squealed when I'd touched the cool, firm limb of the orange star-fish. It had been rougher to touch than I thought. Stronger.

That trip now saved my life as an adult.

The shock of having an entire limb amputated sent my brain into a near-catatonic state. The Collector had, ironically, saved my life when she'd zapped me into shifting. No doubt that had been part of the plan.

If I'd stayed in my human form, I would have died from blood loss and probably shock, but as a starfish, my mind sways silently along the currents of the tank created by the electric motor.

I must be still.

I must be silent.

Every ounce of energy goes into re-growing my severed limb. Because one of the first things a healer learns is that without a hind limb, a wild animal is dead.

And I let the silence take me, until, that is, at some point, when my three mates stride into the room outside my tank.

I have no ears to hear them with, but I do have tiny eyes on the tips of my remaining limbs. So when I sense them enter the room, my eyes perk up and I see three large shapes through the glass.

"Savage," I whisper to myself. *"Scythe, Lyle. My mates. The parts of my soul."*

My anima cries out, desperate and longing. If I had human eyes, they would have filled with tears, and if I'd had a human throat, I would have screamed their names.

I need them. I want them.

"Savage!" I scream to no one but myself. *"Scythe! Lyle!"*

I need you, I need you, I need you. Please save me. Please love me. Please forgive me.

One of the figures moves closer and I feel my wolf hovering right before me.

"Savage!" I scream into the void. *"Please, Savage! See me! I'm here! See me! See me!"*

He moves away and I weep and I scream and I curse myself

for my choices, for my fucking self-sacrifice, for my complete and utter idiocy.

And then he's back. The current shifts and I feel my wolf disturb the water as if he might actually be reaching for me.

"I'm here, Savage!" I cry with such desperation it actually might break me. *"Down here! Please!"*

And then he's gone, and they are gone, and the voice in my head screams on and on. My heart goes silent. Any hope I had, any dream that once was, is gone with those three figures.

I am but a lonely starfish, lost in the dark.

There is nothing left for me here, in this world, nor in any other.

The Boneweaver lineage dies here, with me.

I am sorry.

Chapter 64

Xander

Make It Bun Dem — Skrillex, Damian Marley

Francesca and I return from our trip four days later. Her parents were insistent on showing me their properties and businesses. For some reason, and despite my lack of interest, they were eager to please me. As if pleasing me would get me to actually love their foul daughter.

My alleged wife insists on reporting to my father's office with me, despite me saying that I'd prefer it to be private.

When we find him, however, standing at his desk with his hands on his hips, he's quite smug when he sees the both of us.

"Welcome," he says, far too happily.

His glee is fully reserved for Francesca alone, and I don't even feel jealous as I take my regular seat.

"You will be pleased to hear that we've had a successful exchange," he says to me after kissing the dragoness on both cheeks.

Francesca claps and looks between us.

"What exchange?" I frown.

"Lady Crocodylus," Francesca says, grinning at me with her

teeth. "She placed a winning bid for the Boneweaver. We're considerably richer!"

My stomach turns.

"Yes, she was quite excited," Father says wryly, sitting in his chair and gesturing for Francesca to do the same. "She has quite a few plans, Lady Katerina."

I go still. At his words. At Francesca's giddy joy. At the scent that suddenly wafts my way.

"Urgh, what is that?" Francesca says, wrinkling her nose as it hits her too. "It's coming from that cabinet."

I've already turned towards the old baroque thing. It's heavy and ancient, like the rest of the furniture in the room, passed down from father to son. Hints of gold line the scroll-work at the top. Father's upgrade to it leaves a mechanical hum in the air.

"Yes, I have it refrigerated for the new scientists, but I wanted to keep it in here for a bit."

There is no other thought in my mind, only singular purpose as I rise from my chair and stride towards the cabinet. A dull roar grows in my ears.

A voice comes to me through the din, like an old echo. *Don't open it.*

But I've gotten used to ignoring the voices in my head. My father doesn't stop me when I wrench it open.

Francesca screams.

When I speak, my voice emerges dragon-guttural, heat pouring from my skin and flooding the room. My shoulders heave in a breath. "Who did this?"

"Oh, you recognise it, do you?" my father drawls, sitting back in his chair. "I suppose you would. We'd charged you and that General Ghoul to break the girl. And when you both failed in the matter, I had—

My shift is explosive.

When my dragon tears from my skin, we destroy the entire tower. Stone and dust explode in every direction. I barely hear

Francesca's screams, barely care as I launch into the twilight with a shower of fire pouring from my throat.

There is only one image in my mind: the sight of Aurelia with her leg missing from the thigh down, her screaming and pouring blood.

Her dying.

She doesn't deserve this. Never deserved this, no matter who her father is, no matter who her mother was. No matter what she was to me.

"You have severed our connection to her," my dragon seethes to my human self. *"We cannot track her."*

"We don't fucking need to," I snarl back. *"We know where The Collector's dwelling is."*

"They are protected."

"And I will tear down every fucking reptile on the property."

"For once, we are of the same mind."

At full, terrible speed, it only takes me one hour before the white eaves of Katerina Crocodylus' house come into view.

So much fucking white. I will make it black today.

I announce my arrival with a furious roar. The crocodiles and alligators in the rivers surrounding the property look up before diving under the water for protection. Even so, I sweep low and spew fire above them.

Find her first, find her first, find her first, I remind myself.

Aurelia will have protected herself with her powerful Boneweaver magic, and what condition she's in, I cannot even guess. She's alive, that is the only guaranteed thing.

I land on the now-smouldering roof of the central building, lean down and grip a part of the roof in my mouth before wrenching it right off. It comes away with a terrible metallic shriek. I shrink into human form and jump down into the top floor. Everyone is scattering as I charge through them.

"Where is she!" I roar. "Where is Aurelia?"

Those of her servants who don't run freeze in place like prey.

"You!" I cry, pointing to a young woman, staring with eyes

wide, the whites visible all the way around. She has a port wine stain above her steel collar. "Poultry. Where is she?" She doesn't answer, merely stares at me with a terror unique to prey in headlights. I take her by the shoulders and shake her. In a quieter voice, I say. "Tell me where she's keeping the Boneweaver."

She swallows. "Downstairs."

"Show me," I command.

I have to give her a little push to get going, but she ends up stumbling down one set of stairs and then another until we're on the ground floor.

The rumble of engines sound out the front, followed by many car doors slamming. "Hold on," I tell the girl.

Striding quickly, I open the front door on its useless modern swivel hinge and am met by a group of four crocs armed with rifles, cocked and ready.

They are resistant to most types of magic, because that is their order's power, but I'm a motherfucking dragon.

With a flick of my wrists, their guns clatter to the floor. I lash out with my hands and four ropes of fire whip out of each one, securing around each of their necks. They grunt under the heat but don't fall. I have to yank at the ropes to get them to tumble.

I curse under my breath because the fire isn't burning through their skin. Rolling my eyes, I stride outside, dragging them with me. Fixing the four ropes under my bare foot, I push at the marble crocodile statue. It groans and grumbles in protest, but it eventually gives way and I roll it on top of the four ropes.

That should keep them from interfering for a while, at least.

Making sure the guns are out of their reach, I then run inside, where the chicken is waiting for me, hugging herself in fright. I follow her once again into a big room that's supposed to be a throne room. Steam leaves my nose in a haze of black, but I frown when she leads me to a very ordinary-looking fish tank in the corner next to the throne.

"What is this?" I snap.

"It's not a joke," she says, finally finding her voice. She points to something in the tank. "She's that one."

With my heart pounding, I peer through the glass. She's pointing to a starfish, a pale blue thing, as if leeched of all its colour. It only has four arms, its fifth is but a horrid stub.

Even without the tiny golden ring around its topmost limb, I would know that shade of sapphire in any lifetime. Even sickly and pale. Even if I were blind and powerless. Even with a severed bond, I would know her.

"Get me a container," I command. "A small one with a lid."

She runs off at full speed. Holding my breath, I reach into the tank. She twitches when I touch her, and it makes me want to destroy the entire house. But my hands are gentle as I lift her out of the water and behold her.

"You are safe now," I whisper. "You are safe with me, Aurelia."

I wonder if she will believe that.

The chicken comes back with a tupperware container. I take it from her and fill it with water from the tank before placing Aurelia inside of it.

Then I look around the room.

"Please don't burn the house," she says, tears filling his eyes. "My bond-sisters are locked up below ground. They can't leave."

I'm too full of fury, too vengeful and empty of any care for other creatures to deign to give her a verbal answer. I only charge out of the house without another word, explode into my dragon form, and in one big claw, clutched safely, is Aurelia inside her container.

I tear across the land, to the one place of safety my heart desires. The one place where I keep all my treasures and jewels safe and away from the rest of the world.

Deep into the heart of the Blue Mountains, where my horde lies hidden.

Chapter 65

Aurelia

In my head, a woman screams.

She does not stop. Her agony is infinite. Her agony is madness.

And so, I must retreat into the darkness, far, far away from her, to where the pain recedes into nothing because everything becomes nothing.

I sway in the darkness. I sway in the shadows. I sway in a place that is only for me and my despair. There is nothing left to me. Of me. I have no desire to claw my way back to the reality of those screams. There is nothing left for me there except pain. I have no parents. I have no mates who would want me. I have no friends. These things are only memories. They exist in the past. And the past can't be real.

I just want everything to stop.

Chapter 66

Xander

The Last of Her Kind – Peter Gundry

Deep in the mountaintop cavern where I keep my horde, I set Aurelia's container down on a gilded tray. Then I sit down and watch her, breathing deeply to catch my breath.

She lies so very still in there, my magical sight telling me she's pulled her power in so close it's buried under her skin.

How she thought to shift into this form bewilders the mind.

The golden ring, *collar*, around one of her limbs seems ridiculous. As gently as possible, I open her container and reach in, stroking a finger down the collar and letting my magic open it. A seam appears and I slip it off.

Her skin is cool, and it makes my fingers tingle to touch her.

I also quickly realise that this container is too bloody small, so I set about building her a new home. I have many unique things within my coins, treasures, and jewels, but nothing with which to look after a starfish. Once I've made sure she's hidden, I fly to the nearest town and purchase as many things as I can carry. There's a shiny new glass tank with a bag of fresh, briny water, sand, and after researching on my phone, I approach the local pet shop to get her the right flora, the right nutrients. I even bring her a couple of gentle clown fish for company. A man on YouTube recommends a UV light for a sick starfish, so I get her that too.

Once my setup is complete, I carefully pull her out of the Tupperware container and set her in the new one, ensuring adequate temperature control. Then I sit down and watch her.

Every day from then on, I sit before her tank.

I've learned many things in my research about starfish. They have no ears, but they do have rudimentary eyes. I wave my hands in front of her, press my face close to the glass to see if the tips of her arms might recognise me.

I watch her amputated leg like a hawk. I measure its length daily and write it down in a notebook as well as notes about her colour and condition.

She doesn't move. She doesn't change colour. I try to contact her telepathically, but I get nothing back. At the end of the second day, I try to feed her. I bring her fresh crab meat from the sea. I buy some clams and prepare the meat for her, place it under her stationary body and wait to see if she gobbles it up, a twisting sensation in my own stomach as I wait.

If she is to re-grow a whole limb, she needs food.

To my dismay, she doesn't eat my first offering. I eventually fall asleep next to her tank, and I wake up with a start a few hours later. The food is no longer underneath her.

For the first time in what feels like months, I grin.

The next day, when I measure her amputated limb, it has grown five millimetres. Her colour is slightly deeper blue.

Success! I exhale with relief and write the details in my notebook.

The happiness is short-lived, however, because after a few days, I see no other change in her colouring or size. She eats very small amounts of what I offer and still overall looks unwell. So I start to brainstorm other ideas.

My eye catches on the golden grand piano I keep in the

corner. Excitedly, I tune the ancient thing then place Aurelia's tank on top of it. At first, I play my favourite Beethoven, mostly to calm myself.

With a grimace, I play something girly. Something she and Minnie would likely dance to when no one was looking. Or when *everyone* was looking. I snort at the memory of the two of them, thinking they were sneaking past me on their way to the Bouncing Bazookas nightclub. I'd let them go because I didn't really care at the time and couldn't be bothered trying to stop them. If they were stupid enough to go against Scythe's orders, they deserved whatever consequences came afterward.

But as I watch Aurelia now, and can't help but think that there is something devastatingly sad about how she has reduced herself to something so small. So fragile. She is as beautiful now as she always was, and there is a great power in a creature that can re-grow an entire limb, but she is still so vulnerable.

Any other beast could just come and devour her and that would be the end of...her.

I realise that my fingers have trailed off mid-song, stopped playing at the thought of her simply not existing in this world.

Some pain at the centre of me blooms anew and I press my lips together as I watch her. In this time, in this place, the Wild Goddess saw it fit that her care be designated to me.

I strike up the song again, the sounds filling me up, intoxicating me, making me sway. There are only two of us in this place, so far from the rest of the world, listening to this song. I wonder what she's thinking in whatever is left of that mind of hers. Does she even know that it's me who has her? Does she think it's someone else?

The thought angers me, of course. The idea that my efforts could be attributed to some other bastard. She needs to know that it's me. That I'm the one who's making sure she gets better.

And yet, if I can claim *that*, I should also claim that I'm the one who made everything worse.

My fingers shift into a new song, a beautiful, moving one that means something to me. It might mean something to her. Might be enough to pull her back to us at the end of this.

Chapter 67

Aurelia

The woman in my head is still screaming.

But something calls to me in the darkness. Something familiar.

Because I am desperate, because I am lost, I reach out to it.

And regret it immediately.

Chapter 68

Xander

Something changes on the third night.

There's a giant smash and I awaken with a start, leaping up to standing from my spot on the cavern floor next to the piano.

It's dark but my eyes can see the tank I'd set atop the piano is on the floor in shards, water everywhere.

Debris, plants and rocks lie in between the clear shards, and when I round the corner, Aurelia is there, in her human form, choking out water from her lungs. She heaves and coughs, eyes squeezed shut, chest wheezing.

Immediately, I can see her amputated leg has re-grown to the knee, but the end of it is red and raw.

"Aurelia!" I cry, rushing through the glass and skidding to her side.

She opens her eyes, takes one look at me, one look at her leg, and *screams*.

"No!" I say, pulling her wet body into my chest. "No, it's okay! It's—"

She doesn't stop screaming. She doesn't fight me. Her body is limp, and I don't know how she's doing it, but she doesn't stop for breath. Her scream continues on and on and on.

The sound pierces my ears, but still, I clutch on to her.

"Aurelia!" I shout, rubbing her wet, naked back. "Aurelia!"

She can't hear me.

"Shift!" I scream back. "Shift, damn it!"

She continues to scream in that awful, high-pitched sound of pure terror.

I see what I have to do. I set her down onto the floor, where her mouth opens wide with that scream up into the cavern ceiling. Then I hit her with a bolt of fire right to the neck. She violently flinches, her scream stopping for a second. "Shift!" I command.

She obeys.

Immediately, her body shrinks, her skin turns blue and knobbly, her arms and legs becoming uniform as her head disappears into the starfish. Quickly, I pick her up.

But now I realise we have no water. She's going to suffocate within seconds.

"Fuck!" I shout. "Shif—" I cut myself off short because what should she shift into? My stomach heaves as I realise that there is only one solution.

"Shift into a snake!" I shout, pushing a pulse of power through my voice. "Do it now."

She must feel the command because her body changes, growing longer, her skin smooth and cool. A head and eyes appear again, a hood expanding on either side of her face.

In my hands now, Aurelia lies tightly coiled in her serpent form. A form that has no amputated leg for her to look at. To scream at.

I cradle Aurelia against my chest, and for the first time in eight years, I weep. Only it's not tears that leave my eyes. "I did this," I whisper, the liquid tracking down both sides of my face, burning as it goes. "I did this to you."

I have to hope her Boneweaver magic will heal her leg while

it lies dormant. I take her to my pile of blankets in the corner of my cavern and set her on my bare chest.

The image of her human face when she'd laid her eyes upon what remained of her leg will be forever seared into my memory. The memory of that sound she made... The sheer terror still rings in my ears. It was more than just physical pain.

It was the sound of someone being tortured.

My hand trembles when I place it gently on top of her soft body. I allow my healing power to seep into her scales like sunlight soaking into her skin. "I'm sorry," I whisper, but my voice comes out as brittle as a scorched leaf. "Aurelia, I'm sorry."

Perhaps now she can finally hear me.

* * *

Days pass in much the same way. I place Aurelia's cobra form on my chest and focus my power into her. I rush away to take care of my own physical needs before rushing back and healing her again. I offer her food and sometimes she'll take it. I catalogue the feedings in a notebook with the accuracy of a scientist. I'd been around them enough to know the level of detail that was best. So basically everything.

It's in my close observation of her that I notice she stops responding altogether. Panic almost consumes me before I notice her scales look dull and wrinkled. I quickly search up serpent shedding images and sigh in relief.

Over the course of a few days, Aurelia sheds her skin, but because she is unmoving, it appears difficult. They usually rub themselves against rough surfaces and she can't do that right now.

So I help her.

I keep her warm with my power and get a shallow bowl of warm water. I've bathed her before, but never in this form, and after some debate, I gently pick her up and set her in the pool I've made.

Her muscles seem to relax with that, and satisfied, I gently rub her at her scales. She wriggles a bit, and I wonder how much of this is conscious.

Suddenly, this feels very intimate. Something Savage or Lyle would jump at the chance to do. Or perhaps, something she'd prefer to do alone.

She'd never let me help with something like this if she was fully aware. Swallowing that thought down, I gently rub behind her head with a washcloth. New scales appear beneath the old sleeve, and something in me sighs with relief at the sight of it.

It takes two days of my ministrations before her skin is fully shed, the old skin a crispy off-white material in my hand. After some thought, I find one of my trinket boxes and empty it of its contents before placing the skin inside and locking it with my power.

Glancing at her coiled form in the nest of blankets, I swallow the lump in my throat. This will just have to be between me and Aurelia's cobra for now.

Perhaps this entire thing will have to stay just between us. Because I can sense that it's almost time for her to wake up and become fully aware. And when she does, it won't be me she wants to see.

Chapter 69

Aurelia

It's a dragon that appears before me, black tinged with blue, with golden eyes so wise, so ancient. So ferocious. "My queen. My jewel of jewels, what torments you? Let me know its name so that I may destroy it."

"They tried to break me," I whisper. "Body and mind, I am torn apart."

"Never. Not in this life nor in any other did you succumb. You said as much yourself."

"But it hurts so terribly," I whisper.

"You are queen of the darkest beasts. It was always going to hurt. But you are stronger than you know and more powerful than even your enemies know. Get up."

"I cannot."

"We endured for millennia together. We endured betrayal and death. We endured through blood and fire. You are the last of your kind in this world. Do not leave it lying in a pool of your own misery. Leave it fighting. Leave it with the blood of your enemies in your teeth. Leave it raging. Get. *Up.*"

Chapter 70

Xander

You'll Be in My Heart — Phil Collins

The next day, I rise at dawn and look over to see Aurelia still curled up and sleeping in cobra form. My hand still rests on her, and with a grunt, I realise she'd been soaking up my power all night. Tentatively, I whisper her name, and to my surprise, her eyes open.

Something lurches in my stomach to see those blue king cobra eyes staring back at me. Her forked tongue sneaks out, tasting the air, and I observe her condition. She doesn't uncoil, nor move any other muscle.

"Are you hungry?" I ask. "I still have some clams."

I remove myself carefully from the nest and retrieve the starfish-safe food I'd brought back yesterday. I put it on a clean plate and set it down where she can see it.

"You can eat it in your own time," I reassure her. "I won't watch you if you'd prefer me not to."

Turning around and pretending to tinker with other plates, I listen carefully for signs of her movement, but she remains still.

I turn around and look at her again, right in those eyes. This is her anima I'm looking at, not human Aurelia. I know what I have to do.

Chapter 71

Aurelia

The cursed dragon watches me with those supernatural, golden eyes. He is eager to care for me, eager to allow his ancient powers to heal my broken body and mind.

I accept it hungrily.

Much has been taken from me. Much is owed.

He lies next to me, his massive heat comforting to my cold bones, and he curls his big wing around my body as if he's trying to shelter me from the pain. Old, volcanic power seeps through my scales and down my long spine. It settles into the crevices, the fractured places, and soothes away the pain that lies so deep into my core. Like lava moving in the hollows of the earth, it moves slowly and deliberately.

Under his power, the screams in my mind fade away until they are faint, as if smothered by a heavy blanket.

It allows me to peep past my anima and see what he does in between staring at me.

The cursed dragon nudges forward food on a tray with his big snout. It has the air of a disciple setting down an offering to his patron goddess.

Sometimes I choose to take it. Sometimes I do not.

One day, alongside the fresh, dragon fire-seared meat, he sets down something wrapped in red foil. A small, familiar sweet.

I rear up and hiss at it.

White smoke streams from his nostrils and he uses his power to snatch it up and take it away from my sight.

Handsome bastard creature.

His massive head snaps towards me as eyes flare a brilliant gold.

I go still, staring at him because I had not meant to communicate.

The cursed dragon edges closer on those big claws, sniffing the air. Sniffing me.

With no intention of entertaining this, I lower myself to the floor and coil up, ignoring him.

He snorts in annoyance before lumbering away to a pile of gold coins in the corner.

It's pitch black at night in the cavern where we are. That evening, when he finally settles down next to me and places his wing in its usual position, I wait until his breaths turn deep and slow.

Sliding away, I let the edge of his wing thump onto the blanket and venture out of the nest. This is my first time looking around at this location. I sense we are high above, in mountains where the air is a little bit thinner, encapsulated and isolated in mountainous rock.

And within this rock are piles and piles of treasure.

Stacked high on gilded tables, on the rocky floor, on antique chairs are things that smell of gold and jewels. In one corner, gold bars are stacked as high as a human male, and in another corner, antique paintings that must be worth millions. One corner glints with a silver engine, and upon further inspection, I find a row of motorcycles.

With a distant shock, I realise this is a dragon's treasure horde.

Exploring further into the maze of shining trinkets, I taste the air and sense the direction it blows. The cavern is huge, big enough that I become weary travelling to the other side. Finally, fresh, cool night air brushes my face.

I surge forward until a gaping maw opens up into the night. The cavern entrance is circular and easily three stories tall, big enough to fit a dragon, and just as wide. Lifting my gaze, I finally get to see just how high up we are.

A sky of stars shines above us, the full moon bright. Before me, a mountainous expanse stretches out, peaks and valleys covered with dark foliage. There is no snow as we're headed towards the end of summer, but the mountain air is still cool on my scales.

A soft, draconian snort sounds.

My entire body whips around as Xander, quiet as a predator even as a dragon, has come up behind me.

I let out a breath before looking out over the misty land. But my human eyes would reveal a little more colour...

Swallowing the lump of fear in my throat, I concentrate on my body and feel myself elongate. Scales disappear and make way for human skin. My hood disappears into my head, making way for human hair to come through. And limbs. Four limbs grow from my body. I flex my fingers as they appear, but as for my feet—

Pain burns through the length of my right thigh and I immediately raise my foot, shifting my weight onto my healthy left one.

I feel different. I cannot be the same person I was before. This Aurelia feels like glass. As if all it will take is one decision and I will shatter. They have not broken me. That, is a privilege only I am allowed.

Holding my breath, I look down at my newly grown leg. It is, thankfully, whole, if a bit pale compared to my other, but anatomically identical. The only difference is the pain. I gingerly set the foot flat, testing the feel of it. Bone deep pain shoots like lightning from my heel to thigh and I hiss in agony.

The dragon growls with worry.

I look over my shoulder at Xander, looming over me, his dragon's head swooping low to peer at my face, golden glowing eyes flickering just slightly with some emotion.

"It hurts," I mutter. "Obviously."

I don't know how to reconcile the dragon I felt in my head with this dragon. With this Xander who looks uncertain.

He makes a rumbling sound that turns up at the end like a question.

Frowning at him, I ask, "Are you in a treasure haze again?"

He blinks, those glowing eyes disappearing just for a second before they reappear, lowering his head even closer. He's showing me his eyes are clear.

Silence stretches between us as we stare at one another. Does he hide in this form, as I did just before? Is the human side too painful? Too...distasteful?

I hope he doesn't shift back.

He suddenly leans down, draconian nostrils flaring as he sniffs me. Without another word, he turns around and shuffles away into the cavern.

After a moment, I follow at a snail's pace, limping so I don't place too much weight on my right leg. Each step makes pain shoot through the length of the limb and I grimace, irritated at myself. How many days had I spent healing?

The dragon ahead of me turns around and takes a step towards me before indicating my leg with his snout and then making a strange, polyphonic sound from his chest. It's high and low at the same.

Is he...whining?

"It's fine. I can do it," I say through gritted teeth.

He watches me, standing by a circular black stone basin with a spout that looks like it was made with dragon magic.

The dragon indicates it with his snout. The spout magically turns on, crisp mountain spring water gushing out.

I cup my hands and place it under the water and let it fill, before bringing my hands up to my lips to drink. It's cold, mountain spring water that feels perfect against my hot, parched throat. I wipe my lips with the back of my hand, suddenly weary.

My hand slaps onto the edge of the basin before I fall, steadying myself as a wave of dizziness slams into me.

Xander makes that whining sound again before lowering his head right next to mine. With infinite slowness and great gentleness, he presses the side of his snout against my cheek. I close my eyes against the feel of his mighty power, his warm, rough skin against mine. His breath fans out against my back, hot and wet, and it sort of reminds me of when Henry used to sit on my shoulder, guiding me to breathe.

I don't even know where my little nimpin is now.

The tears start, barrelling over my cheeks in thick droplets. My nose runs and I press a hand against my mouth, trying to stifle the sobs.

Warm air wraps around me and I screw my eyes tightly shut, hugging my arms around my body. Something hot and sharp digs into my sides, but it doesn't hurt me. I'm tilted sideways, and before I know it, I'm moving slowly and steadily through the air. I don't open my eyes as Xander's mouth encompasses my body, carrying me like a pup and setting me onto the soft blankets of his nest. Only then do I crack open my eyes, snot and tears running down my face, to see golden light staring back at me.

Then he opens his mouth—

And the tip of a giant red tongue snakes out and licks my face, wiping away my snot.

"Ew, stop," I say, throwing up my arms and turning away with a grimace. When I'm sure he's put his tongue away, I frown at him. "That was disgusting."

He snorts like he disagrees.

Sighing, I make sure my new leg is bent at an angle so I don't trigger the pain and rest my head on my arms.

When I wake up, it's to something warm and wet gently scraping against the skin of my thigh. Rubbing the sleep out of my eyes, I sit up to see the dragon curled about me, licking my leg.

"Not again," I mutter.

My leg is warm with his magic, the skin glowing like he's been filling my muscles with his power. He makes that strange whining sound again and nudges my face with his massive snout.

"I know," I say. "It's not all the way right yet."

My stomach grumbles.

His head snaps to attention, his eyes wide and alarmed.

"It's just my stomach," I say quietly, rubbing across my abdomen. "Don't look so panicked."

With the type of agility only dragons have, he uncoils himself from around me and bounds away at breakneck speed.

I shiver against the cold, my naked skin erupting with goosebumps. "Do you have any clothes around here?" I ask, looking around at the tall piles of treasure.

The dragon reappears, lumbering back with multiple items levitating before him. He sets them gently before me: a plate of cooked, cut vegetables, and a length of red material.

I place a piece of sweet potato in my mouth and begin chewing before I reach for the material. He's seasoned the vegetables with salt, paprika and oregano. When did he have time to cook this?

The material is a soft type of cotton, and when I hold it up, I realise it's a dress, except the stitches look like they were done by hand and the hem is very uneven. Without looking at him, even though he sits on his haunches staring at me, I shove my head and arms through it.

He doesn't try to help me, which makes me believe he really isn't in a treasure haze. If he were, he'd be stuck to me like mould, fussing and fluffing about. Instead, he maintains a sort of distance, even though his eyes are stuck on me.

Finally covered, I tug at the dress, wiggling to the feel of it. It's strange being covered after so long of being a naked animal, and one part of me doesn't even like it.

But the mountain air is cool, and human skin isn't nearly as protective as scales or fur, so I don't have a choice.

I eat from my plate as Xander watches, snorting softly when I finish and removing the plate with his power. We both watch the white porcelain sail away onto a stack of other dishes by the black stone basin. Dragon eyes then turn to me and he proceeds to coil around my body carefully once again, forming his own sort of nest, his head falling in line with my new leg.

Exhaling a slow breath, I lie down, and using his claw as a pillow, fall into a slumber.

The next time I wake up, it's a human male body coiled around me.

Chapter 72

Aurelia

There's a tanned, male hand under my cheek that I've drooled all over. Another hand rests on my right thigh.

My heart pounds with the reality I now have to face. Carefully and quietly, I extract myself from him and, primarily using my left leg, slide out of his hold.

Rolling onto all...threes, I keep my right knee above the ground and push myself to standing.

Xander sleeps naked on his stomach, having absently shifted in his sleep.

I'd hoped I'd get longer with the dragon. I'd hoped I'd get longer before I'd have to deal with the thing that makes my soul bleed.

Why had Xander saved me? Looked after me as if he cared?

I stand over his nest, watching his muscled sleeping form, the rise and fall of his back as he lies on his side, that arm outstretched, tattooed with his ancient, tribal family markings.

It's jarring seeing him again.

My stomach knots and I have to tear my eyes off him.

My brain feels heavy. My limbs sore, but rested. I can smell the night outside, and I'm sure with a bit of effort, I could get out of here. A cold breeze strays towards me and I sway into it.

"Aurelia?"

I close my eyes against the pain of hearing his voice. The way it cuts so deep, even now. My own voice is small, but a paper cut carries its own sting. "Am I not 'Spawn' any longer?"

He stiffens as that settles between us. And when he does speak, his tone is like nothing I've heard before. "You... You were right. My sister was right. I am a monster. I was fashioned into one by my...anger. My choices. Only I am to blame for..." He struggles for a moment. "For everything that happened to you."

I can't bear to look at him. Can't bear to hear his cursed words. Can't fucking believe this. My hands tremble and I clutch them together. "I want to go home."

His silence bleeds with disappointment. With what seems like great self-control, he says quietly, "I know."

He looks at me, and it's not like before. I should be used to his gaze by now, as I've sensed his attention on me for long, long hours. But I'm not, and I can't. It burns like the worst type of poison.

I look around at his secret home, at the place he's brought me, and likely not brought any other. It's impossible that he regrets what he's done. He can't understand what he's saying. Perhaps he doesn't even understand what he's doing.

So I tell him the truth and let him see it with his magical eyes as I stare at the cavern wall. "I can never forgive you."

From my periphery, he bows his head. I close my eyes and turn away from him.

There will be consequences for this. What he's done. The Collector won't be happy that Xander's taken me away for yet a second time. And there are also consequences for me.

I have failed. Utterly. Irreconcilably. My return will be laced with poisonous shame.

"Aurelia, they will be hunting for you."

Every time he says my name, I die a small death. I want to curl up in a hole. I want to shed my entire human skin until there's nothing left of me. I want to dissolve into water until there is no memory of who I was before.

But one thing calls to me. As old as the stars that forged us, my soul turns its head towards the mates who I have tormented for months with my silence.

Do they hate me now? Do they wish they'd never laid eyes upon me? And worse still, do they regret claiming me as theirs?

I have few options. Little hope for much else beyond them. They are everything to me and I have to try. If they want to reject me, I may as well know sooner rather than later.

So I call, in a quiet, tentative voice across the land. *"Savage? Scythe? Lyle?"*

"REGINA!" comes the immediate triple reply.

I want to cry. *"I... I rescind my orders."* There's a sigh on the other end and it feels like violent relief. *"Would you..."* I take a breath and say in a small, uncertain voice, *"Would you come and get me?"*

"Where are you?" comes Scythe's cold, cold, rasp.

I hesitate for a moment, wondering if calling them here is a good idea. But I've had worse ideas.

"We don't need her to tell us," comes Lyle's predatory growl. *"Regina, we are coming."*

An age-old ache, suppressed for these last months, burns like the sun. I move towards the cavern entrance and shift.

Wings stretch out from my body, my head elongates, human skin turns to feathers, and a beak tears through my nose.

I flex the claws of my new leg.

"Be careful," Xander says. That note of panic in his voice is so new. So fragile. "You have not tested it. There's not enough muscle to carry your weight."

Pain laces through my claw and I immediately raise it and tuck it safe into my body, shifting my weight to the left.

I don't turn to look at him. Instead, my wings flare out as a counterbalance, and I hop towards the cavern's ledge.

I don't turn back.

Once I'm at the lip of the rock, I peer down into the long drop, my heart leaping at the thought of flight after so long.

Home. I am going home.

"Aurelia," Xander says. Again, that desperate, glass-like thing in his voice claws at me. Demands my attention.

I don't turn back.

Raising my wings, I let myself fall over the edge, snapping my wings out as I catch the wind and soar into the night. To home. To the three other pieces of my soul I go—

And leave behind the cursed dragon with the bowed head.

Chapter 73

Scythe

Lyle has been driving non-stop the entire night, refusing to give up the wheel. Even for the police that follow us.

I've had to faint three patrol officers already, and this fourth one brakes in time to swerve off the road, its driver unconscious, the dust kicking up in a pale red cloud. Exhaling in irritation through my nose, I search the blue, cloudless sky above us, searching for any signs of our regina.

She'd finally contacted us. She finally called for help...and she didn't sound good. I'd waited for this day for months, and now it was finally here. That tight fist of pain and rage within me has softened.

But I won't feel true relief until I have her in my arms. Until I have her mouth on mine.

My phone rings, and when I see who it is, I answer immediately. "Katerina," I snap.

"I just thought I'd let you know," Lady Crocodylus purrs, her voice filled with smug satisfaction that makes my skin crawl, "that two hours ago, Mace Naga put out a search warrant for, um...what was it again? Ah yes..." She drags it out for her own humour. "A wedge-tailed eagle with...*one leg*." She chuckles and hangs up.

My phone drops to the floor. Unbidden, my teeth elongate and my vision turns red.

The car speeds up as Lyle drives the pedal to the floor and the entire car fills with his enraged growl.

"No," Savage whispers, from the seat behind me. "No, no, no, no, no!" And then the rage comes. Hot and hard. His power flares out, so enormous that I feel it rush over me like a real wave. He punches through his passenger window and it shatters under his fist. Savage sticks his head out into the wind. "XANDER DRAKOS!" he screams, broadcasting his voice with such violent force it tears through not only the town ahead of us but through the entire fucking state. *"I condemn you to death. Your execution will be done by the claw of Savage Fengari!"*

Whether it was done by his hand or not, Xander is responsible for this. We all silently agree on that.

Chapter 74

Aurelia

The night welcomes me with loving arms as it always has. The cold mountain air on my face, sweeping over my feathers and brushing away at the bad thoughts heckling inside my skull.

As ambrosial as the open sky is, it can't take away the pain.

There is the pain in my thigh, marrow-deep from where the femur was broken, and the occasional bolt of lightning that goes down the entire leg as if it protests its own existence. I cringe against the sensation of the new limb, the ache, the untested bone and muscle. The entire thing might have re-grown, something I hadn't been sure I was capable of, but it cannot bear my full weight right now.

It's as good as useless.

My heart drops as I do, losing altitude as I follow my beak north-west. With my mating mark shield and other protections removed, I can feel my mates and their direction, and no doubt they can also feel me. These look like the Blue Mountains, and if I'm right, I have a distance to travel to get to the academy. Hopefully my mates will meet me halfway.

I'm still tired from the healing and what was no doubt a catastrophic level of blood loss, my stamina at its lowest point. So

I drift lower and lower into the trees below me, choosing a steady branch to nest in for the night. I should have left in the morning, after I was well rested, but I just couldn't stand it any longer in that place. With him. All I want are my mates—the ones who actually love me. I tumble into a heavy sleep, pure luck that no one came upon me in the isolated bushland.

The next morning, I drink water from the river nearby and sigh before taking flight again, this time into a stormy grey sky. The rain makes my leg ache all the more, but I keep it tucked tight against my body as I fly towards my mates.

Excitement mingles with fear as I feel us growing closer. I block telepathic communications, because though I feel requests multiple times, Savage the most insistent and impatient, I'm just not ready for talking.

It's probably why I don't notice the three falcons swooping in behind me in hunting formation.

* * *

At first, they follow at a distance, letting me know they are there, letting me see their numbers. They each carry a bag in their claws, probably with weapons or tools for hunting.

I have no doubt in my mind they are from the council's retrieval team. No doubt they've been scouting the state for me this entire time, probably under some false crime allegation. It's an old game between us.

These are full-grown males, practised in taking down wild, criminal birds, and as one, they decide to catch up to me. Two of them line up on my left and right, and the third takes up position right over me. From the trees below, a fourth spears towards a lower altitude, right under my belly.

We fly for a few crucial seconds where I decide what the hell I'm going to do. Council birds, at the end of the day, work for Mace Naga and Flores Drakos.

They're here to take me back.

The screaming in my head starts up again, and I cringe against it. This can't be happening. My mates are close, I just know it. But if these guys keep me to the wind, none of them will be able to help me.

Reaching my power out to the one below me, I find his beating heart and squeeze it ever so gently until he falters in mid-air. He quickly folds away, falling towards the trees.

I nose-dive, dropping into the line of trees with the hopes of shifting into something not falcon-friendly.

But they follow without hesitation and one of them drops from the sky, piercing my back with his claws. A screech leaves my beak, and I let myself fall through mid-air, pulling us both right towards the treetops. A second falcon joins in and digs its claws into my neck. But he's too late to bring us back up and I cry out again as we hit the canopy and tumble through branches and leaves. Pain erupts through my back and I screech, desperately wrenching at my attackers with telekinesis.

We are a jumble of feathers and leaves as we hit the ground, and despite the pain exploding through my spine and leg, I summon the energy to shift. My wolf form morphs slowly into being, but the falcons are ready for this.

One of them shifts and becomes a naked man holding a navy bag and points to me.

"Aurelia Boneweaver, you're surrounded. Cease your fight."

I growl in fury, taking a step forward and realising too late my right hind leg can't take any weight. Growling in frustration, I raise it up and hobble forward three steps. The two falcons continue to dig their claws into my back, searing pain suffocating my thoughts. I trip over my own feet and they take the opportunity to wrestle me to the hard packed earth. The pain in my leg forces me to shift back into my eagle form, where I tuck it safely underneath me and away from further harm.

Someone's beak stabs at my neck, another digs his claws into my spine. I came all this way just to be felled at the last minute.

The falcon in human form opens his bag, takes out a small dart gun.

There's a moment between us, hunter and prey. Where we both acknowledge that I've lost. That despite everything, despite being the last Boneweaver I don't have the strength, or the cunning or the wiles to get out of this. Defeat slides through my body like sludge.

"Mace Naga will be so happy to see you," he says, hoisting up the gun and aiming it at me.

Something sounds in my head. Like a knocking. Distant screaming begins. But my body has no strength for this.

I accept my fate.

The gunsman exhales, his finger flexing on the trigger—

Right before his head explodes in a shower of flesh, bone and blood.

Chapter 75

Savage

My head is out the window, my hair flapping wildly as I scan the sky because I know our regina is close. The road is empty this early in the morning, with dense forest on either side of us. I listen carefully to my spirit.

A hint of phantom pain hits me like foreign claws in my spine. *It's her.*

"Next left!" I shout to Lyle. "They've found her!"

Lyle doesn't answer. Instead, the car lifts off the road completely and I let out a whoop as our lion shoots us down the road like a bullet. The very skin of my face seems to fly backwards under the force of it, and I have to open my eyes wide to maintain vision. A dirt road appears through the forest on the left and Lyle swerves violently. I hold onto the edge of my window with all my might, the aggression of it riling me up, getting me ready to reclaim my regina.

"*Slow down,*" Scythe commands. "*We're near.*"

Lyle halves his speed and I scan the forest for any sign of movement.

In the distance, a falcon shrieks in pain.

"*Aurelia!*" I scream.

Lyle and Scythe let out snarls of pure fury and I feel Scythe go cold.

I almost break the door wrenching it open. Lyle stops us and drops the car abruptly and my brain rattles as I slam into Scythe's seat from the force of it.

Lyle and Scythe are already out of the car and leaping into the forest as I explode into my wolf form and dive after them.

We run like the devil himself is on our tails, desperate, enraged. We come on them quickly and I crash through the bush into a small clearing, leaves crunching under my paws.

It's not every day you see a lion fly through the sky and take down a falcon in its jaws, squeezing it until it squirts blood and guts.

But we are the Boneweaver pack.

"Give me a go!" I cry to Lyle.

The lion's rabid eyes flick to me while he gnaws on the bird and I feel myself lift. "There!" I indicate to one of the birds and Lyle doesn't make me fly, the bastard *piffs* me, like a football, right at the thing.

Soaring in a giant, deadly arc, I open my jaws wide as I slam into the mass of feathers, chomping in every direction until I feel flesh and bone. The birdy screeches and I throw him down to the ground, just as I hurtle for the ground too.

"Lyle!" I growl.

He catches me in the air just before I hit the ground and then lets me plonk onto the dry grass. I immediately jump back up onto my paws, my head snapping left and right, looking for more enemies.

"Where is she?"

That primal instinct guides my nose left and forward, where Scythe is already bent over a falcon, a human male lying with its head in pieces next to him. My heart near flies out of my chest and I shift into human form, rushing towards them. "Regina!"

Scythe holds up a hand to pause me and it makes me rage to

think I'm being stopped from getting to her. But I realise he's telling me to be careful.

My growl spreads out through the clearing as Lyle comes up next to me, breathing hard. Scythe cradles Aurelia to his chest as he stands, turning around to show her to us. Lyle and I immediately crowd him, cooing and reaching out to pet the feathers of the one we live for. Her eyes are closed where she rests against Scythe's chest, her beak slightly open, panting for breath.

She's in pain.

"*Aurelia,*" I say telepathically, panicking a little. "*My regina. Are you okay? You are not okay, I'm sorry, I know that, we'll make you better, you'll see—*"

Lyle puts a heavy hand on my shoulder. "Hush, wolf. Don't overwhelm her."

"But I want to tell her that I love her." Then I realise that I actually missed that part and turn back to her. "*I love you.*"

"She has both her legs," Scythe says, angling her up so Lyle and I can see two powerful eagle claws. I bend down, inspecting her body.

"That one looks different," Lyle says, adoringly brushing her right leg with the back of his knuckle. "It's lighter in colour. The skin is softer."

She pulls it away from him, tucking it under her like a lame wolf.

"It hurts her!" I exclaim. "Baby, what did they do?"

"Let's get her out of here," says Scythe, pushing between the two of us and heading back through the forest. "We need to get to safety. The hunting wolves won't be far behind the falcons."

"Right," I say as Lyle goes flying past us to take the lead. When we see the coast is clear, he throws himself into the car and guns the engine.

Scythe gets into the back seat and I run around to get into the other side. We take off with screeching tyres back the way we came. I scoot over to the middle seat so I can be close to my regina. My little chompy. Scythe holds her like his life depends on it, one of his thumbs caressing her wing.

I lean in and run my finger down her face, then lightly kiss the top of her beak. *"Baby, I need you to respond to me,"* I whisper into her mind. *"I need to know you are okay."*

"I'm sorry," the reply comes, small and frightened.

My face scrunches up of its own accord and I wipe a tear from my eye before pressing my forehead against hers. *"I love you. You know that, right? You know you could take out my heart and eat it and I would still be madly in love with you. Everything will be okay now."*

"Regina," Scythe's rough-as-cut-class-voice-says, "you will be okay."

Her body relaxes into him then. *"You came back,"* she whispers.

His silver brows crease a little. *"For you, I would do anything. For you, I gladly curse the world with my presence."*

"You're not a curse," she says, her voice tight like she wants to cry. *"I think I am."*

Three angry growls fill the car.

"None of that, regina," Lyle admonishes. "None of us hate you for leaving us."

"In fact, it gave us something to do," I say, settling back into my chair and nodding at her even though her eyes are still closed. "Didn't it, Scythe?"

"We had a great time," Scythe says flatly. "Very productive."

"We did lots," I snort. "And now I'm full of joy again!" Unable to help it, I lean over and nuzzle her neck with my nose. Her mating mark shines bright and I kiss her there three times. Once for love, once for luck, and once because I'm horny.

Lyle glances at me, fully jealous because he can't kiss her from all the way over there. "One kiss for Lyle," I announce, kissing the top of her head because it's something our lion would do. "When will you turn human again?"

Scythe cuts me a sharp look, to which I sit back, like an admonished pup.

"Take your time, Aurelia," he says, stroking her wing. "You are safe now."

He's so possessive, I'm sure I'm not going to get a turn holding her in the car, so I make do with giving her kisses on different spots once every while.

Once we get to one of our city hotels, it's night time and Lyle parks in the staff car park so we head in from the back. We'd fed Aurelia cheesy nuggets and fries in the car, but Lyle isn't happy with that nutrition, and so once we've snuck into our hotel room, he goes down to the kitchens to supervise the cooking of Aurelia's meal. Scythe has to send the hotel manager after him so he doesn't scare the kitchen staff into pissing their pants. I take a quick shower to wash off the dirt and blood, and then we both put Aurelia in the bath.

It's there we discover that she can't, or won't fully stand on her right leg, so I get to hold her under the shower while Scythe washes her up a bit. She still won't open her eyes and I have to wipe my own eyes a few times because I can tell that her leg hurts.

"She's not injured anywhere else, is she?" I ask as Scythe wipes her beak with the washcloth.

"There is some marking under the feathers around her"—he exhales in anger—"neck."

The thought makes me hold her tighter and I press my lips together to stop from saying something that might upset my regina.

"It's okay," I coo after a minute, kissing her crown again. "It's okay now."

We gently dry her and ourselves off and head into the bedroom. Lyle returns with a trolley of covered food, but Scythe already has our regina in bed.

Lyle and I eat our food on the bed, watching over our sweet eagle until sunrise.

* * *

As the first blue light of morning eases the night away, I rub my eyes and look back to Aurelia. Her sleep was troubled. Through the night, she twitched and flinched, and at one point, she stuck her right leg out and moved it around like it ached her.

"Should we get her a wheat bag?" I asked Lyle at the time.

He shook his head and went back to staring at her as if he couldn't believe she was here now. I can hardly believe it too. But whatever luck we've come by, I'm not going to ruin it by questioning it.

Early in the morning, just as dawn's bright rays shine through the curtains, she finally, *finally* blinks her pretty eyes open. I gasp softly and peer into them. Blue as the deep sea, but heavy with sadness. "Oh," I say. "Oh, regina." I cup her face with my hands. Lyle has fallen asleep at the end of the bed and Scythe is also dozing, so it's just me and her.

"I'm sorry," she whispers into my mind.

"I'm sorry too, baby."

Her beak opens and shuts and I want to tear a hole in the universe at the pain and longing I see.

"I missed you so fucking much."

She blinks at me, soft and sad.

"Look what Lyle made for us." I turn around and grab the plate on the bed behind me. "Fairy bread!" I hold up the triangle with the butter and coloured sprinkles. "I think they use the good butter here, too."

"Savage?" she whispers.

I drop the bread and lean in towards her. "Yes, regina?"

"I..."

I wait for her. Hang onto the end of that first word like a man hanging onto a cliff's edge by his fingernails.

"I missed you too."

My grin is wide and triumphant. "See! I knew you didn't *want* to leave me."

"*Savage?*" she whispers.

"Yeah, baby?" I pick up the fairy bread and tear a chunk off before chewing it happily.

"*I was in the tank.*"

My entire body, my entire mind, freezes, and all I can do is stare in horror at those eyes, pleading with me. Calling to me. The tank in the corner of The Collector's throne room had drawn me in, and I hadn't known why. I'd wanted to take a swim in it and see what had been at the bottom, even though I'd known it was too small. I had dipped my fingers in it, wondering if I could somehow take it home, or empty it of the plants and see what else had been in here.

Something in me had known my regina was in there.

"Excuse me one moment," I whisper.

Very carefully, very gently, I get off the bed and exit the room, padding down the long corridor of the penthouse to the elevator. I take it down five levels and head to the end of the corridor, my bare feet silent on the thick red patterned carpet.

Red like my vision.

At the end of the corridor is a window, with two chairs and a table for people to sit on and admire the view.

I pick up one of the chairs and slam it with all my might through the window, roaring with all the rage of a mate who did not see his regina, who did not save her when he should have.

Who'd completely failed her.

Guilt and shame rip at my heart and I tear my throat open, screaming into the awful, ugly dawn. Once I have no more breath in my lungs to spare, I thud my ass onto the floor, slumping against the wall, and crying into my hands.

Chapter 76

Aurelia

I don't know where Savage went, but about fifteen minutes later, he returns, his eyes red. He's quite calm as he comes to lie on the bed next to Scythe and me, Lyle being draped across the end of the bed, lightly snoring.

Savage looks so sad with his face pressed between Scythe's arm and the bed that I wish I hadn't told him about the tank. I'd just felt like I had to tell him *something*, and it was the first thing I could think of. My aching, tired mind hadn't seen it was the worst possible thing and had likely hurt him.

Fear fills my heart, but I have to comfort my mate. He is more important to me than my own fear, and so finally, I shift.

I stretch my legs out, letting them elongate, letting the feathers and wings disappear and gritting my teeth against the ache as my femur bone from my right leg lengthens along with my shin. Savage watches me, his mouth slightly open, and when he sees me in my human form, his face crumples.

"Aurelia," he whispers.

I climb onto him, leading with my left leg, my skin hungering, so desperate for his that when I lay my naked skin upon his bare chest, I whimper with need. Burying my nose into the crook of his neck, I inhale him into my lungs and savour the feeling of his arms snaking around me, holding me with equal desperation. He whispers my name again, his hands tracing down, then up my back as if remembering the curve of my spine, the shape of my hip, the span of my shoulders. His breath is heavy as I cry into him and he sweeps my long length of hair away, laying kisses on my shoulder. Only when he whispers my name for a third time, pained and insistent, do I raise my head and look at him, and find Scythe looking at me too. There is nothing but tenderness in both of their eyes and it shakes me to my core.

I let out a sob.

"No," Scythe whispers, as my tears run down my face. "No, Aurelia." With a deftness that I shouldn't be surprised by, Scythe whips up and crushes his lips to mine. Another sob leaves me as I open up to him and he opens too. Our tongues twine, seeking each other, admonishing each other.

I sob, easing back. "You left me."

He growls in annoyance, grabbing the back of my neck and seizing my mouth again. But he had come back. For me. As I'd hoped and planned in my wild, insane head.

"You *both* left *me!*" Savage cries, pushing between us and grabbing my face in both hands. My wolf's mouth is rough and hard against mine before he remembers to be gentle. He pursues my tongue and lips like prey, first licking and sucking with mad hunger, before slowing down to savour me properly. I hold his face, feel the stubble of his chin, the stud on his left earlobe. I'm desperate to remember him, to reacquaint myself with his body and soul.

Hands slide up my calves, gently exploring, feeling, checking. I reach a hand out, finding Scythe's thigh before my fingers find themselves buried in Lyle's thick mane.

"Angel," he says, voice thick with emotion.

I tear away from Savage long enough to twist and find my lion, but my right thigh burns with pain.

I hiss, my hand instinctively rubbing at the shooting pain in my healed leg. Three heads, one silver, one blond, one almost black, immediately fall upon my leg, showering it with light kisses and gentle touches. I run my hands through Savage and Lyle's hair. "I re-grew it myself," I say, half with pride, half with shame. Xander helped, but I won't bring that up here.

Three heads snap up. "You...*re-grew* it?" Lyle says, as if he cannot fully compute the meaning of my words.

They all look down at my limb in wonder.

"It looks perfect," Savage says, stroking my knee before laying a gentle kiss. "So perfect."

It's Scythe who runs his finger along the faint demarcation line that runs around the middle of my thigh, seeming to understand. His finger trembles, but I watch my incredible shark put his rage away for the moment. For me.

"My incredible regina," he says, placing a palm on the side of my face and pressing his cheek against mine. "I am so sorry for what you went through. So very sorry."

There are more kisses down both my legs as I reach up to Scythe's face. He pulls away to look at me, searching my eyes. It's my turn to take his face between my palms, those ice-blue eyes thawed with emotion. "Thank you for coming back."

He caresses my cheek with his thumb, taking a deep breath as if taking his fill of the sight of me. "I love you too much to ever truly leave you, and your power saved me."

My tears flow again and he kisses me, sneakily licking up my tears while he's at it. Somehow, Savage and Lyle manage to nudge my legs open and they both silently fight over who gets to lick my pussy first. There is much growling and shoving until I feel Lyle's greedy mouth on my core, lapping up the evidence of my desire. I sigh under his care, as Savage kisses along the old scars of my stomach.

Lyle finds my clit, his tongue weaving fine magic that makes me tremble. I cry out into Scythe's mouth, grinding against my lion's face. He grabs my left thigh, moaning his approval.

There's a wild desperation that's worked up in me now, a

feral need that demands my mates in the most primal way. It's been far too long and too many nights away from them.

I tear away from Scythe's mouth long enough to make a breathless demand. "Cocks. I need you all to fill me up." I turn to Scythe first. "Please?"

His smirk is unabashedly all male and all-satisfied as he takes off his shirt and slacks. Then he gently picks me up around the waist and settles himself under me. We are careful with my right leg and I bend it a little more than usual as I straddle Scythe's hips.

Scythe grabs his cock in one hand and cups my cheek in the other, pinning me with his shark's gaze. "I claim you," he says, easing himself into me. The first rounded stud of his piercing slides against the inside of me and I press my forehead against his. "Aurelia Boneweaver, my regina, my queen." I moan as he becomes fully sheathed, stretching me out after what feels like millennia. After so much torment and pain, this sweet burn, this fullness, feels so right. For the first time, I feel Scythe's power twine through me, icy cold and hungry for union. I gasp at the sensation and he kisses me with a tenderness that makes my insides melt as he gently slides in and out of my wet heat. "Aurelia," Scythe says, and I ease back to look at him as sheathes himself into me again. His eyes bore into mine and hold my gaze. "I'm never leaving you," he says. "Ever. You have me for all of my life and more if I can give it."

I come then, falling into the crook of his neck, shaking and crying as Scythe Kharkorous fucks me through it and whispers that he loves me, that he will always love me, and that I can never get rid of him now. Our powers merge and dance like waters from different oceans mixing, glimmering and dancing like sunlight under water.

A regina who found her mate again.

Scythe runs his warm hands up my spine as Savage appears with the lube and carefully manoeuvres behind me, his patience apparently exhausted. He presses himself against my spine and kisses my shoulder blade before the cool press of his lubed fingers find my ass. Scythe slows the movement of his hips as he strokes my hair and listens to the moans Savage evokes from me, that band of muscle in my ass loosening and singing with pleasure. My wolf kisses the cleft of my ass before he removes his massaging fingers and presses his cock against me. I sigh as I receive him, then cry out his name as his rock-hard length fills me.

I sit up a little then, placing my palms on Scythe's tattooed chest to ease backwards onto both wolf and shark. Savage moans his pleasure into my ear.

"Such a perfect regina," he whispers, flexing his hips just after Scythe. "The most wonderful, perfect girl."

Lyle lies down next to Scythe with his arms behind his head as if happy to watch. But I reach out to him.

He smiles at me, soft and happy, and suddenly, I'm overwhelmed with emotion. The fact that I get to have all of these beasts and call them my own...despite what I did to them. My face must show my shift to sadness because Lyle loses his smile and rushes to sit up.

Scythe strokes my hips with his thumbs and Savage kisses my shoulder, but it's Lyle who says, "We all forgive you, angel. How could we not? You showed *us* so much forgiveness." He presses his forehead against mine and I reach up to his bare shoulders. His breath tickles my lips. "You are the best thing that's ever happened to me. You know this, but I'll tell you a thousand times over to make sure you remember it. The *best* thing, by far." He plants a soft kiss on my nose and toys with my hair before he frowns. "Who has been washing your hair?"

"Lyle, really?" Savage says. "Aurelia, put his cock in your mouth. That'll shut him up."

Scythe's chest rumbles, and all three of us look at him, lying beneath me, a human Adonis, only tattooed perfection with the corners of his lips turned up. Scythe's chest heaves, and another rumble vibrates through him.

"Are you laughing?" Lyle asks incredulously.

A soft smile touches my lips. "They're right," I say. "I want your cock in my mouth."

Lyle leaps to his feet, and we bounce on the bed from the impact. Savage steadies us both as I reach for my lion's thickly veined cock, standing erect at the thought of me. My mouth waters and I eagerly slide my tongue along the underside, tasting a vein before taking him into my mouth.

He grunts, calling me angel as I savour the taste of him, tasting the man and the amber power that reaches for my own.

We find a delicious rhythm, then. Having the three of them, touching me, in me, around me, soothes three broken pieces of my heart. This is where I've belonged. Where I've always belonged.

Lyle comes in my mouth quicker than ever before, shuddering and clutching my face. I know now that he's been holding out since I left, and I gulp his cum greedily, squeezing the base of his shaft.

"Every drop sweetheart," Scythe says as Lyle clearly struggles with his words. "He's been waiting for you."

My muscles squeeze of their own accord and Savage groans into my neck, clutching my hips and coming with a shout. The movement jerks me around and Scythe grabs my right leg, supporting it through the jerking movements of my wolf and lion emptying themselves into me.

"More," I groan into their minds.

Scythe pumps into me, short, firm strokes, unblinking eyes boring into mine, as if he'll blink and I might be gone.

"I'm never leaving again," I tell them, before Scythe gasps and comes as well, his back bowing, power shifting into me, claiming me.

"And don't you ever fucking forget that promise," he growls.

Chapter 77

Lyle

Aurelia doesn't speak much after we wake tangled in each other's arms. She's not her usual attentive, mouthy self. There are no retorts for me, no playful expressions on her face. Her black mane of hair is thinner than before, her human skin papery, those eyes dull.

It speaks of great and terrible suffering.

I want to bundle her up and hide her away from the world, keep her safe in my arms so that none of the motherfuckers can hurt her again. But it also confirms that we did the right thing during her absence. That we murdered and maimed for the right reasons.

Scythe catches my eye, worry bleeding through those once cold icy blues. We both know what was likely done to her. She's not pregnant—we all knew that straight away, nor has any foreign male forced his way inside of her.

The world was saved from our furore due to that, at least. The things we would have done to the male who'd touched her would have made the devil himself gape in horror.

But we do have *one* particular male who may get a similar treatment, and to our luck, that bastard presents himself this afternoon, right at our hotel doorstep.

To his credit, he refuses to step inside the property, as relayed by the hotel manager. Scythe sighs when he gets out his phone to look at the security camera footage.

"He couldn't give her a day of peace," I mutter. "Just one fucking day."

"Savage, stay with our regina," Scythe orders over his shoulder. "Lyle and I will be back."

I cannot tell what my shark-brother is thinking, but a great cold descends upon him, wafting in a hoarfrost around him.

We take the elevator down in silence, neither of us wanting to leave our regina, but also wanting to wring the neck of the dragon who haunts us.

Exiting into the lobby, we find the security guards milling about, unsettled by the dragon's arrival. Scythe placates them with his mere presence, having quiet words with the head of security before we stride across the marble tiles towards the main hotel entrance.

I can't sense Xander like I used to, his volcanic presence missing from a space in my spirit and mind, but every animalia in the lobby knows there's a dragon outside because Xander is no longer masking.

He's let his power out, wanting to be known and, no doubt, wanting to be heard.

Scythe exhales heavily through his nose, another tell that he's troubled by this. I cannot even imagine the level of betrayal he felt the night Xander left.

I narrow my eyes when I see him, my lion letting out a low, threatening growl.

The betrayer waits beyond the revolving glass doors, standing in the middle of the drive through, his arms loosely by his side. His clothing of choice is a pair of track pants and a black T-shirt, unusually casual for him as well as the wind-swept, loose hair. His glowing eyes shine with an otherworldly golden light that makes me scowl. Is this some side-effect of the severing? The human porters have long fled, their scents nothing but weak flutters in the air.

His eyes flicker as he sees us, his face deadly serious, no trace of his usual sneer.

"Scythe. Lyle," he greets in a tone like flat, packed earth.

To prevent us from enticing our beasts, we stop a distance away. Scythe has stopped breathing, likely to avoid filling his sinuses with the smoky embers of Xander's scent.

If it's angering me, Goddess knows what it's doing to him. A beast who had once been more than a brother.

"You have a death wish, dragon," I warn, pushing my lion down.

Xander presses his lips together in a moment of irritation, before saying, "I just want to see her."

"No," us brothers growl in unison.

"What fucking right do you have?" My voice is nothing but a rumble, hardly decipherable as my lion shoulders forward. "The only right you have is to a space we've reserved for you six feet under the Mariana Trench. Curse you, Xander Drakos. And curse your entire family."

His throat bobs up and down, and for the first time since I've known him, Xander has no retort. To my second surprise, the light of his magical eyes falters. "I deserve that. I know I do."

"Then why the fuck would you even try?" I ask. "In what universe would we *ever* let you near her after what you did?"

"I have to try," he replies. "Scythe—"

"Do *not* speak to him," I snap.

Xander ignores me. "Scythe, it's good to see you're back."

Until now, my shark-brother has remained silent this entire time, simply staring at the dragon. But he speaks now, in a low, dangerous voice, his power cyclonic in a cold wind. "The only thing I will permit, Xander Drakos," Scythe says with full venom, "is your death. Nothing more."

Xander flinches at that—actually visibly flinches. Scythe and I stare at him in disbelief. At what he's become.

"I'm sorry." Xander pauses, seeming to struggle for a moment. "Out of respect for you, I want to inform you that I will be shadowing you. Shadowing Aurelia—" I growl at his audacity to use her name and he puts his hands up. "I have to ensure her safety. I don't want anything further to happen to her."

"You...want...to ensure her safety," I say through clenched teeth. "I can't believe this."

"I'll stay out of sight," he urges, spreading his hands out as if this is a reasonable thing to say. "You know you can't stop me."

Scythe and I go still before Scythe unfreezes himself. "There are many ways to stop a dragon," Scythe rasps.

Xander blinks at him for a moment, registering the threat. He takes a deep breath. "I deserve everything that comes my way. But I'll protect her if it's the last thing I do." He takes a few steps backwards before turning around, putting his hands in his pockets and strolling down the driveway. His power leaves the vicinity, its dominating presence fading, allowing us to breathe normally again.

Scythe and I exchange a look as we watch him leave down the street until he's out of magical ear shot.

"What the hell happened to him over there?" I mutter.

"They wanted to break her," Scythe says, shaking his head. "Instead, they broke him. But Xander made his bed. Now he must lie in it and he knows that." He looks at me and I turn to face him. "If the time comes. If Aurelia cannot, will you..."

"Help you kill him?" I nod. "Of course, brother."

* * *

We are quick to get Aurelia out of there. Animus Academy is far safer for her, both in its regional location and with the magical protections around it.

I want her to see Minnie, Sabrina, and her friends too. It will be good for her to have female support. As it is, when we get ready to leave, she silently shifts into her eagle form. Savage pouts for a moment before he picks her up and cradles her like a babe, swaying back and forth. She rests her head on his bare chest but keeps her eyes open, flicking around and alert to her surroundings.

We take her through the loading dock again, while Scythe gets the car. I know he's agitated because he insists on driving, needing to do something with his hands and mind before he gives into the urge to destroy something.

Half way through the trip, I announce that it's my turn with Aurelia. Scythe stops at the side of the road and I hurry into the back seat, almost tearing the buttons of my shirt off as I get ready for her. I have to prise her out of Savage's hands, and she makes the smallest, sweetest sound of greeting as she opens her eyes.

My smile feels like a new thing as I settle her on my bare chest. "There you go, my sweetheart," I murmur.

She snuggles into me, making my heart swell and glow with pride and satisfaction. For the first time in what feels like an age, I feel whole.

"*I love you, angel,*" I remind her. "*We'll be home soon. Sabrina and Minnie will be so happy to see you.*"

"*Sabrina is there too?*" she asks softly into my mind.

"Yes. After the attack on The Lily Institute, we had to relocate the survivors."

"*And the twins?*"

"Blair and Blade never leave her side."

"*That makes me happy.*" After a few seconds of silence, she says hesitantly, "*I promised Sabrina I would kill them all. But I didn't. I didn't achieve anything over there. If anything, I just made it worse, Lyle. If I never gave myself up, they never would have gone after The Lily Institute.*"

"The Clawsons are the only animalia responsible for that, and they're a whole different problem," I say firmly. "Don't worry. We're dealing with it."

She sighs, long and sad, and we settle into listening to each other's breathing. Hours later, under cover of darkness, we drive through the cast iron gates of Animus Academy.

Aurelia feels it immediately. Anyone who approaches the academy can sense the concentration of feral, volatile powers rumbling through the place. It forces the animal in us to go on alert.

I extract myself and my regina out of the car and follow my brothers back to our room. Back home.

Chapter 78

Aurelia

The next morning, I wake up with a start. My heart rapidly slams into my chest as I expect to see the bars of a cage around me. Expect to hear the voice of Flores Drakos as he fucks his daughter-in-law. My body trembles, my thigh burns and my eyes prickle with tears.

But none of the things I expect to see are here.

Instead of cold, I am warm. Instead of Flores Drakos filling my nose, I scent comfort.

And instead of the bars of my cage pressing against my body I am enveloped by three warm, muscular bodies. My mates' scents wrap around me, nothing but warmth and comfort soaking deep into my feathers. I realise I've been sleeping shifted and that I'm lying on Lyle's bare chest with Scythe and Savage cuddled up on either side of us.

I scratch at an itch in my side, my beak scraping between my feathers. The movement wakes up Lyle and I turn my head to peer at him.

The sunlight comes through the window in a beam, turning his hair into gold, his eyes into coins. When I first saw him, I thought he looked like the Archangel Michael, come to weigh my worth. But there is only love in his eyes now and a warmth I feel all the way down to the end of my claws as he strokes down my back.

"Let's shower before these animals wake up," he murmurs, smiling lazily at me.

"I heard that," Scythe mutters, rolling over to give us space.

Their voices centre me and my heart attempts to slow its pace. Once we get into the bathroom, I realise I'm reluctant to shift from the comfort of my eagle form, but a single, meaningful look from Lyle has me shedding my feathers and beak for human skin. I let him haul me into the shower, where he gently pushes me against the wall, gets onto his knees, and hungrily devours my pussy whole.

"Is this an approved therapy technique?" I sigh, running my hands through his unbound hair.

He chuckles into me, sending sweet vibrations twirling right up into my stomach. "For me, yes."

Lyle takes his time with his ministrations, during the shower and after, as he dries my hair and gently rubs moisturiser on my face. I try not to look at the black and gold tiles of this bathroom. Try not to see Xander in the dragon spouts. Try not to be reminded of Drakos Estate in the golden hardware.

"I am in Animus Academy," I whisper to myself, touching my neck. "I am safe now."

Lyle looks up at me from where he's carefully rubbing moisturiser into my right thigh. His eyes are stitched with pain. "You are with us, regina. There is only love here."

I close my eyes, nodding in agreement as he stands and warms me with his presence.

Voices from outside make me open my eyes and put my hands over his where they press against my cheeks. We quickly dress and head out into the main sitting room.

I'm met with a tableau. Minnie is jabbing a finger at her phone, showing the screen to Scythe, as tears flow down her cheeks and her face is screwed up in an expression of such pain that it breaks my heart.

"Min?" I whisper.

Her head snaps towards me, her eyes widening all the way around as she stares. Her eyes flick down to my legs, then back up again. "Is it really you?" she breathes. "Is that my Lia?"

My own face scrunches up and I nod. She doesn't run at me. Doesn't cry out. She walks slowly, as if underwater, her movements careful. When we are toe to toe and I can smell the incense on her skin, the silver bangles on her wrists chime as she raises her hands and gently holds the sides of my face.

"Goddess," she whispers. "Thank the Goddess."

My legs give away and I fall into her arms. Even though she's so much smaller than me, she catches me with feline strength. My head lands on her boobs and there is something about laying your head on the soft mounds of your best friend's tits that heals one of the cracks in my tired heart.

I'm coughing through my crying, sagging and clutching onto her for dear life, because I missed her scent, I missed her friendship and I simply...missed *her*. I can tell Minnie is using her telekinesis to keep me up when Savage ends up having to hold me up from behind. Yeti and Marduk stop Minnie from falling backwards too, and it's a strange, wonderful group hug. Just the thing I needed.

"I love you," Minnie murmurs into my hair.

"You don't hate me?" I say, wiping my nose and adjusting my head on my new pillow.

I'm pretty sure Marduk is wiping Minnie's nose for her, because she's muffled as she says, "I always knew you'd try to run away from here. I haven't forgotten that botched escape attempt, after which Savage held me *hostage*."

"I would never!" Savage gasps in horror.

"Liar!" Minnie and I say at the same time.

"What were you showing Scythe on your phone?"

The room goes deathly silent then and Minnie's chest stops moving. I heave myself off her so I can see them all properly. Minnie takes my hand, clearly not wanting to let go just yet. She flicks at her phone with her thumb and holds it out to me.

It's a legal notice on the *Animalia Today* app, in the section with the list of wanted ferals.

Hunting Warrant Issued: Aurelia Boneweaver, 21-year-old female, wedge-tailed eagle, likely rabid, one leg.

My nostrils flare at the last two words. Someone had wanted to advertise that they'd taken my leg. That they'd turned the mythical Boneweaver into food.

Marduk is trying hard not to stare at the leg I'm very obviously keeping the weight off. I'm only letting my toes touch the ground.

"What did they mean, Lia?" Minnie asks.

I clench my teeth and gesture to it, shrugging. "Well I fucking grew it back, didn't I?"

Minnie's mouth drops open and her two tiger bodyguards go goggle-eyed.

"By the Goddess!" Marduk shouts, running a hand through his hair. "What a miracle!" He goes over to Scythe and slaps him on the back. "Who are we killing, friend?"

Everyone in the room turns to look at me.

"We can talk about it later," I say. "For now, I want to see my friends."

I can see Scythe and Marduk making the calculations. Lyle and Savage exchange a look. They know the type of mythical strength it would take to wrench a leg clean off. And they know which beasts would have the audacity to even try something like that.

But I don't want to think about that right now.

I pull Minnie into the TV room, with orders for Savage and Yeti to fetch our anima gang.

Minnie takes my hand again, "I'm not going to call you amazing, or anything like that," she says quietly, "because you already know I think you are. But that is fucked, Lia. What happened to you is fucked up and awful, and I'm sorry."

We turn the TV on for background noise, something meaningless and not too cheery. The others arrive before long, and it's Sabrina who appears first, standing in the doorway. She looks less like a ghost than before, but still wears her favourite black hoodie. It looks clean this time though, and as she wanders through the door, her hand goes to her mouth. I reach for her and she comes to sit next to me. Stacey comes next and squeezes herself between Sabrina's leg and my left one, holding onto me like she can keep me together.

Sabrina lays her head on my shoulder. "We'll kill them all, Lia."

The words echo through time. I rest my head on hers and sigh. "But not today," I whisper.

"Today," Stacey sniffs, "we eat junk food and watch sappy regency romance."

A regency couple appear on TV, staring with great yearning at each other from across a dining room table.

We sit there until our stomachs start to grumble, at which time Lyle pops his head through the door, and using his headmaster's voice, tells us to come to the dining table as Marduk, Yeti, Blair and Blade bring up hot food.

Stacey and Sabrina give a girly "Yes, sir!" all the while looking at me with suggestive grins.

Around halfway through my burger and chips, a feeling makes me look out the window for a third time. Scythe runs a gentle knuckle down my cheek. "Aurelia."

I blink slowly at him and his touch. "He's here, isn't he?"

His own eyes scan the sky through the glass. "How can you tell?"

I look out the window and it comes out as a whisper. "I just can."

"I won't let him near you. He knows to keep his distance. You do not owe him any forgiveness. Even if he rescued you from that place. Even if he...helped heal you. You owe him nothing."

Something in my stomach twinges. Scythe had surmised the truth. I suppose he knows Xander even better than I do. "I know that. I just...." My hands tremble and I clasp them together.

Savage, who has his arm around me from the other side, nuzzles my mating mark. I want them close to me. All of them. Every time Savage nuzzles me, I feel home. This time, however, I can tell it's for his own comfort.

The Boneweaver pack remains fractured. When Xander betrayed me, he betrayed them all. Something in me wants to fix that. To mend it and make it whole except for the fact that...

We will never be whole.

Xander created a permanent fissure. One that can never be healed. Somehow, I have to learn to live with that.

Something inside me twists in pain and I double over, clutching at my chest as my vision blurs. My hands tremble where they clutch my body. This is too much. Too much for one person to handle.

"What is it?" Savage says.

Something makes me look at Scythe. Those sky-blue eyes are brimming with pain. As if he knows exactly what I feel. He feels it too.

"What do I do?" I plead.

"I cannot tell you," my shark whispers. "But the Xander we once knew is gone."

Chapter 79

Xander

When the Party's Over — Billie Eilish

I'm flying over the dark, empty regional road that eventually leads to Animus Academy when a familiar, tiny, black spot on the earth makes me do a double take. The small creature is attempting to drag itself over the dirt.

My magical sight shows a red-grey aura. This bird, nothing more than roadkill, is close to death. But I know how much he means to Aurelia and Savage.

I dive towards him, tucking in my wings and spearing towards the sorry bird. At the last minute, I snap my wings out and bank. As I near the ground, I shift into human form and fall the last few feet, landing in a hazy dust cloud. I drop the duffel bag that holds my pants and T-shirt.

"What on earth are you doing?" I say in disbelief, crouching down and peering at his tiny, bedraggled body.

Eugene is covered in dirt and blood, his eyes half shut. His wings reach out to the sides and they tremble with exhaustion. He's terribly dehydrated, and no doubt has heatstroke with the summer sun beating down on him for unknown hours.

"Did you walk all the way from Drakos Estate?" I say aghast, brushing the ants climbing all over him.

He makes a feeble, squeaking sound. The vicious predator in me wants to squash him, but I know Aurelia wouldn't like that.

"Fool of a bird," I mutter before sending my power into him.

Only when I've swept Eugene away from death's doorstep do I shift once again, then take him in a gentle claw and fly towards the academy.

* * *

An hour later, I find Lyle's SUV speeding down the road and I'm only satisfied to leave when I see them drive safely through the gates of the academy. For the first time, I tense as I approach the protective dome that surrounds the entire place. Its magic vibrates as I near it, shimmering dangerously in warning. I rear up before I hit it, staring at the lethal magic my instincts are now telling me will fry my skin.

Something crucial sinks in my stomach. I make do with patrolling around the barrier a few times and once satisfied, I leave for the night.

I head towards the small town nearby and don't bother dressing when I enter the sole hotel in the town. I'm too irritated by the wheezing bird under my arm and the fact that this place is only three and a half stars. I wave my credit card and the manager hastily gives me a key without asking for my name or ID. I take the stairs instead of the elevator because despite the flight, I'm wired to the bone.

In my room, I set Eugene in the bathroom sink and force water down his throat, before ordering room service and washing the creature.

Apparently, my new occupation is a nurse. But instead of being angry at Eugene, I find myself wondering what Aurelia would look like as a chicken. What colour would her feathers be?

Would they be a combination of colours or solid black like her wolf form?

The food arrives, and I set Eugene to sleep on the sofa as I take my plate to the window and stare at the night outside, thinking about what must be going on at the academy.

I stand by the window the entire night, not wanting to go to sleep and have Eugene accidentally die on me. I heal him twice more and make him drink until his heart's rhythm steadies and his lungs sound dry.

By the time morning comes, he wakes up and gives a merry crow, although his voice is scratchier than normal.

"It'd still hurt a basilisk," I reassure him when he gives me a worried look. "Anyway, I need you to do something for me."

I take him to the academy with a written message tucked into his beak. From afar, I see that the guards let him in without question, on instructions from Savage when we first arrived here.

That seems like an entire lifetime ago.

An hour later, Eugene roosters out of the front gate with a new piece of paper in his beak. I take it from him with apprehension, but the news is good.

By some miracle, Celeste Agnis agrees to meet with me in town. After circling the academy a few times, Eugene and I wait for the headmistress in the hotel restaurant. The rooster gets his own spot on a booster seat adjacent to me, and I slide a plate of greens towards him.

When Celeste arrives, I stand to greet her.

"You look as awful as I feel," she mutters, sitting down as I hold her chair out for her. Despite the summer warmth, she wears a heavy orange-patterned shawl.

"Serves me right," I mutter in turn.

She doesn't actually look *bad* per se, in her usual white suit and shining red hair. She's always been a nice-looking woman, she's just pale and slow-moving today. But that does worry me, because we can't have her acting like prey at a time when powerful beasts might be coming after the academy. After Aurelia.

"I know my presence here is unwelcome," I begin.

She neither confirms nor denies, which is confirmation in and of itself. Her golden eyes study me in a way I find unsettling. "I can't imagine what I can provide for you."

I glance down at my empty bread plate and fidget with the cloth napkin in my lap. "I'll get straight to the point, then. I need to know if a mating bond can be repaired."

The question stretches out between us until it's so fine it may as well be dust. Her pupils dilate and constrict until, finally, she lets out a tired breath. Suddenly, I see it. The strain under her eyes, the fine veins around her nose, the weight she carries on her shoulders. A regal bird, but an exhausted one. She feels what I did, not in the same way Aurelia does, but she certainly feels the weight of it. Her pain is also my fault.

"You made a choice, Mr Drakos. I imagine you did not do it lightly. Titus—"

"Do *not* compare me to that monster," I grit out.

She raises her brows. "And yet the two of you belong to an exclusive club, whose members, in my extensive knowledge, number only two."

I feel the pain of it like a fire-strike to the face. But it's lucky I've been hit in the face a lot, courtesy of Savage. "I want to repair it, Lady Agnis. I need to know if there is a way. I...made a mistake. A terrible one. I know I don't even deserve it. I don't deserve...*her*."

Her eyes soften in sympathy, and she studies me for a long moment. I wonder what heinous picture I make on the bonding plane. "Never did I imagine that we would end up here, Xander. What happened to that excited boy I met so long ago?"

I lean forward. "So many dragons don't even find their mate in this life. But I have. That has to mean something, doesn't it?"

Her brows knit together. "It did mean something. But I don't know if it can mean anything now."

Now that I've ruined it.

"What is the reason for this...change of heart?"

I cast my eye out of the restaurant window, where the glow of the day almost hurts my eyes. "I've realised some things."

She eases back in her chair, some of the tension in her body leaving. And then finally, she says the words I've been dreading. "Xander, there is no known way to reinstate a broken soul bond. Not in this life. It's never been done. You will always be severed."

Chapter 80

Aurelia

The sound of my own screaming wakes me up. I thrash out of my sheets, my legs shaking as Lyle's arms band around me. "You're home, angel. You're safe. You're safe."

I suck in air, reorienting myself through the darkness, clutching at Lyle's strong arms as he rocks me gently back and forth. I'm home. I'm home. Of course, I'm home. There is no collar on my neck and there are no bars around me. Savage rubs my legs in soothing strokes, and Scythe sits close, pressing his cheek to mine.

Their combined scents and their touch on me quickly grounds my mind. I sigh, long and loud. "I'm sorry."

Scythe kisses me on the cheek, then my mating mark. That soothes me more than he'll ever know. "We love you so much, Aurelia."

"It'll take time," Lyle says. "Now and again, I wake up and have to remind myself I'm not in a cage."

"Still?" I ask in surprise.

"Still," he confirms, resting his cheek on my crown. "Sometimes these things stay with you, rearing their heads to remind you they're still there. But it doesn't mean they have to control you."

I gulp down the cold water Scythe passes me, then watch him as he opens the lace curtain, allowing morning light to flood the room. "I dream of fire sometimes, and black smoke."

Savage rubs at his eyes, looking forlornly at the blank wall. "Last night I dreamt I was a mermaid, and I was happy because it meant I could swim with you and Scythe."

An unexpected laugh bubbles up my throat, and I double over, clutching my stomach. Savage is deadly serious when he says, "I had a blue tail and it was really long."

That makes me laugh even more and I land sideways on the bed, wiping at my eyes as the emotions mix in my brain and the laugh turns into a sob. It erupts out of me like a broken fire hydrant, the building pressure suddenly finding release and I cry loudly into the air, screwing my eyes shut as pairs of arms come around me and bodies spoon mine from both sides.

I can't control it. The despair, the agony, the loss. My cries are full of the pain of Lorian, leaving him behind. They are full of Raquel's whimpers as I left them behind too. My cries are for Henry, Selena, Lady Drakos, Delilah and Emmerson...and for a dragon I crave to see again and yet *never* at the same time.

My body eventually gives out, and I lose the energy to sob after my ribs begin to ache. It's only then that I feel the strokes upon my hair, the calming words in my ear. They lull me into a state between dozing and dissociating.

To move means to feel the pain.

"Then don't move," Scythe says in my head. *"Be still until you can't anymore."*

* * *

A few hours later, well after the academy breakfast service, I wake up hungry and Lyle has food waiting for me on a foil-wrapped plate. He plays the mother hen, making me sit in his lap as he feeds me avo toast and cherry tomatoes. Then I brush my teeth and shower in preparation for a visit with Raquel.

The others are all in class, so I go with my mates to the medical clinic. It's slow going, because I insist on hobbling along the entire way, so Lyle takes the time to counsel me.

"It may be disconcerting to see them," Lyle says. "They're administering pain relief because it became clear Raquel was uncomfortable."

"I saw them chained in the dungeons of Drakos Estate," I say darkly, the memory painfully sharp now. "Nothing could be worse than that...or meeting Ruben's regina."

Savage freezes, swivelling around to stare at me. His face darkens as he realises what this means. That Xander has consorted with his enemies.

"When you slaughter a mated beast, it's best to slaughter the entire pack," Scythe rasps. "Otherwise, the others tend to come after you."

Ice trickles into my heart at that. Of course they've done this before. It's easy to forget your mates' occupation when they're giving you sweet kisses and feeding you avo toast. "She would have killed me," I say carefully as Scythe holds open a door. "I got out of there just in time." *Xander* had gotten me out.

"Our hit list is long," Savage sighs, cracking his knuckles as we head inside the medical centre. "But my urge to murder them all is longer."

I grumble something dark under my breath. How many enemies do I have, exactly? I need a journal or a planner of some sort to keep track of them. I can get Minnie and Stacey to help me with a colour-coded spreadsheet.

Hobbling into the medical centre, some of the healthcare staff passing by give me worried looks. But if dragon healing couldn't completely fix my leg, then they certainly aren't going to be able to help me, and I'm not up for talking about it.

Scythe leads us into the section where they keep the private rooms for more sensitive or unstable patients and knocks on a door. A chair scrapes and footsteps hurry to the door. It opens to reveal an older nurse, her silver hair tied back into a bun. Her sharp eyes take us all in.

Lyle asks her for some privacy and she grants it, taking her notes with her. It's not until I step into the room that it hits me.

The room, Raquel lying effectively comatose on the hospital bed with multiple monitors and IVs running reminds me of my mother under Naga House.

My breakfast threatens to depart my throat and I clutch at my chest, turning away for a moment. It's too soon. And this is my fault. I lunge for the bathroom door, and barely make it in time to the toilet, managing to twist my right leg in the process. I heave and scream into the toilet, waving Lyle away when he tries to comfort me.

I don't deserve the help, not when I made this happen. Savage pulls my hair off my face and I allow it. Someone hands me tissues, which I clutch as I stare unseeing into the porcelain. I think of all the possibilities, all the times I could have tried to save my friend, tried to make a difference somehow.

"You were a prisoner there," Savage says softly. "You couldn't have done anything."

I wipe my face, the acidic burn in my throat sharpening my focus. "I did this," I say firmly. "If I hadn't left, Raquel wouldn't have come after me."

Savage exhales heavily. "I was with them, Aurelia. This is on me."

I frown up at him, pushing to my feet. "What?"

For the first time that I've known him, Savage averts his gaze, and watching him closely, I see that his neck is slowly turning pink. His voice is tight when he says. "I took Raquel to Drakos Estate and they never even thought to say no. I...saw the trap too late and couldn't get them out in time. They screamed, but I couldn't— I couldn't—"

Fuck.

I pull my wolf into my arms. Savage has taken this personally.

"He comes here every day," Lyle says into my mind, *"to see how Raquel is. He managed to find a specialist and they'll be coming from interstate in a few days to do an assessment. He's really trying, angel."*

And I'd just made this worse. "I'm sorry," I say to Savage. "But this will always be on me."

I take his hand and we head back into the main room, where I sit next to Raquel's still body, taking their hand in mine as Savage sits next to me, his face solemn.

After ten minutes, the nurse returns to do Raquel's half hourly observations, so we have to leave. In silence, I squeeze Savage's hand and he squeezes mine back.

After the medical clinic, my leg seems to hit the end of its threshold for working properly and Lyle ends up having to hover me through the academy hallways. I feel like a ghost, my toes floating two centimetres off the wooden floor, passively travelling through the hallways. It makes me want to shift into a bird, but some of these hallways in the oldest part of the academy aren't wide enough for outstretched wings.

"The headmistress isn't feeling her best these days," Lyle says as we get into the elevator that will take us to the executive offices. Lyle has apparently taken up his old office again, but his old apartment remains unused as he's been staying with his bond-brothers. "Something about the bonding plane being darkened."

My gut roils again when I hear it. I haven't actively used my phoenix powers since The Collector's house, but think I understand what Lyle means. And I can't help but feel this is also my fault.

The effects of what happened between Xander and me feel like sinister tentacles that have stretched out in every direction. So many people have been affected by it.

When we reach the headmistress' office, she opens the door with an orange shawl wrapped tightly around her shoulders, bluish circles under her eyes.

Alarmed, I examine her appearance and the power around her. It feels tight, like dry skin. The phoenix in me flares outward, golden fire sparking up, recognising her pain.

"Aurelia," Celeste says in welcome, and to my surprise, she pulls me in, her arms wrapping tightly around me. Why does her grip feel desperate?

"Celeste," I say quietly.

She holds my face in her hands. "There are many things I want to say, but the first is that you must not let your guard down."

I search her golden gaze. "What do you mean?"

"They have hurt you," she says. "I know that. I can see that. Your strength is profound, Aurelia, but do not let them take your light."

The backs of my eyes burn. Suddenly, I am reminded of Selena and Lady Drakos.

Lyle shifts behind me. "Celeste—"

"No, let her finish," I say. "This is important."

Celeste's hands slide down to grip my arms. "Did you see him? Did you see Lorian while you were there?"

My heart skips a beat. "Yes. Yes, I did."

"Was he alive? Was he well?" Her eyes are frantic as they search mine.

"Yes, he was. I... I helped heal him." Her hands drop from mine and she steps back, suddenly looking ashen. I follow her, worried that she might collapse or worse. "He spoke to me. He was the only light there."

Celeste's hands reach for her mouth. "Could you show me?"

I hesitate. My only memory of him isn't exactly positive, but the desperation in those phoenix eyes makes me nod. I warn her about his condition before sending her a telepathic picture. I've not had to do it in a while, so it takes me a second, but I know she receives it when the tears slip from her eyes. Lyle helps her to her chair.

"Phoenixes do not have soul-bonded mates, Aurelia," she explains quietly. "We wander alone or choose our own. I met Lorian many years ago when—" her eyes flick to me in shared understanding—"he was passing through." Her shoulders seem to sag, heavy with history. "I knew he'd come back, but Katerina also came across him. Became infatuated with him. I had hoped he'd find me first, but..."

I feel sick to my stomach. Perhaps this is another reason Celeste is unwell. Damien certainly hadn't been so affected by the darkness on the bonding planes.

"Can I try to help you?" I blurt out.

The headmistress twitches in understanding and surprise. "I wouldn't think that—"

"May I try?" I urge. "I'm not physically unwell, as you can see." I have a fuck tonne of other issues, but I can use my powers just fine.

She gives me a small smile. "Please."

I nod, coming to stand before her and taking one of her cool hands in mine. My power floods towards her, keen to push away the dark in someone, even if it's not me. Celeste shudders. There is no exact physical illness I can sense, but much like Lady Drakos, there is something ephemeral that my power seeks out and purges.

Celeste squeezes my hand and sighs, her cheeks flushing. "I feel better, Aurelia. Although I'm not sure what you did."

"Me neither," I admit. "But some type of healing was achieved."

"Thank you." She studies me with great interest for a while, but under her kind eyes, I don't feel so much like an interesting bug like I did at Drakos House. Perhaps I feel seen by her, one of the few people to have known Lorian.

Celeste rubs her eyes. "Unfortunately, there is a related matter we must discuss."

Somehow, I already know what it is.

"Xander is here, Aurelia. And he has a request to make of us."

Chapter 81

Xander

Helvegen — Wardruna

I fly towards the academy, Eugene in one of my claws while we watch over Celeste's car as she drives through the gates. The shadow I cast is huge.

With the dome intent on keeping me out, I have no choice but to land outside the gates and shift into human form, dropping my bag onto the bitumen. The academy guards hoist up their rifles, and for some reason, Eugene sticks by me.

"What, going to use those on me?" I snap.

"S-Sorry, Mr Drakos," calls one of Scythe's employees. "Protocol, you know."

"Of course I fucking know. I helped set up those protocols,"

"R-Right, sorry!" he calls again.

I quickly dress and cross my arms, glaring at the two of them until they break eye contact and shuffle closer to one another. Sighing, I turn away from them to lessen the threat. I don't know if Celeste will meet my request. She has no obligation to, of course. I just have to rely upon the fact that she's a good person.

Sort of in the same way Aurelia relied upon the fact that I

was a bastard of a person when she asked me to help her into the hands of her own enemy. It was a risk for her to rest her plans on me because I could have stopped her at any point. I could've stopped Ghoul, too, if I'd wanted.

But she'd known.

Known me so well that her entire plan hinged on me being a complete asshole. I glance at my bag and what I have in it. The offer I have to make.

They make me wait, of course, and it's hours later before Lyle, Yeti and Marduk stalk down the driveway.

The look on Marduk's face tells me he'd happily hang me by my colon in the way he's done to many before. He uses the colon so you have to smell your own shit before you die. Crafty asshole. But I deserve that look.

Yeti, his snow-white hair worn loose, looks like he let Minnie trim it. It's still long but a bit uneven around the front. He's smoking a joint and his pale blue eyes avoid mine like the plague.

Lastly, the head feline of the school vibrates as if he's smelled an enemy and is trying to keep the lion's chain tight in his grasp. He's impeccable in his regular three-piece, today a stormy grey, but the tamed violence in his aura is an even darker shade.

I wonder if I should let them have at it with me. It might help my old friends feel better to draw some of my blood. I'd gladly give it to them.

They come right up to the gate, but don't open it.

"Nice hair, Yeti," I smirk.

"Fuck off," he says in disgust.

I clench my teeth against the pain of that. But how can I expect any sympathy from them when their own bond-brother did the same thing to their regina?

"Your request," Lyle says coldly, "has been accepted on one condition."

Relief pours through my chest, a cool mountain stream. "Anything."

"You come to her crawling."

I barely give it thought. "Done."

I feel the dome around the school change for me, it's a dangerous sizzle burning down to embers.

They open one gate a fraction, and although Eugene hurries through it easily, I'm left to squeeze through it, and in the way of prisoners, stride past them to take the lead, so they can do what they want to me. They don't of course, but a strange feeling enters my chest as I walk through the familiar grounds and down the path to the animus dorms.

Though our bond is broken, I know she's in this dorm, waiting for me, and it's the sole thing that makes my heart pound as I lay my hand on the glass door.

"Look who's back," sneers Bastien, the gargoyle above the door. "The disgraced dragon lord." He looks down his nose at me from where he sits above the door, stick-like legs dangling down.

"That's right," I say evenly. "I've come to make amends."

"Your mistake," he says, adjusting his monocle. "You'll be leaving in pieces."

Already am.

Marduk presses his ID tag to the electronic sensor and the lock deactivates. I wrench the door open and head inside the foyer and left, down to the recreation room.

Savage and Beak stand at the ready before the double wooden doors.

My heart twists at the hate on my wolf brother's handsome face. At the pain that lies under it. It feels like I have not seen him in years and the sight of him makes me blink back the burning in my eyes. He still wears the black stud I gave him many years ago. I'm surprised he still has it on but honestly with Savage it's more likely he'd just forgotten that I'd been the one to gift it to him. Still, it's my only consolation as he looks upon me with such contempt. I'd heard his vow on the day Aurelia was returned to them. I was sure he'd try to slash my throat as soon as

I'd come in the door. "I have orders not to kill you, dragon," he spits. "Otherwise, your head wouldn't be attached to your body."

Savage would never keep a cabinet of body parts like my father. No, he'd just chuck my head straight into the bin, never to be seen again.

The thought makes me want to laugh for some reason.

"Eugene?" Savage says in disbelief.

The rooster clucks happily and pecks Savage on his bare foot. Savage lifts him up to check on him. "Mate, I thought you were dead."

"Almost was," I say drolly. "But I fixed him right up."

Savage frowns deeply in my direction.

"On your knees," Lyle sneers from behind me, snatching up my bag and rudely opening it for an inspection.

My ears tell me the room beyond is full of beasts. They've prepared an audience for me, likely gathering the entire animus dorm. So they should have. I would have done exactly the same, and it makes old pride swell in my chest.

I drop onto my hands and knees, immediately noticing the dirt and grass particles on the linoleum. They haven't swept in over a week, I bet, and half these ferals walk around barefoot.

Savage and Beak open the doors, before striding in and announcing my name, in growling, mocking voices. The room goes silent, over a hundred heartbeats thrumming in my ears.

I begin crawling.

It's not so foreign, I suppose. I'm on all fours as a dragon anyway. I ignore the boot marks, toe prints and dirt on the floor, the dark whispers and mutters. The only thing I focus on is who I see when I raise my head.

They've sat her like a queen on the stage. Her animas, including Minnie and excluding Raquel and Connor, stand around her, Scythe standing at her right-hand side. I grimace under Sabrina's glare. Her scent is all over one of the dungeons in Drakos Estate.

Aurelia wears a long blue dress with no sleeves and a high neckline. Her hands are curved around the ends of the armrests, her chin high as she watches me with those blue eyes that are seared into my mind.

The only thing she's missing is a crown.

I hasten my pace a little, and rather quickly, I reach the front, getting off my hands and planting a foot in front of me.

"Uh-uh!" Savage says to me like a stray dog as he and Beak come to stand with their backs against the stage like guards. "You stay on your knees, betrayer."

"Fair enough," I mutter, swinging my foot back.

"Oh my god!" Minnie shrieks, pointing at Savage. "Eugene!"

Aurelia gasps and Eugene wriggles out of Savage's arms and flies onto the stage. The animas make cooing and crying sounds, huddled around him. After each one has had a kiss, Aurelia cuddles him to her chest. But Eugene won't stay there. He proceeds to hop off the stage and comes back to me, standing sentinel by my side.

Savage exhales irritably. The animas frown at his behaviour.

"Why have you come here?" Scythe asks, in his distinct voice that sails easily across the pin-drop silent room. "What right have you to speak to my regina?"

"Go back to your family," Savage snarls. "The one you chose over us."

Lyle growls, "The ones who gave you that tattoo you wear so proudly on your arm."

I glance at Aurelia, listening to her. That heart of hers beats fast, though her breath is controlled by her concentration. Her lips part gently with breath; I miss seeing her on a daily basis.

"I have no right," I say to her. "But I've come here to try to repent for what I've done."

How does a man repent for something like this? How do I come back from hurting her so badly? "Nothing on this earth can make up for what I did," I continue. "But I will tear through eternity trying to figure that out. And the first step is offering myself to you." I glance at Lyle over my shoulder. "Give her what's in that bag."

Lyle stares at me for a moment. He's seen it, what it is that I'm offering his regina. But I ignore his gaze and turn back to Aurelia. She needs to know I mean what I say.

Chapter 82

Aurelia

The sight of Xander Drakos, crawling to me as fast as he can, his eyes desperately fixed on me, is something I'd never thought in my wildest dreams I'd ever see. It makes my breath seize; it makes my hands tremble.

And then Lyle is approaching the stage with a strange look on his face as he reaches into Xander's bag. Scythe steps forwards to accept it. Gold glints as it changes hands and something crucial in me goes still as Scythe stiffly holds it out for me to see.

A gold collar and chain.

Scythe turns it so I can see what's etched onto its surface in the same way my own was.

PROPERTY OF AURELIA BONEWEAVER

Shock and horror winds through my heart and I inhale a sharp breath. "I don't know what to do with this," I whisper.

"Oh, I do," Minnie says loudly, her hand squeezing my shoulder.

"We can all give you ideas, Lia," Sabrina says.

"I can put together a colour-coded action plan," Stacey nods.

I glance up at Stacey, whose beautiful face is taking in the gold collar with the seriousness it deserves. And Minnie, who's staring not at the collar but at Xander. They understand the choice I'm being given. What is at stake.

Xander remains still as I deliberate over this. This thing he is offering me is beyond belief. I glance at Scythe, his face pale, as he holds the hunk of valuable metal. *"How is this even possible?"* I say into the minds of our mates. *"Is this even Xander?"*

"Oh it's him, alright," Savage replies quietly. *"This is something only he could have come up with."*

"Savage is right," Scythe says evenly. *"Only he'd make himself a collar of solid gold with rubies."*

"He's giving you his ego on a platter, regina," Lyle says, sounding troubled. *"Willingly."*

"Should I do it then?"

A small smile curves Scythe's lips. *"He's the one asking for it."*

My collar looked exactly the same. That was by his design. That was by his desire to repent.

I nod as regally as I can. I'm clutching the arms of the chair to hide the fact my hands are trembling. "Put it on him."

Somebody in the crowd cheers and then everyone joins in as Savage takes the collar and snaps it into place around Xander's neck. The beasts in the hall roar with approval, shouting and howling and stomping their feet as Savage takes Xander by the lead and parades forward, holding up the chain like it's a trophy.

I hold out my hand for the golden chain and Xander nimbly frog leaps upon the stage, making Beak and a few others snort. Scythe takes the lead and reverently hands it to me. I take it, and Xander crouches by my feet, looking up at me as if seeking approval. I look at the chain in my hands.

"I am your slave," he says above the din of the crowd. "And I want everyone to see it."

Minnie exhales slowly behind me. "And you'll do whatever she wants?"

"Anything," Xander confirms.

"We should make a list," Minnie murmurs as Savage and Beak hurry everyone out of the room.

"Tomorrow," I say distractedly, looking down at the giant dragon, whose eyes are fixed on me. "We should get to bed."

My friends bid us goodbye, giving Xander glares as they go. Yeti takes Minnie's hand as they leave, and I can't help but feel sorry for the Siberian tiger. He'd been friends with Xander once. I don't know if they will ever be able to heal that.

With one action, Xander had destroyed his own life, and I think that's finally hitting him.

"Regina." Scythe's voice next to my ear makes me flinch in surprise, but I am quick to smile at him.

"Let's go." The chain in my hand is a cold and foreign thing.

"Regina!" Savage says loudly, holding his arms out for me.

"Yes, my love?"

He beams as he takes me by the waist and lowers me carefully from the stage to the floorboards. "Can I have a turn tomorrow?"

I realise he's indicating to the golden chain. Xander leaps down from the stage and begins bear crawling as we walk out of the rec room. Lyle has a frown on his face and I agree.

"You don't have to crawl," I say. "We won't get anywhere fast if you do."

Xander rises to his full height and I know we must look ridiculous, him at almost seven feet, being led by me, at five foot seven. "Thanks."

Savage scowls at Xander and prances on ahead, leading the way to our rooms. When we get to the stairwell, I grimace at the sight of the three flights.

"I can carry you," Xander says.

"You will not," Scythe says with a lethal softness.

I've regina commanded them not to attack or kill him, because even without the controlled violence oozing from Scythe, I know it's a very real possibility. I can only imagine how painful being forced to interact with him is going to be. It's painful enough for me.

Lyle's power surrounds my body like a hug and I lift off the floor, letting him levitate me up the stairs. I feel pretty stupid flying up like that because it's *nothing* like being a bird and so embarrassing. When we have three steps to go, I ask him to put me down.

"I need to build up the muscle," I say calmly, even though I'm already grimacing from the anticipated pain. "Better to get started now."

Four pairs of eyes and Eugene watch me like hawks as I heft my bad leg up and set it on the next step, shifting my weight onto it. Gripping the rail, I stifle a cry as lightning shoots through the bone. I manage to get my good foot up just in time, grimacing and panting from the agony.

"You should stop if it hurts!" Savage calls down to me with alarm.

"No, she shouldn't," Xander says. "You need to push past it, Aurelia. That's the only way it will heal."

"Who the fuck asked you?" Lyle snarls.

"Be thankful my regina stands between me and you," Scythe says quietly.

Xander shuts his mouth.

"I'm alright," I say, suddenly hot. I try for the next step, and this time, I can't stifle the cry at the pain that almost floors me. "Shit. No, I'm not."

Xander's hands come around my waist and three pairs of growls echo in the stairwell. He doesn't take his hands off, though. "Maybe avoid stairs for now, Aurelia."

Lyle's furious power snaps around me and hoists me up the final stair. I cast him a dark look over my shoulder as I hobble down the corridor and he gives me an apologetic one. Savage reaches down to put an arm around me, but I put up a hand.

"I'm okay." I don't know if I'm telling him or myself, but suddenly I'm angry.

Savage nods, following along beside me at my snail's pace while I scowl at the floor. "How are we going to sleep tonight, regina?"

"Xander's bed is still there," Lyle says. "There's no need to *change* anything for him."

"You could always put me in a cage," Xander offers.

"There's an idea." Savage rubs his chin. "I say we take him up on it. It might lower my urge to murder him a teensy bit."

I whip around and glare at them all. "A cage isn't comfortable."

Scythe can't help it. He takes my hand and finding it unusually warm, my anger melts away. I've seen his memories. This is just as hard for him. I squeeze his hand in reassurance.

"You care about my comfort?" asks Xander casually.

It's not often that I growl but tonight it's audible. "I think it's best if you stop the chatter."

"As you wish."

I turn to look at him suspiciously for a moment before continuing on. This is going to take a lot of getting used to.

* * *

After my mates have all showered for the night, and Eugene has found a spot to roost on a pillow, I unclip Xander's chain. It's a traditional clip on, because I wasn't going to figure out the wrist flicky thing so quickly. He leaves for his turn in the bathroom and I see my three mates staring at Xander's back with their arms crossed and their faces set into furious lines.

I smile softly at the sight. "So grumpy," I say, hobbling towards the bed. "Someone cuddle me before I combust, quick."

They suddenly come out of whatever murderous daydream they're collectively having and hurry for the bed. I'm wearing a silk chemise tonight, because it'll only be dresses for leg purposes from now on, and as I settle into the middle of the bed, Scythe and Savage scoot themselves next to me. Lyle crawls up my body, slowly, and so feline-like that I suck in a breath at the heat in his eyes.

He reaches my face and his lips brush mine as he speaks, his breath minty from our toothpaste. "I'm so proud of you." He kisses me three times on the mouth before sliding down my body again. He has tiger balm in one hand and he starts gently rubbing some on my knee.

It's the type of pain that feels good and bad at the same time. What I probably need is Xander's dragon healing. I'm not going to ask for that, so I allow my own power to funnel down to my thigh, easing the inflammation there.

Savage takes the opportunity to kiss me, one hand cupping my cheek. His mouth is heaven on mine. It's a huge comfort after a long day, combined with Lyle's massaging hands and Scythe's thumb stroking my left thigh.

Savage releases me, resting his head on my shoulder as he draws in his writing and poetry book.

Scythe hands me my book from the bedside table, and it's then that Xander strolls in with nothing but tiny black boxers, his taut muscles rippling as he dries his long hair with a towel.

"You should get an e-reader for the evening. My sister has one," he says as he strides past our bed.

My mates follow him, their heads like three camels, turning as they stalk his movement.

"Eagle, remember?" I say as he throws himself onto the single bed by the window.

"Are *you*," Savage snarls, "implying that we haven't provided for her *every* need?"

Xander raises his hand and ticks a list off. "Let me see. In my brief observation, I've seen that she's almost out of hair conditioner, there's no water on the bedside table, and no one's thought to wrap her knee."

"Oh, stop it," I say. "I can do those things for myself."

Xander rolls his eyes. "It's not your job?"

"I think he should sleep outside," Lyle mutters, getting out of bed to no doubt fetch water. I don't know if we even have bandages for my knee.

"If we forgot those things," Savage gruffs, "it's only because your gnarly presence distracted us. Once again, you're at fault."

"Pull up your socks, Savage," Xander retorts.

Savage whips his head towards me and presses his palms together like he's praying to me. "Can I kill him, regina, *please?*"

"Honestly, I just want to read my book in silence, if that's okay with you all?" I raise my brows at Savage, then Xander, who throws his head back onto his pillow. Then I turn to Scythe, who's holding out a foil strip of painkillers for me.

I kiss him on the cheek before taking it. When Lyle returns with the water, I swallow down the oxycodone tablets, then open up my smutty witches book to the first chapter.

Xander's snide voice is a boom through the silent space. "Also, there's only one tampon left—"

"I'm the pad monitor, you giant eyeless bastard!" Savage cries.

"Well who's the tampon monitor, then?" Xander grumbles. "They're doing a shit job."

"Why don't you strangle yourself with your collar?" Lyle says, surprising me. "Do us all a favour."

"Don't worry, I've thought about it," Xander mutters, before rolling over and apparently going to sleep.

"Does he expect us to feel sorry for him?" Savage asks incredulously. "Because I fucking don't and I never fucking will."

"Nor will I," I say softly, glancing at Xander's back.

Chapter 83

Ghoul

"Well, it certainly knows what it's doing."

Mace Naga, Flores, and the dragoness Francesca Hellfire watch the Drakos Estate tower rebuild itself. I remain behind them, my arms crossed firmly about my chest, observing the powerful dragon magic with great interest. If I built a house like this, would it have magic too? The thought intrigues me.

Flores took his time to call us after Xander's apparent *rescue* of the snakelet. I mean, Mace had been very happy the day the money was wired into his account, and we'd been concentrating on other things after the sale, so Aurelia's whereabouts had not concerned him too much.

But then The Collector, shaking with rage, turned up here, demanding to speak with the lord of the house. Only then did Flores call a meeting with the rest of us.

Flores Drakos turns to me, his face contorted with wild rage. "The rumours that Xander is back at Animus Academy cannot be true."

"They are true," Mace says simply. "Our spies there have never been wrong. He has been seen there, and talking to Celeste Agnis no less."

"It would have been easier if he'd just wanted her for himself," Lady Hyena says dryly. "But it seems he's changed his colours once again, foolish boy."

"Foolish is *one* word," The Collector hisses. "Dead, is another. It will take me months to repair my property!"

"You will be compensated handsomely," Flores says, "if the plan works well."

"They'll never see it coming." The Collector smiles with her teeth and it gives me goosebumps. "None of them will be able to stop it, will they, Lady Hyena?"

"Precisely." Unlike the crocodile, the elderly woman's face is deadly serious, and that, above all, makes my fangs drip.

Chapter 84

Xander

Skin and Bones – David Kushner

My ears wake me up in the middle of the night, Aurelia's soft—to my ears, loud—moan jerking me to attention. I've turned to face the bigger bed in my sleep, and if I open my eyes, they'll light up the room, so I keep them shut and listen carefully. She's trying to be quiet, I can tell by the strain in her throat, and it's Scythe's sharp intake of breath I hear, and the rapid beating of his heart.

Lyle and Savage remain fast asleep, their breaths steady and slow in deep NREM.

The curiosity is killing me. Eating at me, in fact, so I crack open one lid, completely risking it.

What I see makes me salivate. Scythe's eyes are closed, his head tossed back as Aurelia moans around his pierced cock; the lower rungs of his Jacob's Ladder glint under the light from my eye. Aurelia is in the perfect position for me to see her, lying between Scythe's open legs, her own long legs hanging off the end of the bed. Scythe's breaths come in stutters now, his hand buried in her dark mass of hair. She takes the entire length of him, swallowing him down to the base just before she gags, then comes up and licks the side of his cock.

It's then that she pauses, her open eyes seeing the light from mine.

But she doesn't stop. Doesn't look away from me either. As if she knows it's torturing me, she opens her mouth wider, lets me see her tongue as it traces the length of Scythe's dick, the piercings reflected by the warm, golden light of my eyes. She maintains that angle, holding my gaze as her hands run up Scythe's bare abs, her nails scraping gently. Those plush lips suck on the tip of him before she flicks his Prince Albert with her tongue. I exhale slowly, fighting the urge to sit up and watch them more closely. Her chemise slides up her ass, showing me her bare skin. Though I've seen it before, obsessed about it before, this moment feels so intimate, and I imagine myself crawling up behind her, kissing her beautiful thighs and finding her wet and ready. Her scent fills the room, heady and intoxicating, calling me in.

I don't know when my eyes fully opened up, but they are now, and my hand is clutching my cock for dear life. Aurelia's eyes bore into mine, catching my light and reflecting it back to me. Her eyelids lower seductively as she pops Scythe's cock out of her mouth and uses that sinful tongue again, but I can't turn away, and I can't help the hard-as-obsidian-cock that pulses with each rapid heartbeat. I run my hands down my length until I come to my new gold cock ring, imagining myself buried in her, feeling that gorgeous wet heat and the moans that come from that perfect mouth as I fill her completely.

She bobs faster on Scythe, clutching at him, moaning softly as he pulls at her hair. Faster and faster she takes him and faster and faster my own hands go, my breath coming in pants now. My balls tighten, begging for release. For release into *her*. Scythe makes a sound of pure pleasure and his head tilts back further as she sucks him tightly.

"Aurelia," he breathes as he comes into her mouth.

Her throat bobs as she swallows him eagerly down, a look of

pure bliss on her face as each wet swallow fills my ears like the sweetest song. When he's done, Aurelia withdraws slowly, making him shiver, milking the last drops from him and audibly swallowing. Scythe opens his eyes and sits up, helping her carefully crawl up to his body. They kiss passionately, him holding her face, her holding his shoulders as they devour each other like they've spent a lifetime apart.

It may have very well felt that way because even the days she wasn't a constant presence by my side felt long to me. I see it for what it was now.

Her pink tongue snakes into his mouth and I explode into my own hand, trying to keep silent as the thought of her mouth tears me open. I don't know if they hear me, hell, I don't even care at this point, but she ends up draping herself on top of Scythe, and shortly after, they both fall asleep.

I lie there for a few moments, just to make sure, before I get up to head to the bathroom.

* * *

The next morning, after everyone is dressed for the day, Savage gets an evil glint in his eye and has a telepathic conversation with Aurelia. Her jewel-eyes are uncertain for a moment before she nods.

"You have to listen to Savage's commands," she says to me.

Fuck.

Savage takes the gold chain from Aurelia's hand and bares his teeth. "Hands and knees, lizard," he snarls with hate.

I drop to my knees and barely get my hands down before the mad wolf lunges for the stairs. I have half a second of mental preparation before I face plant, sliding along the carpet and thudding down the stairs in rapid succession. My shirt wrenches up and I feel each blasted wooden stair like a punch to my ribs.

Savage rounds the staircase and flies down the corridor at a near mythical pace, shouting, "Wolf on the loose!" as he goes. I'm left to slide along the linoleum, my skin burning, making a god-awful squeaking sound.

Beasts jump out of the way, some snarling as they see me, some whooping with excitement. I don't even bother to try to get my hands and legs under me; we're going too fast, and it'll only satisfy us both if I bleed.

Savage rounds the corner, and instead of leaping over the rail to get down the three flights of stairs, he takes them the hardest way for me. My head bangs against the corner of the first rail and I end up flipping under my own weight and am rapidly dragged down the stairs on my back. My skin finally tears halfway down, the burn sweet and cruel as the next steps hit it in the exact same spot.

Savage's shouting and singing draws an audience, and by the time we get down to the ground level, the entire animus dorm is vying to get a view. Someone holds open the glass front doors and I manage to flip over again.

The concrete path awaits me.

Suppressing a grimace, Savage hits the path running, and I go, shirt tearing, skin shredding, leaving a trail of blood behind me. He skids to a stop before the dining hall, barely breaking a sweat, hardly panting as he looms over where I lie on my back, squinting up into the sky.

"It'll do," he says in a quiet, lethal voice he usually reserves for our most hated enemies. "For now. Up!"

I only let out a little grunt as I haul myself to my feet. My magic is already healing my skin where the concrete grazes turned into lacerations.

"Hm," Sabrina hums, sauntering up with her two quiet leopard bodyguards, Blade and Blair. "Sort of looks like someone took a massive cheese grater to it."

We all look down at my bare abs. She's right, there's more blood than skin.

"That was my doing," Savage says proudly.

"Well," Minnie's voice comes from behind them, Marduk

and Yeti scowling at the sight of me. She brandishes a new purple binder thick with typed papers. "We've got the list."

They're plotting my demise.

A sharp intake of breath tells me Aurelia has finally waded through the crowd with Lyle and Scythe. Savage proudly hands her the golden chain, and she takes it, her face carefully blank.

Avian power brushes against me before snapping back as if she's remembered herself.

Her natural instinct is to heal me.

I clench my jaw as I follow her into the dining hall, to stop the stabbing pain that's suddenly assailing my chest, worse than the pain of my burning skin. Her hand is clenched tight around the gold, her knuckles white. She trembles.

I want to say I'm sorry, again and again ad infinitum. But words are of no use here.

Only my blood is. Only my pain is. That's the equivalent of what I dealt.

"Surely he's not allowed food," Sabrina says, her mouth twisting as she lines up behind us at the buffet.

"They used to give me dog food," Aurelia says quietly. "Kibble."

A cold, shocked silence seeps like a festering wound through the buffet line. Blood drips from my shredded skin, splashing onto the floor. Suddenly, I can't breathe.

"I won't eat," I say.

"Hunger strike, is it?" Minnie says, her binder tucked under her arm. "Let's see how long he lasts. I'm sure we have dog kibble around here somewhere."

I watch Aurelia collect her food, which isn't much this morning. Toast, eggs, some blueberries, and an iced coffee. Theresa and Ronald are supervising the line, and towards the end of it, Theresa comes around and hugs Aurelia.

"We'll talk later," the cassowary anima says, a happy light in her grey eyes. "Minnie has requested a few things from me for this morning."

That tigress works fast.

Theresa glances at me, a completely disturbed and unsettled look on her face that makes me feel like she wants to kick my soul out of my body.

Everyone stares as we sit down at the usual group table towards the back. Chairs have been added for Sabrina and her new mates and Minnie makes sure Aurelia takes a seat at the head of the table. Without conversing about it, I take up my spot, kneeling next to her.

"Such a good boy," Sabrina says viciously. Having lost her own mates, she's also taken the severing of my bond to Aurelia personally.

Because of my height, even kneeling, my head is well above the table and I get to smell everyone's food as they eat. Savage ends up strategically sitting next to us, but Lyle's and Scythe's reactions interest me. Both have been caged—Lyle literally, Scythe figuratively—but he watched his mother caged for many years. It unsettles them to see me with a collar on, but not because they think I don't deserve it. It's too close to home, but they endure it because it's what I deserve.

It only validates my need to do this.

After breakfast is finished, we leave for our first class, which is group therapy with both animas and animuses. If I thought Savage's physical treatment was bad, it's nothing compared to the thrashing the animas have prepared for me.

Chapter 85

Aurelia

"I'm not comfortable with this," our male counsellor, Ryland, says as I enter the class with Xander on his golden leash.

"Well it's a good thing nobody asked you, Ry Ry," Savage says lightly.

Ryland's pupils dilate as Scythe enters behind me. "Is there a problem?" my shark asks in his quiet rasp.

"N-No, Mr Kharkorous. Not at all." Ryland purses his lips and shuffles the papers he's holding.

Theresa is more subtle with her words, and I think a part of her thinks Xander deserves this. "There is a lot to talk about," she says slowly, indicating that I should take my seat. I do so, and Xander silently kneels before my chair. "But I don't want him bleeding all over the carpet. It's not hygienic."

"That's fair," Lyle says. "Heal it just enough to stop the bleeding."

I have a good view of Xander's back and the freely bleeding, red raw skin from his ride over the lino, stairs, and concrete. He should have stopped bleeding by now, which indicates that he's suppressing his own healing. I wiggle the chain and Xander's magic pulses in tiny vibrations around him, his immense power kept close to his skin to knit the bottom layer of ruined tissue.

"Right, well," Theresa says, "Lia is back, everyone!"

"And thank fuck for that!" Sabrina cheers. Everyone claps after that and I give the circle of them a small smile.

"How *did* you get out?" one of the more clueless jaguars asks, frowning at me. "Didn't he have you captive—" he trails off and turns pale under the combined flat stare of Savage, Lyle and Scythe. "Sorry."

"Lia won't be answering any questions," Theresa says sternly. "But I believe Minnie has a request."

"Right!" says Minnie, jumping up and saluting Theresa like a soldier. She opens her binder and reads from it. "Xander's first task is to give a formal apology to Lia in front of the entire school. And he has to do it naked."

Ryland makes a choked sound but says nothing. Xander glances at me over his shoulder. "Of course."

"Oh, and he has to cut his hair before the speech—"

"No!" the word blurts out of my mouth without warning and I clamp my lips shut as everyone, including my mates, stares at me. I try to shrug it off casually. "What? I...like his hair."

"Fair enough, Lia," says Minnie kindly, then glares at Xander as if to say, *'See? She's a better person than you'll ever be.'*

"There's a lot of pages in that binder, Minnie," Scythe says. "What else is in there?"

Minnie's cheeks turn pink as Yeti and Marduk grin with pride. "Well, we spent the night brainstorming, Scythe. There was a lot to think about."

Scythe nods in approval. His voice enters my head. *"May I have my own orders for Xander, regina?"*

"Of course."

He smiles at me. I blush every time Scythe asks my permission for something, or smiles. Or does anything, really. I doubt I'll ever get used to the fact that he's here and mine.

"You're staring, angel," Lyle says into my head, a hint of jealousy in that baritone.

I blink in surprise and smile sheepishly at them both. *"I'll stare at you in the next class,"* I reassure my lion.

"And me in the next," Savage interjects.

It's then that I notice Xander is staring at me from over his shoulder. I can't decipher the look on his face, but the smile fades off mine, and he purses his lips.

I'd been an outsider once. I know how that feels to be at the edge of everything, cast aside like something less than. Rotten. Unwanted. Watching from the outside as everyone else enjoys company. My father had done that to me. And then Xander had done that again. The walls of the classroom close in on me like the bars of my cage in Xander's room. My lungs collapse, my ears turn fuzzy. I have to get out. I need the air, the open air and nothing else. I need to be free.

Before my next breath, I drop Xander's chain and am hobbling out of the room and out the door. I can't do this. I can't be at the academy and pretend that I'm fine. I'm not fine. I'm a mess. Mentally and physically.

Lightning strikes my leg again and my sob turns into a yelp. My eagle has no choice but to burst from my skin and it feels like a sweet release to be off my leg and flying through the corridors with the speed I desire.

My mates call after me, but I need to keep moving. I need the air. I back flap to turn a corner and use my beak to butt open a glass door. Warm air meets my face and I move my wings in the way I love best. Sweeping and catching the wind, feeling it move over my feathers in powerful movements.

My chest opens up and I can finally let in air again, the spring air blasting past my face, refreshing me and keeping me focused. I sigh in a long exhale and wheel high above the school. The tall gum trees that line the perimeter look welcoming, and I choose the tallest, settling into the highest branches, the ones that sway like a pendulum under my weight. Gently I ease my weight onto the branch, my left claw secure around it and my right lightly clasping it for stability. I take a deep breath, closing my eyes for a moment and calming the braying of my broken soul.

"*No fair, regina,*" comes Savage's voice in my head. He's in wolf form, a black mass of fur at the base of the tree. "*I can't get up that high.*"

"*She wouldn't be up there if she wanted your company,*" Scythe says firmly. "*Give her a moment.*"

I can feel Savage's sulking from up here, but he ends up settling on his belly. Lyle is in his shifted form to my surprise, telling me he's feeling my pain and probably his own too. He sits on his belly next to Savage, and they face away from me as if protecting the tree from enemies. Or maybe one enemy in particular.

Scythe lights a joint and sits down next to Lyle, stretching out his muscular legs and resting his back against the smooth trunk of the gum.

With the three of them settled, I cast my eye up to the open blue. There are a few clouds scattered through the periwinkle and not much else. I scratch at an itch under my wing, yanking at the feather that sits on top of it. The burn is sweet.

"*Sabrina and Minnie are asking if you need them,*" Savage says, likely talking through another wolf.

I don't know what I need. There's a dark feeling inside my chest and I don't think anything is ever going to make it go away. I pull at an irritating feather below my wing again, the sensation of the burn as I pull at it grounding me. The feather comes out, the sting hitting two parts of me, knitting them together for a few short moments. I drop the feather from my beak and watch it fall before I sweep it behind the tree with my telekinesis.

A prickle of awareness makes me cast my eye over the academy grounds. From the dining hall entrance, the tall figure of Xander, shredded abdomen and all, emerges. He pauses at the entrance, uncertain if he should move closer.

It's then that Scythe gets up and makes his way over to the dragon, silver hair rippling in the breeze, making it look like it has a silver halo, which should be funny given that it's Scythe, the grim reaper himself. But I don't have it in me to laugh as the two of them have a conversation I wish I could hear. Scythe's shoulders are tight, as if he doesn't like the idea of being that close to, or talking to Xander.

My chest clenches at the sight of them. Xander nods and waves a hand, dismissing something, but I can't read the words his mouth is making.

They both turn away and head in opposite directions, except Xander stops to take a seat by the doorway of the dining hall, taking out a joint and lighting it with his finger. Scythe returns to the base of my tree.

Eventually, my left leg gets sore from carrying the brunt of my weight and I spread out my wings, fluttering down and back flapping to slow my landing right onto Savage's back. He raises his head, ears pinning back, and I flop onto my belly on top of him, turning my head to the side and resting it on his warm, thick fur.

Scythe comes over and checks my leg. "You need to rest it, regina," he says.

"I like being high in a tree."

My shark tilts his head back, looking up into the branches above us. "Next time, I'll climb up with you."

"Really?"

He looks down at me, smiling. "Yes, regina. You know we'll do anything you need, and"—he shrugs—"I'm guessing you'll catch me if I fall off."

"You wouldn't fall off," Lyle says. "Not how I've seen you on the back of—" He cuts himself off, an air of disgust forming around him.

A dragon, is what he meant. Riding the back of Xander for so many years made Savage and Scythe agile in high places.

I make an annoyed, tired sound through my beak.

"Let her sleep," Savage admonishes. *"She's tired."*

* * *

Late in the afternoon, I wake up, cocooned in Lyle's arms in the TV room, with Savage wafting a ham and cheese croissant under my nose. My wolf grins at me.

"See, I knew it would work. She loves these." He breaks a piece off and offers it to my beak. I pluck it from his fingers, gobbling it down. Savage licks those same fingers and offers me another piece.

Lyle strokes my wings in a soothing motion. "They'll assemble for Xander's speech soon. Do you want to be in human form or eagle form for that?"

How could I forget the formal apology Xander was supposed to be writing? I sigh. *"Human form, I suppose."*

I shift in his arms, bringing my human legs up and curling myself in Lyle's lap. He holds me close, burying his nose in my hair and inhaling. "Angel, you know you can talk to us about what happened. We promise not to react adversely."

"How can you make that promise?" I murmur, toying with a piece of bread. "How do I know you won't want to kill him?"

"Do you not want him dead, regina?" Savage asks. "It's your right."

My chest goes tight again, my heart suddenly pounding as if it wants release. I squeeze my fists to avoid the tremble I know is coming. "Where is Minnie?"

Five minutes later, Minnie and Eugene are walking into the TV room, leaving Yeti and Marduk with Savage and Lyle in the dining room. Eugene was doing the rounds with the animas since Xander disappeared for the afternoon and Stacey took him to visit Raquel.

My tigress curls up on the couch next to me. "They're making popcorn downstairs," she muses. "You can smell it all the way to the second floor. And someone has a spit roast going on the front lawn. I don't know who approved that."

I can barely crack the smile she's trying to coax out of me. "I don't feel like laughing tonight, Min."

She takes my hand and drops her head back onto the headrest. "I know. Of course I bloody know. I wouldn't wish this on my worst enemy, Lia, let alone my best friend."

A tear slips down my cheek. "I can't handle this pain, Min. I just can't."

She clutches her own chest. "I feel mine here. Like something inside of me is torn, and the frayed pieces are flapping hopelessly in the wind. Like fingers reaching out for someone who'll never reach back."

I can't bear to tell her about the last time I saw Titus. She already knows the type of person he is. I brush at my cheeks. "What the fuck do we do? A part of me doesn't want to live, Min. Every time I look at him, I just..."

"It feels like it's breaking all over again, I know." She puts her arms around me, resting her temple against mine. "I don't even have to look at Titus this frequently and it still hurts like a bitch."

"He wants forgiveness, Min."

Minnie sighs as she considers this.

It's Lyle's voice that sails into my mind. *"Guilt doesn't entitle someone to forgiveness, regina. Neither do his words, and what he says in a speech. It'll be what he does that will tell you if you should trust him."*

I remember something Scythe said to me long ago, when Sabrina was taken. *Judge a man by his actions.*

"Are you ready?" Minnie asks.

"I don't have a choice, do I?"

She grins. "Yeah you do. We can cancel this whole thing if you want. But...a little birdy called Marduk tells me you'll want to see this."

Chapter 86

Xander

*Peer Gynt, Op. 23: IV. In the Hall of the Mountain King —
Edvard Greig*

It's been more than a hundred years since a dragon has been seen with a slave collar. My ancestors might be rolling in their graves, but I wear mine with determination as I fly through the afternoon sky towards my mark. After checking in with Celeste, it's an hour's flight by dragon wing to the location Scythe wanted me to infiltrate today before my speech.

I have no idea if he's helping me or trying to get me killed, but either way, I'm up for it. Normally, for a mission like this with a high-powered beast, I'd have backup of some kind, often both Savage and Scythe.

But Scythe wants to test me. Probably wants to see me bleed as well.

The mansion is a crimson structure, likely regularly painted from the bright colour under this harsh sun, which enables me to see if from far away. This mission requires stealth to begin with, so I wheel behind the property and drop into the bushland, shifting into my human form and donning military camo gear.

I trek for an hour through the sweltering bush, shouldering

my heavy pack and wiping sweat from my brow. By the time I get to the outskirts of the property, I'm thoroughly irritated and ready to blow someone's head off.

It's just as well that there are three snipers hiding in the evergreens at the front of the property. They're in their shifted forms, one loaned snake and two birds of prey, well camouflaged high in the trees with their planted weapons at the ready on specially made stands. If I couldn't hear their hearts beating, I might have missed them.

Pew, pew, pew, I recite, as if I can pretend Savage is with me.

Well out of their eyesight, and the serpent's thermal recognition, I get out my phone and detonate a small explosive I've set a few hundred meters away. It's not big enough for human ears, but just big enough to be heard by the three snipers whose heads snap in the direction of the blast.

I take the opportunity to lasso the first two guns from the trees. The birds give warning cries, but they're cut short as I catch one of the guns and shoot both of them between the eyes. The serpent has to shift to shoot his gun, but by the time I swing to him, he's pulled the trigger. I lunge out of the way, rolling to a stop just in time, and shoot his naked ass right in the left cheek. Deciding that guns may as well be my backup today, distasteful as they are for a beast like me to carry, I hover two of them in front of me, ready to fire. The cast iron main gate has the family name declared atop of it and is locked with magic. I consider it for a moment.

My skin itches with the need to get back to the academy. It needs a dragon to protect it, and that means I can't dilly-dally here.

The stealth attack I've planned will likely take an hour or so. The alternative, however...

I drop the guns in a bush and head to the intercom, pressing the doorbell.

"Who is this?" comes the curt voice.

I wave at the camera lens. "It's Xander Drakos. I've come to have tea with the master of the house."

"We were not expecting you."

"Tell him I have information on Scythe Kharkorous, if he wants it."

There's a moment of silence before the gates creak open and I get to stalk through them and up the straight driveway. Two birds come out from the door, guns pointed at me.

"How did you get past the snipers?" one of them shouts.

I look around uncertainly. "Pardon? What snipers?"

"Get inside!"

"That's where I was going," I drawl, striding through the arched doorway.

A white suited Damien Agnis waits on the other side, four guards on either side of him, guns with red lasers aimed at my head. He's scared these days; I've never seen an animus with so many guards, and honestly, it's embarrassing for him.

"You are a wanted man," Damien admonishes. "Where have you been?"

"You're so sweet to be worried about me." I examine my fingernails, stepping forward.

"That's close enough!" one of the guards shouts.

I stop in my tracks, smiling at them and spreading my hands out like a benevolent king. "Of course."

"What do you really want?" Damien asks. "I know you don't have information on Scythe. He has not accepted you back into the fold."

"You've always been intelligent," I nod. "I've come to rescue the nimpins."

"What?" he spits. "They are my property."

"I know. But I want them to be my property, you see." And what Aurelia wants, she gets.

"You can't have them! I claimed them and I will need them for when Aurelia is returned to us."

The thought of that heats the blood in my arteries. "Very confident of that, are you?"

"I am," he says firmly. "And I'll be contacting your father now. He is *very* interested in talking with you, as are the rest of the council members."

"I was worried you'd say that," I reply darkly. "Now, how many guards do you have?"

"Why do you want to know?"

"Let's see." I tap my finger on my chin. "There's six down here, and you've got another five, six, *ten* up in the wings I can hear."

Sixteen venom guns. Scythe knew about this, no doubt about it. Bastard.

A smile curves my lips and I wave forward at the first group. "Come along, gentlemen. Let's get this over with."

Chapter 87

Aurelia

When we arrive at the recreation room, it's already packed with most of the school. Beak and some other birds are directing the traffic, making everyone squeeze together. There's a live band with a full set of drums and electric guitars.

Beak throws a smirk our way, his eyes scanning the four of us and Eugene.

"Alright there, ladies?"

"Yes," we chime.

"I've put seats for you at the front." He catches my eye, a certain knowing in them. I'd been wondering how much Scythe had told him. How much he knew about my shark's plans to replace himself with Beak. Now I'm sure he knew at least some of it. I wonder what he thinks of all of it now.

"I need to talk to you after this," he says.

The backs of my eyes prickle, moisture filling them. Embarrassed, I glance away and nod. Beak has always been kind to me, right from the moment I'd first met him that day in Halfeather's mansion. Now I know the truth about his past, about how his regina had been murdered for refusing to help Halfeather and he'd sworn himself to Scythe for revenge. It makes me look at him in an even more positive light. I want to help him, but I have enough problems to keep me busy for a lifetime.

As Minnie and Sabrina lead us forward, Stacey takes my hand as if she knows I'm having a moment. "What do you think he wants?" she asks me. Our little lioness wears her ombre hair in a braid tonight, a black shift dress and sandals, but my eagle eyes tell me she's been crying, no doubt over Raquel and Connor. It may be why Eugene chose her to be his carrier for the night.

"Nothing good," I say darkly. "It's never really ever been good when someone asks to talk to me. Just once, I'd like a fortune cookie joke or something, you know?"

She huffs a laugh as we reach our seats, right at the front of the hall, in the first row before the stage. Beak has left four seats on either side of the middle walkway, and we take the row on the left.

"I'll prepare some jokes for you," Stacey says, "and then schedule a formal meeting so we can discuss them."

I remain clutching her hand, because I need to for this ordeal that's about to happen. The clock above the stage ticks over to eight, and Beak calls for everyone to settle down as Savage, Lyle and Scythe walk in. I don't even have to look behind me to know they're here, the regina in me raising her head and keening in appreciation as they stalk towards us.

Savage bounds up first, quickly falling to my feet to sit on the floor.

I scratch him behind the ear and he grins at me, before protectively putting his arms around my calves to cuddle my legs. Lyle comes over and kisses me on the head and Scythe kisses me on the cheek before the two of them take their seats next to Marduk and Yeti on the other side. Scythe catches my eye and there is a glimmer of something there that I can't quite place. It's similar to satisfaction, perhaps, but darker.

My stomach flops upon itself.

"*Where is Xander?*" I ask the group chat. Everyone around us is casting their eyes toward the door.

The clock strikes eight, and almost immediately, the floor vibrates at the impact of something terribly large landing on the building. He's here.

"Did he leave the academy?"

Savage sniffs the air, growling under his breath. He clutches me tighter. The very air around us becomes taut with tension. Expectation. The instincts of every beast in the room are firing off and they all go still in anticipation.

One minute passes, then another, before finally there's a thump on the ground floor and the sound of something heavy being dragged over the threshold to the rec room.

Someone gasps.

I don't turn around. I refuse.

Instead, I grab onto Stacey's hand and she clutches onto mine with both of hers as the dragging sound gets closer.

The reek of blood hits my nose, along with Xander's volcanic scent. My right leg starts to tremble and Savage growls softly, caressing me with his thumbs.

My heart pounds faster and faster, and still, I don't turn around. Scythe lights a cigarette and blows smoke into the air.

When Xander's giant, naked form appears in my periphery, I still don't turn around, do not look at what he's brought with him. He rounds my chair and comes to stand before me, forcing me to look at him, but not at what he's dragging. His hair is neatly tied back, and his eyes glimmer with pleasure. There are also multiple bullets lodged in his torso.

Stacey makes a strangled sound, and Sabrina covers her mouth.

"Is that a cock ring?" someone in the audience asks in a hushed voice.

"It's fucking solid gold," someone replies. "Is he semi hard or is that—"

Someone shushes them.

When Xander speaks, his voice is soft, almost intimate. "An offering to you, Aurelia. And the academy."

He gestures at the thing on the floor. But in his other hand, he's holding a drawstring bag and the handle of a large square box covered in a black cloth. This he sets down on the stage. My heart freezes in recognition.

Only then do I look down to see Xander's offering.

There is no head on the body, but the deceased wears a starched white suit. Xander removes the black cloth from the box on stage.

Stacey, Sabrina and Minnie leap to their feet at the same time, shouting in shock and alarm.

Instead of the expected nimpins in the carbon monoxide chamber, the severed head of Damien Agnis sits in there, pale in death, eyes open as if in shock.

Xander opens his drawstring bag and five nimpins zip out. I cover a sob as Henry, shrieking and squeaking in paragraphs, bolts towards me like a bullet. He smacks into my chest, vibrating as I gather him up.

The others are doing the same with their nimpins, Stacey sobbing fat wet drops onto her orange nimpin, Sabrina consoling Raquel and Connor's green and pink nimpins and Minnie crying over Gertie.

"Henry," I whisper, cuddling him to my cheek. He chirps his version of my name. My ball of soft blue fur rubs himself against my skin as if he can bury himself into me and never be kidnapped again. I pull him away from me to look at him, holding him in both my palms, his massive liquid black orb eyes blinking at me with a million different emotions. "I'm never letting you go, ever again."

He chirps in happiness and I hold him to my chest, where he buries his face with a big sigh. Finally, I look back at Xander, and am surprised to see his lips curved into a small, pleased smile. He seems to shake himself the second my attention is back on him, however, before swinging himself onto the stage. There is something about the way he does it that makes me stare, though. A small wince is the only sign he gives of pain as his body curves and rises to standing despite the bullets. I push that aside as Xander comes to stand at the lectern.

The last time he stood at a lectern was at the kangaroo court that condemned Sabrina and me for stealing Titus' laptop. He'd passed judgement on us then, and now it's our job to pass judgement upon him.

How the tables turn.

My friends calm down enough to settle their nimpins and move their gazes to Xander. The dragon holds the sides of the lectern as if bracing himself, the corded muscles of his arms bulging. When he speaks, it's directly to me, glowing eyes serious and firm.

"I am one of the worst people you will ever meet. I've done reprehensible things. Hurt people. Killed people. Some who didn't deserve it, some who did." He gestures to Damien's body and head beneath him. "But..." He clears his throat. "But the worst thing I did, by far, the thing that condemns me the most, is —" He casts his eyes down as his Adam's apple bobs. My chest grows tight. Xander takes a deep breath. "Is the fact that I made my regina bleed and severed our bond."

I thought I knew everything there was to know about Xander Drakos. I'd spent every day for months with him, watching him and his family. But the one thing I didn't know was that when Xander cries, he cries blood. A crimson drop tracks down from his right eye, trailing down his cheek. Henry coos softly into my chest as my own vision blurs and that crucial part of me cries out. The urge to shift into the safety of feathers and claws is strong, but I push it aside as Xander fixes his attention onto me.

"It doesn't matter how much I repent for this," he stresses. "Nothing I do will *ever* repay what I did. Nothing will ever make up, ever heal, ever resolve this. I will always be a walking, dead beast." Stacey is quietly crying next to me, and I think Sabrina is too, as she holds Minnie in her arms. "Aurelia," Xander says. My hands tremble. "I am sorry for what I did to you. You were the best part of me. Kind and strong." He grimaces and his voice wavers. "And *good*. And I couldn't let myself have that. I didn't know what to do with that. So I broke it." He shakes his head, his voice strong once again. "I won't ask for death; I don't even deserve that. I don't deserve the dirt from your shoe." His eyes bore into mine, and he breathes as if in pain. A fine sheet of sweat coats his forehead. "There is only one thing I will not accept. I won't accept it if you send me away. I *need* to be near you. Scenting you hurts me, but I still crave it with everything I am. I crave your voice in my ears, your beautiful gaze on me." He puts his hand over his heart, leaning over the lectern, his voice almost desperate. "I *need* to protect you, and I pledge to do it, body and what's left of my soul. Anyone who comes after you will meet a bloody, violent end. Even if it is my own family."

A thousand emotions pummel through me as a chill runs down my spine at the intensity of his voice. I have no doubt in my mind that he means every word he speaks.

Xander leans back from the lectern, stepping away and letting his hands drop from his heart. Then he leaps down from the stage and kneels before me, his hands resting in his lap. "I don't deserve your forgiveness, but I will beg for everything else. I beg you to let me stay."

The room is silent. No one claps. I think everyone is far too shocked. Maybe their chests feel hollow, like mine does. Maybe their beasts are screaming in maddening protest too. I tear my gaze from Xander's and look at Minnie. Sabrina has her arms around my best friend, holding her together as Minnie trembles, her mouth parted in distress. Gertie, her nimpin, huddles against her neck, quietly chirping reassurance in her ear. Both of them had lost their mates. What right do I have to deny a living one who clearly repents?

"*His guilt does not absolve him, regina.*" Scythe's voice is firm in my head. "*These are pretty words.*"

"*And,*" says Lyle, "*no action of his will ever undo this damage. A mate bond cannot be re-made.*"

My anima screams at that. Screams and shrieks for the bond

to be re-made, re-joined. But we scream for a future that cannot be. What is dead cannot be brought back to live.

"Am I never to be whole, then?" I ask my mates. *"Are we always going to feel this emptiness?"*

"When he condemned himself, he condemned us all," Scythe says. *"There's no coming back from what he did."*

It confirms what I'd suspected. Scythe is not the forgiving sort. He will never forgive Xander for this.

"I've had enough," Savage announces to the room, getting up and holding his hand out to me. "We're done here."

I glance at my animas and take Savage's hand, letting him lead us out from the rec room and away from the naked dragon on his knees. With every step, my heart sinks deeper into the catacomb that used to be my chest.

Chapter 88

Savage

Out in the foyer, Marduk and Yeti whisk Minnie away after a little hug with my regina and her friends. Blair and Blade take Sabrina away to comfort her and then Stacey stands by the door, with two nimpins on her shoulder and Eugene by her foot, but otherwise, she has no mates.

Sadness pangs through my organs.

"Go and see Raquel," Aurelia says, opening the door for her. "They could use a visit."

Stacey wipes her nose. "Yeah, good idea, Lia."

At least she has her nimpin with her now. Even then, as I pull my regina into my arms and carry her bridal style, I send a message to Mutton, one of my messengers. *"Send Beaky to guard Stacey in the medical ward. I don't want her to be alone."*

"And a lion as well, boss?"

I look down at my regina's face as I climb the stairs. She's already watching me, and one of her hands reaches up to run across my chin. *"Nah. An eagle fixed my heart. I reckon an eagle can fix Stacey's too."*

"Aye-aye, boss."

"I sent Beak to watch over Stace," I proudly tell my regina.

"Is that so you don't have to look at him?"

I grin. "Maybe." Then I frown. "I wish I was born as an eagle so we could fly together. Then I could heal you too."

She smiles softly. "I love your wolf. This way we can speak secretly. Birds can't do that."

My heart shines like a full moon and I howl into the ceiling to let her know how I feel. "I love you too, baby." Henry gives a squeak, rolling around to look at me with his big, black eyeballs. "Yeah, alright; I love you too, Hennie."

He squeaks with satisfaction. I still want to eat him, but you can still love something and want to eat it, right? I might ask Lyle about it later.

"I hope someone cleans the mess downstairs," I frown. "Phoenix blood is spicy in the nose." I wonder what it tastes like.

"Yeah," my regina says, drawing my eyes back to her face. She looks sad. There's more colour in her cheeks compared to a few days ago, but there's a great tiredness under her eyes. Like she's been hunting all night and needs to go to bed. Only I know she's been sleeping even more than she used to. "I want to give Henry a bath. He smells."

Henry clucks sadly.

"We can do it together!" I say excitedly. Henry turns around to give me a worried look, but I ignore him. "Do you feel better or worser after Xander's speech, regina?" We reach the empty third-floor corridor and I head towards our hidden stairs.

"Worser," she sighs. "Definitely worserest."

"Is that a word?" I ask.

"It is now."

"Good." I climb up our hidden stairs and put my regina down, taking her wee little face in my paws. "Are you happy that old turkey is dead?"

She closes her eyes briefly, putting her hands over my own. "Yes."

I remove my hands and wrap my arms around her, pulling her close so she can feel how my heart beats for her.

Lyle, Scythe and unfortunately Xander, now with clothes

on, make their way up the stairs as we part. Lyle is holding Xander's golden chain and I give them both a dirty look. *"She needs to recover from that fucking soppy sop speech,"* I tell them. *"Get the blind lizard out of here."*

"We all need to recover from that soppy sop speech," Lyle replies. *"But Xander wanted to say something to Lia in private."*

My regina is not paying attention to us, giving Henry kisses and petting him by the dining table. I suddenly get the urge to eat the furball again.

"Aurelia," Scythe says, going over to them. He pets Henry with a finger.

She looks up at him with admiration. "You did this, didn't you?"

Scythe puts a possessive arm around her and kisses her lips. "Thank you."

"You're welcome."

Lia turns to Xander then, her eyes flicking down to his collar and the chain still in Lyle's hand. Our lion offers it to her.

She places Henry on her shoulder and strays towards Xander, eyeing him. "Take off your shirt."

"Excuse me!" I cry.

She casts me a look and I sigh. "Now," she commands.

Xander fiddles with the shirt. I don't understand why there's so many buttons on those things, but eventually, the black shirt opens and he drops it to the floor.

I roll my eyes and throw my hands up in the air in annoyance.

Xander looks like he has chicken pox except with bullets. They're all lodged across his torso, shoulders, and even a couple in his arms. I hope there's a few in his ass too.

"Unless there's one in his dick, I don't get what the problem is," I say, irritated because my regina, *my* regina is stepping forward. I want to pull her back to safety, but she only steps closer to the betrayer.

"Why don't you heal yourself?" she asks in a softy voice.

I narrow my eyes at the dragon. He says nothing, his chest heaving, all shiny with sweat. I'm glad he's hurting.

My regina raises her palm, but it's as if she doesn't want to. Like she's fighting herself, she rests her palm on his pec. Her power ripples through the air like the downdraft of one of her wing beats. It goes into him and I scowl as, one by the one, the bullets pop out and fall to the carpet.

"That's for Henry," she says.

"Of course," Xander says tightly.

"Shut up," I drawl, stepping forward myself to sniff suspiciously at the both of them. I inspect Xander's skin. Skin that once bled for me. Skin I once bled for. Skin that covers the creature that ripped my heart out of my body and ate it whole. His right arm is covered with his family's tribal tattoo. The one he got after his mating mark came in and he became a man in the eyes of his ancestors. I snarl, "I should skin that family tattoo off your fucking body."

Xander's head snaps to me from where he was rudely staring at my regina. "Would you?"

"What?" I snap.

"Will you flay it off me, Savage? The tattoo."

I meet his eye, letting him see the hate I have, the distrust. Letting him see the place my soul used to be and the damage he did. How I wish I could murder him with my teeth. I growl, dark and intent. "You fucking know I would."

He smiles, but there is no happiness, no humour there. "Do you have time now?"

Ten minutes later, Aurelia is in the shower with Lyle and my shark-brother watches on as I take a claw to Xander's skin. He sits on a dining chair with a plastic drop sheet underneath us, his dripping sweat the only tell that he's in great pain.

I savour it like a full roast dinner.

"She wasn't sure," he says through gritted teeth. His first words in ten minutes. "She wasn't sure if she should let us do it."

"It's not her choice," I say, squinting at the red muscle under the tattooed skin I'm slicing away. I'm pretty good with my claws, very precise if I want to be. Scythe has many knives, but I'm old-fashioned. I'm also only doing it slow to drag it out. I can skin a lot more quickly in a regular situation. "How long will it take you to grow a new lizard skin anyway?"

"Don't know."

"I give you three weeks," I say. "Because I'm going to pour salt on it after and bandage it tight."

Xander's jaw clenches and he takes a deep breath as I cut a particularly deep slice, cutting a bit of muscle for good measure.

"Yeah?" he says, voice strained. "How much do you want to bet she'll try to heal me?"

I growl, tugging on the flap of skin in my left hand so hard Xander makes a sound in his throat. "Fuck you, Xander. Fuck your dad. Fuck your entire estate. I should skin your whole body and make crackling out of it."

Xander tilts his head back and laughs like a madman, sweat dripping off his temples. "Fuck," he drawls. "I fucking missed you, Sav."

I drop his skin and step back, frowning at him, then at Scythe. "He's gone off." Sometimes that happens when you torture someone past a certain point. They go delirious and mad.

"We'll take it up again tomorrow," Scythe says, straightening off the table he was leaning against.

"No." Xander shakes his head. "Get it done. Today. I want to show her."

I roll my eyes. "This is a performance for him!" I say to Scythe. "Completely showing off."

Scythe eyes Xander in an assessing way. "If he wants to do it. Let him."

"It's not fun for me if he wants it," I complain, crossing my arms.

"Come on," Xander groans. "You can't stop now."

I glare at him.

"I'll do it," Scythe rasps, unsheathing a small knife and coming to my side. "And I'm not stopping for anything." There's a determined look in his eye that scares me, so I put my claw away and head into the bathroom to find my regina, my only comfort in this life.

Chapter 89

Xander

Scythe has just finished with the last piece of my skin at my hand when Aurelia comes into the dining room, freshly showered and smelling sweet and fresh. She freezes in the doorway.

I stand up, showing her the bloody mess of my arm, skinless and free of the tattoo that shackled me. That told the world I belonged to something I abhor. Her eyes flick from my arm to the silver bowl full of my tattooed skin Scythe has on the floor.

Her eyes grow wide, her pupils dilate, and she makes a strangled sound before she whirls around and flees for the bathroom, a hand covering her mouth.

"Aurelia," I cry, rushing for her, my arm outstretched.

"Don't you fucking dare," Scythe says, pushing his body into my way.

I snarl, "Give me a moment with her, for fuck's sake!"

Lyle shoulders past Scythe, meeting me nose for nose. He snarls, the rabid in his eyes on full display. "Push me, Xander. I fucking dare you to push me."

For a moment, I wonder if we should let our mad monsters at

one another. My mouth twitches in annoyance and pain of a different sort. "I did this for her."

"You did this for yourself," he says, his lion's voice deep and guttural. "Like everything else you've *ever* done."

I blink, stepping away from him, wondering if that is true. "No, I..."

Two pairs of eyes are on me, one amber, one ice cold. Under their gazes, I sit back in my chair, staring at my empty hands. "You're right. It was for me. To show that I'm..."

"You think you're different because you said sorry?" Lyle asks, aghast.

I stare at him. "People can change, Lyle, you know that! I just beheaded a phoenix for her!"

"Maybe," he says, amber eyes shrinking as his human side assumes control. "Your little speech was a good one, I'll give it that. But it'll only ever be that. A speech."

"Every word was true," I say firmly.

Lyle takes a deep breath and looks at Scythe as if waiting for confirmation. My shark-brother nods, assessing me. "He was speaking the truth."

"He can't have spoofed you?" Lyle asks, almost desperately. "Tricked your psyche in some way?"

It hurts, this questioning of my words. Of me. As I sit here bleeding, with the blood of Damien Agnis on my hands. Not that I care about him, it's that they don't think it means anything.

"He cried, you know," I say softly. "As he died. Damien. He thought he was invincible for so long. Told me he was a protected species. Told me I'd pay for it. Told me it was a curse to kill a creature as pure as a phoenix." I laugh darkly. "Do you want to know what I said?" I slump back in my chair, not even knowing why I'm even telling them, just that I have to get it out. "I said...'tell my regina that'." My laugh is even crazier this time. "'You know who she is?' I said. 'Aurelia Boneweaver. And after I made that perfect soul bleed, no curse could ever beat that one.'" I look up at the ceiling, to wherever Damien's spirit now is. "Did you hear that, you fucking old duck? My curse trumps your curse!"

Light footsteps sound, and Aurelia is hobbling up to me, her eyes wet from the stress of vomiting. I raise a bloody hand, then drop it uselessly. "Don't feel sorry for me."

"I don't," she says simply. "But I feel sorry for anyone who has to listen to you feeling sorry for yourself."

I gape at her.

"You heard me." She walks right up to me and grabs my face in one hand, squeezing my cheeks together. I gaze at her in delight and wonder. "Stop it. Right now, stop this. I'm sick of it. Sick of being sad and lost. I want it to stop, and you're not helping." She lets me go and I sit up in the chair.

"How can I help?"

"Go back to your normal, arrogant self."

Savage gapes at her and Lyle looks at her in surprise. My brows fly up. "But...why?"

She puts her hands on her hips. "Because then things will at least *feel* normal. No—" She puts her hands up to Savage's protests. "I know they're not normal. I know that Xander did something I can never forgive. I just need normalcy for a second." She shifts uncomfortably and I know her leg pains her. I want to heal her. I want to help.

"What about this?" I hold up the golden chain still hanging from the collar at my neck.

"I don't want it," she frowns. "I appreciate the sentiment, but I'm quite done with it."

"Fine, but I'm keeping the collar on."

"Wild Goddess, *fine.*"

"Are you...*exasperated* with me?" I breathe.

She shakes her head in dismay. "Yes, you overgrown gecko." She looks around at the rest of them. "Look, I don't think he's going to turn around and betray us, and in all fairness, he can't hurt me any fucking more than he already has. It's not like he can cut the bond again."

Goddess that hurt. Something in me erupts in violent protest at her words, but with one look from her, I shut my mouth.

"So..." she says on an exhale. "Can we just...go back to normal for one fucking day?"

"Whatever you want," Lyle and I blurt at the same time.

We scowl at each other.

"But," she says, turning towards me, her chin raised. "You don't really have the right to call me regina. I'm not."

My insides deflate, my soul along with it. This cut is deeper than any other. I swallow the sudden lump in my throat. "What can I call you then?"

She narrows her eyes at me, no doubt running through the list of names I used to call her. The bad ones...and the good ones. "Just...my name is fine."

I nod. "Of course. Whatever you like."

She raises a brow at me.

"I'll make up for it, you'll see."

She sighs and I'm not sure if she believes me. "Let's just get to bed. Do you need to see a healer?"

"No, Aurelia."

Savage rolls his eyes, putting his arm possessively around her. I narrow my eyes at it. "I need a moment alone with you. Will you grant me that?"

The three lethal animuses wait for a response.

Her chest expands with breath. "Alright. You three head into our room and don't come out unless I say so."

None of them are happy, but I don't care. I need to be closer to her, if just for a moment. And as they leave, casting me murderous looks over their shoulders, I rise from the chair and step off the plastic.

"Will you help me with this?" I hold up the white bandage roll.

She takes it, because it's second nature to her, and sets the end against the back of my hand. I enjoy her attention on me, depraved as it is. Enjoy her small, gentle touches.

Fuck. I always had. I'd just never allowed myself to really feel that.

"Was the speech too much?" I ask in a low voice. Gods, her scent is the most perfect thing. Up close, I can smell her toothpaste.

She swallows. "I'm not sure." Her hands are so gentle, so soft, even though she's not touching my skin. I let her get to my bicep, savouring her movements, her breathing, her face, before I speak again.

"I meant all of it," I whisper. "Every last word. And even if you hate me, I'm glad you feel *something* for me. I can hold on to that."

"Xander," she whispers, blinking hard at my bleeding arm.

"Gods, say my name again." I raise my hand, ready to risk it all just for one touch of her cheek. My fingers brush her soft skin, tingles flooding all the way down my good arm.

She inhales, closing her eyes.

I lean closer, wanting to share her breath. "Just one more time."

A tear trails her cheek, but she graces me with her eyes, lids fluttering open, long dark lashes drawing me in. I want to covet these jewels for myself. I want to take her away to my horde again.

She inhales deeply and I revel in the joy it gives me to see that she enjoys my scent. I lean closer, letting her smell me. "Give me what I want," I whisper. "Please."

That seems to interest her. She pulls back, looking into my eyes. "Beg for it."

My cock hardens. Holding her gaze, I slowly drop to my knees on the blood-splattered plastic. We're so close that I can't help but press my forehead to her stomach, my hands coming around to brush my fingers against her calves. She shivers. I look up at her, enamoured by the power she has over me. To make me this hard, this desperate for her touch.

"Please," I whisper. "*Please* let me have you."

She gives a tiny shake of her head that excites me to no end. "Not good enough."

"I can't live knowing I can't have you," I say, watching those sapphires glimmer. My fingers skim the backs of her thighs. "Your skin is so soft. I beg you to let me taste it. To lick it. To suck on it."

Her breathing is heavy, but still, she shakes her head. My insides burn. I make tiny circles on her skin. "Aurelia," I breathe. "If you let me taste your pussy, suck your clit just once, I can live happy knowing I've tasted heaven one last time. I'm *desperate* to bury my face in your sweet cunt. If I don't hear you moan in pleasure, it'll destroy me." I gently squeeze the backs of her thighs. "My life depends on having your mouth on mine. Fuck, my cock is so hard."

She looks down for the evidence, track pants tenting as my cock strains. "You want to eat me out, Xander?"

I rest my chin on her stomach, inhaling her scent and revelling in my name on her lips. "I'll kill every beast in this academy just for one lick. One kiss of that precious pussy, Lia. I'll burn this entire state alive just for one look at you, splayed naked on that dining table."

She hums, stepping away from me and pulling her dress over her head. I can't breathe, can't think as she tosses her dress to the floor and undoes her bra. That too drops to the floor and my mind seizes in maddened desire.

"A gift," I whisper, reaching out to run a finger against her thigh. "You're a gift to the fucking world. To me."

"Take this off." She indicates to the tiny blue thong she's wearing.

"Can I kiss here?" I breathe, pointing to her lower stomach and hoping against hope she'll permit me.

"Yes," she says quietly, stepping forward.

I lean in, wrapping my arms around her thighs and pressing my lips against the place where cloth meets skin. Soft, sweet heaven. I can't help it, and open my mouth, dragging my tongue against her perfection. I skim my fingers up the back of her thighs, all the way up to her bare ass. She moans softly, leaning into me, burying her hands in my hair.

I hook my fingers into the thong and gently tug it down, sending healing into her right leg as I go and licking the soft skin above her pubic hair. Surrounding her with my power, I lift her off the ground and set her on the dining table. Her eyes are heated as she puts her hands behind her knees and pulls them up.

If I wasn't already on my knees, I would've dropped at the sight of her. A glistening sweet cunt is splayed before me. The finest jewel that, for these next moments, if she permits, I get to worship.

My mouth waters, and as I move forward, she peers down at me.

She halts me with her voice. "And if I told you just to look?"

I grip the leg of the chair next to me, needing to steady myself. "Then I would worship you at the altar of your pussy by kneeling here."

She looks at me, and I drag my eyes away from her core to look at her. There is challenge there, and it makes me lick my lips.

"Please," I beg. "Just one lick."

"Just one lick." She nods.

I swallow in anticipation, my breathing strained as I ready myself. I shuffle forward and hover my mouth over her, inhaling that heady scent that makes me want to fall into her and never leave. I let my breath tickle over her clit and she shivers.

She's biting her lip now, clutching the table like it's going to save her from me. I lean forward and drag my soft tongue up the entire length of her core, from cunt to clit. She tilts her head back and whimpers.

"Just one, you said," I murmur over her clit.

"Maybe just one more," she whispers.

Smiling, I delve my tongue between her, running it through

her juices, savouring every divot and curve, flicking her clit at the last moment. "So good," I whisper, my lips brushing that sensitive spot. "So perfect. Open yourself for me."

She does so with her left hand. "Another one," she breathes.

"Always," I say, licking under and over her clit, swirling my tongue around it and then all the way down until I find that tender hole. I enter her with my tongue and she gasps, dropping back onto the table, like the feast she is, displayed for me and only me. I use my lips then, sucking on every part of her, tasting each and every sweet inch of flesh and finally sucking her clit. She writhes on the table, moaning loudly and I grin, knowing the others are hearing her and are furious about it but forbidden to come out and see.

I flutter my tongue over her core, forcing her to feel all of my desire.

"In me," she breathes. "In me, now."

I freeze before raising my left hand and brushing my fingers against her. She whimpers and I rise to my feet. She's splayed out before me, naked, her curves made for my hands, her skin made for my tongue. I tease her pussy with my forefinger and she meets my gaze, a mixture of emotions glimmering through her eyes. She doesn't want to like this, but she *does*. She's dripping onto the table, right where Lyle was sitting not long ago. Raising my fingers to my mouth, I suck on them, closing my eyes to savour her taste before easing my first finger into her dripping heat.

Her back bows from the table and I lean over her, wanting to be close. "This is how you make me feel," I whisper, closing my eyes as her slick, wet heat grips onto my finger. "This is how much I need you. Give yourself to me. I don't fucking deserve it, Aurelia, but—" I grab the back of her neck with my other hand, and despite the pain of it, kiss her deeply, my tongue entering her just like my finger, her lips around mine, my mouth desperate. I ease back to murmur against her lips, "I want you to give yourself to me anyway."

"You're mad," she says. "You don't deserve any of it."

"I know," I say, pumping my fingers until her eyes roll back. "You're right. You've always been right. I'm a depraved fucking asshole that the devil doesn't even want in hell, but all I want is you. All I can fucking think about is you."

"Less talk, more tongue, asshole."

I exhale at the command, thoroughly pleased as I drop to my knees again. I add my tongue to her clit, sucking softly at first. She's swollen with pleasure and I grin against her, working her until she's trembling and gasping. I pursue her orgasm like a predator on a hunt.

When she comes, the sound of her wetness against my finger is loud and messy and I don't relent, groaning against her sweetest spots, wringing every last bit of satisfaction from her until her back thumps against the table and she goes limp and breathless.

There is a moment, when she and I are simply breathing, when my finger is still inside of her and my face is still buried in her pussy, that I finally feel a slither of satisfaction. It's fleeting, but it's there.

I clean her up with my tongue. Lapping up every last bit of evidence of her desire for me, keeping it for me and my greedy dragon. Then I get to my feet and see that Aurelia's eyes are closed as she catches her breath. A hand supports her right leg and I immediately gather her into my arms, supporting her behind both knees.

Thankfully, she lets me, probably spent and wanting to revel in the golden afterglow, a small reprieve from all the pain she suffers.

Then I carry her into the bedroom.

I find the three of them pacing the room, glowering and muttering under their breaths, in a nest of violence. I'm unsuccessful in hiding my smirk as I lay her gently on the bed and cover her, tucking the blankets tight along her sides.

They surround me, sniffing aggressively and checking their

regina for any sign of harm. Savage gives me a violent shove, and I let him.

"Don't worry, I did a good job," I reassure them.

And because they fucking heard that I did, they say nothing more.

Chapter 90

Xander

8 years ago

Selena is on her hands and knees on the hardwood floors of the bedroom of her husband's home, her body trembling as she sobs into a hand.

"Sissy!" I cry, running over to her.

"Xander!" she screams. "Oh my god, Xander!"

I take her face in mine and immediately step away in horror as I see the giant black eye blooming across her face.

There are more bruises on her arms, her legs. Her chest.

There is no longer a question in my mind as to who has done this to her. Who has been doing this to her for the last eight months. I roar in fury. "I'm going to kill him!"

"No!" she cries. "I need you to help me, the babies are coming early—" she gasps, clutching her stomach and sticking a foot out at an angle like a woman about to give birth.

"Shit, Sissy, who should I call?"

"It's too late!" she grunts, bearing down like she's constipated. "They're coming now!"

My head whips around the room and I remember what they do on TV. Towels.

"Where are the towels?"

Red-tinted water pools on the floor under Sissy. "There!" She points at the chest of drawers behind her and I run for them, pulling out five because I have no idea how many we'll need.

I run back to Sissy and she tells me to put two underneath her.

A contraction ravages her body just as I get them in place and she grabs onto my shoulders, crying out, her body shaking violently. "Support the head!" she cries.

I look around as if there's someone else who can do this. I really don't want to be seeing—

"Xander!" she cries, tears leaving her eyes now.

Without thinking about it more, I flip her dress up, only to see something big and round sticking out from between her legs. My heart near flies out of my chest before I realise it's a head. Of course it's the hatchling's head.

Sissy puts one hand on the baby's head and screams again. "Catch her!" I grab a towel just as the hatchling slides out of Sissy in a big gush of water. I catch her in the towel.

"Dry her off," Sissy gasps, looking at the hatchling but groaning again, going onto all fours. "The other one won't be far."

I set the baby in the towel and on the carpet, the cord still connecting her to Sissy, and gently rub her dry. Her little face is screwed up like she's in pain.

She gives a little, gurgling cry and I roll her onto her side, patting her back to try to clear the water in her throat.

Sissy gives a low moan of pain. Quickly, I wrap the first hatchling in the towel and set her aside.

"Is the other one coming?"

The second hatchling comes a few minutes later, this time legs first. I stare at the little blue legs in horror until Sissy screams and the baby's head finally comes out. I catch him in the nick of time.

This time, the little boy is blue and limp like a ragdoll. Panicking, I blow into his face. "Sissy, what do I do!"

But she's not answering me, crumpled on the floor on her face. "Sissy!" I cry. My power whips out in two directions and the little baby in my arms draws its legs up and gives a tiny cry. I set him down beside Sissy and roll her onto her back. She's pale as a sheet, but her eyes flutter open.

"Thank you," she says.

The first baby cries and she perks up, looking for her hatchlings. "Pass her to me."

At that moment, the room door slams open and Ragnar Firewing storms in, the midwives and doctors rushing in behind him, their eyes wide in urgency.

"Why are you here?" Ragnar says to me, his yellow eyes wide with fury. "Get the fuck out!"

"I was helping her give birth, you fucker!" I snarl as a midwife pushes me out of the way with her elbow. Ragnar grabs my collar and hauls me to my feet, looking between me and Sissy. "Did you—" he snarls as he realises what's happened and he hauls me out of the door, getting out his phone. "You'll pay for this."

"You'll fucking pay for what you did to my sister, you sick fuck! We'll kill you! My father will kill your whole family!"

Ragnar presses his hands to my face, and it feels like hot irons on my skin. I scream, stumbling away from him. "You think your dad is going to be happy about you being inappropriate with your sister? That you saw her, *touched* her?"

"What?" I gasp in horror. "I was helping the hatchlings!" I leap onto him, throwing a mighty fist drenched in fire.

Ragnar cries out as I strike his jaw, before he grabs me around the waist and takes me to the floor. I throw punches left and right, but Ragnar is bigger, stronger and dodges two of them, his hands finding my throat and squeezing.

I choke under his fiery pressure, kicking and grabbing at his wrists. But it doesn't matter. His face is red, his mousy hair flopping over as he focuses all of his rage into my neck. Within seconds, everything goes black.

* * *

Some time later, my Uncle Fabian and Ragnar throw me at my father's feet in the entrance hall of Drakos Estate.

Groaning, I roll onto my side, rubbing my burnt neck. My father glares down at me, towering and imposing as heat waves roll off him, scalding my sore face.

"You've brought great shame to our family on what was supposed to be a happy day," he booms.

"I was helping," I choke, rubbing my throat as I get to my feet. "She was giving birth early because *that* asshole beat her up and I was helping."

My father strikes me across the face, making my head snap so hard to the right that I fall to the ground. "That was not your place."

"He covets her, he always has," Ragnar snarls.

I right myself, gaping in outrage at the lies. "I do not! She's my *sister*. It's my job to protect her from monsters like you!"

My father's eyes glimmer. "You've always been unstable, son. But this is a step too far. You attacked your sister's mate, the father of the hatchlings."

"Fuck you!" I cry at Ragnar. "And fuck you, Father! You let him beat her! You married her off. She has bruises all over and she's pregnant! You told me we need to protect our women at *all* costs!"

Father glances at Ragnar, irritation flashing across his eyes. "I will deal with you later." He returns his dark eyes upon me and I see the force growing behind them, becoming massive. Possessive, dominant draconic power fills up the room, overwhelming me, pushing on my shoulders so hard.

"You can't do this!" I say, panicking at the silence in the room. "I'm your heir. I'm going to take your throne after you. You know I'm going to be more powerful than the other dragons. You know it!"

He narrows his eyes, the words registering as a threat, and I know I've made a grave mistake. His visage turns ugly. "And yet you won't even be rex of a nest. You have a *regina*."

Ragnar chokes with shock and amusement at this new information.

"I want his eyes burned out of his skull for looking at my mate," Ragnar says with new vigour. "I never want him to look at my female again."

Uncle Fabian steps forward. "Surely that's a step too far," he says. "A disowning is enough."

My heart misses a beat and my head whips back at my father. He stares at me, assessing. I see what his dragon is thinking. In a few years, I will challenge him for his crown. But disowning me, removing me from the family, would make me an enemy. An enemy who might come back for him. This needed to be dealt with permanently, but differently.

My mother appears by the doorway behind Father. The sight of her in her night gown, the thought of never seeing her again, makes my brain scramble in panic.

"Father, I was trying to help," I plead. "Please, there was nothing else I could—"

There's nothing but dragon-deep magma in his voice as he cuts me off. "Hold the boy still."

I shake my head, not believing this, not believing my eyes when Ragnar and Uncle Fabian take positions on either side of me, their big hands around my biceps like impossible shackles.

My father advances upon me. There is something worse than death in his eyes, something I've never seen in my sire. But it's been growing for months now. At some stage, he'd stopped seeing me as a hatchling and begun seeing me as a rival. A threat to him and his household.

Nobody spoke about the fact that the dragon population had been dying off because dragon animuses were killing their sons out of rabid, possessive greed. It was a nasty cult secret. But my father was made of nastier material and mere death held too little satisfaction.

"Mother!" I cry.

She blinks at me. Uncertain. Confused.

I clench my teeth, refusing to show my fear.

"Keep your eyes open, Xander," Ragnar says smugly.

Father holds my face, placing his thumbs just beneath my eyes.

But no, not this. Not this way. I try to wrench out of his grip. Try to save myself from a fate worse than death.

"All the way, Your Majesty," Ragnar says. "They shouldn't be able to grow back."

Father's eyes snap with irritation to Ragnar. "Your punishment is coming in a moment. Shut up and hold him still."

Ragnar's obedience is the only thing that saves him from a fate like mine.

A dark warmth takes over my eyes as my father's power tunnels into my skull. Suddenly, there's blinding white light. My vision twinkles, a thousand stars appearing in my world, taking over completely. Agony sears through my face, excruciating like knives penetrating my skull.

And an acrid, putrid smell like burning flesh fills my sinuses.

Those screams can't be mine. That scent of burning flesh can't be mine.

Chapter 91

Aurelia

I wake with a shout, sweat dripping off my chest, the sheets soaked and twisted under me. Someone is shouting, shaking my shoulders.

Gasping, I grab at the hands on me, and when my eyes adjust, my vision is filled with four worried faces. My hand reaches up to touch my eyes.

But it wasn't my eyes that were being burned. Wasn't my head that was filled with agony. Xander's glow catches my attention, and I hastily avert my gaze.

Scythe touches my face, worry etched in his, before he glances at Xander.

Lyle rubs my sore leg. "You're okay, regina. You are safe. No one can hurt you now."

Not true, but I'll take it for the moment. I try to smile before reaching for the water on the bedside table. Savage quickly hands it to me and I gulp it down.

"Eugene alerted us before you started shouting, actually," Savage says proudly.

Chicken shifters can see the future five seconds ahead, but it comes randomly to them, usually when something unexpected is about to happen. I guessed he'd seen me come out of my vision.

"Thanks, Eugene," I say. "It was just a bad dream."

He clucks sleepily from Xander's bed.

Savage strokes my leg, calming my beating heart.

"Sorry I woke you up," I murmur.

"It's sunrise anyway," Lyle says, kissing my shin. "What can I do?"

I set the glass on my leg to avoid the way it trembles in my grip. I swallow, trying not to burst into tears because they'll all ask why I'm upset. I take in a shaky breath. "I'll be okay."

"Regina," Savage says slowly, having never taken his eyes off me. "Can we...go to the pool today?"

"Why?" Scythe asks, sitting closer to me and running his fingers gently through my hair.

Savage glances over his shoulder at Xander and speaks into my head. *"I want to hold you as a starfish, please."*

I can't help it then. The tears slip out, my throat thickens, and Scythe takes the glass from me so I can hide my face.

"Fucking hell Savage," Xander snarls.

Savage ignores him, arms coming around me. "I'm sorry, regina, we don't have to. I was being stupid."

My memories of being a starfish are not good. My hands tremble as I remember the darkness at the time, the loneliness.

But I've never hated a form before, and I don't want to start now. Xander's presence in the room flutters along my skin. Perhaps it would be healing to have Savage hold me. I look at my wolf, his eyes slightly pink, his hair mussed from sleep. It would be healing for him too.

"No, you weren't being stupid," I whisper into his mind. *"We should do it. We should play mermaids with Scythe."*

Savage takes my hand and nods seriously.

* * *

Half an hour later, we file into the underground pool area that

Scythe rebuilt after Marduk broke it that one time. It was glass and steel then, but now it's set into the ground like a proper pool.

Everyone except Xander strips off and gets into the water. Savage eagerly stands in front of me, but there's an uncharacteristic nervousness in his eyes.

"I have no hearing in that form," I warn him. "So don't be bad-mouthing me while I can't hear you."

Savage grins wolfishly. "It'll only be dirty things, regina."

I smile. "Will you catch me?"

His face turns serious. "Always."

The shift has the potential to be triggering, but with my mates around me, watching with so much love, I pat my right leg to remind myself that it's still there and take a deep breath. Lowering myself into the shallow side of the pool, I suck in a breath at the cold until my thighs kiss the water. I tear off my dress and toss it at Lyle, who sets it carefully at the water's edge.

Turning back to the water, and feeling Savage close behind me, I shift. My arms are forced outwards as I become smaller, my vision becoming blurry and my hearing going fuzzy until it disappears completely.

True to his word, as I flop onto the water's surface, Savage scoops me up, holding me under the water while his big face peers at me. Three blurry giants hover above the water, their movements in the water fluttering around me.

For a moment I struggle to breathe. The memories come crashing back. The fear returning anew, that feeling of being lost, forgotten—

"What a sweet princess you are," Savage coos into my head. *"What a pretty star you make."*

My thoughts still as I concentrate on his words, my tiny heart rate slowing.

"Which part is your head?"

I lift the limb at the top and Savage strokes me there. *"Your mating mark is so small!"* he exclaims. *"How cute."*

I focus on my mate. I am here. I am not forgotten. Savage is holding me.

"*So clever,*" Scythe murmurs, dipping his fingers in the water to stroke my left arm. "*So perfect.*"

His touch is like heaven to my frayed nerves. They are all here with me and I am never leaving them.

"*If you turned into a barnacle,*" Savage says, inspiration striking him. "*You could stick to Scythe and ride around the ocean with him!*"

"*Can't do a barnacle,*" I reply faintly. "*Never touched one.*"

They take turns holding me under the water and I bask under my mates' attention. Eventually, dark thoughts start to filter through my brain. My leg might be back, but this form is too powerless, too passive for my tastes. Without warning, I shift in Scythe's hands, my beast of choice a surprise for them all.

Quickly, he brings me above water and I curl my long body around his thick wrist and forearm, rearing up to peer at him.

His lips twitch into a smile and he lowers his head, kissing my hood before setting me down on the concrete next to the pool.

Xander sits on the floor off the side, watching us from afar with a carefully blank expression. I slither up to him and his eyes lighten with hope. Goddess, the way it makes my heart pang to see him like that. I'm aware of my other mates watching us I slither right up to his booted feet. I bare my fangs and hiss at him.

The bastard smiles and lowers his hands to the ground. I consider him for a moment before slithering into them. There's a stunned silence behind us as Xander carefully raises me to his face. He's shaved this morning, the skin of his cheek smooth and soft.

I strike.

Sinking my fangs into his cheek, I pump venom into him, hoping it stings, hoping he understands that I want him to hurt for everything he did and did not do. Luckily, he doesn't drop me, just barely stiffens under the pain I'm inflicting.

I lift my fangs out of him, letting them fold back into the roof of my mouth and easing back to hiss at him again. The two puncture wounds drip blood down his cheek.

His eyes are keen on me, glimmering with different colours under my vision. "I'll take it, Aurelia," he says. "I'll take anything you deign to give me."

Xander walks around with those puncture marks on his face all day. Teachers and students stare, and even when he gets rude remarks, he simply ignores them. My animas raise their brows at both the bite and his bandaged arm and Minnie gives me a significant look, before turning back to Marduk and grabbing his hand for comfort.

"Nice one," Sabrina says with approval.

But I can't take my eyes off Minnie and the way Marduk pulls her into him and kisses her on the cheek, whispering something in her ear. They walk off together and I hope he's going to eat her out or something similar. That always makes a person feel better.

"So!" Sabrina says, glancing at Xander, who's taken a knee by my seat at the lunch table. Stacey procured the dog kibble for us and Xander picks at the bowl. Sabrina opens Minnie's folder. "Take a look at these and see which one you like. We're calling it the torture menu."

Lyle chokes on his coffee, but I chuckle under my breath.

Accepting the folder, I check out the tabs Minnie has placed to section the papers. There is green, yellow, orange, and red. I flip to the yellow section and see she has written in her neat bubble cursive an addition: *Dog kibble (the cheapest kind)*

The dragon in question is trying to peer at what's written, but I have the front of the folder angled upward so he can't see.

"You should eat actual food," I say, picking up a blackberry and offering it to him.

But Xander doesn't take it. "Naughty boys should be fed by hand."

It's Savage's turn to choke on his lamb shank. "Is he serious? Are you serious, regina?" He gapes at me.

Xander licks his lips by my side, and I can't help but remember his tongue last night. The way it teased and coaxed tingles from me. I suppress a shiver, knowing the entire table is staring at me, though Blair and Blade are trying not to out of respect for their bosses.

Without a word, and holding my breath, I hold up the berry to Xander's lips. It's a fat, juicy one, and Xander leans forward and places his lips around the berry, skimming my fingers. His eyes flick up to mine and he drags his lips over my fingers as he takes the berry. My fingers hang in mid-air, now stained purple, as I watch him chew.

Savage lets out a jealous growl. "You never feed me by hand, regina."

Xander gives him a vicious smirk.

"I'll feed you your dinner, sweetheart," I say.

Savage presses his lips together, but I know he's placated, if not excited now.

After lunch, Sabrina falls into step with me and pulls me aside. Her hood is drawn up, and she still has a little pallor from her time in captivity. "Lia, I get it, he's hot. If you were to *boink* him, I wouldn't judge you at all."

I snort.

She pulls me to a stop, leaning against the notice board behind her. "Are you going to forgive him?"

Nausea rolls through my stomach and the halogen lights above us are suddenly far too bright. "I don't know if I can," I say honestly. "I don't even know if it's the right thing to do."

The males stop to wait just ahead of us, out of earshot.

"Fuck the right thing," Sabrina whispers, grabbing my arms, her eyes suddenly bright. "Fuck everyone. Do what's right for you." She glances at our males down the corridor, and the leopard assassins who follow her everywhere, despite being too old to be at the academy. "Blair and Blade have made me see things a different way. You know what they do for a living."

I nod. They're Scythe's assassins. Hitmen. They kill people for money.

"They didn't use to feel guilty about their job. But since they've been away from it while they've been with me, they're reconsidering things. Blade cuts himself sometimes, when it gets really bad. Blair smokes way too much. We have each other. We understand how it feels to feel so much pain you want to go to sleep in a permanent way. How maybe we'll fight that feeling for the rest of our lives."

My hands tremble, and Sabrina's voice turns thick as she grasps them in both hands. "You've lost a lot. I've lost a lot. But Xander..." She casts a glance at the dragon, standing with his hands in his pockets, looking anywhere but us, then down at Minnie's folder tucked under her arm. "If he truly regrets what he did. If he *truly* hates himself for it, then..." She looks at me meaningfully, then grins. "I mean, we'll make him pay for it, but then, what after?"

My stomach churns at her words, my mind a tumult of dark emotions.

"We'll be late," Savage calls.

Sabrina gives me a hug and we hurry after them. "Since when are you worried about being late?"

After the next class, Scythe leans over to me and says, "Aurelia, I made an appointment for you with the academy physio."

"Oh no," Xander says. "I also made an appointment for tonight."

Shark and dragon stare at each other over the table in challenge. I wait patiently, before Xander's glow flickers and he nods. "I concede." Scythe takes my hand. "This time."

Minnie snorts from the table next to us. She catches my eye and gives a dramatic eye roll.

"They should have picked up the double booking," I say reasonably. "It's no one's fault."

"Maybe they thought Xander's appointment was for him," Savage says. "Eyeball physio or something."

"I have no eyeballs, you fuck," the dragon retorts.

"Eye*lid* physio, then," Savage clarifies.

My chest goes tight as the vision of Xander's torture flashes through my mind. His father's pure malice and the screams that followed. "Let's go," I say, heaving myself to my feet before the panic attack starts.

"Can I come?" Xander asks politely. Hopefully.

It's Scythe's shark that turns his gaze to Xander, the temperature in the room suddenly dropping. I stroke a hand down my great white's muscled back, and he cracks his neck. The other students flee the room, rubbing their arms.

"The choice is always yours, regina," Scythe says in my mind, but the hand that comes around my waist is fraught with tension and possession.

"Next time, Xander," I say softly.

The dragon nods, but his eyes flash with something I don't really want to see right now.

Scythe helps me to the medical ward, but just before we get there, he pulls me aside in the corridor. His mouth crashes onto mine, dominating and intense. He possesses my body with his own, picking me up and pressing me against the wall.

"Mine," he growls into my mouth. "Always mine." His tongue snakes down my mating mark.

"Yours," I reassure him with a sigh.

He makes a purely animal sound and hikes up my dress. "I need to be inside my regina," he rasps, his movements jerky with need. "I need to claim you again."

Breathless, I let him rip my thong in two before his hand slides down my new leg. "Leg up or down, beautiful?"

"Um...down."

He swivels me around and I press my cheek against the wall as the sound of his zip coming down makes my pussy weep with joy. Scythe bands one hand around my hips to find my clit, and on the other, he spits, rubbing his cock before easing it into me.

"My perfect woman," he says, voice haggard. "My perfect regina."

Gasping his name as his girth finds me, I grind against his hand and cock. "Never leave me again," I pant.

Scythe's other hand stabilises my new leg. "Never," he agrees. He fucks me hard and fast then, desperate, stuttering strokes that make me cry out.

Someone walks past us with a small cough—a doctor, I think —but neither of us care, too caught up in each other.

My shark grunts, thrusting hard enough that he has to hold me in place against the hard plane of his body. I take it all with relish, letting him fuck away my dark, troubled thoughts. Teeth scrape my shoulder as he lifts me up completely. My power searches for his, and his cold waves penetrate my insides, demanding union, demanding that he claim me.

I look at him over my shoulder and find his eyes are wild with desire as he captures my mouth.

The vision of Scythe Kharkorous losing control because of me makes me come and I scream, leaning back into him and squeezing my eyes shut as I feel all of him inside me. My muscles contract and Scythe growls into my shoulder, lifting me off the floor and violently emptying himself into me with each grunting thrust.

"Give me all of it," I moan, contracting around him again. "I need all of it."

"All of what?" he demands into my ear. "Tell me what you need."

"All your cum," I moan. "Give me all your cum, Scythe."

He stills as he finishes, both of us panting against each other. Eventually, he slides me down his body so my shoes touch the floor once again.

"You mean everything to me." He kisses me much more softly now, his tongue exploring my mouth, taking care of me as he always does. I stroke his chin and he melts into my touch. "I needed that, regina," he whispers against my mouth.

Heat floods my face like it always does when Scythe is being sweet. "I did too."

"Next time you come up with an insane plan," he smiles and it stuns me for a moment. "I want in on it. I was born for a little insanity."

My breath feels haggard. Perhaps the weight of long, isolated years finally dropping off my shoulders. "I don't want to keep things from you any more."

"Thank the Goddess for that. Promise me we'll scheme together from now on."

It's my turn to smile. The image of us both bent over a table, pointing at papers under a spotlight flashing through my mind. "I promise."

He tugs my dress back in place and brushes my hair off my temples. Then he bends down and picks up my thong, pocketing it. Without a word, he takes my hand and kisses the back of it, before we continue on into the medical centre.

Chapter 92

Xander

Aurelia returns to a private dinner in our suite full of Scythe's cum. I can practically hear it as she hobbles towards the dining table, her leg more mobile after the physio, but in more pain. Savage picks her up and whirls her around before showing her the food he's demanded from the kitchen. Lyle makes her a plate, and she sits in Savage's lap, tucking a serviette into his T-shirt, fulfilling her promise to feed him tonight.

I watch jealously as Savage kisses her between the breasts as she cuts up his steak and feeds it to him with her bare fingers.

It's then that I catch Lyle staring at me, his lion's eyes sizing me up like he wants to eat me for his dinner. He looks like he wants to rip my throat apart first.

Giving him a knowing nod, I continue to eat my meat and vegetables. I miss Selena. I miss the hatchlings and Mother. Our night time meetings in the family drawing room without Father were some of my happiest moments amongst the darkness of being there. Glancing at Aurelia, I wonder if she secretly misses my family too. If she thinks about Delilah and Emmerson and the way Emmerson forced me to play cards with her. The way Delilah clung to her after the kidnap attempt.

The dragon community would know that I have left the estate by now, removing any reason for another attempt. Father is bodyguard enough for the hatchlings and the Chens will have been adequately threatened. I know no one will try anything like that again.

But the academy is a different matter.

Everyone separates after dinner, Savage and Lyle sweeping Aurelia into the kitchen as Scythe goes off to speak to some of his people. I head to the bedroom and pick up my phone to check the academy's security cameras. It was an old habit of mine at Drakos Estate and it's followed me here. I check the feeds almost compulsively, searching for suspicious activity, then scanning the sky for signs of danger. Scythe, now almost as possessive as a dragon, has avians patrolling the skies on a twenty-four-hour roster. We want to be able to see any dragons coming in from a distance.

Mace has brought his forces here before, and he has the audacity to do it again. My own father would avoid a public attack and would probably rely on Mace to do the dirty work for him. I'm sure it's one of the reasons why he collaborates with Mace at all.

I've heard nothing from Francesca. I have her blocked on everything, but no doubt my father is keeping her quiet anyway. Selena wouldn't dare reach out to me when the estate monitors her so closely.

Pure darkness drapes around me like a blanket and I throw my phone aside. The others lope in some time later, and once they've brushed their teeth, they climb into bed, cuddling up all cosy.

That darkness thickens until it becomes stifling. My ears echo with Aurelia's high-pitched screams. My bed feels like spikes are embedded into it and I can't take it anymore. Rolling to standing, I head out of the suite and leave the four of them tangled in each other behind me.

I scowl at the beasts I pass on the way down and, despite the two fang marks on my face, they still blanch and stumble at the sight of me. A hyena drops to the floor and pencil-rolls into the nearest room. All beasts are taught to stop, drop, and roll when they see a fire. I suppose that counts for fire-breathing dragons too.

Outside, Bastien the gargoyle is silent, as is the hunting games field. Telling the guards to shut their mouths, I climb up onto the wall and sit there, my legs dangling down over the long drop.

The night is cool, the stars covered by clouds and the scent of lemon eucalypts fills my nose. I can't even see the moon, so I settle for listening to the night instead.

Mice chitter in the bushes a few meters away. A guard is blowing his nose in the tower closest to me. In the anima dorm, someone gives a high-pitched scream as she finds a huntsman in her toilet.

I flinch, these sounds only irritating me further. I get the urge to take out my earphones and let loose on the world. To tear it apart and see what remains at the end of the day. It's tempting, but all I do instead is think of the young woman in the arms of my ex-brothers back in the animus dorm.

Late into the night, my ears pick up the swoop of an eagle's wings. I know it's not Beak or one of the other scouts, because I would know the sound of *her* wings if I were deaf. The way she moves through the air is unique, like she finds joy in it, like she relishes in every rustle of her feathers.

I turn as she descends upon the parapet, her lilac silk chemise clutched in her beak. There are little bows at the sides. But my eyes slip past this to the space under her left wing, where a bald spot has appeared.

Aurelia has been plucking her own feathers. I tamper the

agony in my being at the realisation. That she is still hurting. That she will likely always be hurting because of me.

"How did you sneak out?" I murmur.

She shifts, the chemise levitating upwards as she settles on the wall in her human form. I respectfully keep my eyes forward as she pulls the material over her body. Her skin smells of the herbal rub Lyle massaged into her muscles before bed.

"I was sneaking around for years before I met you," she says quietly, absently rubbing her thigh. She does that often now.

"For your father," I clarify.

She nods absently. "Why are your eyes gold now?"

I peer at the clouds as I wonder how to answer her. "We fought in ancient wars together," I say quietly. "On ancient battlefields, I was your general. In a different body, but it was me. All of us. My dragon showed me pieces of our lives together."

"You told me that on the day of my trial."

I exhale at the memory that surfaces like a whale breaking through the water. My dragon had hidden things from me and it should feel like a betrayal, except it doesn't. "When I gave you the sapphires. I remember that now. I guess I'm...listening more."

She shifts on the concrete to face me, whispering her next question. "Does he...speak to you now?"

"Yes," I whisper, eagerly turning to face her. "He's...much happier."

"Would you shift?"

"I would slit my own throat if you asked it."

"Don't say that!" she exclaims. "I expect you to have—to be your own person."

I get to my feet on the narrow concrete of the wall. "Everything I do is my own choice, Aurelia," I say darkly. "You know that."

My shirt is off in one movement, and to my amusement, Aurelia looks away as I slide my pants down. The corners of my lips turn up before I leap right off the wall.

She stifles a beautiful gasp as the sound of cartilage

crunching explodes in the air and a dragon rises up in place of a human. My big head and golden eyes are in line with her as I stand before the wall. I step forward slowly to show her I mean no harm, and to rest the edge of my muzzle on her knees gently. There's no weight on her, only touch, only warmth and my power seeping into her tired bones.

Blue eyes glisten by the light of my own and I know I take that deep-ache away from her injured leg. I scent her, nostrils flaring, my inhale so mighty that it sounds like a gale. She smells like sun and sky, like summer and a cool mountain spring.

She raises her hand and my heart leaps. Tentatively, she reaches out and rests her hand on my snout. I want to leap into the sky and roar in triumph. Instead, I close my eyes, so the only thing I feel is her.

"None of this should have happened, you know," she says. "None of this is the way it should be," she sighs. "I suppose it's useless to think about that."

No, it would be better to burn everything to ash.

On the top floor of the animus dorm, there comes the sound of three furious snarls. Aurelia straightens as no doubt three voices in her head demand to know where she is. I remove my head from her lap, missing the touch immediately. Grunting in annoyance, I shift back, flinging myself upward at the last second to land on the wall. Giving my clothes a moment of thought, I push them to the side and sit down, this time facing the academy.

It takes the three predators all of sixty seconds to sprint across the academy grounds towards us and I tense my abs a second before I'm brutally wrenched off the wall.

Chapter 93

Aurelia

"You don't get alone time with her," Lyle snarls, shoving Xander flat on his back and punching him in the nose. There's a sickening crunch. "You haven't *earned* the right." Lyle punches him again on the same spot.

Naked and bloody, Xander does nothing. I stand on the wall and cry, "Stop!"

Xander raises a hand as if to stop me. "It's past time, Aurelia," he says in a nasally voice. "Let them have at it."

My three mates set upon him.

I've seen brutal fights in my time. Awful, bloody matches where participants edge near the threshold of death.

But this? This is unlike anything I've ever seen. It's not only brutal and bloody, it's as if I'm watching three rabid monsters let go of all inhibitions and tear into a piece of meat. They pummel Xander like they hate him. Like they want to follow him into hell and destroy his soul. It makes my heart bleed; it makes me see stars, but I don't look away.

Even when Lyle breaks Xander's right thigh bone, right in the middle.

Even when Scythe wrenches both arms out of their sockets.

Even when Savage sinks his teeth into Xander's gut and shakes him like a ragdoll.

Xander's face and body resembles something closer to an open jar of jam. There is blind rage in their eyes and they don't look like they're going to stop.

Xander is no longer responding with grunts and groans. He is silent. His breath nothing but a wet and raspy wheeze.

"Enough," I say.

They don't, or can't, hear me. They continue as if I'd said nothing. The regina in me flares in anger, and I pull off my chemise and shift into an eagle, coming to land just behind them before shifting back.

There's power behind my voice as I scream, *"Enough!"*

My three mates pause, Lyle's clenched fist is raised and trembling as he stares daggers at Xander's body, no part of him left unmaimed. Savage and Scythe heave with breath, but vibrate with rage.

They're trying to fight the regina command. Not on my fucking watch.

I shoulder past Savage and Scythe and cover Xander's body with mine. I look up at my three mates, their faces contorted with violence so profound it makes me shiver to be under it.

It's truly terrifying to be on the receiving end of those expressions of utter primal fury, but I know it's not directed at me, but past me to the beast who'd wronged them so badly.

"Enough," I urge.

Xander coughs beneath me, a drowning, heaving sound. I turn to him and send healing through to his shattered nose and throat. His eyes flutter open and I realise he's still completely conscious. He says something, but through his broken jaw and damaged vocal cords, I can't make it out.

"You ask for mercy, regina," Scythe says, his shark in full control. "But when did this beast ever show you any?"

There's only one language my mates will understand right now. Gentle Aurelia is of no use here. I get to my feet, hopping up to protect my leg. I hobble up to Scythe and grab a fistful of his shirt, pulling his face down towards my snarling one. Nose to nose, I hiss. "He gave me mercy when I needed it most, Scythe Kharkorous, and that's what counts. Stand. Down."

I let him go, and he straightens, studying me. "Scythe Boneweaver," his shark says.

"What?" I snap.

"I have claimed you, regina, I am Scythe Boneweaver."

It's not easy to glare at someone when you're craning your neck to look at them, but I manage it. "We're not married."

"Not yet."

Annoyed, I whirl around and hobble up to Lyle, shoving him in the chest. "Enough, lion."

He lowers his hand, albeit begrudgingly. "As you wish, regina." Savage is next, frowning deeply at Xander and refusing to look at me. I force his face to turn, but his eyes stubbornly strain away from me. I kiss him on his snarling mouth. "Stop, my love."

His whole body seems to relax and his shoulders sag when he sighs, "Yes, regina."

I turn to Xander and carefully kneel again, recommencing my healing, one body part at a time.

* * *

It's well past sunrise by the time I finish, but I'm not tired. My mates won't leave my side but can't watch as I work. Once the last students stream into the dining hall for breakfast, I levitate Xander to waist height and head back to our dorm. There's no one else to see us climb up to the top floor, and even my mates stay outside as I drop Xander onto his bed. Henry wakes up from where he's sleeping cuddled against Eugene and he chirps in greeting as I go to the sink and get a bowl of water and wash-cloths. I get the two of them their own bowl, setting it on the shower floor where Henry happily plonks himself in and shoots water out of his beak.

Xander's eyes are closed as I dip the washcloth into the water and begin cleaning the crusty blood off his face. His brow is furrowed, but I smooth those lines away and find that his face is, luckily, back to its normal handsome, if arrogant, state.

His eyes remain closed as I work my way down his body and still when I change the crimson water twice over. It's not until I get to his lower stomach that I hesitate. His cock is thankfully the only part of him not covered in blood, and there's no damage to it. But I can't help but glance at the golden cock ring he wears at the base.

"Pretty sure Savage thought about ripping that off a few times," Xander muses. I turn to see him watching me staring at his now semi-hard dick. "I've seen him do it before."

My cheeks flush. "Luckily, he didn't. You, unfortunately, can't shift into a starfish and grow one back."

Xander is silent at that, simply gazing at me.

I can't read his gaze, so I settle on avoiding it and washing his legs. "I think you did this better than me," I say quietly.

"I was...thorough."

He shifts and his cock lengthens. "Did you see what it says?"

"What?"

"My cock ring."

I raise my brows at him. "What does it say?"

"Take a look," he says gently.

Swallowing the lump in my throat, I shuffle up the bed and peer at the base of Xander's cock where ink dark curls are cropped close to his skin.

He may have listened when I told him to remove the slave collar from his neck, but he's only put it on a place no one else could see. The collar sits at the base of his dick now, the same words, PROPERTY OF AURELIA BONEWEAVER, etched along its golden surface, just in miniature.

I'm struggling to breathe.

"I won't touch you unless you tell me to, Aurelia," Xander

says. " But I want you to know that it's yours. I want you to claim it."

I can only stare at him, my body heating with each passing second. His voice, his offer, eliciting something new in my core.

Xander drops his voice. "The power you have over me is something I crave." He licks his lips. "I...miss you, when you're not near me."

The taut expanse of his body, his masculine perfection, offered to me, almost in the same way he used to offer me food in his dragon's lair. I suck in a breath. "Are you still in pain?"

In one smooth movement, Xander sits up and swings his legs over the side of the bed. I step backward to give him room, but he shakes his head and reaches for me—before his hand drops. "Touch me, Aurelia." His voice is haggard, a beast at the end of his patience. Yet he holds on...for me. "Please."

And because I do want to, because that urge in his voice triggers some long-lost instinct in me, I raise a hand and, stepping between his legs, I let my fingers brush along the dark stubble of his jaw. It's deliciously rough against my fingertips, and his massive chest expands with stuttered breath.

Xander closes his eyes. I lean into his face, experimenting with the feeling of being so close to him.

"You can give me one kiss," I murmur. His eyes snap open, but I warn, "Just one, and that's it."

His hands clench on his knees. "Just one."

I can smell the soap on his skin. Xander closes the distance between us and brushes his lips along mine. "You'll grant me just the one?" he murmurs against me.

"Yes," I whisper across his mouth.

Steam exhales from his nose, fluttering around me like a smoky cloud. "You really know how to test a beast," he growls before crushing his mouth against my own, forcing my lips open, devouring me whole. I make a startled sound but don't back away, gripping on his face and meeting his energy with my own.

I raise my left knee and place it around his hip and onto the bed, intending to straddle him, but when I raise my right, it's stiff and sore. I pull away, reaching down for it—until I see Xander's trembling clenched fist still on his knee.

He really won't touch me until I tell him to. In the back of my mind I understand what he's doing. That he's giving me complete power. Showing me what it's like to...command a dragon.

I straighten and meet his gaze. "Help me lift my leg, Xander."

His eyes flash with pleasure and he reaches around my knee and gently positions me. Pressed against him, I see it when he remembers I'm not wearing any underwear. His hand clenches around my thigh.

"Touch me here." I brush my neck with my finger, trailing down between my breasts.

Xander seems to stop breathing as he brushes my neck with his own fingertips, his soft touch trailing down and leaving shivers in its wake.

"Lie down," I instruct.

He lifts me a little with his telekinesis, swings his legs up onto the bed and lies down. I watch his hard abs tense as he adjusts himself, his unbound hair splayed out around him like a halo of black.

"You can hold me here." I indicate to my hips, lifting my chemise a little.

He grabs me so fast that I have to steady myself for a second, his hands hot against the bare skin of my hips.

But then I hesitate.

"I want to be inside of you, Aurelia," he whispers. "I've needed it for ages now, and it's been killing me to watch *them* have you and not... I've been hiding my hard cock all week."

And I've been purposely making it worse.

I lean forward, lifting my ass up and reaching behind me to grab the base of his cock. My hand hits metal, reminding me of the ring. I have to lean forward more than I usually have to, but when his wet head hits my soaked entrance, Xander lets out a feral sort of sound. His entire body tenses but doesn't move.

Looking down at him, I rub his head against my entrance. "Do you like it when I do that?"

"Yes. Oh Goddess, yes," Xander grits out.

"Do you want more?" I ask, fascinated, squeezing the base of him.

"Please. Yes." His hands are clenching my hips, supporting me but telling me he's struggling.

I nudge his head into me.

"Fuck, are you wet for me?" he pants. "You're soaking."

"No," I say ever so slowly, easing him in a little further.

"Ah gods, don't fucking lie to me, Aurelia. Not now." His voice cracks and I take mercy on him, sitting back on his cock, easing it into me and breathing hard as I accustom myself to his girth.

I can finally say that old wives tale about dragons is true.

Xander's head tilts back, and he lets out a cry, his entire body vibrating as I allow him inside of me.

"Don't come," I warn. "Until I say so."

He breathes hard and I enjoy watching him fight the pleasure, eventually looking back at me. Slowly, I reach for the hem of my chemise, watching his eyes widen as I pull it up and over my head.

"You're going to kill me," he breathes, rubbing circles on my hips with his thumbs. "I'm going to die today, Aurelia."

I run my hands up his body, working my way up, watching him tremble, then vibrate as I lean over him, pressing myself against his chest. I lick up his neck. "So dramatic," I murmur against his skin.

"Aurelia," he moans. "Please."

"Please, what?" I whisper over his mouth. I raise my ass, almost groaning at the feel of extracting him from me. "What if I told you that was it?" I unsheathe him further, his head now the only part of him inside me. I tease it a little, fucking it just enough to elicit a moan from him.

"Don't," he growls, eyes flashing the deepest gold I've seen yet. "Please don't take it out."

My confidence grows. "Such good manners."

His throat rumbles. "I want another kiss. Please."

I ease his cock back into me, slowly, because he's far too big for a hard fucking. "I said it was just the one, remember?"

"You're going to kill me," he moans. "I might already be dead. I don't think you healed me, I think you sent me—"

I suck on his lower lip to shut him up and he reciprocates immediately, his tongue slipping into my mouth, demanding to taste, to explore. Pulling back, I say, "Run your hands up my back." He does so and I let him feel me as I grind my clit against him, then gently fuck his massive girth.

It's difficult work, given my sore leg and his size. Eventually I straighten, placing my palms on his chest, riding him. My thighs burn as I look down at him. His jaw is clenching and unclenching, his hands supporting my hips.

"Fuck me," I say.

"Come here," he groans, pulling me down on top of him. He rolls us onto an angle so he's not quite on his side and I'm wrapped around him, my right leg supported on his hip.

It's then that one of his earphones falls out. It lands between us and I pick it up. He's staring at it like he hates the thing.

"Take the other one out," I say.

He takes a deep breath and does so. There's a moment of silence then, when he's inside of me and there's no music in his ears except the sound of the both of us panting.

Then Xander wraps his arms around me, buries his nose in my neck and thrusts into me like it's the last time he'll do so.

I cry out, folding my arms around him and brushing his hair away from his neck. The side where the mating mark used to be.

Xander whimpers as he sheathes himself fully in me and stops there, his entire body vibrating.

"It's alright," I whisper. He pulls his face out of the crook of my shoulder and looks down at me, something shining in his golden orbs. Regret, shame, guilt...and something else too.

Even unable to hear his thoughts, I know what he's thinking. I give him a small smile and brush a finger over the side of his neck, sketching the mark we once shared. "See? I drew it back on."

He falls over me again, this time pressing his lips to my neck, for once, unable to find the words as he fucks me, slowly, with long, languid strokes, my clit grinding against him with each thrust, his lips fluttering over my sensitive neck. He fills my body so completely, I gasp in wonder at the stretch, at the way my body adapts to his size and the way I soak him so completely it's not long before every thrust makes a satisfying sound.

"I want to come inside of you, Aurelia," he groans against my skin. "I want to fill your womb with so much of my cum that you'll be full of it for days, so that there won't be space for anyone else. I want to keep you in my lair and feed you and heal you and fuck you for days. It wasn't enough time, Aurelia." His voice lowers into his guttural dragon form as he continues that deep languid thrust. "I want you soaking in my cum at all times. I want your pussy to be dripping *me* every second of the day, and I want to taste every part of your skin while you're covered in the jewels I brought you, on a bed of gold that I made. I want that for eternity and whatever comes after that."

My body spasms as I explode into a bunch of multicoloured sparkles the colour of Xander's eyes. I'm nothing but fractals of myself, floating above our bodies; pleasure and pressure make me scream around him.

Xander thrusts into me deeply and comes right against my cervix like he wanted, holding me tight and emptying himself with stuttering, short thrusts.

The dragon eases back. Tucking my hair behind my ear as he searches my gaze. "We should stay like this forever," he breathes.

It's at that point that Savage, Lyle, and Scythe find us when they burst into our room.

Chapter 94

Aurelia

"No!" Savage dramatically clutches his face, his eyes wild. "That's not fair, regina! We were trying to kill him!"

I extract myself from Xander, sighing as his still-hard cock leaves me. Carefully, I crawl over him and step onto the carpet. My mates stand before me with bated breaths, barely containing themselves. Planting my hands on my hips, I raise my chin in my air.

"This was *my* choice. I know you might have some big feelings about it and I guess so do I. But it's happened now. So…" I inhale deeply, my gaze softening as I meet Scythe's eye. I can't read his expression. "I didn't want to hurt you."

Scythe exhales a slow and measured breath before he reaches for me, pulling me into his arms. "You haven't hurt me," he whispers into my hair. "I just don't want *him* to hurt *you*."

My throat thickens as he kisses the top of my ear and I feel Lyle's caress, then Savage's hand tugging at mine. "Take me away before I try to kill him again, regina," my wolf says.

I let him lead me away, casting a backward glance at Xander, who has remained silent the entire time. He lies on the bed, leaning on his elbows, his golden eyes following my every movement. Something tender in my heart grows at the sight of him. It's new and strange, but...I like it.

Lyle follows us into the bathroom, undoing his tie. "Minnie wants a sleepover tonight," he says unhappily. "She wants *everyone* there."

I get the feeling he's trying to distract himself. I can work with that. "Not an animas night?" I ask, as Savage turns on the shower.

"No, I get the feeling she wants to speak to Xander specifically. Titus and his followers have been harassing her."

My heart twists for my friend, angry heat spiking through my veins. "What's that bastard up to now?"

Savage pulls me into the shower, growling to himself as he soaps my body.

"He sends her videos of the explicit variety of him with other women."

There is nothing but fire in my veins as I let Savage take care of me. "Can't we stop that? Have we not blocked him on every platform?"

"They use different numbers and accounts each time," Savage says. "I think we made it worse after we destroyed the Clawson businesses."

"Either way, she wants her friends around her," I nod. "Pack your things, then. I'm guessing this'll be your first slumber party, Lyle."

My lion's lips twitch. "I'll get my hair rollers."

* * *

We arrive at the Devi pack room to find Marduk hanging pink heart balloons over the windows. He greets us with a sombre bow, before offering Scythe and Lyle whiskey on a liquor trolley he's prepared. Yeti brings out a pile of board games behind Minnie, who's wearing a new, pink sparkly onesie with her mates' names written in rainbow cursive across the ass.

Minnie's pack bed lies in the middle with new pink sheets, while the mattresses on the floor make it clear who is to sleep where.

"This is our bed of love," Minnie says, gesturing to her bed. "But it's animas only tonight."

Stacey snorts when she enters the room with Eugene tailing and her orange and yellow nimpins chirping in greeting. I immediately loop my arm through Stacey's, deliberately turning my face away from Savage in faux dismissal. He growls and hijacks Eugene, immediately going to inspect Yeti's board games.

Sabrina and her cheetah twins arrive straight after, their arms laden with food they've nicked from the kitchen, including a super-sized bag of caramel popcorn and a metal tray bursting with hot, juicy burgers.

We have a great time as we eat dinner, chatting about harmless things like hair and the nimpins. It's exactly what we all needed, despite the fact that my eyes keep straying to Xander, sitting by himself with his half-eaten burger, trying to keep his eyes off me.

"You smell like Xander," Minnie says quietly, delicately wiping her mouth with a serviette. She's the only one who uses his name these days.

I nod. There's enough buzz in the room from male voices that I hope Xander can't hear us. "We had a moment before."

"Smells like more than a *moment*," Sabrina muses.

Heat fills my cheeks as I attempt to hide behind Henry. "Don't look at my face."

Minnie huffs a laugh. "I'm not one to judge, Lia, you know that." She gives a shuddery sigh, glancing at the strangely calm dragon. "If you'll allow it, I'd like to talk to Xander."

"Of course." I turn to look at said dragon, who I can tell is trying hard not to listen in. "He wants to help where he can."

When he realises we're all staring at him, Xander finally regards us. I beckon him and he smoothly gets to his feet, that whiskey glass dangling from his fingers. I can't help the way he takes my breath away as he stalks over. I know he doesn't mean to walk the way he does, but he could never get rid of that arrogant dragon's stalk, no matter how humbled he might be feeling.

"You may sit," I say regally, patting the end of the bed. "Minnie has some questions she would like to ask of you."

It starts to rain outside. On our top-floor dorm room, it sounds like bullets pelting down overheard.

"I need to hear it from you," Minnie begins. Her voice is brave, but her eyes glimmer with sorrow. Suddenly, I'm reminded of Lorian, lying on his side in the Collector's dungeon. My heart clenches. "What did it feel like when you broke your bond with Lia?"

I suppress a flinch. I've never asked him. Never wanted to know. But this is important, Minnie just realised it before me.

Xander stills, as do the other males in the room. Minnie clutches my hand and I shuffle in next to her, with Stacey close on her other side, holding her other hand. When Xander speaks, it's gentle, as if he's trying to save us from the truth. "It felt like fading away. Like a song that's come to its end and all that's left is silence."

Minnie's face crumples as she lets out a sob, heart-wrenching and awful. I release her hand and she covers her mouth. I put my arms around her, hiding my own flood of emotions.

"And," Xander continues, "every day I found myself growing emptier and emptier. As if...if I lost focus for a moment, I'd become nothing. Like a shadow. Barely a beast at all. Barely human."

I blink into Minnie's hair. Had I known this? Had I seen it in his anger, his rage, as he held on to his old life with everything he had?

"What makes you different from Titus?" Minnie asks in a hushed voice. "Why do you want Lia again?" There's no jealousy in her question, not even envy. Just sadness, pure as grief.

"I fell in love, Minnie," Xander says. "I fell in love with Aurelia, that's what's different."

Minnie and I inhale sharply at the same time. My heart pounds, the shattered pieces chiming like glass shaken in a bottle.

"Titus is not capable of love, Minnie. There's too much hate in him," Xander says, gravely.

"But why?" Minnie chokes. "Why does he have to be like that when he could have me?"

Xander looks out the window, where the rain turns the world grey. "Choices. He chose that path. Willingly, knowingly. Just like you choose to love people, he chooses to hate them." His eyes glow with that golden colour, mesmerising in the way it seems to glitter. "Mate or not, regina or not, it's our choices that make us who we are. Not some idea you have of him in your mind. Consider him dead to you, Min. Your heart is too precious to have it tainted by someone who can't see its beauty."

My vision blurs as I hear Xander's kind words to my best friend. This side of him we rarely see, that he rarely shows to the world, is something I'll hold like a gem in my own secret horde of Xander's goodness.

We're silent after that; some of us in shock, some of us in grief. The rain hammers the roof now, less like bullets and more like an assault of sadness. When it finally eases, leaving a hush in its wake I stare at Xander, and he silently gazes back at me.

"If Raquel had mates," Stacey whispers into the quiet. "They might have gone to save them."

I wipe my eyes as guilt strikes me right in the sternum. "Is there a way?" I ask Xander. "Can you not do anything at all for Raquel?" Xander's eyes flicker and I can tell he wants to. That he feels guilt for our wolf anim. "Please, Xander?"

He sucks in a breath at that. "Let me see what I can do."

"You'll get to her telepathically, like last time?" Sabrina asked quietly.

"Yes." Xander gets off the bed and seats himself on the floor.

"In that case, I want to come as well," I say, placing my good foot onto the carpet. "I need to see Raquel again."

"No, Lia!" Minnie cries, lunging for me. "I won't risk anything happening to you as well!"

I pat the small hand gripping my arm. "I need to do this, Min. I left Raquel there. I can't stand the thought of that."

"Aurelia is more powerful than Raquel, Minnie," Xander says, watching me hobble over to him. "Don't forget that the only way anyone ever captured her was because she went willingly."

The room is quiet for a moment. Well thank fuck he finally remembered that. Stacey shivers, rubbing her arms. "Be careful."

"I'll be there, too," Savage says, making his way over to me and pressing himself against my side.

I nod and we take our seats opposite Xander. Sitting cross-legged makes my knee ache, but I nudge it out a little and Savage puts a comforting hand on my thigh.

"There's a chance we can bring Raquel back with us," Xander says, closing his eyes. It's strange how much I miss that light when it goes out like that. "But that'll rely upon me actually getting in and shoving aside the Lunaris wolves."

"They might still obey you?" I ask.

Xander exhales through his nose. "That'll be up to them. Savage better stay back in that case. Your presence may rile them up."

Savage growls. "I'm going where my regina goes. If I'm staying at the perimeter, then so is she."

"I'll make that decision," I say in a disapproving voice. "Now let's go."

I close my eyes and immediately feel Xander's cavernous power expanding towards me. A smoky scent fills my nose and we're off, my mind lifting off skyward. Xander shoots us out into the night, across the barren, regional land that spreads out so far into the distance. The sky is still overcast, but that heavy rain over the academy has stopped. The speed of travel makes me giddy, my burger threatening to vault out of my throat, but just as I clutch my stomach, Xander slows and the power of Drakos Estate unfurls before us, vast and more powerful than before.

The dragon king has been strengthening his shields.

I don't mention it, however, as Xander loiters at the edge, testing the boundary of it. Savage stays close to my side, and in the distance, I feel Scythe's psychic presence monitoring me.

"Will it let you in?" I whisper into the room, growing impatient. Minnie and Sabrina whisper to each other, and Lyle shifts uncomfortably. My mind remains honed in on the dragon before me, whose own power feels taut now.

"Only one way to find out." Xander surges through the shield, and without hesitation, I follow.

"Stay, wolf," I command.

Savage growls in protest, but I place a hand over his where it still sits on my thigh.

Xander slows for me as we breach the protections of Drakos Estate with only a mild burn in my brain.

I sense unrest in this place I was held captive for so many months. Wild power moves irregularly, like a boat unbalanced at sea. Xander senses it too, and we go on high alert.

"Something's not right," I tell the room.

Xander says nothing as he hooks a mental finger into me so we remain close as we fall into the castle.

But we end up in a different part of the castle than intended, and what we see sends a shockwave through the both of us.

Lady Drakos lies on the sweat-soaked sheets of her four-poster bed, all four limbs shackled with obsidian, her eyes wild and her mouth snarling as she strains at her bonds.

Flores Drakos and Francesca, with her arms crossed, stare at Xander's mother with frank observation. Ragnar Firewing and Fabian stand behind them. Selena frets in the corner, wringing out a cloth and hurrying over to the bed and wiping her mother's forehead. Selena leans down and whispers something in her ear. Lady Drakos falls back for a moment, sighing and closing her eyes.

"How long?" Francesca asks bluntly.

"If the potion is no longer working," Flores says, "then nothing will help her. I will end it myself."

Lady Drakos' eyes suddenly fly open, looking directly at us. "Xander?" she cries. "Xander!"

The heads of the observing dragons snap towards us.

I grab Xander in a mental fist and launch us out of there. "Out!" I cry. "Xander, run!"

Although he lets me pull him out of the castle and completely out of the estate, Xander growls. "I don't *run,* Aurelia."

Scythe and Savage wrap me in their power and fly me back across the land. "What happened?" Savage demands. "What did you see?"

"My mother," Xander answers quickly. "She's lucid, the potion that keeps her Berserker genes at bay has stopped working and they've bound her to her bed. My father will likely execute her."

"What?" Minnie asks. "He can't do that!"

"He can," Marduk answers darkly. "That was agreed upon by the council. It was a condition of their marriage."

I blink my eyes open as my mind re-enters my body.

"I didn't realise you knew so much about my family," Xander says to Marduk. He's on his feet already, pacing the room.

"If the council knows about it, I know about it," Marduk replies coolly. "What will you do?"

Xander runs his hands through his hair as Savage helps me to my feet. I wipe the panicked sweat off my forehead. "This is my fault," I say. "I...tampered with her entire supply of medicine. I thought it was making her sick."

Xander stops his pacing to stare at me. I can see his golden eyes shift as he remembers how Lady Drakos always asked me to prepare her medicine. How she'd always asked me specifically, and I'd never questioned it. Finally, that day when we'd cooked together in the Drakos kitchen, when she'd shown me the entire supply, and hadn't stopped me when my power flared outward.

As if that's exactly what she'd wanted.

Lady Drakos may have been delirious and drugged, but somewhere inside of her, she'd known what I was capable of. That I might be the one to free her from the slump her mind had forced to endure.

But at what cost?

Xander finally shakes his head, his eyes dull. "It *was* making her sick. That's how the potion works. But it doesn't matter now, Aurelia. This is a long time coming. I..." He looks at me, his eyes flashing with leashed emotion, telling me what his mouth won't.

So I give him what he needs. "You should go," I say. "Go now. And quickly."

He takes a single step towards me before seeming to think better of it and grinding his teeth as he turns on his heel.

We all watch Xander leave with a dead sort of feeling. Then we hear him as the top of the dorm shudders under his shifted weight. And then there's silence, that mighty presence now launched into the sky, back to where he came from.

I feel bereft now. Feel a niggling, nagging feeling inside my heart. Savage is frowning at the ceiling; Scythe has stopped breathing.

Then Marduk, bearing that strange wisdom that comes from a beast weaned into the underworld, says, "You all know this is a trap for him, right?"

Chapter 95

Xander

What Could Have Been – Sting ft Ray Chen

The castle is dark as I arrive, only flickering candles lighting the entrance hall, as if the estate is already in mourning.

The thought lights a fire in my arteries and twists my face into a snarl as I ascend the stairs and charge through the corridors.

One of the maids shrieks and drops her bundle of linen as she sees me coming. I step over the tumble of sheets and continue to my mother's room.

To my continued annoyance, it's Francesca who stomps out of the room to greet me.

"What the fuck do you think you're doing?" she grouches.

"Get out of my way," I snarl.

She stands her ground, crossing her arms, an ugly twist to her mouth. "This is no longer your home."

I lean down and get into her face. "It never fucking was. And you were never my fucking wife."

Her face, that I'd once thought was beautiful, now turns horrendous as her power flares like knives about her.

"If you keep me from my mother, I will kill you."

"It's alright, Francesca." My father's drawl carries a dark weight tonight, and it makes my dragon bristle. "Let him in."

I stare at her hard as she steps aside, her head still somehow tilted in an arrogant manner.

They all stand in my mother's room, three male dragons: my father, Fabian, and Ragnar. I hate the fact that they're in her private space, watching her like some performance as her night gown rides up her legs.

My mother pants, sweat pouring off her as she snarls softly. Her head whips towards me as I appear and she frowns, baring her teeth. I wonder if she can see me.

"This is inappropriate," I say flatly to the males. "Get out of my mother's room."

Ragnar has a smirk on his face as Francesa slides around me to hurry to my father's side. Selena is nowhere to be seen, likely having been kicked out to attend to the children this late at night.

Uncle Fabian is the only one with the decency to pretend to look troubled. "You have some nerve appearing here, Xander, after everything you've done to betray us."

"Well, you betrayed me as a child, so I don't know what you expected."

"Your father gave you a second chance," Fabian says.

"A second chance," I muse, approaching my mother. The yellow glow from the overhead lights makes her skin look sallow. I feel her power, her need to be free and rage. I remove one of my headphones and put it in her ear. But music had never worked for her in the way it has for me and she thrashes again. She'd never managed to find that one thing that calmed her, save for the potions. "Designed by Mace Naga."

"Damaged," Francesca spits. "I should have known."

I crack my neck against my need to kill them all. My fingers crave to tear their flesh to pieces, my teeth needing to taste their blood. The sheets are hot as I pull them up to cover Mother's legs and preserve her dignity in front of these intruders.

"What happened to your eyes?" Fabian asks.

"I respected you once," I say in disgust to my father, who, all this time, has remained seething and silent as he glares at me. "But I was a fool to think you were honourable like our ancestors."

"Our forefathers?" My father rounds on me, his eyes wide and draconian. I step away from the bed. "Our ancestors stole and cheated and killed to possess their wealth. A wealth that *I* own now. One that you will never deserve."

"What do you know of *deserving*?" I ask, stepping in time with him as we stalk each other around the room in an arc. "I never deserved the punishment you gave me, and you know it."

He scoffs. "You were the son I never wanted. I wanted a leader, someone who the Wild Goddess deemed worthy of his own nest." Never mind Fabian and *his* crimes. I cast my uncle a disgusted look. Ragnar had been punished by having Selena and the hatchlings removed but Fabian had never been punished for his crimes.

"No one here was deemed worthy of a regina," I counter. "No one here has so much as a single mate to their name."

Now it's Fabian's turn to snarl as I hit a nerve. So I dig deeper. "So much so that some of us resort to exchanging money for *teenagers*."

Father cuts a look at Fabian. "I thought you stopped that nonsense years ago."

"That's no one's business but my own," Fabian says, clenching his fists. "What a dragon does in the privacy of his own lair is his own—"

"No," I say simply. "That's not how it works at all. Let's just say I found some transactions of yours, Uncle." I smirk at him. "And let's just say they're being uploaded to the internet this very evening. All your little politician friends will want nothing to do with you."

It's then that Fabian and Ragnar join Father in our little dance around the room, their eyes locked onto me as his prey.

"Perhaps," my father says through clenched teeth, "we deal with this the old-fashioned way."

"What are you saying, brother?" Fabian asks, not taking his golden eyes off me.

"That this is something I should have done a long time ago."

Three older Drakos dragons plus Francesca against one.

The odds are not ideal.

Am I resigned to death? I deserve it, yes. Perhaps this is the way my regina gets justice. The only right way to close the crime that is my current existence. I didn't see this solution before. I look at my father, into those dark eyes. This is the beast who hurt Aurelia. Who tore her leg right off her body and kept it in his cupboard of treasures, hoarding it for his own pleasure.

"No," I snarl. A sudden draconian rage rises up within me. Possessive, dominant. Vengeful. "You have yet to pay for all the things you've done, Flores Drakos. If you intend to kill me, I intend to travel to hell with you by my side." My snarl is purely vicious. "Two of us will die tonight," I vow. My eyes flick to Uncle Fabian and Ragnar. "If not four."

Their eyes flare in reciprocal challenge. The room fills with dragon smoke and flecks of embers stir within it.

Given what I'd done, I should want to die. Except for one crucial thing:

The thought of Aurelia existing when I'm not is a thought I cannot bear. I need to be here watching over her, even if, after all her wanting, she decides to live her life without me. I can't leave her again. Not ever.

Something booms from the east. Like a plane breaking the sound barrier. Like sacred fire formed into a spear.

And then I feel her, like a ruthless summer monsoon. A young woman who'd burned down her family home because of what her father did to her mother. A young woman who'd healed a broken dragon.

She'd come for me.

My heart near shatters in my chest, and even as my vision

blurs and the roar in my head turns into a scream, I turn and glance at my mother.

And meet her eye. She smiles at me, and it's not sweet or gentle or motherly, but full of anger. Full of the endless rage of her bloodline. The rage we share.

She nods and I nod back, waving a hand and sending her shackles falling open onto the bed.

Chapter 96

Aurelia

We sit in silence for a while. Well, my pack and me. The Devi and Panthera packs chat amongst themselves, unsettled by the events of tonight. We'd gone in to save Raquel and did nothing for her. Instead, I've lost Xander to what Marduk thinks is a dragon-sized trap.

I stew in it. The look in his eyes, the gentleness of his voice. The way Lady Drakos fought against her bonds, that familiar look of berserker rage I'd seen in Xander so clear on her face.

Something ignites within me, and it blazes through my muscles and tendons. It flashes through my core and my power flares like wings.

There is only one path for me now.

I rise to my feet and meet the gaze of my mates, one at a time. Somewhere in the distance, perhaps in ancient memory, there comes the sound of war drums.

The hairs on the back of my neck rise. The regina in me snarls at her mates. "Do you stand with me?"

As one, they stand. Scythe's teeth elongate. "You know we do, regina."

I nod with approval. "Then we go to Drakos Estate. Xander does not die tonight. Not on my watch."

"Your will is mine," Lyle vows, his amber eyes wide and ferocious.

Savage crouches as if ready to spring. "My soul is yours, regina," he growls.

I see it then, as Xander would have in the visions his dragon gave him. The way we might have won battles in other times and places. The way we would fight in a battle to come.

"Lia?" Minnie whispers, her eyes gleaming as she stands from Yeti's lap. "But how will you get there? You have no dragon."

"True enough. But dragons weren't the only beasts who could carry incredible weight." I swallow. "The thought came to me when I rescued Delilah Drakos from the clutches of a dragon. I'd carried her as an eagle, but she was too heavy for me then. It was just the wrong form."

Stacey's mouth forms an 'o' and she grabs Savage's notebook and pen, scribbling something onto it. She shows her picture first to Minnie, Marduk and Yeti, then to me.

I smirk and nod.

"But your leg," Minnie frowns.

"I have two legs," I say simply.

"Can you take us as well?" Marduk asks excitedly.

Lyle's brows shoot up. "Will you share with the rest of the class?"

That fire in my body makes me burn with urgency and I grab Lyle's hand and pull him outside, calling for everyone else to follow.

I hobble down to the elevator that's thankfully in the pack dorms, and before I know it, I'm rushing outside.

"Regina," says Scythe in disapproval.

"Come, come!" I wave a hand at him as I exit onto the field at the back of the academy, looking up at the overcast sky.

There are no stars tonight. No moon. Just the faint blue glow of the security dome.

"Regina, tell us what you're trying to do," Savage urges.

"No time!" I say, whipping my shirt off.

Marduk yelps and turns around as Minnie and Stacey step forward. My power is so irritable that when I explode into my phoenix form, I shower my friends with glittering, crimson feathers.

"No," Scythe says, understanding immediately. "I should never have told you about Celeste."

But he *had* told me how Celeste had broken the sound barrier carrying him back to the academy after I'd left.

Too bad, so sad. He'd given me a gift.

Stacey finally shows my mates her illustration. "What in the chamber of secrets is that!" Savage exclaims, wildly gesticulating at the drawing.

My beak is smirking, but no one else but me can tell. I'm too jittery, too full of fire to even joke about it. "I'm going with or without you." I spread my wings, flapping so they get battered with air, before I angle them downwards and launch into the sky.

"Regina!" Savage screams in panic as I gain height. "I'm coming!"

"*Good boy,*" I tell him as I tip, ready to swoop. "*Lyle, strongest first.*"

Lyle frowns and glances at Scythe. I know they hate this, but they have no choice as I dive towards Lyle, my right leg bent up to protect it, my left claw ready to receive. Lyle shouts out, but he reaches for me, Henry clutching onto his hair as I shove my claw in Lyle's face. He grips it in one hand. Savage leaps to attention as I sweep Lyle into the air and he catches Lyle's legs just as he's lifted off. Scythe snarls up at me, but I ignore him as he adds his weight to Savage's

"Quick!" Marduk says as I bring them up higher, pulling Scythe above the ground with my teeth clenched against this new power. The Caspian tiger grabs Scythe around the legs, and with a loud *fuck* that comes out as a high-pitched cry, Marduk's feet leave the ground. He's followed by Yeti. There's no physical force keeping me afloat, all power, no physics as my irritated, immense strength is let out in near-full force, my anima finally getting what she wants.

We wobble in the air, the males hardly keeping still as I beat my powerful wings.

"Ready?" I ask everyone, taking a deep breath as I head for the dome.

"Wait for me!" Minnie exclaims.

We all look down at the same time to see Minnie leaping up and wrapping herself around the front of Yeti like a koala joey.

"No, regina!" Marduk cries.

"It's a chain of friendship!" Minnie happily shouts up at me, pointedly ignoring the protests of her mates. "Go, Lia, go!"

Blair and Blade let out a *whoop!* as Stacey and Sabrina cheer me on. Honestly, it's lucky my friends are as crazy as I am.

My power cushions Minnie and Yeti from underneath, but the combined feline telekinetic powers keeps the entire chain stable for me. They sway in a long chain below as I beat my wings to gain more height.

I close my eyes as we touch the protective dome, but just as I'd suspected, given its mistress is a phoenix, it lets another phoenix out. I envelop everyone in my power, and only once Minnie and Yeti are safely through do I pause and stare into the dark distance.

My power gathers around me like clouds gathering before a cyclone and I funnel all my rage, all my need for vengeance, and all my pain into that power. Lyle swears beneath me, his hands tight around my leg.

"Someone count me in," I say tightly.

Funnel. Funnel. Funnel.

"One!" Minnie cries.

I think of Lady Drakos in her bed and Selena thrashing on the floor under her father's power.

"Two!" Savage cries.

I think of Lorian, lying on the floor of The Collector's dungeon, no light, no moon shining on that fair face.

"Three!"

Xander's face fills my vision, of the light going out in his eyes and his world going dark as his father hurt him.

I scream and let my power go.

Like a slingshot being released, there is a mighty sound that snaps at the ears and we are catapulted through space. There is silence for three scary heartbeats as we hurtle towards Drakos Estate. The wind might have cut us into pieces if it wasn't for the power I'd bound around my friends and their combined powers assisting mine.

Only when dark opens up to tiny lights, do I release my speed back to normal.

Everyone swears in their own way, loudly and proudly, except Scythe, who silently looks up at me to see if I'm okay.

"Your ass is going to be so sore for this," he threatens.

I sure hope so.

Gaining a bit more height so that Yeti's feet don't hit the top of the black stone wall around the estate, I sail beak first over the grounds. Drakos Estate lets me in. I defended her once, saved one of her hatchlings when she could not, and she seems to remember it.

Everyone lets go in a wave after that. Yeti takes Minnie, rolling onto the grass, followed by Marduk. I lose height, letting Scythe and Savage drop off next. Lyle lets me go and lands on his feet in a crouch, leaving me to land smoothly on the grass.

My mates sprint towards me as I shift into human form, Scythe handing me my PJ shorts and tank top.

"Are you alright?" Lyle asks quietly.

"Are you mad?" Savage exclaims.

"Yes to both," I pant. In fact, I'm pumped.

That flight should have taken everything out of me. Instead, my vision is acute, my muscles taut like springs, and there is a power in me that still demands to claw and maim.

I lead the way into Drakos Estate without another word.

"We're completely out of our depth in a dragon fight," Lyle says.

Savage barks, skipping merrily to catch up to me. "Those are fighting words, lion."

"Wolves don't bark."

"I'm a special wolf.

"I suppose you are."

As I stumble up the steps to the castle, I glance over my shoulder to see Savage grinning in delight as he picks me up around the waist and runs up the stairs. "My regina says so too."

I growl in my chest, nothing more than a deep rumble, and Savage growls back. Scythe and Lyle flank us with Marduk, Yeti and Minnie bring up the rear.

It's at this moment we hear a mighty, earth-shattering *roar* followed by the explosion of brick and mortar.

Chapter 97

Savage

"Oh no," Minnie says as we freeze.

I pick my baby girl up as we run back the way we came. She's stiff in my arms, rigid with that Godzilla-sized power in her body. It smells like a bushfire. It smells like my Aurelia.

We pass through a shower of rubble, my regina putting up one of her shields like a giant beach umbrella, making the tiny rocks and dust slide down around us. Overhead, a dragon bursts out of the castle like a circus cannon.

"Who is that?" Yeti cries. "That's not Xander, but—"

But she is huge and black like Xander, and where Xander's scales are tinged with blue, hers are tinged with gold.

She roars, fire from her open mouth lighting up the night sky as she circles around, looking for her prey.

Another dragon bursts from the castle, this one I know to be Flores Drakos from the pictures Xander's shown me. Deep green like an emerald overcast with shadow, the dragon king barrels after his wife, smashing right into her in a full body punch.

But Lady Drakos is not swayed so easily.

Finally free in her true form, they tussle in mid-air as another two dragons join the mix, one a deep red, the other one smaller and green like spearmint chewing gum.

"I bet that's Francesca." Aurelia points to the chewing gum one. "And that's got to be Ragnar." So the red one is Selena's bastard husband. We'd been trying to get at him for ages, but he'd been a hard one to catch out with all his security.

"What's that saying about bringing a knife to a gunfight?" Minnie says, gaping at the sky of overgrown lizards breathing angry fire.

"They still have soft bits, Minnie," I say defensively, squinting as I try to get a look at Ragnar's underside. His dick and balls have to be hidden in there somewhere, right? I'd never really tried to find Xander's in this form.

"Their eyes, yeah," Minnie says, not understanding me at all. "It's just their big old fire-breathing mouths that get in the way."

My regina glances around and I know who she's looking for. Meanwhile, the three dragons surround the black one and Flores Drakos lands a solid kick to her underside. She roars, stumbling a little in mid-air.

"They're going to kill her," Aurelia says through clenched teeth. "What do we do?"

"Who?" I ask.

"That's Lady Drakos," answers Scythe.

Suddenly, I'm angry too. "No! We have to help her!"

Something high on the castle walls amongst the rubble lets out an angry, screeching sound. Two more dragons burst into view, spewing fire at one another. I'd recognise Xander anywhere, dark as midnight, big as a monster, and the other one...

"Fabian," Scythe growls, nodding at the foresty-green dragon.

"Many enemies," Marduk says. "I'm taking my regina inside."

Minnie ignores his tug on her elbow and catches Lia's eye. "Between the three of us, we can take that red one down."

Lia nods. "Do it, Min. I'll hide you."

The little tigress pulls her mates towards the shelter of the castle before they disappear into one of my regina's shields. I imagine the three tigers with their hands up, making angry faces at Ragnar, who's snapping his big jaws at Lady Drakos's neck.

A moment later, Ragnar shudders and falls back, looking around in panic as something he can't see takes control of his wings.

"Lyle!" my regina says like a military commander. "Take Francesca."

Lyle steadies himself before raising his hands and aiming at the slender chewing gum dragon who's flapping around Flores like a fly.

"Xander can take care of himself, but Flores is pretty strong." My regina looks at me and Scythe. "I've made one of them faint before."

Without another word, she shifts into her phoenix form. *"Hold on to me."*

We both hesitate, glancing at the heavy clouds above us. Normally, I'd be right up for this type of thing. I mean, imagine sinking my fangs into a dragon's soft eyeballs or belly? But I won't have control in the sky and it's my regina at risk here.

My chompy sweetie rounds on us, a light in her blue eyes I've never seen before. She shifts back into human form to hiss in a low, dangerous voice, "I never did tell you who tore my leg right off my body with no warning, did I? Who lay me down on a hospital bed and put his hands on my bare leg?"

Scythe and I go dead silent.

"It was Flores *fucking* Drakos."

That does it.

Me and my brother descend into our animuses before we realise it. My wolf takes over, my canines growing as I rumble in lethal rage.

Aurelia shifts back into phoenix form and tucks in her new

leg, launching into the sky. Scythe lunges first and I leap after him. As she takes our weight, Aurelia falters for a short moment in mid-air, but her phoenix strength kicks in, and almost straight away, we're flying right up to the two pummelling dragons.

Lady Drakos is not holding back. I watch in awe as she, exactly like Xander without his headphones, fights like she was made for it. It's easy to follow, brutal movements, and the trained fighter in me doesn't blink, watching eagerly as they dance with claws and teeth drawing blood. A light spray of rain makes the air cooler as we watch and I swing my feet in mid-air, my muscles wanting to get in on the action.

On our other side another dragon fight is taking place, just as brutal, with the feeling of old enemies finally coming to a head.

"Wheel around and drop me on Fabian," Scythe says.

"What?" comes Aurelia's surprised voice.

Scythe's voice is filled with raw command. *"Savage, climb up, take my spot. Aurelia, do as I say."*

Hand over hand, I climb up my brother's body until I reach my regina's pretty leg. Aurelia obediently wheels around, surging towards the two warring dragons as I wrap a hand around her leg and Scythe slides down my body, latching onto my bare ankles just in time.

Aurelia lets out a warning cry, smooth and golden as we approach Xander and his golden eyes flick towards us.

I can't imagine what the fuck we look like to him, I'll probably never hear the end of it after this, but everything is wiped from my mind as Xander's claws dig into Fabian's chest and force him to rotate so that Xander is under him like a kid on monkey bars, leaving Fabian's back exposed.

Aurelia flies over the pair of them and Scythe lets me go.

My brother lands on Fabian's back in a practiced crouch before scuttling up his back like a crab, keeping low.

Aurelia makes a wide arc, letting us get a good view of Scythe, ready to dive in case he falls. But Scythe's feet are steady even as Fabian bucks, trying to wrench Xander off him. Xander's teeth appear, snipping at Fabian's leathery neck. The older dragon roars in Xander's face, and Xander roars right back.

It's then that Scythe reaches Fabian's head, the dragon's eyes going wide as Scythe's power penetrates through his chest and into his heart and blood vessels.

Xander takes the opportunity to snap at Fabian's muzzle, his teeth sinking into Fabian's lower jaw. Scythe unsheathes a dagger and leaps over Fabian's head with the knife raised high over his head—

And buries it right into the dragon's eye socket.

Fabian roars as blood spurts and Xander rips a chunk out of his uncle's jaw. The three of them thrash in mid-air and Scythe loses his balance, slipping right off Fabian's head.

Aurelia shrieks and shoots towards them, but Xander's power whips out and Scythe is slapped back into Fabian's nose, where Scythe whacks his knife into the flesh there.

Scythe roars into the face of the dragon who'd once hurt him, his face red, the veins in his neck bulging, right before blood explodes out of Fabian's eye socket and the dragon goes limp as a dead fish.

Xander plucks Scythe off Fabian with his teeth before the green dragon's wings upturn and go crashing, lifeless to the grass. It seems to take forever, but when he does land, it's with a mighty thump that shakes the earth.

Aurelia speeds for Scythe, my legs swinging back almost horizontally, but my brother is already scuttling down Xander's back and seating himself there, waving us on.

Together, we head back towards Lady Drakos, who's still tangled with her husband.

Lyle and the Devi pack still have the chewing gum dragon and Ragnar thrashing against themselves in mid-air.

But while we were focusing on the fight in the sky, we'd forgotten one thing. Suddenly, Ragnar rights himself, pulling free of his invisible bonds and angling his maw straight for Xander.

Marduk lets out a shout of warning and I look down to see wolves spilling out of the castle like ants, two of them knocking Lyle right off his feet.

Chapter 98

Scythe

A tsunami fills my body, roaring, whipping me up on the high of a successful kill. A mortal enemy finally dead. Finally dead. The creature who had haunted me for near on a decade is finally gone.

Rain splatters across my forehead as, on the back of my new ally, Xander, we fly towards Lady Drakos.

Bonds are forged in battle, and this is one battle I won't ever forget.

There is a shout below as the wolves, likely hiding inside the castle until now, join the fight on land.

But they have four powerful felines to contend with, and neither Marduk, Yeti, or the most powerful tigress I know will be overcome by mere grunts, Lunaris wolves or not. But this means that the two previously occupied dragons, Francesca and Ragnar, are now free of their telekinetic shackles. And free to charge right for us.

Xander roars in challenge and charges right back. I tense to ready myself for impact, except Francesca, being smaller and more nimble, banks at the last second, the side of her wing skimming down Xander's neck.

Sharp scales hit me as Xander banks away from her, and the

force of the blow, combined with the inertia, sends me sliding down Xander's side, my shoulder and arm blossoming with pain.

"Scythe, hold on!" Xander's cavernous dragon's voice is an emotional and psychic mallet into my head, and I scramble to keep my seat, my fingers getting cut on his scales.

Aurelia's phoenix screech of panic is another sort of blow as her power picks me up and plonks me onto Xander's back. Panting in relief, I settle back in place to see Savage pointing towards Flores and shouting something that's lost to the crosswinds.

A high-pitched draconian roar of pain fills the air, and I turn in time to see Flores ripping a giant chunk out of Lady's Drakos' side. He swallows the flesh as Lady Drakos' wings upend and she falls to the earth.

It's then that Ragnar's head crashes into Xander's ribs, sending us careening in mid-air. From our other side, Francesca breathes fire right into Xander's face, making him flip vertical. But Ragnar was prepared for this and sinks his teeth into Xander's shank.

I grip onto Xander's neck with all my power as roars fill the night air; I don't know how we're going to win this.

Aurelia's sudden scream in my head makes light burst across my vision.

Chapter 99

Aurelia

My mates are being attacked on all fronts. Lyle is bleeding on land, Scythe is clutching onto Xander's back for dear life, and my dragon has just been attacked by Ragnar, his teeth still deep into those blue-tinged black scales, tearing, *ripping* his tough hide.

I see defeat. I feel fury, and I embody it.

The Wild Goddess knocks inside my head, a sound from deep within the earth. *BOOM BOOM BOOM goes the* ancient sound, full of primal rage.

And this time, I answer.

The scream that tears from my lungs makes my throat bleed as it turns into a colossal, draconian *roar*.

Chapter 100

Lyle

Everything suddenly stops. Both on the ground and sky. The remaining wolves all cease their fighting to look up. Ragnar abruptly lets Xander go, wheeling around. Francesca too stops her pursuit of the black dragon and spins around in surprise. Flores stops mid-dive and wheels around to stare. Even Lady Drakos rights herself where she lies on the grass and angles her head up.

All to look at my regina.

Aurelia, my angel of light, is growing in size, her crimson plumage darkening to a bright and terrible blue, and becoming something much harder and sharper. Her beak morphs into a muzzle full of sharp teeth. And her *wings*. Her wings reach out and grow to an impossible size, now strong with leathery skin and cartilage.

She opens her blessed, mighty mouth and roars fire right over Flores' head.

Aurelia's dragon form is magnificent. There is no other word for something so phenomenal as my regina has done the impossible. Everyone had thought Boneweavers were simply not capable of shifting into a dragon. Even Xander had never broached the subject; we'd all just accepted it as a given.

But she takes to it like a being born to reign over the sky.

"That's my regina!" Savage shouts excitedly, now held tightly in a car-sized blue claw. "*My* regina!"

Aurelia's grand spell is broken with that and the dragons above us round upon Aurelia.

But my blue angel is ready.

And so is Xander.

Savage scrambles up Aurelia's leg and onto her back with great familiarity. Xander approaches the two younger enemy dragons from the east and Aurelia hones in from the west, catching them in the middle. Both dragons open their mouths with the full force of their great chests, and let out a pure storm of dragon fire. Where Xander's fire is a vicious red, Aurelia's is a deep, almost ultraviolet that stings the retinas.

I don't look away as my own eyes burn, but no doubt the pain of it is what makes the green and red dragon shriek in pain as they lose their vision and direction in the sky. The mint green one veers towards the ground, while the red tumbles as far away from my regina as he can.

It's then that Flores Drakos charges for Aurelia, his jaws aimed for her neck.

I scream my regina's name, but just before impact, a black mass intercepts. Xander takes the full force of the bigger dragon's charge and Flores' jaws close around his son's neck instead.

Scythe goes flying from Xander's back.

I catch my shark-brother with my own power and lower him to the ground. Aurelia rages at the sight of the two dragons, diving after them as Flores uses his larger weight against Xander. When they hit the turf of Drakos Estate, Xander is crushed beneath the force of his father's sheer size, the sound of breaking bones reverberating in my ears. Something else also reverberates through the air. Something made of wild, celestial power. Something that makes my mating mark burn like living lava.

Aurelia lands heavily, teetering to one side as her new leg struggles to take the brunt of her landing. She rights herself quickly and Savage, in his wolf form, appears on top of Aurelia's head and leaps right for Flores Drakos, who's snarling over his son's supine body.

Savage lands on Flores' neck, scrambling to get purchase on the hard scales and uses his teeth instead, sinking them between the heavy emerald plates.

Flores tilts his head up and screeches, stumbling backwards as Savage, as if the bastard was born to do it, buries his entire muzzle into Flores' neck at an angle, digging into muscle, and making blood spurt like a fire hydrant. The massive dragon bucks like a bull and Savage loses his grip, sending him spinning through the air in a wide arc.

I catch him with my telekinesis and lasso him towards where I'm standing with the Devi pack out of the way of the dragons.

Xander groans, his power healing him, but not quick enough to get him back up. Aurelia tosses her head angrily and considers the bigger dragon—

Until Lady Drakos charges in on foot and screams into the minds of everyone in the vicinity, *"You will never hurt my children again!"* She slams right into Flores and they thrash upon the grass, kicking up a violent dirt storm.

"Mother, no!" A voice I don't recognise screams from the castle entrance and a slender, pale woman in a grey dress sprints down the steps towards the fighting dragons. She shifts as she does, deep yellow scales tearing through her skin and clothes. There's a loud crunch of cartilage and her dragon form appears stilted until she stretches out her wings and forelegs. There's a sound of cartilage popping and groaning like her body is waking up after a long time.

"Who is this?" Minnie cries, her hands digging into her hair.

The yellow dragon charges for the fray, but Ragnar intercepts her, landing with his claws extended and brutally kicking her backwards.

Aurelia roars in anger as the yellow dragon shrieks and thuds onto her back.

"That's Selena!" Aurelia cries into our minds. *"Xander's sister!"*

But it's Savage who's already sprinting, nothing but a black bullet as he leaps and lands with a thump on Ragnar's tail, his teeth deep into the hard flesh right at the tip. Ragnar turns in alarm and thumps his tail, but Savage doesn't let go as he's shaken like a rag doll.

I've had enough of watching my regina and brothers fight together while I watch on. I let my power slingshot me towards Aurelia just as she launches herself at Ragnar, teeth bared in rage.

But Ragnar is an older, more practised dragon, and sees the attack coming a mile away. Just as he kicks with his foreleg, I whack him with my power, sending him stumbling backward—

Allowing Selena to leap on top of him, her fangs violently tearing at the flesh of his neck. Blood spurts from the side of my eye and I turn to look as our black wolf, who has crawled up Ragnar's supine body, has ripped into his underside, right between his hind legs.

Savage pulls out something long and fleshy, tossing it into the air. He shifts into human form, his face covered in blood as he catches what's left of the protuberance. "Found it!" He cheers, holding it up like the trophy.

Ragnar lies dead on the grass, Selena still ravaging his neck, focused like she's trying to decapitate it.

Aurelia turns away to look for Xander and Lady Drakos. We spot them close to the estate wall. Lady Drakos thrashes madly under Flores' much larger body while Xander launches himself at his father, teeth and claws outstretched.

My regina cries out as Flores twists just in time, rolling Lady Drakos on top of him as a shield. Many sets of telekinesis lash out, shoving Xander to the side before he crushes his mother. Xander's eyes widen as he barrel rolls through the air in an arc, realising he's being saved by our combined powers. He rotates, landing back on his feet.

The ground trembles under the force of him.

Scythe appears from behind the dragons, sprinting towards Aurelia. I collect him with my power and yank him towards safety. He scrambles up Aurelia's back with the familiarity of long years of practice.

Lady Drakos is injured, bleeding freely from her wounded hind leg, and now we can see multiple other wounds have joined the first. She's groaning in pain, all the while fighting her captor, who's sunk his teeth into her shoulder from behind.

Selena's daffodil-yellow form thunders past us, making Aurelia stumble back on the crosswind. Together, Selena and Xander take one of their father's legs in each bloody maw and force him to roll over.

But Flores won't let go of his wife, his eyes wide and wild as blood spills from his mouth where he's sunk even deeper into her shoulder. Xander roars, tearing at the flesh of his father's side, ripping a chunk of black scales right off his body.

Aurelia takes a step forward.

"*No, regina,*" Scythe says. "*Let his family take him.*"

She rumbles with discontent in her chest, but she knows on land she'll be a liability.

Flores lets out a muffled, almighty sound, but he doesn't let go of Lady Drakos, instead thumping her onto the earth by the force of his thick neck alone.

So Selena does something that's considered taboo amongst winged orders and snaps her jaws around her father's left wing.

Xander immediately lunges for the right.

Together, the siblings dig their claws into the earth and *pull.* Flores Drakos finally lets his wife go and emits a terrible sound that makes Savage and me plug our ears. Tendons groan, bones crunch, and flesh rips as Xander and his sister pull their father's wings from their joints.

Lady Drakos, bloody and torn, leaps to her feet. She snarls at the sight of her husband being torn apart before lunging for his exposed ribcage. She angles her head sideways, and just as I realise what she's doing, blood sprays in a fan, litres and litres of crimson liquid burst from arteries as Lady Drakos tosses the dragon king's heart to the side.

Flores gurgles on his own blood, his dragon's head screeching to a sky that won't help him, before he goes limp and crashes sideways to the ground, dead.

Chapter 101

Xander

I spit what's left of my father's wing onto the ground as my mother roars in triumph. But I'm not done. I rip into my father's right leg at the thigh, gripping the limb in my jaws and snapping it upwards. I've never heard a more satisfying sound than the loud crack of my father's marrowbone breaking.

Tearing it from his dead body, I hold it in my jaws and search for my regina. She stands behind me, with three of our mates watching over my natal family's kill. I stalk towards her, my eyes never leaving her bright blue ones, and lay down my father's hind leg at her beautiful, blue-clawed feet.

If I wasn't already in love with her, I would have fallen in love again at the sight of her as a dragon. Regal as a queen, brilliant as a living sapphire. Her eyes glisten with unshed emotion as Scythe scrambles to crouch on her head, looking down at my gift with bloodthirsty glee.

But Aurelia doesn't say anything. Instead, she takes a step towards me, her scent filling my nose, and presses her forehead against mine.

I close my eyes, accepting this gift, listening to her giant heart thumping in time with mine. I feel my ex-brothers, their powers surrounding me, their auras pulsing, not with hate, but something else.

My throat suddenly feels like it's going to close up. I never thought I'd be on the receiving end of anything other than hatred and violence from them.

I want to fall at their feet. I want to cry.

Aurelia's eyes flick over my shoulder and widen. She cries out and I whirl around just in time to see my mother, now shifted back into human form, crumbling to the ground, her eyes closed, her mouth agape.

Selena, her entire muzzle coated with Ragnar's blood, whines and reaches our mother, her snout hovering over her bare chest. I too join her, allowing my healing power to flood my mother's torn body. Chunks of her skin are missing from her torso and legs, her damaged body fighting to keep its life.

Aurelia makes her way over to us, her gait uneven due to her lifting up her right hind leg, but her power is endless as she lets her own healing join our two streams.

My mother's eyelids flutter open, and despite their golden hues being filled with pain, they crinkle at the edges, the corners of her mouth tilting open. She reaches up to touch mine and Selena's wet faces. "He will never hurt my children again."

Mother's wounds seal up, and she closes her eyes from exhaustion. Her heart beats strong, but she'll take weeks to recover from this battle.

"Take her inside," I order Selena.

Selena grips our mother in a gentle claw and flies her up to the dragon-perch. Behind me, Aurelia tiredly sighs and shifts back into her human form. I remember the first time I shifted; being a dragon is a tiring thing. I want to look after her, ask her what it felt like to be a dragon, to breathe fire. To *rage*. The breeze is soft on me as I take my cue to shift back into my human body, suppressing a grunt as the broken bones suddenly register.

Scythe gives Aurelia his shirt, her pyjamas lying tattered

across the grass as the Devi pack runs up to us, sweaty and bloody from their own exertion.

"Raquel is free," Savage pants. "Marduk forced one of the maids to show us where they were. We undid all the shackles for good measure."

The far-away rumble of a heavy engine reaches my ears and I go on high alert. This is not yet over. I clench my teeth and gesture to the road leading to the estate. "Someone's coming," I say. "I don't know who it is, but it's a convoy."

"Fuck," Savage mutters, brushing at his still bloody face. "Regina, we have to get you out of here."

Aurelia blanches as we all look at her. "I've just realised," she said quietly. "We don't know where Francesca is."

Fuck, she's right. I stride towards the open gates of Drakos Estate. Ragnar and Uncle Fabian's cars are parked in the driveway near the front stairs, hence the reason for the gates being open. But as I near the spiked iron gates, the rumble of the trucks is loud enough that I recognise the make of them immediately.

Four open Jeeps with armed guards are led by the Collector, in a red silk jumpsuit and matching headscarf.

Scythe and Lyle realise it quickly, and Minnie helps shove Aurelia behind her own pack. The Collector's eyes light up as she spots the three dragons lying decimated on the grass. She screeches to a stop and swings out of her Jeep on black calf-hide boots, shaking a finger at me. "Naughty little dragon," she says, eyes raking down my naked body. "Did you lot just kill three of the most powerful dragons in the state?"

My ribs are broken and there's the start of a pneumothorax on the left side, but I lazily cast my eyes over the convoy and realise it too late—

The final Jeep holds a group of hyenas and Lady Hyena herself, a tiny black cauldron in hand, throws a white powder at me.

I stumble back, but my shoulders hit an invisible wall. Beady black eyes gleam, and she croaks, "It's not your night, Xander Drakos. Not your night at all."

The scent of the powder hits me. White power. Bone white.

As Savage, Scythe and Lyle sprint towards me, I struggle to find the voice to warn them what I've scented in that powder: they are going to use the power of our regina to bind us, harvested right from her very bone.

"*Run!*" I cry to my brothers.

But Lady Hyena throws a fistful of the powder over Savage, the fastest to reach us. He stops in his tracks, trapped against the energetic bubble. Lyle and Scythe are stopped next, crashing heavily into their invisible cage.

The Collector tuts as she stalks around us in a circle, a cigarette smoking in her hand. Lady Hyena circles us in the opposite direction, sprinkling the bone powder as she goes, calling to the moon and stars with her heinous magic.

"Black moon, red moon," Lady Hyena chants. "Black sea, Red sea,"

"Bind these beasts to me," the Collector hisses. "A new regina comes, an old regina goes."

"Bind them by the wind that sows." A fierce wind whips my hair as Lady Hyena finishes the spell, fell whispers filling my ears. A vile tug pulls me towards the Collector and I frown at it, resisting this new alien urge. But purely against their will, Savage, Lyle, and Scythe turn towards the Collector.

I follow suit, copying them as I realise what this means. I clench my teeth against the nausea as I feel the powers shifting in the air.

"I thought it wouldn't work for Xander." The Collector frowns at me. "Scythe, tell me what happened here tonight, and leave no detail out."

Scythe's voice is unusually flat as he immediately gives her a brief rundown of the events, including Aurelia shifting into a dragon, and finally, the death of my father.

Shocked by the smooth obedience of the great white, I remain silent. Lyle and Savage also remain silent and still.

"Is that so?" the Collector breathes, sauntering up to Scythe and kissing him on the cheek.

He doesn't react at all.

"The magic is binding the dragon," Lady Hyena muses, gesturing to my stricken form. "But I do not understand why."

"How wonderful! I get a dragon for free!" the Collector cheers. She runs her hand through Savage's hair, then moves to Lyle, stroking the collar of his shirt.

Aurelia's power crashes into me, protesting, demanding my attention. My breath strains as I fight the urge to turn to her. Something circles around me in a vortex. A wild power that feels heavy and golden. I begin to vibrate, my muscles trembling, my body burning up. I blink at my brothers. Then blink again.

"My my," The Lady Hyena stares me down with those coal-black eyes. "How merciful the Wild Mother is."

Chapter 102

Aurelia

"This is evil magic, Aurelia, you mustn't go there!" Marduk urges me, the combined powers of the Devi pack and he keep me from running to the Collector and my mates as we watch them weave a vile spell that curses the very air. "There are too many of them, even for a Boneweaver."

"Even for a dragon?" I hiss.

"You know as well as I do how hyena spells work!" Minnie furiously whispers up at me.

"I can still kill her!" I say through gritted teeth.

The Collector turns to me, and even over the distance, I hear her gloating voice. "It looks like I have a new pack, Aurelia," she calls, eyes gleaming in triumph. "And I can regina-command them to do as I please."

My insides turn to ice as I stare at my stationary, stiff mates.

"Let's put it to a test, shall we?"

"Savage!" I scream into his head. *"Seythe! Lyle!"*

But I come up against a wall. As if I no longer have a connection to them at all. I scream against Minnie's invisible powers.

"Savage, Seythe, Lyle and Xander," The Collector purrs. "Bow to me if you accept me as your regina."

Silently, the four of them get to their knees before the Collector, bowing their heads. I scream in agony at the sight. Even Xander, his dark head bowed in complete submission. I've never seen a spell like this. Never even known this was possible.

"She's been working on this for a long time," Marduk said. "She has coveted them for even longer. These evil beasts chose the way they hurt you specifically."

The Collector tilts her head back and laughs. Then she smiles at me. A crocodile's smirk. "Now, for your first regina-command, my new mates. *Kill* Aurelia Boneweaver."

My heart drops as Scythe, Savage, Lyle and Xander turn around, their eyes dark and fixed upon me. As one, they begin advancing.

The sight of them, eyes glazed and determined, chills me to the core.

"Lia, we have to go," Minnie desperately urges, tugging at my arm. "*Lia.*"

Lyle's power lashes around me and I cast it off with an angry cry.

"How can I leave them?" I cry to my best friend.

Scythe's power is next, folding around my heart, flooding the chambers.

"They don't know you anymore," Marduk cries, also desperately tugging at my arm now. "You must!"

Yeti blocks my vision and shakes me by the shoulders, his light eyes furious. "Shift into a dragon and get us out of here, Lia, or we're all fucking dead."

I scream in his face and he goes stumbling back as I shift. It hurts. God, it's an awful pain that assaults my leg, my heart, every piece of shifting cartilage and bone as I become colossal again. The three tigers use their powers to levitate themselves onto my back.

"Go!" Minnie cries.

I let her voice guide me as my vision blurs and I shoot into the air with painful force.

Leaving my mates, the pieces of my soul, behind.

As I cast one last look at them, my eye catches on Xander, the way he's looking up at me like he's seen the first light of dawn, and the way something new mars his neck. Infinitely black as the void between stars, stark against his fair skin: a skull with five beams of light curling from it.

Chapter 103

Ghoul

I turn away from the camera feed that our spies have set up at the perimeter of Drakos Estate, stroking my chin with a gloved hand.

"So the dragons ended up destroying themselves as we planned," Mace Naga says, nothing but pure triumph in his voice.

"Yes, Your Majesty." I bounce on the balls of my feet, adrenaline pumping through me from the sight of what happened tonight. "You pitted them against each other and they never had any idea."

Mace smiles at me as he looks out the window of his new home, the picture of a proud king. A job well done. "Now we have no opposition to do as we please."

He turns around and regards me. "Commence the final phase of our plans. It's time we showed the world what we are made of."

I bow low. "With pleasure, my king."

The End of Her Tortured Beasts

About the Author

Ektaa P. Bali was born in Fiji and spent most of her life in Melbourne, Australia.

She published her first novel in 2020, the beginning of a middle grade fantasy series, before going on to pursue her true passion: Young & New Adult Fantasy.

Her Vicious Beasts is her fourth series set in the Chrysalisverse and Her Tortured Beasts is the fourth in the series.

She currently lives in Brisbane, Australia.

facebook.com/ektaabaliauthor

instagram.com/ektaabaliauthor

youtube.com/ektaabali

Also by E.P. Bali

<u>New Adult Fantasy Romance</u>

A Song of Lotus and Lightning Saga:

#1 *The Warrior Midwife*

#2 *The Warrior Priestess*

#3 *The Warrior Queen*

#1 *The Archer Princess*

#2 *The Archer Witch*

#3 *The Archer Queen*

Her Vicious Beasts

#0.5 *The Beginning*

#1 *Her Feral Beasts*

#2 *Her Rabid Beasts*

#3 *Her Psycho Beasts*

#4 *Her Tortured Beasts*

#5 *Her Monstrous Beasts*

<u>Upper YA Dark Fantasy</u>

The Travellers:

#1 *The Chrysalis Key*

#2 *The Allure of Power*

#3 *The Wings of Darkness*